QUANTUM NIGHT

BOOKS BY ROBERT J. SAWYER

NOVELS

Golden Fleece

End of an Era

The Terminal Experiment

Starplex

Frameshift

Illegal Alien

Factoring Humanity

FlashForward

Calculating God

Mindscan

Rollback

Triggers

Red Planet Blues

Quantum Night

THE QUINTAGLIO ASCENSION TRILOGY

Far-Seer

Fossil Hunter

Foreigner

THE NEANDERTHAL PARALLAX TRILOGY

Hominids

Humans

Hybrids

THE WWW TRILOGY

Wake

Watch

Wonder

COLLECTIONS

Iterations
(introduction by James Alan Gardner)

Relativity
(introduction by Mike Resnick)

Identity Theft
(introduction by Robert Charles Wilson)

For book-club discussion guides, visit **sfwriter.com**

QUANTUM NIGHT

ROBERT J. SAWYER

ACE BOOKS, NEW YORK

An imprint of Penguin Random House LLC
375 Hudson Street, New York, New York 10014

This book is an original publication of Penguin Random House LLC.

Library of Congress Cataloging-in-Publication Data

Sawyer, Robert J.
Quantum night / Robert J. Sawyer.
pages ; cm
ISBN 978-0-425-25683-1 (hardcover)
1. Psychologists—Fiction.   2. Violence—Psychological aspects—Fiction.   3. Quantum theory—Fiction.
I. Title.
PR9199.3.S2533Q36 2016
813'.54—dc23
2015028314

FIRST EDITION: March 2016

PRINTED IN THE UNITED STATES OF AMERICA

10   9   8   7   6   5   4   3   2   1

Cover design by Rita Frangie and Danielle Mazzella Di Bosco.
Cover art: statue of Lady Justice © Christian Mueller / Shutterstock; abstract technology
background © arleksey/Shutterstock.
Interior text design by Kelly Lipovich.

Penguin
Random
House

FOR
CHASE MASTERSON

BEAUTIFUL INSIDE AND OUT

AUTHOR'S NOTE

The Canadian Light Source synchrotron, the University of Manitoba, and the Canadian Museum for Human Rights all really exist. However, except for certain public figures used satirically, all the characters in this novel are entirely the product of my imagination. They are not meant to bear any resemblance to actual people who hold or have held positions with these or any other institutions.

The real public figures who feature in this novel include Canadian politicians Naheed Nenshi (the current mayor of Calgary) and Justin Trudeau (the current prime minister), as well as Russian president Vladimir Putin. Given this is a story in part about quantum physics, if they don't like the future portrayed here, they can rest assured that in some other quantum reality they have different fates.

Although my fictional characters refer to the work of many real academics, including philosopher David J. Chalmers, consciousness-studies expert Stuart Hameroff and his collaborator physicist Roger Penrose, and psychologists Bob Altemeyer, Angela Book, Robert D. Hare, Kent Kiehl, Philip Zimbardo, and the late Stanley Milgram, the extrapolations and sometimes contradictions of the findings of those academics presented by my characters are also products of my imagination.

ACKNOWLEDGMENTS

Thanks to **David J. Chalmers**, PhD, Director, Centre for Consciousness, Australian National University; **Kevin Dutton**, PhD, author of *The Wisdom of Psychopaths;* **John Gribbin**, PhD, author of *In Search of Schrödinger's Cat;* and **Stuart R. Hameroff**, MD, Director, Center for Consciousness Studies, The University of Arizona, Tucson.

Thanks also to **Jeffrey Cutler**, PhD, **Lisa Van Loon**, PhD, and **M. Adam Webb**, PhD, of the Canadian Light Source, Canada's national synchrotron, in Saskatoon, and to **Matthew Dalzell**, who used to work there. Thanks as well to **Jeremy Maron**, PhD, Researcher-Curator, Canadian Museum for Human Rights.

Thanks to clinical psychologists **Christopher Friesen**, PhD, **David Nussbaum**, PhD, **Jill Squyres**, PhD, and **Romeo Vitelli**, PhD; clinical psychiatrist **Norman Hoffman**, MD; and neurologist **Isaac Szpindel**, MD.

Many thanks for stimulating conversations and wonderful feedback to **Alisha Souillet, Elizabeth Cano, Nick DiChario, Vince Gerardis, Walter Hunt, James Kerwin, Kirstin Morrell, Sherry Peters, G.W. Renshaw, Don Thompson,** and **Matt Whitby.**

Thanks, as well, to my wonderful beta readers: **Robb Ainley, Ted Bleaney,** Rev. **James Christie, David Livingstone Clink, Shayla Elizabeth, Dan Falk, Paddy Forde, Marcel Gagné, Belle Jarniewiski, Herb Kauderer, Rebecca Lovatt, Kayla Nielsen, Virginia O'Dine, Lynne Sargent, Hayden Trenholm,** and **Sally Tomasevic.** Thanks for other assistance to **Paul Bishop, Dan Brook, John Dahms, Fingers Delaurus,**

Matthew Pounsett, and Jamie Todd Rubin. Thanks also to copyeditor Robert L. Schwager, PhD.

Huge thanks, as always, to the Aurora Award–winning poet Carolyn Clink, who helped in countless ways; to Adrienne Kerr at Penguin Random House Canada's Viking imprint in Toronto; to Helen Smith, also at Penguin Random House Canada; and to Jessica Wade at Penguin Random House USA's Ace imprint in New York (and also to Ginjer Buchanan, who commissioned this book for Ace before retiring). And, of course, many thanks to my agents: the late Ralph Vicinanza, who negotiated the contracts for this book, and Chris Lotts, who saw it through to publication.

Finally, most of all, gigantic thanks to my wonderfully patient readers. I had a twenty-year run of averaging a novel a year, but leading up to and following the death from lung cancer of my younger brother, the Emmy Award–winning multimedia producer Alan Sawyer, I took time off. It's been three years since my last novel, *Red Planet Blues;* I hope you'll think this one was worth the wait.

It may be a requirement for a theory of consciousness that it contains at least one crazy idea.

—David Chalmers

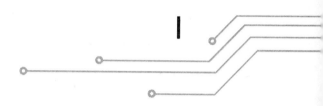

1

Several of my colleagues in the University of Manitoba's psychology
department considered teaching to be a nuisance—"the ineluctable
evil," as Menno Warkentin used to call it, resenting the time it took
away from his research—but I loved it. Oh, maybe not as much as
I loved bananas, or binge-watching old episodes of Curb Your
Enthusiasm *or* Arrested Development, *or photographing globular*
clusters with my telescope, but as far as things that people would
actually pay me to do are concerned, it was right up there.

    Granted, teaching first-year classes could be overwhelming:
vast halls filled with stagnant air and row after row of angst-
soaked teenagers. Although my own freshman year had been two
decades ago, I vividly remembered signing up to take introductory
psych in hopes of making sense of the bewildering mélange of
anxiety and longing that swirled then—and pretty much now,
too—within me. Cogito ergo sum? *More like* sollicito ergo sum—
I fret, therefore I am.

    But on this gray morning, I was teaching The Neuroscience
of Morality, *a third-year class with fewer students than February*
had days—and that allowed for not just lecturing but dialog.

Last session, we'd had a spirited discussion about Watson and Skinner, focusing on their notion that humans were nothing more than stimulus-response machines whose black-box brains simply spit out predictable reactions to inputs. But today, instead of continuing to demolish behaviorism, I felt compelled to take a dark detour, using the ceiling-mounted projector to show the Savannah Prison photos WikiLeaks had made public over the weekend.

Some were individual frames from security-camera video, the guards caught unawares from on high. Although what those depicted was brutal, they weren't the most disturbing images. No, the really disquieting ones—the ones that knotted your stomach, that made you avert your eyes, that you just couldn't fucking believe—were the posed *photos: the picture of the officer with her boot on a prisoner's back while she gave a jaunty thumbs-up to whatever asshole was holding the iPhone; the still of the two uniformed men tossing a naked, emaciated prisoner so hard against the ceiling that his skull, as x-rays would later show, had fractured in three places; the snapshot of the mustachioed sergeant straddling a downed man while defecating on his chest, one hand clamped over the inmate's mouth, the other flashing a peace sign, the image then having been run through Instagram to make it look like an old-fashioned Polaroid, white frame and all.*

My stomach roiled as I stepped through the slides, one atrocity giving way to the next. It was now sixteen years after Abu Ghraib, for God's sake, and a half century since Philip Zimbardo's Stanford Prison experiment. Not only were guards supposed to be trained about situational pressures and how to avoid succumbing to them, but two of those shown in the photos were studying to be wardens. They knew about Zimbardo; they were aware of Stanley Milgram's shock-machine obedience-to-authority experiments; they'd read summaries of the Taguba Report on the Abu Ghraib atrocities.

And yet, despite being specifically taught to recognize and avoid the pitfalls—a word that at first seemed innocuous but, if one reflected upon it, suggested tumbling into the abyss, following

Lucifer into the very fires of hell—each of these men and women had dehumanized the perceived enemy, and, in the process, had lost their own humanity.

"All right," I said to the shocked faces of my students. "What can we take from all this? Anyone?"

The first hand that went up belonged to Ashton, who still had acne and hadn't yet learned that it was permissible to trim a beard. I pointed at him. "Yes?"

He spread his arms as if the truth were self-evident. "Simple," he said, and he flicked his head toward the screen behind me, which I'd left on the last slide, the one showing a gangly guard named Devin Becker killing a naked prisoner by holding his head under water in a jail-cell sink. "You can't change human nature."

THE call had come just about a year ago. "Hello?" I'd said into the black handset of my office phone.

"Professor James Marchuk?"

I swung my feet up on my reddish-brown desk and leaned back. "Speaking."

"My name is Juan Garcia. I'm part of the defense team for Devin Becker, one of the Savannah Prison guards."

I thought about saying, "Well, you've got your work cut out for you," but instead simply prodded him to go on. "Yes?"

"My firm would like to engage you as an expert witness in Mr. Becker's trial. The prosecution is seeking the death penalty. We're likely to lose on the facts—the security-camera video is damning as hell—but we can at least keep Becker from being executed if we get the jury to agree that he couldn't help himself."

I frowned. "And you think he couldn't because . . . ?"

"Because he's a psychopath. You said it in your blog entry on Leopold and Loeb: you can't execute someone for being who they are."

I nodded although Garcia couldn't see it. In 1924, two wealthy university students, Nathan Leopold and Richard Loeb, had killed a boy just for kicks. Leopold considered himself and Loeb to be exemplars of

Nietzsche's *Übermenschen* and thus exempt from laws governing ordinary men. Supermen they weren't, but psychopaths they surely were. Their parents engaged none other than Clarence Darrow to represent them. In a stunning twelve-hour-long closing argument, Darrow made the same defense Garcia was apparently now contemplating: claiming Becker couldn't be executed for doing what his nature dictated he do.

I took my feet off the desk and leaned forward. "And *is* Becker a psychopath?" I asked.

"That's the problem, Professor Marchuk," said Garcia. "The D.A. had a Hare assessment done, which scored Becker at seventeen—way below what's required for psychopathy. But we think their assessor is wrong; our guy squeaks him into psychopathy with a score of thirty-one. And, well, with your new procedure, we can prove to the jury that our score is the right one."

"You know my test has never been accepted in a court of law?"

"I'm aware of that, Professor. I'm also aware that no one has even tried to introduce it into evidence yet. But I've got your paper in *Nature Neuroscience* right here. That it was published in such a prestigious, peer-reviewed journal gets our foot in the door; Georgia follows the Daubert standard for admissibility. But we need you—you personally, the lead author on the paper—to use your technique on Becker and testify about the results if we've got any chance of having the court accept the evidence."

"What if I show that Becker *isn't* a psychopath?"

"Then we'll still pay you for your time."

"And bury the results?"

"Professor, we're confident of the outcome."

It sounded worthwhile—but so was what I did here. "I have a busy teaching schedule, and—"

"I know you do, Professor. In fact, I'm looking at it right now on your university's website. But the trial probably won't come up until you're on summer break, and, frankly, this is a chance to make a difference. I've read your *Reasonably Moral* blog. You're against the death penalty; well, here's a chance to help prevent someone from being executed."

My computer happened to be displaying the lesson plan for that afternoon's moral-psych class, in which I was planning to cite the study of Princeton seminary students who, while rushing to give a presentation on the parable of the Good Samaritan, passed by a man slumped over in an alleyway, ignoring him because they were in a hurry.

Practice what you teach, I always say. "All right. Count me in."

Shortly after I came off the Jetway into the international terminal at Hartsfield-Jackson Airport, I went into a little shop to buy a bottle of Coke Zero—here, in Atlanta, headquarters of Coca-Cola, there was no sign of Pepsi anywhere. Without thinking, I handed the woman at the cash register a Canadian five.

"What's this?" she said, taking it.

"Oh! Sorry." I dug into my wallet—I always have to carefully look at US bills to make sure of the denomination, since they're all the same color—and found one with Abe Lincoln's face on it.

There was no one else waiting to buy anything, and the woman seemed intrigued by the blue polymer banknote I'd handed her. After examining it carefully, she looked up at me, and said, "There's no mention of God. Ain't you a God-fearing country up there?"

"Um, well, ah, we believe in the separation of church and state."

She handed the bill back to me. "Honey," she said, "there ain't no such thing." She frowned, as if recalling something. "Y'all are socialists up there, right?"

Actually, until recently, Canada had had a much more conservative leader than the United States did. When Stephen Harper came to office in 2006, George W. Bush had been in the White House and, to liberal Canadian sensibilities—the kind found on university campuses—he seemed the lesser of two evils. But once Barack Obama was elected, Canada had by far the more right-wing leader. Harper managed to hold on to power for almost a decade, but Canada was now ruled by a minority coalition between the Liberal Party and the socialist New Democratic Party.

"Kind of," I said, although I suspected her understanding of the term "socialism" was different from mine. I handed her the American five, got my Canadian bill back plus my change, and took my pop, or soda, or whatever it was here.

This was my first time flying in the States since Quinton Carroway had been sworn in as president, and I was surprised to hear that the constant warnings about terrorist threats over the public-address system were back; they'd disappeared under Obama but had returned with a vengeance. The old wording had invariably been, "The Homeland Security threat level is orange"—which was only semi-effective propaganda because you had to have memorized the code to know that orange was the new black—the thing white folk were supposed to fear most—being one step shy of an imminent attack. The new message, which played every three minutes or so, was much more direct, and, unless I missed my guess, the voice was the president's own distinctive baritone: "Be on guard! A terrorist attack can occur at any time."

And speaking of propaganda, despite Atlanta also being home to CNN, Fox News was on the big-screen TV hanging down like a steam-shovel scoop from the ceiling as I arrived at baggage claim. Orwell had been right that mind-controlling messages would be pumped twenty-four hours a day through telescreens, and he'd have recognized the ones in the airport with no way to turn them off. What would have astounded him is that many millions of people would voluntarily tune into them in their own homes, often for hours on end.

I recognized Megyn Kelly although I usually only saw her in unflattering clips on *The Daily Show*. "Look," she said, "it *is* a fact that this guy was in our country illegally."

"And for that he should have died?" said a man—clearly the day's sacrificial liberal lamb.

"I'm not saying that," said Kelly. "Obviously, what these three men did was not the way to handle it."

"No?" said the man. "What they did was *exactly* what Governor McCharles intended, isn't it?"

"Oh, come on!" snapped the other woman on the panel. "The Texas governor simply meant—"

"The whole point of the McCharles Act," said the man, "was to provoke attacks like this. Redefining homicide as the killing of a *legal* resident! What is that, except a wink-and-a-nod to every yahoo out there that the cops will look the other way if an undocumented immigrant turns up dead?"

"The point," said the same woman, "was merely that these illegal aliens can't flout the law and then expect to be protected by it."

"For God's sake!" said the man, who was getting red in the face. "McCharles is setting things up for a pogrom!"

I grabbed my bag, then headed off to find a taxi, grateful to be leaving the arguing panelists behind.

I beheld the monster.

One of them, anyway. There were six according to the indictments; nine, if you believed the *Huffington Post,* which argued that three other corrections officers who should also have been charged had gotten off scot-free. But this one, everyone agreed, had been the ringleader: Devin Becker was the man who had incited the other guards—and he was the only one who had actually killed somebody.

"Thirty minutes," said a burly sergeant, as Becker folded his lanky form onto the metal seat. The irony wasn't lost on me: Becker himself was now in the care of a prison guard. *Quis custodiet ipsos custodes?* Who indeed watches the watchers?

Becker had high cheekbones, and the weight he'd lost since the notorious video had been recorded made them even more prominent. That the skin pulled taut across them was bone white only added to the ghastly appearance; put a black hood over his head, and he could have played chess for a man's soul. "Who are you?" he asked, a slight drawl protracting his words.

"Jim Marchuk. I'm a psychologist at the University of Manitoba, in Winnipeg."

Becker curled his upper lip. "I don't wanna be part of any damn experiment."

I thought about saying, "You already have been." I thought about saying, "The experiment has been done time and again, and this is just another pointless replication." I even thought about saying, "If only this were an experiment, we could pull the plug on it, just like Zimbardo finally did at Stanford." But what I actually said was, "I'm not here to conduct an experiment. I'm going to be an expert witness at your trial."

"For the defense or the prosecution?"

"The defense."

Becker relaxed somewhat, but his tone was suspicious. "I can't afford fancy experts."

"Your father is paying, I'm told."

"My father." He sneered the words.

"What?"

"If he really cared, it'd be him, not you, sitting there."

"He hasn't come to see you?"

Becker shook his head.

"Has any of your family?"

"My sis. Once."

"Ah," I said.

"They're ashamed."

Those words hung in the air for a moment. The *New York Times* front-page article about the Savannah Prison guards had been headlined "America's Shame."

"Well," I said gently, "perhaps we can convince them not to be."

"With psychological bullshit?" He made a *"pffft!"* sound through thin lips.

"With the truth."

"The truth is my own lawyer says I'm a psychopath. Norman Fucking Bates." He shook his head. "What the hell kind of defense is that, anyway? Y'all must be out of your minds."

I didn't have much sympathy for this guy; what he'd done was horrific. But I *am* a teacher: ask me a question, and I'm compelled to answer—that's *my* nature. "You killed someone in cold blood, and the court would normally call that first-degree murder, right? But suppose an MRI showed you had a brain tumor that affected your behavior. The jury might be inclined to say you couldn't help yourself and let you off. You *don't* have a tumor, but my research shows that psychopathy is just as much a clear-cut physical condition and should likewise mitigate responsibility."

"Huh," he said. "And do *you* think I'm a psycho?"

"I honestly don't know," I replied, placing my briefcase on the wooden table and snapping the clasps open. "So let's find out."

"Professor Marchuk, were you present when my learned opponent, the District Attorney, introduced one of her expert witnesses, psychiatrist Samantha Goldsmith?"

I tried to sound calm but, *man*, this was nerve-wracking. Oh, sure, I was used to the Socratic method in academic settings, but here, in this sweltering courtroom, a person's life was on the line. I leaned forward. "Yes, I was."

Juan Garcia's chin jutted like the cattle catcher on a locomotive. "Sitting there, in the third row, weren't you?"

"That's right."

"Do you recall Dr. Goldsmith giving a clinical opinion of the defendant, Devin Becker?"

"I do."

"And what was her diagnosis?"

"She contended that Mr. Becker is not a psychopath."

"And did Dr. Goldsmith explain the technique by which she arrived at that conclusion?"

I nodded. "Yes, she did."

"Are you familiar with the technique she used?"

"Intimately. I'm certified in administering it myself."

Juan had a way of moving his head that reminded me of a hawk, pivoting instantly from looking this way to that way; he was now regarding the jury. "Perhaps you can refresh the memories of these good men and women, then. What technique did Dr. Goldsmith employ?"

"The Hare Psychopathy Checklist, Revised," I said.

"Commonly called 'the Hare Checklist,' or 'the PCL-R,' correct?"

"That's right."

A quick pivot back toward me. "And, before we go further, again, just to remind us, a psychopath is . . . ?"

"An individual devoid of empathy and conscience, a person who doesn't feel for other people—someone who only cares about his or her own self-interest."

"And the Hare Checklist? Refresh the jury on that, please."

"Robert Hare identified twenty characteristics that define a psychopath—everything from glibness and superficial charm to promiscuity and lack of remorse."

"And, again, remind us: to be a psychopath, do you need to exhibit all twenty of the traits he identified?"

I shook my head. "No. There's a numerical scoring system."

"The subject fills out a form?"

"No, no. A person specially trained in Professor Hare's technique conducts an interview with the subject and also reviews police records, psychiatric reports, employment history, education, and so on. The expert then scores the subject on each of the twenty traits, assigning a zero if a given trait—pathological lying, say—is not present; a one if it matches to a certain extent—perhaps they lie all the time in personal relationships but never in business dealings, or vice versa; and a two if there's a reasonably good match for the trait in most aspects of the person's life."

"And the average total score on the twenty items is?"

"For normal people? Very low: four out of a possible maximum of forty."

"And what score do you need to be a psychopath?"

"Thirty or above."

"And do you recall the score Dr. Goldsmith assigned to the defendant Mr. Becker?"

"I do. She gave him a seventeen."

"Professor Marchuk, were you also here in this courtroom when we—the defense—presented an expert witness, another psychologist, prior to bringing you to the stand?"

I nodded again. "I was."

"That psychologist, Dr. Gabor Bagi, testified that he, too, administered the same psychopathy test to Devin Becker. Do you recall that?"

"Yes."

"And did Dr. Bagi come up with the same score as Dr. Goldsmith?"

"No. He gave Mr. Becker a score of thirty-one."

Juan did a good job of sounding astonished. "Thirty-one out of forty? Whereas Dr. Goldsmith came up with seventeen?"

"Correct."

His head snapped toward the jury. "How do you account for the discrepancy?"

"Well, although Professor Hare's checklist is supposed to be as objective as possible, his test is prone to some inter-rater disagreement in non-research clinical settings. But a difference of fourteen points?" I shrugged my shoulders beneath my blue suit. "I can't account for that."

Snapping back to me: "Still, our score of thirty-one puts Mr. Becker over the legal line into psychopathy with room to spare, while the score Dr. Goldsmith obtained leaves Mr. Becker far away from being a psychopath, correct?"

"Correct."

"And, given that the State is seeking the death penalty, the question of whether or not Mr. Becker is a clinical psychopath—whether or not he had any volition in his behavior—is crucial in determining his sentence, which puts the good men and women of the jury in the unenviable, but regrettably common, position of having to choose between conflicting expert testimonies, isn't that so?"

"No," I said.

"I beg your pardon, Professor Marchuk?"

My heart was pounding, but I managed to keep my tone absolutely level. "No. Dr. Goldsmith is dead wrong, and Dr. Bagi is right. Devin Becker *is* a psychopath, and I can prove it—prove it beyond a shadow of a doubt."

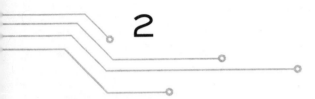

2

"A simple yes-or-no test for psychopathy?" Heather said as she looked across the restaurant table at me. "Surely that's not possible."

"Oh, but it is. And I've discovered it."

My sister was one of my favorite people, and I was one of hers; I think we'd have been friends even if we hadn't been related. She was forty-two, almost exactly three years older than I, and worked as a corporate litigator in Calgary. Every now and then her work brought her here to Winnipeg, and whenever it did, we hung out together.

"Oh, come on," she said. "Surely there's a spectrum for psychopathy."

I shook my head. "Everyone wants everything to be on a spectrum these days. Autism is the classic example: 'autism spectrum disorder.' We have this desire for things to be analog, to have infinite gradations. But humans fundamentally *aren't* analog; life isn't analog. It's digital. Granted, it's not base-two binary; it's base-four. *Literally* base-four: the four bases—adenine, cytosine, guanine, and thymine—that make up the genetic code. There's nothing analog about that, and there's nothing analog about most of the human condition: you're either alive or dead; you either do or don't have the genes for Alzheimer's; and you either are or aren't a psychopath."

"Okay, fine. So how do you know? What's the binary test for psychopathy?"

"You ever see *The Silence of the Lambs?*"

She nodded, honey-colored hair touching her shoulders as she did so. "Sure. Read the book, too."

I was curious as to whether she'd picked it up after she'd started dating Gustav. "When?" I asked offhandedly.

"The movie? When I was in law school. The book? Maybe ten years ago."

I resisted shaking my head. Gustav had only been on the scene for six months now, but I was sure he was a psychopath. Not the violent sort that Thomas Harris had depicted in his novel—psychopathy was indeed binary, but it manifested itself in different ways; in Gustav's case, that meant narcissistic, manipulative, and selfish behavior. A self-styled actor—IMDb had no entry for him—he apparently lived off a succession of professional women; my ever-kindhearted sister, so sharp in legal matters, seemed utterly oblivious to this. Or maybe not: I'd attempted to broach the topic a couple of times before, but she'd always shut me down, saying she was happy, all right?, and I should let her be.

"Well," I said, "in the movie *The Silence of the Lambs,* remember the first interview between Clarice Starling and Hannibal Lecter? Anthony Hopkins absolutely nails one aspect of psychopaths—at least as much as someone who actually *isn't* one can. He looks right at Clarice and says"—and here I did my best impersonation of Hopkins's cultured hiss—"'First principles, Clarice. Of each particular thing ask: what is it in itself? What is its nature?' And then, the most memorable part, as his eyes drill into her and he says, 'What does he do, this . . . man . . . you . . . seek?' Remember that?"

Heather shuddered a little. "Oh, yes."

"Jodie Foster's response—'He kills women'—is supposed to be the chilling part, but it isn't. It's Lecter's stare, the way he looks right at Clarice, unblinking, unflinching. I've seen that stare in the flesh, from real psychopaths in jails. It's the most unnerving thing about them."

"I bet," said Heather. She'd ordered mozzarella sticks as an appetizer; I'd been out with her and Gustav and seen him veto her choices of anything fattening. She took one of the sticks now and dipped it in marinara sauce.

"But, you know," I said, "good as he is, Anthony Hopkins is only simulating the psychopathic stare. He can't do it quite right."

"How do you mean?"

"A real psychopath looks at you not just without blinking much—although that certainly adds to the reptilian effect—but also without performing microsaccades."

Heather had heard me talk about them before. Microsaccades are involuntary jerks as the eyeball rotates two degrees or less; they occur spontaneously whenever you stare at something for several seconds. Their purpose is debated although the most common theory is that they cause the neurons perceiving an object to refresh so that the image doesn't fade.

Heather's eyebrows rose above her wire-frame glasses. "Really?"

I nodded. "Yup. The paper's coming up in *Nature Neuroscience*."

"Way to go!" But then she frowned. "Why would that be, though? What have microsaccades got to do with psychopathy?"

"I'm not sure," I admitted, "but I've demonstrated the lack in forty-eight out of fifty test subjects, all of whom had scored thirty-two or above on the PCL-R."

"What about the other two?"

"Not psychopaths; I'm convinced of it. And that's the problem with the PCL-R: it's not definitive. Bob Hare got pissed several years ago when a pop-sci book called *The Psychopath Test* came out. It implied anyone could properly assess whether their neighbors or bosses or even casual acquaintances were psychopaths. As Hare said, it takes a week of intensive training to be able to score his twenty variables properly, and that's on top of formal psychological or psychiatric education. But his test *can* have false positives if a clinician miscategorizes something, or assigns a score of two when only a one is really warranted—or if the psychopath is good at evading detection."

"Ah," said Heather. "But, um, how do you know Anthony Hopkins isn't a psychopath?" Her tone was light. "I mean, think of the parts he's played—not just Hannibal Lecter but also Alfred Hitchcock, a guy who was obsessed with making a movie *about* a psycho and who had a lot of callous traits himself. Maybe it's typecasting."

"I actually thought about that. Hopkins also played Nixon and Captain Bligh, after all—arguably a couple of other psychopaths."

"True."

"So I got the 4K Ultra disc of *Silence of the Lambs*. That film was shot in thirty-five millimeter, and 4K scanning is sufficient to capture all the resolution of the original film stock; it was sharp enough in the close-ups when he's staring at Clarice to check. His eyes were indeed performing microsaccades."

Heather smiled. "So much for Method acting."

Her mozzarella sticks looked yummy, but I couldn't have one. "Yeah. Still, Hitler had an unnerving stare, too. He'd lock his eyes on people and hold the gaze much longer than normal. There's no footage of him clear enough to show whether or not he was doing microsaccades, but I'm sure he wasn't."

"But I still don't get the *why* of it," said Heather. "What has the lack of microsaccades got to do with being a psychopath? I mean, okay, I can see how it could account for the stare . . ."

"It's more than that," I said. "You know, a lot of the world's most-cutting-edge work in psychopathy has been done here in Canada . . . which says something, I'm sure. Not only is Bob Hare Canadian—he's emeritus now at UBC—but so is Angela Book. She published a study in 2009 called 'Psychopathic Traits and the Perception of Victim Vulnerability.' That study and subsequent ones have shown that psychopaths have an almost preternatural ability to target already wounded people.

"In one of my own experiments, I made high-resolution videos of a group of female volunteers, some of whom had been assaulted in the past and some of whom hadn't, milling about in a room with some male grad students. I then showed the footage to a group of men, asking them to pick out which females had been previously assaulted. For normal men, the success rate was no better than chance: they simply couldn't tell and so just guessed. But the psychopaths averaged eighty percent correct.

"When I asked the psychopaths *how* they could tell, their answers ranged from the not-very-helpful 'it's obvious' to the significant 'I can see it in their faces.' And apparently they *could*. Human faces are in constant, subtle motion, exhibiting fleeting microexpressions that last between a twenty-fifth and a fifteenth of a second. When a psychopath turns on the psychopathic stare, free of microsaccades, he can clearly see the microexpressions. In the case of the previously abused women, an ever-so-brief look of fear might pass over their faces when a man looks at them, and not only do the psychopaths notice it, but they gravitate toward those exhibiting such things."

"Holy shit," said Heather.

"Yeah."

The server arrived with Heather's Cobb salad. "Go ahead," I said.

She took a forkful. "What about sociopaths as opposed to psycho-paths?"

"Po-tay-toe, po-tah-toe. Although some clinicians—mostly Amer-icans, come to think of it—still try to distinguish between the two, the *DSM-5* lumps them together. You know, much of the dialog in the movie version of *The Silence of the Lambs* comes straight out of the novel, but in the book, Lecter is described as 'a pure sociopath,' whereas in the film, they changed it to 'a pure psychopath.' The distinction, if there is one, either comes down to etiology—those like me who prefer the term 'psychopathy' think the cause is mostly a difference in the brain; those who prefer 'sociopathy' think society must have shaped the person—or down to how the condition manifests itself. Some say the classic glib and charming but totally heartless guy—that's a psychopath; if it's more of a regular schlub who just happens to lack conscience and empathy, he's a sociopath. Regardless, my technique detects them both. Still . . ."

She looked at me expectantly. "Yeah?"

"You know the difference between a psychopath and a homeopath?"

She shook her head.

"Some psychopaths do no harm."

"Ha!" She ate a forkful of salad, then, "So, how precisely does your method work? How do you conduct the test?"

"Well, microsaccades are a fixational eye movement—they occur only when your gaze is fixed on something. And to get a really solid, really good track, I don't normally use film. Rather, I use a modified set of ophthalmologist's vision-testing goggles. I get the suspected psychopath to wear them and simply ask him or her to stare for ten seconds at a dot displayed by the goggles. Sensors check to see if the eyes stay rock-steady or if they jerk a bit. If the former, the guy's a psychopath, I guarantee it. If the latter—if the subject *is* performing microsaccades—he isn't. You can't fake microsaccades; the smallest volitional eye shift anyone can do is much bigger. As long as the person doesn't have an eye-movement disorder, such as congenital or acquired nystagmus, which would be obvious before you did the test, with my technique, there are no false positives. If I say you're a psychopath, you bloody well are."

"Wow," said Heather. "Can I borrow them?"

Maybe I'd underestimated her; perhaps she *was* onto Gustav after all. "No," I said, "but invite me for Christmas, and I'll bring them along."

"Deal," she said, spearing a cherry tomato.

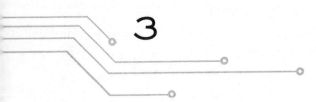

3

"AND so, Professor Marchuk, in summary, is it your testimony that the defendant, Devin Becker, is indeed a psychopath?"

Juan Sanchez had rehearsed my direct examination repeatedly. He wanted to ensure that not only the judge, who had heard psychological testimony in many previous cases, could follow me, but also that the seven men and five women in the jury dock, none of whom had ever taken a psych course, couldn't help but see the logic of it all.

Juan had told me to make eye contact with the jurors. Sadly, juror four (the heavyset black woman) and juror nine (the white guy with the comb-over) were both looking down. But I did connect briefly with each of the others although three averted their gazes as soon as they felt my eyes land on them.

I turned back to him and nodded decisively. "Yes, exactly. There is no question whatsoever."

"Thank you, Professor." Juan looked questioningly at Judge Kawasaki. The best way to use an expert defense witness, he'd told me, was to present direct examination immediately before a recess so the argument would have time to take root before the prosecution attacked it; he'd timed my testimony to finish just before noon. But either Kawasaki was oblivious to the time or he was onto Juan's strategy since he turned to the D.A. and said the words Juan himself had failed to utter. "Your witness, Miss Dickerson."

Juan shot me a disappointed glance, then moved over and sat down next to Devin Becker, who, as always, had a scowl on his thin face.

I shifted nervously in my seat. We'd rehearsed this part, too, trying to predict what questions Belinda Dickerson would fire off in an attempt to discredit my microsaccades technique. But as Moltke the Elder famously said, no battle plan ever survives contact with the enemy.

Dickerson was forty-eight, tall, lithe, with a long, pale face and short black hair; if the pole holding the Georgia flag at the side of the room ever broke, she could stand in as its replacement. "Mr. Marchuk," she said, in a voice that was stronger than one might have expected from her build, "we heard a great deal about your qualifications when my opponent called you to the stand."

It didn't seem to be a question, so I said nothing. Perhaps she expected me to make some modest noise, and, in a social situation, I might have done just that. But here, in this court, with the hot dry air—not to mention an annoying fly buzzing around the light hanging over my head—I simply nodded as she went on: "Degrees, postdocs, clinical certifications, academic appointments."

Again, not a question. I had been generally nervous about being cross-examined, but I now relaxed slightly. If she wanted to go over my CV with forensic glee, that was fine by me; I'd embellished nothing.

"But now, sir," Dickerson continued, "I'd like to explore some parts of your background that weren't brought forth by Mr. Sanchez."

I looked at Juan, whose head did an avian snap toward the jury, then ricocheted back to facing me. "Yes?" I said to her.

"Where is your family from?"

"I was born in Calgary, Alberta."

"Yes, yes. But your family, your people: where are they from?"

Like everyone, I've been asked this question before, and I usually made a joke of my reply, the kind only an academic could get away with. "My ancestors," I'd say, "came from Olduvai Gorge." I glanced at the jury box and also at the dour, wrinkled countenance of Judge Kawasaki.

There was no point in uttering a joke you knew was going to bomb. "My heritage, you mean? It's Ukrainian."

"So your mother, she was Ukrainian?"

"Yes. Well, Ukrainian-Canadian."

She made a dismissive gesture, as if I were muddying the waters with pointless cavils. "And your maternal grandfather, was he Ukrainian, too?"

"Yes."

"Your grandfather emigrated to Canada at some point?"

"The 1950s. I don't know precisely when."

"But he lived in Ukraine prior to that?"

"Actually, I think the last place he lived in Europe was Poland."

Dickerson took a turn looking at the jury. She raised her eyebrows as if astonished by my answer. "Where in Poland?"

It took me a second to come up with the name, and I doubt I did justice to the pronunciation. "Gdenska."

"Which is where?"

I frowned. "As I said, in Poland."

"Yes, yes. But *where* in Poland? What's it close to?"

"It's north of Warsaw, I think."

"I believe that's correct, yes, but is it close to any . . . any *site,* shall we say . . . of historical significance?"

Juan Sanchez rose, jaw jutting even more than usual. "Objection, Your Honor. This travelogue can be of no relevance to the matter at hand."

"Overruled," said Kawasaki. "But you *are* trying my patience, Miss Dickerson."

She apparently took that as license to ask a leading question. "Mr. Marchuk, sir, let me put it bluntly: isn't that village of yours, Gdenska, isn't it just ten miles from Sobibor?"

Her consistent refusal to use one of the honorifics I was entitled to was, of course, an attempt to undermine me in front of the jury. "I don't know," I said. "I have no idea."

"Fine, fine. But it's *near* Sobibor, isn't it? Only a few minutes by car, no?"

"I really don't know."

"Or by train?" She let that sink in for a beat, then: "What did your grandfather do during World War II?"

"I don't know."

"Don't you?"

I felt my eyebrows going up. "No."

"That surprises me, sir. It surprises me a great deal."

"Why?"

"You actually don't get to ask questions, sir; that's not the way this works. Now, is it really your testimony here, under oath, that you don't know what your mother's father did during World War II?"

"That's right," I said, utterly perplexed. "I don't know."

Dickerson turned to the jury and lifted her hands in an "I gave him a chance" sort of way. She then walked to her desk, and her young female assistant passed her a sheet of paper. "Your Honor, I'd like to introduce this notarized scan of an article from the *Winnipeg Free Press* of March twenty-third, 2001."

Kawasaki gestured for Dickerson to come forward, and she handed him the piece of paper. He gave it a perfunctory glance, then passed it to the clerk. "So ordered," he said. "Mark as People's one-four-six."

"Thank you, Your Honor," she said, retrieving the sheet. "Now, Mr. Marchuk, would you be so kind as to read us the first indicated passage?"

She handed me the page, which had two separate paragraphs highlighted in blue. I couldn't make out what they said without my reading glasses, and so I reached into my suit jacket—and saw the guard at the far end of the room move to draw his revolver. I slowly removed my cheaters, perched them on my nose, and began reading aloud: "'More startling revelations were made this week as papers from the former Soviet Union continued to be made public. The newly disclosed documents have a Canadian connection. Ernst Kulyk . . .'" I faltered, and my throat went dry as I skimmed ahead.

"Continue, please, sir," said Dickerson.

I swallowed, then: "'Ernst Kulyk, the father of Patricia Marchuk, a prominent Calgary attorney, has been revealed to have been a guard at the Nazi Sobibor death camp, implicated in the deaths of thousands, if not tens of thousands, of Polish Jews.'"

I looked up. The paper fluttered in my hands.

"Thank you, sir. Now, who is Patricia Marchuk?"

"My mother."

"And, just to be clear, she's your biological mother—and Ernst Kulyk was her biological father, correct? Neither you nor your mother were adopted?"

"That's right."

"Is your maternal grandfather still alive?"

"No. He died sometime in the 1970s."

"And you were born in 1982, correct? So you never met him, right?"

"Never."

"And your mother, is she still alive?"

"No. She passed fifteen years ago."

"In 2005?"

"Yes."

"Were you estranged from her?"

"No."

"And yet it's your testimony before this court that you didn't know what her father—your grandfather—did during World War II?"

My heart was pounding. "I—honestly, I had no idea."

"Where did you live in March 2001, when this article was published?"

"In Winnipeg. I was in second-year university then."

"A sophomore?"

"We don't use that term in Canada, but yes."

"And the *Winnipeg Free Press*, correct me if I'm wrong, is now and was then the largest-circulation daily newspaper in that city, right?"

"I believe so, yes."

"So surely someone must have mentioned this article to you, no?"

"Never."

"Seriously? Didn't your mother say anything to you about this revelation?"

Acid was splashing at the back of my throat. "Not that I recall."

"Not that you recall," she repeated. "There's a second highlighted passage on that page. Would you read it, please?"

I looked down and did so. "'Ernst Kulyk was a local, living near Sobibor. Historian Howard Green at the Simon Wiesenthal Center in Los Angeles says Marchuk fits the physical description of Ernst the Enforcer, a guard notorious for his brutality.'"

"And your work, Professor, as we've heard here in this courtroom, is designed to exonerate those accused of heinous crimes, is it not?"

"Not at all. I—"

"Please, sir. Surely the defense would not have engaged your services if they hadn't thought your testimony could be used to convince the honest men and women of this jury that some people just happen to be psychopaths, that God made them that way, that they can't help themselves, that they shouldn't be held accountable to the highest standard of the law, isn't that so?"

"Objection!" said Juan. "Argumentative."

"Sustained. Careful, Miss Dickerson."

"Mr. Marchuk, sir, how would you characterize the relationship between your family history and your area of research? Isn't it true that the one inspired the other?"

"I told you I didn't know about my grandfather."

"Come now, sir. I can understand wanting to put your family's shame—*Canada's* shame—behind you, but, really, isn't it true that you, in fact, had made up your mind in this case before you ever met Devin Becker? For to find Devin Becker accountable, to insist he answer for his crimes, his perversions, his cruelty, would require you to demand the same of your grandfather. Isn't that so?"

"Even if I'd known about my grandfather," I said, feeling dizzy now, "the cases are vastly different, separated by decades and thousands of miles."

"Trivialities," said Dickerson. "Isn't it true that you've been called 'an apologist for atrocities' in print?"

"Never in a peer-reviewed journal."

"True," said Dickerson. "I allude to Canada's *National Post*. But the fact of the matter remains: is it not true that every aspect of your testimony here today is colored by your desire to see your grandfather as a blameless victim of circumstances?"

"My research is widely cited," I said, feeling as though the wooden floor of the witness dock was splintering beneath me, "and it, in turn, cites such classics as the work of Cleckley and Milgram."

"But, unlike them, you come at this with an agenda, do you not?"

It seemed utterly pointless to protest that Stanley Milgram's family had been Jews slaughtered in the Holocaust—his work was all about trying to make sense of the senseless, to fathom the inexplicable, to comprehend how sane, normal people could have done those things to other thinking, feeling beings.

"That would not be my position," I said, trying to keep my voice steady.

"No," responded Belinda Dickerson, looking once more at the men and women in the jury dock, all of whom were sitting up in rapt attention. "I'm sure it wouldn't be."

Judge Kawasaki finally called the recess, and I exited the Atlanta courtroom, my heart pounding again, which, given my history, is a feeling I hated. Juan Sanchez was going to have lunch with Devin Becker, but I doubted they wanted me to join them. I headed out into the afternoon heat, air shimmering above the parking lot's asphalt, used a shaking hand to put my Bluetooth receiver in my ear, and called my sister in Calgary. The phone rang, then a woman said, "Morrell, Thompson, Chandler, and Marchuk."

"Heather Marchuk, please." My sister's marriage had fallen apart long ago—way before mine had—but she'd always used her maiden name professionally.

"May I ask who's calling?"

"It's her brother Jim."

"Oh, Mr. Marchuk, hi. Are you in town?"

I'm usually pretty good with names, and I suspect if I wasn't so distraught, I would have come up with the receptionist's. I could picture her, though—blond, petite, round glasses.

"No. Is Heather in?"

"Let me put you through."

I saw a husky man looking at me—probably a reporter hoping for a quote. I turned and walked briskly away.

My sister and I talked a couple of times a month—the maximum Gustav would allow—but it was always in the evenings; she was clearly surprised to be getting a call from me during the workday. "Jim, is everything okay? Where are you?"

I couldn't answer the first question in a reassuring way, so I skipped to the second. "Atlanta."

Heather knew me too well. "Something *is* wrong. What?"

"Do you know what Grandpa Kulyk did in World War II?"

Silence for a moment. Off in the distance—here or there, I wasn't sure which—a siren was wailing. "What the hell, Jim."

"Sorry?" A question, not an apology.

"What the hell," she said again.

"Excuse me?"

"Jim, if this is some kind of joke . . ."

"I'm not joking."

"You know full well what he did in the war, at that camp."

"Well, I know *now*," I said. "I found out today. I'm here giving expert testimony in that trial I told you about. The D.A. blindsided me with the news."

"It's not *news*, for Christ's sake," said Heather. "It came out ages ago."

"Why didn't you tell me?"

"Are you nuts? We all knew about it."

My head was swimming. "I don't remember that."

"Seriously?"

"Seriously."

"Jim, look, I've got a client meeting in—well, damn, I should be doing it now. I don't know what to say, but get some help, okay?"

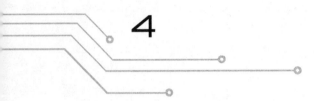

4

I'D have been happy to go home after the morning's evisceration, but when the judge had called the recess, Miss Dickerson indicated she wasn't through with me. After failing to find a vegan entrée in the court-house cafeteria, I'd settled for a packaged salad and a cup of black coffee.

The fireworks began again as soon as court resumed. "Objection!" said Juan, rising in response to Dickerson asking me once more about my personal history. "This fishing expedition has no bearing on the sentencing of Devin Becker."

Dickerson spread her arms as she turned toward the brooding judge. "Your Honor, this is the first time Mr. Marchuk's technique has been introduced in a court of law. With the court's permission, it seems only appropriate to delve into any biases or prejudices—even ones that he himself might not be aware of—that might have tainted his results."

"Very well; objection overruled—but don't wander too far afield."

"Of course not, Your Honor." She turned back to me. "Mr. Marchuk, sir, what's your stance on capital punishment?" I saw Juan clenching his wide jaw.

"I'm against it."

Dickerson nodded, as if this was only to be expected. "Earlier you told us you were Canadian, and our friends to the north don't have capital punishment. Is your objection simply something that goes with your citizenship, like a fondness for hockey and maple syrup?"

"I object to capital punishment on a philosophical basis."

"Ah, yes. When Mr. Sanchez was introducing you, he made mention of the fact that in addition to your three degrees in psychology you also have a master's degree in philosophy, correct?"

"Yes."

"Well, then, given this sentencing trial is precisely about whether Mr. Becker will receive the death penalty, perhaps you could briefly enlighten us as to your philosophical objections to it?"

I took a deep breath. I'd often debated the issue in classrooms, but the palpable disapproval of the jurors was throwing me off my game; the D.A. hadn't allowed anyone who was morally opposed to capital punishment to be impanelled for this case. "They aren't just my objections," I said. "I'm a utilitarian philosopher. Utilitarians believe the greatest good is maximizing happiness for the greatest number. And one of utilitarianism's founders, Jeremy Bentham, back in 1775, articulated several compelling arguments against the death penalty, arguments that still make sense."

I let my butterflies settle for a moment, then: "First, he said—and I agree—that it's unprofitable. That is, it costs more to society to execute people than it does to keep them alive. That was true in Bentham's day, and is even more true today: the extended legal proceedings, including this very one that we're all part of right now, plus the inevitable appeals, make it far more expensive to execute a criminal than it is to imprison him or her for life.

"And, just as important, Bentham said—and, again, I agree—the death penalty is irremissible. That is, there's no way to undo an error. Of course, the unhappiness that results from a wrongful execution is huge for the death-row inmate. More than that, though, if a society executes an innocent man, and that fact is subsequently revealed when, for instance, the real killer is caught, then everyone in that society feels— or, at least, *should* feel—great remorse at the horrible thing done in the name of all of us. And then—"

"Thank you, sir. We get the idea. Now, then, what about abortion? If your argument is that punishing the innocent with the ultimate sanction is debilitating for society, then I'm sure the men and women seated here, in the wake of our Supreme Court having recently overturned *Roe v. Wade,* will be gratified to hear that you're pro-life."

"I'm not. I'm pro-choice." I heard a hiss-like intake of breath from one of the jurors, and saw another one, the bearded white man, shake his head slowly back and forth.

Belinda Dickerson returned to her desk, and her assistant took a book out of a briefcase and handed it to her—and, like every author, I have the ability to recognize one of my own books at just about any distance, even when it's partially obscured. "Your Honor, I'd like to introduce this copy of *Utilitarian Ethics of Everyday Life,* by our current witness, James K. Marchuk."

Judge Kawasaki nodded. "Mark as People's one-four-seven."

"Thank you, Your Honor. Just to confirm, sir, you *are* the author of this book, correct?"

"Yes, that's right."

"As you can see, I've marked two pages with Post-it flags. Would you be so kind as to turn to the first one and read the highlighted passage?"

Post-it flags come in many colors; I use them all the time myself. She'd no doubt deliberately chosen red ones; she wanted the jury to be thinking about blood.

I flipped to the first indicated page, carefully took out my reading glasses, and said: "'As in all utilitarian thinking, one cannot put one's own desires or happiness ahead of another's simply because they *are* one's own, but in the case of a genetically defective fetus which, if brought to term, will live an unhappy, pain-filled life, terminating the fetus is clearly the path that will most increase the world's net happiness, for, as we have observed, there are only two ways to add to the world's total joy. The first, obviously, is to make the people who already exist happier. The second is to actually increase the number of people in the world through childbirth, *provided they will likely live happy lives.*'" Italics, as the saying goes, in the original.

I shifted uncomfortably in my seat then went on. "'The corollary to this is that the world's total happiness is decreased by either making existing people less happy—as raising a disabled child with its attendant emotional and financial costs would doubtless do for the parents—or by allowing more people to come into existence who will be unhappy, as a child born to a life of pain and suffering will be. In such a case, therefore, abortion is perhaps morally obligatory.'"

The argument was more complex than that, and I dealt with all the objections one might raise in the subsequent paragraphs, but I stopped when the blue highlighting came to an end, closed the book, and looked up.

You could hear a safety pin drop in that courtroom. The jurors were all staring at me, some with mouths agape, and the color had gone out of Juan's face. Only Devin Becker looked unperturbed.

Dickerson let the silence grow for as long as she felt she could get away with, then: "Thank you. Now, the next passage, please."

I nervously opened the book again and flipped to the second marked page. At the top of it was a double-indented quotation from utilitarianism's other founder, John Stuart Mill; I knew it by heart:

> *Few human creatures would consent to be changed into any of the lower animals, for a promise of the fullest allowance of a beast's pleasures; no intelligent human being would consent to be a fool, no instructed person would be an ignoramus, no person of feeling and conscience would be selfish and base, even though they should be persuaded that the fool, the dunce, or the rascal is better satisfied with his lot than they are with theirs.*
>
> *It is better to be a human being dissatisfied than a pig satisfied; better to be Socrates dissatisfied than a fool satisfied. And if the fool, or the pig, are of a different opinion, it is because they only know their own side of the question. The other party to the comparison knows both sides.*

But Dickerson hadn't highlighted that. Instead, the blue marking began immediately afterward; I swallowed, then started reading aloud:

"'Mill's key point is that we reasonably and correctly value the lives of a human more greatly than we do that of a chimpanzee, for the chimp, while perhaps enjoying the moment, cannot anticipate future happiness as well as we can—and that act of anticipation is in itself a pleasure.'

"'Likewise, we value a chimp—to the extent in many jurisdictions of outlawing their use in laboratory experiments—more than we value a mouse, a being of demonstrably lesser intellectual capacity. But to be fair, and to avoid a charge of speciesism, we must apply the same standards to our own kind.'

"'Yes, an embryo, from the moment of conception, is genetically fully *Homo sapiens,* but it has no complex cognition, no ability to plan or anticipate, and little if any joy. As it develops, these faculties will accrue gradually, but they clearly do not exist in anything approaching their full form until several *years* after birth. On the bases previously discussed, a utilitarian should support abortion when a prenatal diagnosis has been made that is strongly indicative of an unhappy, painful life; it is on this current basis—the lack of a fully developed mind for years to come—that a utilitarian can additionally embrace not just abortion but also a merciful release when a severe defect is not apparent until after parturition.'"

"'Parturition,'" said Dickerson. "A right fancy word, that." She glanced at the jury. "For those of us more accustomed to plainer speaking, what is 'parturition'?"

"Childbirth."

"In other words, Mr. Marchuk, sir, you believe abortion is okay. You believe—and I find this almost impossible to say aloud, but it is what the indicated passage said, isn't it? You even believe *infanticide* can be okay. But you *don't* believe in capital punishment."

"Well, as Peter Singer would argue . . ."

"Please, sir, it's a yes-or-no question. Are you against capital punishment in all circumstances?"

"Yes."

"Are you in favor of abortion?"

"I'm in favor of increasing utility, in maximizing happiness, so—"

"Please, sir, again: yes or no? In the vast majority of circumstances in which a woman might desire an abortion, are you in favor of letting her have it?"

"Yes."

"And are there even times when infanticide, when killing an already-born child, is, in your view, the right thing to do?"

"On the basis that—"

"*Yes or no?*"

"Well, yes."

"And your goal here is to convince the good men and women of this jury that it would be morally wrong to execute the defendant?"

I spread my arms. "I have no goal other than to explain the screening technique I developed, but—"

"No, buts, sir. And no more questions. Your Honor, I'm very grateful to be through with this witness."

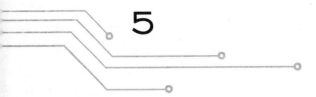

5

I said it didn't bother me if people examined my résumé, and that's true—with one exception. When other academics look at it, they shake their heads when they see I did my undergrad at the same institution I teach at now; that's always considered fishy. Although I love the University of Toronto's "Prof or Hobo?" web quiz, which asks you to identify by their photos whether a person is a vagrant or a faculty member, we tenure-track types are supposed to be more like male chimpanzees: once we reach maturity, and have proven ourselves intractably irascible, we're expected to leave our native community, never to return. *Welcome Back, Kotter* was a bad-enough scenario for a high-school teacher; it was anathema to those of us in academe.

But my own career had brought me from doing my bachelor's degree here at the University of Manitoba—my flight had gotten in last night—back to being a tenured professor at the same institution. When asked why, I cite several reasons. "A fondness for bitter cold," I'd quip, or "An abiding love of mosquitoes." But the real reason was Menno Warkentin.

When I started at U of M, in 1999, Menno was teaching the same first-year introductory-psych course that I myself taught now. Back then, I was eighteen, and Menno was fifty-five. He was now seventy-four and had emeritus status, which meant he was retired but, unlike some of the figurative if not literal bums who were eventually shown the door, was always welcome in his department, and, although drawing only a pension and not a salary, could still do research, supervise grad students, and so on. And, for all those years, he'd been my friend and mentor—I'd lost track of the hours we'd spent in his office or mine, shooting the breeze, talking about our work and our lives.

More than just his age and professorial status had changed since I'd started being his student; he'd also lost his sight. Although he happened to be diabetic, and blindness was a common side effect of that condition, that wasn't the reason. Rather, he'd been in a car accident in 2001, and while the airbag had kept him from being killed, its impact had shattered his beloved antique glasses, and shards had been thrust into his eyeballs. I'd once or twice seen him without the dark glasses he now wore. His artificial blue eyes were lifelike but didn't track. They just stared blankly forward from beneath silver eyebrows.

I found Menno sitting in his office with his headset on, listening to his screen reader. His guide dog, a German shepherd named Pax, was curled contentedly at his feet. Menno's office had an L-shaped dark-brown shelving-and-counter unit against the back and side walls, but he had everything out of the way, up high or pushed to the back, so he couldn't accidentally knock things over. And whereas I always had stacks of printouts and file folders on my own office floor, he had nothing that he might trip on. His office had a large window that looked not outside but into the corridor, and the white vertical blinds were closed, I guess on the principle that if he couldn't see out, no one should be able to see in.

Today, though, in the summer heat, his door was open, and as I entered, Pax stood and poked her muzzle into Menno's thigh to alert him that someone had arrived. He took off the headset and swung around, my face reflecting back at me from his obsidian-dark lenses. "Hello?"

"Menno, it's Jim."

"Padawan!"—his nickname for me since my student days. "How was your trip?"

I took a chair, and Pax settled in again at Menno's feet. "The D.A. really worked at discrediting me."

"Well, that's his job," Menno said.

"Her job. But yeah."

"Ah."

"And she brought up some stuff about my past."

Menno was sitting on a reddish-brown executive-style chair. He leaned back, his belly like a beach ball. "Oh?"

"Stuff that I myself didn't recall."

"Like what?"

"Do you remember 2001?"

"Sure. Saw it in a theater when it first came out."

"Not the movie," I said. "The year."

"Oh." He made a how-could-I-forget-it gesture at his face. "Yes."

"Jean Chrétien was prime minister then, right? And George W. Bush was sworn in as president."

"Umm, yeah. That's right."

"And what were the biggest news stories of 2001?"

"Well, 9/11, obviously. Beyond that, off the top of my head, I don't remember."

"But you *would,*" I said.

"What?"

"You would remember others if you gave it some thought, right?"

"I guess."

"I don't," I said.

"What do you mean?"

"The D.A. surprised me with an article about my grandfather from the *Winnipeg Free Press.* I went to the DaFoe Library this morning, and they pulled the microfilm of that edition. I started looking at other headlines from that day, but none of them stirred any memories, and neither did the front pages of the *Free Press* from other days around then. So I went online and looked at the covers of *Time* and *Maclean's* from 2001. I didn't recognize any of the stories until the summer. Two thousand, no problem. The second half of 2001, yeah, it all came back to me. But the initial six months of 2001 are a blank. The first thing I can pin down from that year is the day after Canada Day. July first fell on a Sunday that year, so people got July second off work. I remembered being pissed that I'd tried to go to the post office on that Monday to pick up a parcel, only to find it closed for the holiday." I spread my arms. "I've lost half a year of my life."

"You're sure?"

"As far as I can tell, yes. I mean, I remember being disgusted when the US Supreme Court handed down the decision in *Bush v. Gore*—but that was in December of 2000. I don't remember Bush's actual inauguration although there *had* to have been protests, right?"

"I imagine so."

"And in June of that year, Carroll O'Connor passed away—Archie Bunker himself! You know how much I love *All in the Family*. I simply *couldn't* have missed that bit of news, but somehow I did. Until today, I'd always assumed he was still alive in retirement somewhere."

"And you just realized you had this gap?"

"Well, it was nineteen years ago, right? How often do we think about stuff from that far back? I do remember 9/11. I remember being right here, on campus, when I heard about the planes hitting the World Trade Center; I'd just started my third year. But other things from that long ago? How often would they come up?"

Menno shifted his bulky form in his chair. "Any idea why you can't remember those six months?"

"Yes," I said, but then fell silent. Menno had known me back then, but I'd never told him about this.

"And?" he prompted, reaching down to stroke Pax's head.

I took a deep breath, then: "I died when I was nineteen. Legally dead. Heart stopped, breathing stopped. The whole nine yards."

Menno halted in mid-stroke. "Really?"

"Yes."

"What happened?" he asked, leaning back again.

I pulled my chair closer to his desk. "I'd gone back home to Calgary for the Christmas break. My sister was off in Europe, and my parents were on a cruise—but I wanted to see my friends. I remember New Year's Eve, of course. Yes, the whole world had celebrated big-time a year before, on December thirty-first, 1999, but you know me: I held out for the *real* beginning of the twenty-first century, which was January first, 2001, right? Not 2000."

"Because there was no year zero," supplied Menno.

"Exactly! Anyway, I'd attended a party at the house of one of my high-school friends, and that night—that is, like 2:00 A.M. on the morning of January first, 2001—when I was heading home, I was attacked by a guy with a knife. It was a cold, clear night. I remember the stars: Orion standing tall, Betelgeuse like a drop of blood, Jupiter and Saturn near the Pleiades."

"You and the stars," he said, smiling; I'm secretary of the Winnipeg Centre of the Royal Astronomical Society of Canada.

"Exactly, but it's relevant, see? I was doing what I always do. Cold night, I've forgotten my mitts so my hands are shoved into my jacket pockets, toque pulled down over my ears, and I'm walking along looking up—not ahead of me, but up, finding the ecliptic, looking for planets, hoping to maybe see a meteor streak across the sky. Sure, I'd checked for traffic before crossing the street, but that's all I did. I wasn't looking to see what was happening on the other side. Oh, I probably registered that there were a couple of people there, but I wasn't paying any damn attention to them. And so I crossed diagonally because I was heading in that direction, right? And when I got to the other side, suddenly this guy wheels around, and he's got this pinched, narrow face and teeth that are sharp and pointy and all askew, and his eyes, man, his eyes are *wild*. Wide open, whites all around. And he shoves me with one hand, palm against my chest, and he snarls—really, it was a total snarl, his breath coming out in clouds—and says 'What the fuck do you want?'

"I look over at the other guy, and, Christ, he's covered in blood. It seems black in the yellow light from the streetlamp, but that's what it's got to be, blood all over his nylon jacket. That guy's been stabbed; I've walked into a drug deal gone bad. I stammer, 'I'm just heading to the C-Train.'

"But it's no good. The guy is crazy or high or both, and he's got a knife. The other guy takes the opportunity to try to get away: he starts running—staggering, really—onto the street. But he's badly hurt, and I see now that he'd been standing in a puddle of his own blood, a puddle that's freezing over.

"But the guy with the knife is looking at me, not him, and he lunges at me. And I'm *me*, right? I don't know jack about street fighting. I don't know how to deflect a blow or anything like that. I feel the knife going in sideways, and I know, I just know, it's going in between my ribs, just off the centerline of my chest. It doesn't hurt—not yet—but it's going deep.

"And then it pierces my heart; I know that's what's happening. And he pulls the knife out and I stagger a half-pace backward, away from the road, clutching my chest, feeling the blood pouring out, and it's hot, it's like scalding hot compared to the chilled air, but it's not ebbing and flowing, it's not pumping. It's just *draining* out onto the sidewalk. I fall backward, and I'm looking up at the sky, but it's too bright here, the streetlamp is washing everything out, and I'm thinking, *God damn it, I wanted to see the stars.*

"And then—nothing. None of that tunnel bullshit, no bright light except the sodium one from the lamp; none of it. I'm just *gone.*"

Menno had switched to leaning forward, and about halfway through, he'd steepled his fingers in front of his wide face. They were still there. "And then what?" he said.

"And then I was dead."

"For how long?"

I shrugged. "No one knows. It can't have been *too* long. Man, if the word 'lucky' can be applied to that sort of situation, I was lucky. I'd fallen right by that streetlamp, so I was in plain view, and it was bitterly cold. A medical student coming home from a different party stumbled upon me, called 911, plugged the hole in my torso, and did chest compressions until the ambulance got there."

"My God," said Menno.

"Yeah. But, given the timing, it has to be what's affecting my memory."

Silence again, then, at last: "There was doubtless oxygen deprivation. You likely did suffer some brain damage, preventing the formation of long-term memories for a time."

"You'd think—but there should be more evidence of it. During my missing six months, if I wasn't laying down new memories, I'd have had enormous difficulty functioning. I was in your class then. Do you remember me behaving strangely?"

"It was a long time ago."

"Sure, but I also was one of your test subjects in that research project, right?"

He frowned. "Which one?"

"Something about . . . microphones?"

"Oh, that one. Yeah, I guess you were."

"You had a cool name for it, um . . ."

"Project Lucidity."

"Right! Anyway, I was helping you with that before the knifing, and—well, I don't know: that's the whole point. Maybe I was part of your study afterwards, too?"

"I honestly don't remember," said Menno.

"Of course. But could you check your files, see if you have stuff about me going that far back? I'm looking for anything that might jog my memory."

"Sure, I'll have a look."

"I *must* have been laying down long-term memories during my . . . my 'dark period.' I mean, how else could I have functioned?"

"I suppose, yeah."

"And I did a half-year course in science fiction then, one semester, January to April. It was required that I take an English course, and that seemed less painful than CanLit."

"Ha."

"Anyway, I found the reading list from it still online. Apparently, we all read this novel about a biomedical engineer who discovers scientific proof for the existence of the human soul—but I don't remember ever reading it; I only know that's what it's about because I looked up the title on Amazon today."

"Well, there were more than a few assigned books I never got around to reading during my undergraduate days."

"Yeah, but I did an essay on this book. I found the WordPerfect file for it still on my hard drive."

"Could you, y'know, have bought the essay? From one of those services?"

I raised my hand palm out to forestall any more of this. "Sure, sure, you can explain away any one of these examples. But *all* of them? Six

months with no new memories laid down and yet me apparently functioning normally? There's no way to explain that."

"All right," said Menno. "But, you know, Jim, if the barrier to your
remembering that period is psychological rather than physical—
well . . ."

"What?"

"If your subconscious is repressing something, maybe you'll want
to just accept that. You're fine now, after all, aren't you?"

"I think so."

"The missing memories aren't affecting your work or your personal
life?"

"Not until that D.A. tore me to shreds."

"So, just keep in mind that the cure might be worse than the dis-
ease." Pax was still at Menno's feet, but her eyes were now closed.
"Sometimes it's better to let sleeping dogs lie."

Pax did look at peace. But I shook my head as I rose. "No," I said.
"I can't do that."

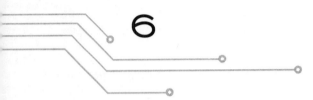

6

As I looked out my living-room window at the Red River, I thought perhaps I'd been unfair back at the Atlanta airport. If Fox News was a thorn in the side of every Democrat unlucky enough to hold public office in the United States, it was perhaps fair to say that the CBC was equally vexatious to any hapless Conservative trying to do his or her job in this country. The irony was that the CBC was a public broadcaster owned and operated, albeit at arm's length, by the federal government. There is little if anything Barack Obama could have done to deflect attacks from Fox News, but year after year of Conservative government in Ottawa had whittled the CBC down to a fraction of what it had once been, and even after Harper was finally given the heave-ho, tough economic times kept the CBC's funding from getting fully reinstated.

I had CBC Radio One on. The female announcer intoned: *"Although their attempt to blow up the Statue of Liberty was thwarted over the weekend, it's been revealed that the two would-be bombers, both Libyan nationals, entered the United States from Canada, crossing over from Ontario into Minnesota near Lake of the Woods eleven days ago. This is the second time this year that terrorists from Libya have entered the US via Canada. President Carroway was clearly frustrated at his press briefing this morning."*

The announcer's voice was replaced by a clip of the president: *"I've expressed my deep concern over this issue to Prime Minister Justin Trudeau. Perhaps if the killers were flowing in the other direction, he'd take it more seriously."*

As the newsreader was moving on to the next story, my iPhone played the *Jeopardy!* theme music, meaning a call was being forwarded from my office line, the one published on the university's website. The screen showed "KD Huron" and a number with a 639 area code, one I didn't recognize. I turned off the radio and swiped the answer bar. "Hello?"

An odd silence for a moment, then a hesitant female voice: "Hi, Jim. I was in town, so I thought I'd look you up."

"Who is this?"

"Kayla." A beat. "Kayla Huron."

The name didn't mean anything. "Yes?"

Her tone was suddenly frosty. "Sorry. I thought you might be happy to hear from me."

It's hard to talk and google on your phone at the same time, but fortunately my laptop was up and running on my living-room desk. I cradled the phone between my cheek and shoulder and typed her name into the computer. "Yes," I said, "of course I'm glad to hear from you . . . Kayla. How have you been?"

The first link was to her Wikipedia entry. I clicked it, and the article came up with a photo that was surprisingly good by Wikipedia standards, showing a pretty white woman in her mid thirties.

"Well," said Kayla, "it's been a lot of years, Jim. Where to start? I mean, I'm fine, but . . ."

"Yeah," I said, still stalling. "A lot of years." The first line of the entry said she "explores consciousness at the Canadian Light Source"—which sounded like some flaky new-age institution.

"Anyway," she said, "I'm here for a symposium at UW." The University of Winnipeg was the other university in town. "And, well, I saw your name in the paper today, and figured, what the heck, I'd see if you might like to have coffee, you know, to catch up . . ."

I scrolled down the Wikipedia entry: ". . . earned her MS (2005) and PhD (2010) from the University of Arizona following undergraduate work at the University of Manitoba (1999–2003) . . ."

"Yes!" I said, much too loudly. We'd been contemporaries here at U of M—including during my lost six months. "Absolutely!"

"Okay. When would be good for you?"

I wanted to say, "Right now!" But instead I simply offered, "My afternoon is open."

"About one? Suggest a place; I've got a rental car."

I did, we said goodbye, and I put the phone down on my wooden desk, my hand shaking.

I took a deep breath. I had several hours to kill before I needed to head out to meet Kayla, and, well, if my memory loss was indeed associated with the stabbing, then starting by researching that event seemed the logical first step.

There were normally numerous hoops to jump through to access patient medical records—even your own—but fortunately I knew one of the staff psychologists at the hospital I'd been treated at in Calgary; she and I had served together on the board of the Canadian Psychological Association. It was noon in Winnipeg, but that was only 11:00 A.M. in Calgary, so it seemed like a good time to try my call. I tapped my way through the menu tree to get the person I wanted. "Cassandra Cheung," said the lush voice in my ear.

"Sandy, it's Jim Marchuk."

Genuine warmth: "Jim! What can I do for you?"

"I'm hoping you can cut through some red tape. I need a copy of my own medical records."

"Your own? Yeah, sure, I guess that's no problem. You were treated here?"

"Yeah. I came in on New Year's Eve 2000—well, after midnight, so it was actually January first, 2001."

"That's a long time ago," she said, and I could hear her typing away.

"Nineteen years."

"Hmmm. You sure about that date?"

"Oh, yes."

"Were you maybe an outpatient? Not all records from that far back are in our central system."

"No, no. It was emergency surgery."

"My God, really?"

"Yeah."

"Were you brought in via ambulance?"

"Yes."

"I'm not finding anything. Do you remember the name of the surgeon?"

"Butcher," I said.

"Ha," replied Sandy. "That's funny."

"That's what I thought!"

"But there's no Dr. Butcher in the system. Are you sure it was this hospital? Could it have been Foothills instead?"

I wasn't sure of much at this point. "I . . . I guess. Um, can you try my last name with a typo? People sometimes put a *C* in before the *K*: M-A-R-C-H-U-C-K."

"Ah! Okay—yup, here it is, but . . . *huh*."

"What?"

"Well, the date wasn't January first—no one gets to have elective surgery on New Year's Day: there's too much likelihood that the operating rooms will be needed for emergencies, and all the surgeons who can be are off skiing."

"Elective surgery?"

"That's right. On Monday, February nineteenth, 2001, you had an infiltrating ductal carcinoma removed."

"A what?"

"It's a breast cancer."

"I'm a man."

"Men can get breast cancer, too. It's not that common, because you guys have so little breast tissue, but it happens. Says here they cut it out under a local anesthetic."

"No, no; that's got to be somebody else—somebody with a similar name. Besides, I was a student at the University of Manitoba then; I wouldn't have been in Calgary."

"Well, what *do* you think you were here for in January?"

"I was attacked with a knife."

"Jesus, really? What'd you do back then? Tell someone you'd voted Liberal?"

"Something like that."

"There's no record of your being treated here for anything of that nature."

"Are you sure?"

"Uh-huh."

"Um, okay. Thanks, Sandy."

"Jim, what's this—"

"I gotta go. Talk to you later."

"Okay. Bye."

"Bye."

I sagged back into my chair, my breath coming in short, rapid gasps.

7

"All right," I said, looking out at the sea of faces. "Is morality subjective or objective? Anyone?"

"Subjective," called out Boris, without bothering to raise his hand first.

"Why do you say that?"

"Because it varies from person to person."

"And," called out Nina, "from culture to culture."

"That's right," I said. "Some people are pro-choice; others are pro-life. Some believe you should always lend a helping hand; others think you make people weak by keeping them from having to struggle for themselves. Right?"

Nods.

"But Sam Harris—who knows who he is?"

"A famous atheist," said Kyle.

"Yes, true; his best-known book is The End of Faith. But he also wrote one called The Moral Landscape, in which he argues that if you define moral acts as those that promote the flourishing of conscious beings, then there is such a thing as objective morality. Consider this: imagine a world in which every single person

*is suffering as much as possible; everyone is in as much physical
and emotional pain as the human body and mind are capable
of experiencing—something like being in hell or, I dunno, Pitts-
burgh."*

Laughter.

*"Now, says Harris, what if we could dial it down a notch?
What if we could take the physical pain from a ten out of ten to
a nine out of ten, even for one individual? Wouldn't that be objectively the right thing to do? Is there any conceivable counterar-
gument, any possible moral view, in which not decreasing the pain
would be the right thing to do? Yes, yes, we can contrive scenarios
in which it's a zero-sum game—I turn down your pain, but somebody else's pain therefore has to go up. But that's not the situation
Harris proposed. He said every person is suffering the maximum
amount possible; there's no way lessening one person's pain could
increase somebody else's. So, given those circumstances, isn't
turning down even one person's pain clearly objectively the moral
thing to do? And turning down two people's pain would be even
better, right? And if you could turn down everyone's pain, even
a little bit, that would be a moral imperative, no?"*

*Boris was unconvinced. "Yeah, but who's to say what the
maximum suffering a human can endure is?"*

"Have you seen The Phantom Menace?"

*Some of the students laughed again, but Boris just frowned.
"If it can be a little less, it can be a little more."*

*"Not if experiencing pain involves neurons," I replied. "If
every pain-registering neuron is firing simultaneously, you're
maxed out. A human brain is a finite object."*

*"Some more finite than others," said Nina, looking pointedly
at Boris.*

*"Anyway," I said, "we'll talk more about moral relativism
later. What I really want to get at today is utilitarianism—and
utilitarianism is striving for the exact opposite of Sam Harris's
thought-experiment hell. Utilitarianism is a terrible name. It
sounds so cold and calculating. But really, it's a warm, even lov-*

ing, philosophy. Jeremy Bentham and John Stuart Mill were its first major proponents, and they said, simply, that all action should be geared toward achieving the greatest happiness for the greatest number of people. The happier people are, the better. The more people who are happy, the better."

I looked at Boris, who was frowning again. "Comrade," I said, "you look unhappy."

Nina and a few others laughed.

"It just all seems so self-serving," Boris said.

"Ah, but it isn't," I replied. "Bentham and Mill are both clear on that point. Under utilitarianism, you are to be neutral when weighing your own happiness against somebody else's. True, it's not a self-sacrificing philosophy—you don't have to give up your own happiness for the sake of another person's. But if doing something will cause your happiness to be diminished a little and someone else's happiness to be increased a lot, there's no question: you have to do it. You can't put your needs in front of those of other people."

"Let me know how that works out for you," Boris said.

WHEN I'd first gone away to university, I'd left lots of stuff at my parents' house in Calgary; Heather had done the same. But when our dad died, Calgary housing prices had been going through the roof, and Mom wished to downsize. I'd gone back and disposed of things I didn't want and moved the things I did to Winnipeg in a U-Haul. And, as with most people's collections of junk they thought was worth saving, I hadn't looked at it since although I periodically added more boxes to the midden—doing my part to give future archeology grad students something to work on.

I drove to the storage unit I rented and began to rummage around. Most of my crap was in identical corrugated-cardboard boxes I'd bought from a moving-supply company, but some of it was in bankers' boxes, and some old clothing—doubtless out of style although I'd be the last person to be able to actually confirm that—was in bright-orange garbage bags. I'd lived in Winnipeg during my dark time, but I figured that there should have been get-well cards from when I'd been in hospital in Calgary, and copies of police reports related to the stabbing. But I couldn't find anything like that.

The two heaviest known substances are neutronium and cartons of books. I shifted several boxes around, getting more of an upper-body workout than I was used to. Eventually, I came across one labeled "Textbks 2000-01" in black Magic Marker. I placed it on the storage unit's floor and used a box cutter to slit open the strapping tape.

Inside were the usual you-could-kill-a-man-with-them texts with titles such as *Social Psychology, Statistics for the Humanities,* and *Freud and Jung in Perspective,* but there were also a few science-fiction paperbacks. Ah, that half-year English elective I'd taken. There were copies of *Frankenstein* and *The War of the Worlds* and *Nineteen Eighty-Four,* which were titles I recognized, at least, although didn't recall having read, and others I didn't know at all. I picked up one with a beautiful cover painting of a steamboat in a green lagoon: *Darwinia* by Robert Charles Wilson. As had been my habit in those pre-ebook days, I'd used the sales receipt as a bookmark. I opened the novel to the indicated page, to see if the prose sparked any memories, but—

The receipt was from the McNally Robinson at Polo Park. That branch didn't exist anymore, but the date—

The date was 31-12-00, one of the few in that format that could be unambiguously parsed: thirty-one had to be a day, and double-zero could only be a year, which meant this book had been purchased New Year's Eve 2000.

Here. In Winnipeg.

And the time stamp was 17:43, which must have been just before closing on a holiday evening; even the nerdiest of nerds didn't ring in the new year in a bookstore.

Of course, someone else might have picked up the novel for me, but—

But, no, the credit-card number was printed on the bottom of the receipt, with Xs substituting for all but the final four digits, and those I recognized; I'd had that number for many years. I must have gone in to purchase the book, planning to get a jump on my class reading over the remaining week of the Christmas break.

Yes, technically, one could be in Winnipeg at 5:43 P.M. and still fly to Calgary in time to shout "Happy New Year!" six hours later—or, actually, seven, if you take into account the time-zone change. But there's no way I would have gone home for New Year's Eve but not Christmas, even if my parents and sister were away. What the hell was going on?

I continued to rummage around and found a Dilbert wall calendar from 2000. I'd hoped there'd be one for 2001, as well, but there wasn't. I flipped to the last page, the pointy-haired boss staring out at me, and looked at the days between Christmas—which had been on a Monday that year—and New Year's Eve. There were four appointments in my handwriting spread across those six days. On Boxing Day, I'd noted "Miles 6ish." I hadn't thought about Miles Olsen for years; he'd been in one of my classes, and we used to get together occasionally for a beer. On the thirtieth I'd written, "Pay dorm fees." And on the twenty-ninth and thirty-first, I'd written simply "Warkentin." There were no classes then, so these must have been related to that research project I'd volunteered for.

I scanned further up the calendar; Warkentin's name was written in three more times in the week before Christmas. The ink was black for the earlier appointments, blue for the later ones. I hadn't added them all at the same time, which meant the later appointments had been made after the earlier ones; he'd asked me back for some reason—and on New Year's Eve, for God's sake . . .

I'd told Menno yesterday that I'd been in Calgary on New Year's Eve 2000. Sure, it's possible he'd forgotten that I was with him on that long-ago date, but he hadn't mentioned a thing.

No, no, that's not quite right. He'd faced me, his blind eyes behind dark lenses, and he'd said, "Let sleeping dogs lie." I'd thought that was odd; he was a psychologist, after all—he should have been fascinated by the challenge of recovering my missing memories.

I'd used Gmail since the days when you needed an invitation to get an account, but those archives only went back to 2004. I'd had a student address here at U of M in 2001, and so I'd called up the IT department on the off chance that they kept email archives going back that far; they didn't. But I used to have a habit of printing out emails I wanted to keep—and, to my delight, I found a file folder containing a bunch of them in the same box that had yielded the calendar: a sheaf about half an inch thick of dot-matrix printouts, one email per sheet, conveniently stacked in send-date order. I worked my way through them: class assignments, a few from my sister, but nothing that stirred any memories.

I reached the end of February and flipped the page; the next email was from March second, and—my goodness!—it was from Kayla Huron to me. The subject line was "Re: Friday," but whatever my original message had been was lost to history; there were no quoted lines at the bottom of what she had written, which was, "Yeah, me, too. And I'd love to! You like Crash Test Dummies? They're playing over at UW next week. Can you pick up tickets?" That was all the email said, except for the number 2.9 at the bottom.

I kept reading messages; there were twenty or so from Kayla mixed in with other things. The other things were all prosaic—I'd clearly only printed out emails that had to-do items for me mentioned in them—and, indeed, the Kayla ones all had action items, too, but they also had something else: flirtation, giving way after a couple of weeks to actual smut. Apparently, we'd been *way* more than just classmates.

And all her messages to me ended with the same number: 2.9. Except the last one, that is—and the action item was clear: "Pick up your stuff, asshole."

Near as I could figure, Kayla and I had been hot-and-heavy for three-and-a-half months, until, apparently, it had all blown up. And, in about half an hour, I'd see her for the first time in nineteen years.

8

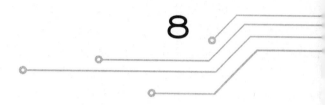

I drove along Pembina Highway, heading for my rendezvous with Kayla Huron, once again listening to the CBC. As I pulled into Grant Park mall, the 1:00 P.M. newscast began:

"Big news from Parliament Hill: Prime Minister Justin Trudeau's Liberal Party has just fallen as his controversial carbon-tax budget narrowly failed to pass a parliamentary vote. It's a situation not unlike the one that briefly ousted his father, Pierre Trudeau, as prime minister in 1974. Canadians will go to the polls next month to choose our next national leader . . ."

I walked across the asphalt, entered Pony Corral, and presented myself to the pretty young woman standing at the lectern. I don't know why restaurants have lecterns; they made me want to teach.

"Just one today?" she said.

I hated it when they said, "Just one?" in that sympathetic tone. *Sorry you're a loser, sir.* But I tried to keep the annoyance out of my voice. "Actually, I'm meeting someone. Do you mind if I have a look?"

She gestured at the dining room, and I went in, looking around— but Kayla spotted me first. "Jim!"

I saw an attractive redhead in a booth. She'd been a brunette in the

Wikipedia photo, but the ginger color suited her. As I approached, she rose. Normally, if I'd been greeting an old friend from that long ago, I'd have gone in for a hug or a peck on the cheek, but Kayla appeared . . . leery, perhaps, and so I simply sat down opposite her.

Her expression changed—via a conscious effort, it seemed—and I realized she was evaluating me in that way you do when you run into someone you haven't seen for a long time: looking for gray hairs, receding hairlines, paunches, wrinkles. On the hair checklist, both boxes were empty for me, and being vegan kept me trim, but, damn it, I preferred to call them "laugh lines." At least I wasn't doing the same thing; I had no old memories to compare the present her to—and I liked what I saw just fine.

Still, because it seemed the appropriate thing, I said, "You haven't changed a bit."

She smiled, but, again, it was a little wan, a tad reserved. "Nor have you." She already had a glass of white wine. "So," she added, "what's new?"

I liked to respond to that question with, "New York, New Jersey, New Delhi," but I didn't know this woman, damn it, I didn't know her at all; I couldn't be sure it would get a laugh. And yet at one time she *had* liked me, and so just being myself seemed the way to go. I trotted out the "New" list, and it did earn me a smile—and, at least for a second, the hesitancy was gone.

"Same sense of humor," she said. "You remember Professor Jenkins? What was that joke you told that got you kicked out of class?"

I was rescued by a waitress in a tight black top, cleavage showing. "Something to drink, sir?"

"What have you got on tap?"

She rattled off a list. I chose a dark craft beer, then turned back to Kayla. Unfortunately, though, she asked her question again. "Do you remember? That joke? Something about an orangutan?"

Christ, I don't think I've ever heard an orangutan joke in my entire life—well, except for *The Simpsons* singing "Help Me, Dr. Zaius" to the tune of "Rock Me Amadeus."

"I don't recall," I said.

She shrugged a little. "Well, it was a long time ago. So, what's up with you? Are you married?"

"I was, briefly. We divorced a couple of years ago. You?"

"Also divorced. I live with my daughter. She's six."

"What's her name?"

"Ryan."

I nodded. One of the many boy's names that had become girl's names in my lifetime. I'm waiting for one of my friends to name their daughter Buster or Dirk.

The waitress returned with my beer. I thanked her and took a sip. Kayla and I had had a fight—a big one that caused her to walk out of my life for two decades—but one that I didn't remember at all. Maybe she'd been justifiably angry with me, or maybe she had wronged me horribly, but in a way that had never quite been so true before, it really was no skin off my nose. "Kayla," I said, "about what happened, you know, all those years ago. I just want to say I'm sorry."

She looked at me for a few moments, as if seeking something in my expression. Then she tilted her head slightly. "Thanks, Jim."

I took a deep breath, then let it out. "Kayla, I need your help."

"With what?"

"I, ah, I had an accident many years ago, about two months before we started dating. I don't know if I ever told you . . . ?"

"Not that I recall."

"Well, I almost died. And apparently that did something to my memory. I—I'm sorry, I truly am, but until today, until you called, I had no memory of you."

"Seriously?"

"I'm sorry."

"Then why'd you want to see me again? You sounded so eager on the phone."

"I am. I lost memories of six months—January to June 2001—and I want to get them back. I'm hoping you can fill in some of the gaps. Earlier today, I read some of our old emails, and—"

She looked aghast. "You kept those?"

"Printouts of a few, yeah."

She took a sip of wine, then set the glass down carefully, as if afraid she might knock it over. "That explains why I haven't heard from you in all the years since."

"I'm sorry."

A waitress glided by. Kayla tracked her movement, perhaps so she wouldn't have to look at me. When the waitress had disappeared from view, Kayla dropped her gaze to the tablecloth. "I've googled you from time to time," she said "You've done well."

"Thanks." Silence for a moment. "Okay," I said, "one thing's been bugging me. A lot of those emails ended with the number two-point-nine. What the heck does that mean?"

A spontaneous little smile—fond remembrance, perhaps? "You really have lost your memory, haven't you?" She reached into her purse and took out a retractable ballpoint pen. She then pulled a paper napkin toward her. "You know how you make a love heart online? The emoticon?" She drew it: <3

"Yes?"

"It's the less-than sign followed by the number three, see? And what's less than three? Two-point-nine. So it's a cute way of saying the same thing."

"Ha! That's really clever."

She smiled again, and this time the warmth was unmistakable. "That's exactly what you said all those years ago when I first used it."

"So, forgive me, but . . . we were . . . we were in love?"

Her eyes tracked across the room again even though there wasn't anyone to follow. "Oh, who knows? I thought we were, back then, but, well, we were just kids."

I took another sip of my beer. "Yeah."

The server came to take our orders—which was a case of opportune knockers, as it helped break the awkward moment. "What'll it be?" she asked.

"Steak sandwich," said Kayla. "Rare. With the Caesar, please."

"And for you?"

"The vegan wrap," I said.

"Very good," she said, and sashayed away.

Kayla's eyebrows arched up. "The vegan wrap? You used to love a good steak."

She was right, but that had been before I'd read Peter Singer. The best-known modern utilitarian, Singer was the author of, among others, *Animal Liberation,* which had kick-started the whole animal-rights movement. Given humans can be perfectly healthy eating only plants, the minor increase in our happiness that we might get from the taste of chicken or beef in no way offsets the pain and suffering of animals raised or slaughtered in cruel conditions. "I've changed," I said affably.

She narrowed her eyes, as if that were still somehow an open question. "You don't mind that I'm having steak?"

"I'm from Calgary. If I couldn't stand being around people eating beef, I'd never be able to go home again."

"Ha." She took another sip of her wine.

We chatted for the next half hour, during which our meals came, and, slowly but surely, she seemed to get comfortable with me, in part due, I liked to think, to my charm, and in part perhaps to a second glass of wine. She mentioned our dates from all those years ago that stood out in her mind, including a road trip one weekend down to Fargo; attending Keycon, Winnipeg's annual science-fiction convention; seeing the Blue Bombers play; hanging out at Aqua Books and Pop Soda's—both sadly now defunct—and going to a traditional Cree sweat-lodge ceremony. I'd hoped something would ring a bell, but I couldn't remember any of them.

Kayla finally fell silent; it's doubtless no fun reminiscing with someone whose only responses are, "Really?" and "We did?" and "Wow, that sounds like it must have been fun." To fill the void, I delicately broached another topic. "So, um, you're a New Ager?"

She practically did a spit-take with her wine. "What?"

"Well, I only glanced at your Wikipedia entry, but it said you were with something called the Canadian Enlightenment Centre."

She had a wonderfully warm laugh. "You mean the Canadian Light Source. It's a synchrotron, Canada's largest particle accelerator; just under three gigaelectronvolts. It's on the grounds of the University of Saskatchewan."

"Oh! But it said you 'explore consciousness.'"

"I do. Psych was your major, but just an elective for me; I was doing physics. But Warkentin's course really got me interested in the mind, which is how I ended up working on the quantum mechanics of consciousness. After graduating from U of M, I headed off to the University of Arizona to study under Stuart Hameroff."

"Who is?"

"An anesthesiologist. He was fascinated by exactly what he was doing when he deprived people of consciousness. Roger Penrose, a physicist who sometimes collaborates with Stephen Hawking, wrote a book that said consciousness had to be quantum mechanical; it couldn't be just classical physics because of Gödel's incompleteness theorem. Stuart read it and got in touch with him, oh, almost twenty-five years ago now. That's why I'm at the Light Source; there's a synchrotron specialist I'm working with there who's got a technique for detecting superposition without promoting decoherence."

"Ah," I said. "Well, one must."

She smiled warmly. "'Superposition' is that uniquely quantum condition in which something is in two states at once: for instance, not either here *or* there, but simultaneously both here *and* there. We call it 'decoherence' when superposition collapses. Anyway, my work builds on what Stuart brought to Penrose. Stuart said, look, an inhaled anesthetic, like halothane, affects the microtubules—the cellular scaffolding—in neurons. There are two-lobed pockets in the microtubules, and each pocket houses a free electron. When you're awake, those electrons are in superposition, simultaneously existing in both the top and the bottom lobe. When the anesthetic is introduced, the electrons lose coherence, collapsing into being in just one or the other lobe—and when that happens, the patient ceases to be conscious."

I frowned, trying to sort this out. "So halothane is used as an inhalant to induce anesthesia?"

Kayla nodded. "Right."

"And anesthesia is a state in which only classical physics occurs in the brain?"

"When it puts you out cold, yes."

"So, halothane is a classical gas."

"Yes?"

"It has its own theme song."

"What *are* you talking about?"

"'Classical Gas.' It's that famous instrumental by Mason Williams." I made *ba-ba-ba-bump-ba-ba* trombone sounds.

"You are a very strange man," Kayla said.

She was not the first to have observed that; still, I guess I looked crestfallen because she reached over and patted the back of my hand. "Which is precisely why I fell for you all those years ago."

I smiled, and she went on: "Anyway, my work is on consciousness as a product of quantum superposition of electrons in neuronal microtubules. And, well . . . that's kind of why I looked you up."

"I, um, don't quite see the connection."

"I saw the news coverage about your being an expert witness."

I looked away. "Oh."

"You know, you *did* know about your grandfather. I remember when the news broke. You were mortified."

"Yeah, so my sister said. But I honestly don't recall it. I—it's so strange, not remembering that period."

"I'm sure."

"And that's why you wanted to see me? Because of my grandfather?"

"No, no, no. I mean, yeah, that's fascinating, but it was your technique that caught my eye—the microsaccades thing."

"Caught your eye. Microsaccades."

"What? Oh."

"I'm here all week."

She shook her head in what I took to be fond exasperation, then said, "No, it was the correlation with the Hare Checklist that interested me. I've been following your work in that area."

"Yes?"

"Yes. Because, just like your microsaccades test, I've found a quantum-superposition state that also precisely corresponds to psychopathy. If you're a high scorer on the Hare Checklist, you'll have this correlation, too."

"Seriously?"

"Yup." She looked at her watch. "Oh, cripes, the time! I gotta go. They're expecting me back at three."

And that should have been that, but the words just popped out of my mouth. "Well, what about dinner?"

Her eyebrows ascended, but then, after considering it for a long moment, she said, "Sure. Sure, why not?"

Kayla and I agreed to meet for dinner at 8:00 P.M., which gave me almost five hours to kill—and time to do some more reality-checking. She and I hadn't started dating until March of 2001, so she couldn't help me with what had gone down the preceding New Year's Eve, but perhaps someone else could.

I suppose the information I wanted was also online, but nothing beat the human touch. And so after returning to my office in the Duff Roblin Building and making a phone call to be sure she'd be in, I wandered along Dysart Road to the office of Sally Mahaffey, who taught meteorology in the awkwardly named Faculty of Environment, Earth, and Resources. That could be a miserable hike in winter, but now, in May, it was pleasant as long as you avoided all the droppings from the Canada geese wandering about.

The interior of the Wallace Building was done in Early Modern Tinkertoy, with red, green, and yellow tubes and pipes everywhere, and its washrooms were bizarre standalone modules like indoor outhouses. Sally's office was off a corridor painted floor to ceiling, doors included, in bright yellow; going down it, I felt like I was inside a French's mustard squeeze bottle.

Although there were lots of faculty members I'd never met, I'd run into Sally a few times in her role as treasurer of the Faculty Association. She was sixty-something, with hair I thought of as appropriately thundercloud gray.

"Hey," I said, entering. "Thanks for making time for me."

Her office had wall-mounted metal shelving she used for a display of vintage weather-forecasting equipment; I was pleased with myself for knowing that the propeller with cups was an anemometer. "My plea-sure," Sally said as she got up from her chair—which didn't do much to increase her height. "What can I do for you?"

"I'm looking for some old weather data."

"How old?"

"Two thousand and one."

She sounded relieved. "I had a history student come here last week, wanting to see the weather report for a key battle in the War of 1812. I had to explain to the poor thing that Environment Canada's records don't go back *quite* that far." She sat down in front of her computer and proceeded to type rapidly, using two knobby fingers. "Location?"

"Calgary."

"Airport or downtown?"

"Downtown, I suppose."

"What date?"

"January first, early in the morning. Like, 2:00 A.M."

She worked away for a minute. Above her desk was a political cartoon showing a trio of baffled old men in baggy golf shorts on an island only a few feet across surrounded by nothing but water. The caption: "Climate-change deniers retire to Florida."

"Got it," she said, rolling her chair aside to let me have a look.

There was so much data on the screen—meteorologists apparently care about all sorts of measurements regular folk don't—that it took me a moment to find my way around. But at last I spotted it: *Falling snow.* "That can't be right," I said, pointing. "Are you sure you've got the correct date?"

She indicated where it was listed; the time was correct, too. "Can you show me the hour before, and the hour after, please?"

She nodded and did so. For 1:00 A.M., the readout was also "Fall-ing snow." For 3:00 A.M., it had changed to "Heavy snowfall."

"But the sky was crystal clear," I said. "I remember that."

"I've seen a lot of wondrous weather in my day," Sally said gently. "Tornadoes, sun dogs, hail the size of grapefruit. But I've never seen snow come down from a cloudless sky. Are you sure you've got the right day?"

"Yes."

"And the right year? It took me to February to stop writing 2019 on things."

"Yes," I said, "I'm sure about the date." I recalled the stars so vividly that night, Orion low in the southwest. I knew my way around the night sky like the proverbial back of my hand; Orion is absolutely visible in Calgary at that time of night in the winter months. Or, at least he *is* when the sky is clear. I took hold of the edge of Sally's desk for support.

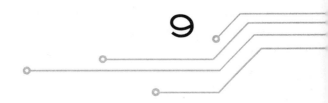

9

MENNO Warkentin was friends with Dominic Adler, a transplanted Torontonian who held the university's Bev Geddes Chair in Audiology. They played racquetball together once a week; there was no doubt Dominic was the better player. "Balance, my boy!" he'd exclaim whenever he got in a return that astonished Menno. "And balance is all in the inner ear!"

Menno had recently bought a carbon-fiber racquet in the vain hope that better equipment would make up for his lack of coordination. He served, and wiry Dominic swatted the ball back. Predictably, Menno missed. As he went to retrieve the ball, he said, "I walked by your lab earlier. Saw a guy delivering a skid full of new computing equipment." He tossed the ball vaguely in Dominic's direction.

Dominic served, and Menno managed to return it three times before he missed. When Menno went to get the ball again, Dominic said, "Yeah, we got a major new research grant."

"From who?"

Dominic put down his racquet and motioned Menno over. "The DoD."

Menno might not win at sports, but he was a demon at trivia. "We call it the DND here in Canada. Department of National Defense."

"Yeah, we do," said Dominic. "But I'm not talking about the Canadian one. I'm talking about the American one: the Pentagon."

"*Ka-ching,*" said Menno.

Dominic smiled. "Wasn't he treasurer during the Ming Dynasty?"

"Ha."

"What do the Americans want?"

"Life, liberty, and the pursuit of happiness," said Dominic. "But they'll never get that, so apparently they'll settle for a battlefield headset that lets soldiers hear over top of explosions and mortar fire. My department is going to try to develop one for them."

"Can't you do what those newfangled noise-canceling headphones do?"

"Sure, yeah," said Dominic. "That's the easy part. The hard part is the microphone. The last thing you want is the soldier shouting to be heard above the explosions. Hostiles might overhear."

"'Hostiles,'" said Menno, amused.

"You pick up the lingo." Dominic tossed the ball into the air and swatted it toward the wall, which was covered with skid marks from previous impacts.

"So how's the project going?" asked Menno after he'd batted the ball back.

Dominic didn't even try to return; he just let the ball zip past him. "It's not. It's damn near impossible to pick up a whisper when there are bombs going off all around you."

Menno glanced up at the analog wall clock, behind a protective mesh. Their time was almost up. "Oh, that's the wrong way to go about it."

Dominic retrieved the ball and started toward the door in the side wall. "What do you mean?"

"Trying to pick up the sound is the problem. Don't do that."

"We have to hear what they're saying."

"No, you don't," said Menno. "Instead, pick up the phonemes as they're being coded mentally. Grab those with a targeted scanner. The speaker doesn't have to say anything aloud that way—nothing to overhear. He just mouths the words. Whether he actually speaks them or not makes no difference to the brain's staging area; they have to be queued up regardless. Grab them from there, then use a voice synthesizer at the receiving end to reconstruct what would have been said out loud."

Dom's eyebrows climbed toward his widow's peak. "And that would work?"

Menno smiled. "Oh, who knows? Actually, it's only supposition that there even is such a staging area. But if I tell you a phone number and you try to remember it until you can jot it down, you'll rehearse it over and over in your head, right? There's a buffer somewhere that holds the data you're repeating. Scan that buffer and pick up sounds that *aren't* being said out loud." Menno smiled. "At least you'll get a good paper out of it."

"Except I can't publish. All the work is under an NDA."

"Huh. How big is your grant?" asked Menno

"Two hundred and fifty thousand—US. Wanna collaborate?"

Menno was more used to grants from Canada's Social Sciences and Humanities Research Council, which tended to be in the low five figures, if not four. But the Department of Defense! Menno was a Mennonite, a pacifist. The idea of working for the military was detestable, and if other members of his church found out, well, there would be devastating consequences. But this wasn't going to be published, and, heck, it wasn't weapons research; really, it wasn't. It was just an intriguing physiological investigation—with a giant research budget.

"Okay," said Menno, at last. "I'm in."

"I don't get it," said Dominic, months later. "It worked fine on our first two test subjects. Why isn't it working with this guy?"

Fine was overstating the case, Menno thought. They could indeed now pick up unspoken phonemes from the brain, but they were still having a lot of difficulty distinguishing many of them. Trying to tell a *tuh* from a *duh* was proving impossible, although Menno suspected they could write software to figure out which it should be based on the preceding and following phonemes. But telling one phoneme from another was predicated on first actually detecting the phonemes—and that had turned into a nightmare with this student volunteer from Menno's second-year developmental-psych class.

Dominic and Menno were on the opposite side of a glass wall from the subject, a doughy-looking Ukrainian kid named Jim Marchuk. Menno pressed the intercom button. "Jim, try again. What was that phrase you were thinking? Say it out loud for us."

"'Making your way in the world today takes everything you've got.'"

"Right, okay. Now, again—but subvocalize, okay? Over and over."

The headset, Menno knew, was large and uncomfortable, and much too unwieldy for battle. It consisted of a modified football helmet with a dozen electronics packs, each the size of a deck of cards, attached to it, and a thick bundle of cabling heading off to more equipment on a table beside the chair Jim was sitting on. But if they could get it working at all with this prototype, slimming the device down would be a task for the DoD engineers.

Menno and Dominic stared at the oscilloscope display, which was showing the reconstruction of the signal being transmitted by the headset. The trace was thick, running almost the height of the scope; it looked more like white noise than anything meaningful.

Dom had taped printouts from the previous two subjects on the wall above the scope. They each showed a single, distinct line spiking and falling. Underneath, he'd written in red marker the phonemes the patterns represented.

Menno shook his head. "I can't even tell when he's finishing one rendition and starting another."

Dominic reached for the intercom button. "Jim, thanks. Just be quiet for a minute, would you? Don't say anything and don't subvocalize. Just sit there, please."

Jim nodded, and Dominic and Menno turned back to the oscilloscope, which was just as active as before.

"Where do you suppose all that noise is coming from?" Dominic asked.

"I don't know. You're certain the equipment isn't overheating?"

Dominic pointed at a digital readout. "It's fine."

"Okay, well, maybe this boy is a freak. Let's test a few other people."

Menno was wearing his heavy winter coat; Dom had on a bright blue ski jacket with a lift ticket attached. It was 3:00 P.M. on a crisp afternoon, and the sun was already well on its way down to the horizon. They were walking along the Memorial Avenue of Elms, a road lined on both sides with trees, leading from the Fort Garry campus to Pembina Highway. Menno liked trees; he hated war. As a psychologist, he understood that this particular part of the university was a physical instantiation of the cognitive dissonance he felt working on a DoD project. The Avenue had been dedicated in 1922 to the men from the Manitoba Agricultural College who had died in the First World War; two and a half years ago, in June 1998, the dedication had been extended to include many who had died during World War II and the Korean War, as well.

"The Pentagon isn't going to be happy with a microphone that can only be used by half their soldiers," said Dominic, the words coming out in clouds of condensation. "For whatever reason, it just doesn't work with some people; why they have all that noise in their auditory cortices is beyond me. I mean, if they were reporting tinnitus, it'd make sense. Or maybe if they'd all listened to super-loud rock music, or something like that. But it seems completely random."

Menno thought about that as they walked past the block of stone with the dedication plaques. "No," he said at last. "Not quite random. You're right that the majority of our sample group doesn't have the background noise, but if you look at the test subjects who came from my class—Jim, Tatiana, the others—most of them *do* have the noise, and . . ."

"Yes?"

Menno continued along, the packed-down snow squeaking underfoot. "Background noise . . ." he said, slowly pursuing the idea as if it were a rabbit that would flee if startled. "In the auditory cortex . . ." His heart was pounding. "Preferentially present in those who study psychology."

"Well, I always said psych students were a little weird."

"It's not just that," Menno replied. "Psych attracts a certain kind of student: kids trying to make sense of themselves. Cheaper than therapy, you know?"

A single puff of chilled air: "So?"

"So, they're obviously chewing things over, ruminating, wondering." He felt his eyebrows colliding with the wool of his cap, and he lowered his voice, as if speaking softly would make the idea sound less crazy. "The background stuff. It isn't noise." He shook his head. "It's—my God! It's *inner monologue*—stream of consciousness! It's the constant background of a normal life, all the stuff you're thinking inside: *I wonder what's for lunch. Jeez, is it Thursday already? Gotta remember to stop by the store on the way home.* Those thoughts—those articulated thoughts—are made of phonemes, too. They're never spoken, they're never even subvocalized or mouthed. But they're words all the same, made up of phonemes. And so the question isn't—"

"The question isn't," said Dominic, coming to a dead halt beneath skeletal branches, "why some people *do* have background noise in their auditory cortices. The question is why most people do *not.*"

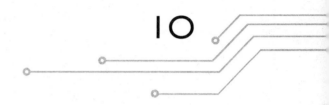

10

I entered the lecture hall in the aptly named Tier Building, rows of first-year students rising in front of me. Some were looking bright-eyed and bushy-tailed even now, at stupid o'clock in the morning, but most still showed signs of struggling to wake up. Tim Hortons had clearly done dynamite business before class: half the students had red cardboard cups on their swing-up desktops.

I tucked my hands into the pockets of my black denim jeans and strode to the lectern. "Okay, ladies and gentlemen, we're going to start with a joke. Stop me if you've heard this one before." I smiled and waited until I had their full attention—or, at least, attention from those who usually gave it. "Here goes: why was the road crossed by the chicken?"

I continued to smile at them, but no one laughed. After a few seconds, I said, "Tough room," and that, at least, merited a few chuckles. "Anybody? What's the punch line?"

A white girl with long red hair in the third row started to say, "To get to the . . ." But she trailed off, apparently realizing that although that worked when the setup was the normal "why did the chicken cross the road," it didn't make sense here.

I tried again: "Anyone? Why was the road crossed by the chicken?"

An Asian boy in the fifth row folded his arms in front of his Winnipeg Jets sweatshirt. "There's no answer to that, Professor Marchuk."

"Why not?"

The boy's tone conveyed that his word choice was deliberate: "Well, this ain't English class"—and that, too, got some chuckles—"but your joke is in the passive voice. There isn't anybody deliberately doing *anything, so there's no one to assign the motivation of 'to get to the other side' to."*

"Exactly!" I said, delighted, as I always was, when a session got off to a good start. "And you're right, this isn't English class; it's psychology. So let me introduce you to a core psychological concept, namely the notion of agency—*the subjective awareness that you are initiating and executing your own actions. And then we're going to talk about why, although we all believe that we do indeed have agency, perhaps we really don't . . ."*

I returned to my condo, grabbed a shower, put on a wine-colored shirt and black slacks, and drove over to The Forks. Once again, I was listening to the CBC; *The World at Six* was on.

"—and the stunning news that the leader of the New Democratic Party has chosen not to seek re-election this time out," Susan Bonner said. *"We reached political analyst Hayden Trenholm in Ottawa. Mr. Trenholm, what do you make of his announcement?"*

A man's voice with a hint of a Maritime accent: *"The NDP were the front-runners in the 2015 election but stumbled badly under then-leader Tom Mulcair, and his replacement certainly also failed to excite. But if they can come up with someone people from across the political spectrum can get behind, the New Democrats could make some inter-*

esting gains. Of course, they've been searching in vain for a person like that since Jack Layton passed away in 2011 . . ."

I parked my car and headed out into the cool evening air. I'd made reservations for us at Sydney's, an upscale place housed in the century-old Grand Trunk Pacific Railway Stable. Kayla was already seated when I got there—gotta love that punctuality—and—what a sweetheart!—she'd already asked the server to bring a vegetarian menu for me. We had a great table by a semicircular window; it arched up from a horizontal sill overlooking the confluence of the Red and Assiniboine Rivers. Kayla was wearing a shimmering blue top and gray pants.

After we'd ordered, I said, "So, at lunch you were talking about the quantum physics of consciousness."

She took a sip of wine. "That's right. My research partner is a woman named Victoria Chen. As I said earlier, she's developed a system that can detect quantum superposition in neural tissue."

"I'm no physicist, but I thought you couldn't have quantum effects like that in living things."

"Oh, it definitely happens in some biological systems. We've known since 2007 that there's superposition in chlorophyll, for instance. Photosynthesis has a ninety-five percent energy-transfer efficiency rate, which is better than anything we can engineer. Plants achieve that by using superposition to simultaneously try all the possible pathways between their light-collecting molecules and their reaction-center proteins so that energy is always sent down the most efficient route; it's a form of biological quantum computing. Vic was curious about how plants manage that at room temperature while we have to chill our quantum computers to a fraction above absolute zero to get superposition. And, well, as I mentioned at lunch, I've long been interested in the Penrose-Hameroff model that says quantum superposition in the microtubules of neuronal tissue is what gives rise to consciousness. So I convinced Vic to let me try her technique on people, to see if there really is superposition in human brains."

"And?"

"And, oh my God, yes, there is. It's not quite what Hameroff and

Penrose proposed, but they definitely opened the door for this line of work." She sighed wistfully. "I suspect Vic and I will have to share our eventual Nobel with one of them—they only allow three people on a Nobel, so Stuart and Roger will have to fight it out between themselves."

"Ha."

"Yeah, see, they think consciousness occurs in the moments of collapse from superposition to classical physics—that each moment of collapse is a moment of consciousness, forty or so of them per second. It was an interesting theoretical model when they first put it forth in the 1990s, but Victoria has shown that superposition in microtubules, unique among body structures, is maintained indefinitely—indeed, probably permanently."

I frowned. "But I thought quantum superposition was fragile. Doesn't it fall apart?"

"Not as far as we can tell. Not ever—or at least not as long as the person is alive."

"Why not?"

"Vic calls it 'entanglement inertia,' and, I've got to say that it's a revolutionary-enough discovery that it might get her the Nobel on her own. See, a single electron will decohere rapidly, falling out of superposition, but, for whatever reason, the countless trillions of superpositioned electrons in a given brain are locked together in a way that defies quantum theory, and so probabilistic laws apply. At any moment, any one of them might wish to decohere back to the classical state, but, unless a majority simultaneously want to, it doesn't happen. We've got computer simulations that show the tipping point never comes, at least not normally. Oh, an external force—an anesthetic, for instance—can cause the superposition to decohere, but without something like that, the superposition never collapses. It just keeps on going on."

I made an impressed face. "Has she published yet?"

Kayla shook her head. "It's out for peer review at *Neuron*."

"Sounds like a great paper."

"I'll send you a preprint. But it's only the first of several papers; she and I also have one coming up in *Physics of Life Reviews*."

I took a sip of my own wine. "Oh? What about?"

"Well, Penrose proposed that each tubulin macromolecule has a single two-lobed hydrophobic pocket with just one free electron. But he also offhandedly remarked that there might actually be *multiple* hydrophobic pockets, each with its own electron. And that's exactly what Vic and I have found: there are actually *three* hydrophobic pockets in each tubulin macromolecule."

"Okay."

"And *all* the tubulin macromolecules in a given brain are quantally entangled, meaning collectively they're all in the same state: the combination of superpositioned and classical electrons is the same in every tubulin in the brain of a given individual."

"Ah."

"That means that each person is in one of eight possible conditions: all three pocketed electrons in the classical-physics state; all three in superposition; or six possible combinations of one or two electrons in the classical state and the remaining ones in superposition."

"Very cool."

"Thanks. Now, we don't think it matters which electrons are in superposition and which aren't; electrons, like all subatomic particles, are fungible. So that means there are really only *four* states not eight: no electrons in superposition, any one of the three in superposition, any two in superposition, and all three in superposition. In other words, there's the classical-physics state, plus three states with quantum superposition: Q1, Q2, and Q3."

"Got it."

"And it's the Q2 state that caused me to look you up; that's where my research dovetails with yours. I ran a couple of hundred volunteers through Victoria's beamline—the test doesn't take long—and found that everybody's got at least one electron in superposition. Nobody was in the classical-physics state; everyone was either Q1, Q2, or Q3. And the three cohorts are each successively smaller, a 4:2:1 ratio, each group half the size of the one before it. In round numbers, sixty percent of our test subjects had only one electron in superposition; thirty percent—half as many—had any two in superposition; and about fifteen percent had all three in superposition."

"I suppose it's like juggling," I offered. "Easy to keep one ball in the air, harder with two, and a bitch with three."

"Yeah, that's our thinking, too. Assuming those ratios hold true for the entire human race, if you think of Earth's population as seven billion people—it's really more like 7.7, but for convenience's sake let's assume abstinence-only sex education actually worked, and round down—that means there are four billion in the first cohort, two billion in the second, and just one billion in the third."

"Right."

"Anyway," said Kayla, "I was curious if there were any psychological differences between the cohorts, and so I administered a standard five-factor-model personality measure on each subject and—*bada-bing!*—all our Q2s had scores that correlated with psychopathy."

"Ah," I said, finally getting it. "You came up with a triad suggestive of psychopathy: low conscientiousness, low agreeableness, high extraversion."

"Exactly! Got essentially the same results when I tried HEXACO, too, so we moved on to the Lilienfeld Psychopathic Personality Inventory and the Hare Psychopathy Checklist, and found an almost perfect correlation between psychopathy and having any two of the three electrons in superposition. Didn't matter which two—that's how we confirmed the fungibility notion—but if you had two out of three, you were a psychopath." She raised a hand, palm out. "Not necessarily a violent one, mind you. You were just as likely to be one of those Hare calls 'a snake in a suit,' a ruthless businessperson. Still, it's a clear-cut relationship, just like your microsaccades thing."

"You said about thirty percent of your test group were Q2s?"

"Yup, and evenly split between men and women."

"My microsaccades test shows the same percentage and gender balance. Did you get the kind of flak I did about that being a much higher prevalence of psychopathy than is generally assumed?"

She smiled. "We cited you in our paper on that very point, but, yeah, we're expecting the reviewers from *Physics of Life* to challenge us on it."

I nodded. As I'm sure Kayla knew, most older estimates put the prevalence of psychopathy at between one and four percent of the general population of men, and about a tenth of that among women. But those values were due to sampling problems. Take Kent Kiehl, one of Hare's last grad students, who did the first-ever scans of psychopaths' brains— great work, that. He did his initial studies at the University of British Columbia, where, with the extraordinary cooperation of the Canadian Department of Corrections, he was able to routinely transfer violent criminals who had scored high on the Hare Checklist to a hospital where they could be scanned by fMRI; the precautions taken against the prisoners escaping were worthy of a Hollywood film.

But when Kent was lured to Yale with a sweetheart offer—he asked for double the salary his colleagues in Canada were getting and was told, "Oh, we can do better than that"—he immediately became frustrated. He'd hoped to work with psychopaths at large in the New Haven community: people with criminal records but now released from prison. But he found—*duh!*—that psychopaths weren't good about keeping appointments for scientific experiments, and those rare times they *did* show up, they were often too drunk or too uncooperative to be of any use.

Anyway, one of the chapters of Kent's book *The Psychopath Whisperer* begins by baldly declaring, "Fact: There are over twenty-nine million psychopaths worldwide." If you flip to the endnote, it turns out he reached that figure by assuming the percentage of psychopaths found in prisons accurately reflected the prevalence of psychopathy in the population as a whole. But the ones behind bars are just the ones dumb enough to get caught; with their skills at manipulation and deception, psychopaths almost certainly are captured at a rate much lower than that of normal people—my pal Devin Becker notwithstanding.

Likewise, Kent claims that there are ten times as many male psychopaths as females. Why? Well, see, he says, there are ten times as many male psychopaths in prison as females ones—which is true, but there are also ten times as many male left-handers in prison, and male redheads, and males who like anchovies on their pizza—simply because there are ten times as many men behind bars as women.

Before my work, and now Kayla's, *no one* knew how many psychopaths there actually were. Twenty-nine million? Nuh-uh, Kent. It's more like *two fucking billion*—thirty percent of Earth's population, two out of every seven people.

The waiter came with our entrees. When he was gone, I said, "What about the other two cohorts—you know, just one electron in superposition, or all three in superposition?"

Kayla lifted her shoulders. "I couldn't discern any difference between Q1s and Q3s. No, as far as we can tell, there are only two types of consciousness, at least from a quantum-mechanical point of view: psychopathic Q2s, and everyone else."

"Do you think you inherit your state?"

"It doesn't seem to run in families. Oh, some people are the same state as their parents, siblings, or children, but that's not disproportionately common. And, as far as we can tell, people don't change states— we've done as much of a longitudinal study as we can so far, and no one has ever switched."

"Fascinating," I said. Marveling at the circumstances that had brought us together again after so much time, I added, "Quite a coincidence, you and me both ending up working on psychopathy."

Kayla's tone grew cold. "It's not a coincidence, Jim."

"What?"

She stared at me, and I met her gaze—until I couldn't. "I got interested in psychopathy because of you," she said. "Because of the horrible things you did all those years ago."

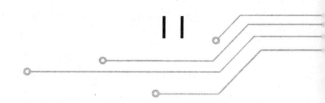

TWO DECADES AGO

"**G**OOD evening, Jim. Thanks for coming in again."

Jim Marchuk was carrying a plastic bag with the green McNally Robinson logo. "No problem, Professor Warkentin. Bit surprised anyone's working on New Year's Eve."

"Oh, Christmas break is my favorite time on campus," Menno said. "Peace and quiet. Summers are great, too—the campus is mostly empty, and the weather's nicer then, but Christmas is the best; the place is dead."

Jim's tone was light. "Universities would be wonderful if it weren't for all those pesky students."

"No, no, no," said Menno. "It's *faculty* that drive me up the walls. Departmental meetings, committee meetings, so-and-so's retirement dinner, somebody else's birthday lunch. Here, with almost everyone away, a body can finally concentrate."

"Huh," said Jim.

"You got a party to get to?"

"Kinda. Bunch of friends, we're going to Garbonzo's—hang out, watch Ed the Sock do *Fromage*."

"I'm sure that means something," said Menno. "Anyway, we'll get you out of here long before midnight."

"I'm happy to come in," said Jim. "Dorm's kinda lonely. But my parents are off on a cruise for their twenty-fifth wedding anniversary, so not much point in going back to Cow Town."

Dominic Adler entered the room, carrying the Mark II. "That's not the same helmet as before," said Jim, but there was nothing suspicious in his tone; he was just making conversation, and it beat talking about the weather.

"True," said Dominic. "Completely new design." They were hoping that by using transcranial focused ultrasound—a new brain-stimulation technique the DoD was experimenting with—they could boost the phonemes enough to punch through the background noise.

"Great," said Jim, reaching for the helmet. It had different modules attached to its surface, and, in addition to ones that looked like decks of cards, there were two—one on either side—that looked like green hockey pucks.

"Put it on," Dominic said.

Jim pulled it over his head, and Dominic loomed in to make various adjustments. "It's a snugger fit than the old one," Jim offered.

"Yes. We thought maybe we were losing alignment with the previous setup." Dom pulled on the chin strap, cinching it. "How's it look, Menno?"

Jim glanced toward Menno, as if expecting an assessment of his appearance, but Menno was peering at the oscilloscope, which showed the thick, chaotic trace of the para-auditory scan. "I think it's fine," Menno said.

"Okay," said Dominic. He glanced at his calculator watch, then: "Take your seat next door, Jim."

Jim headed out into the corridor and went into the other room, lowering himself onto the swivel chair on the opposite side of the glass.

Menno turned on the cassette recorder, which had a little microphone on a plastic stand. "Project Lucidity, stage two, test number fourteen on thirty-one December 2000, 7:49 P.M. PIs: Dominic K. Adler and Menno Warkentin. Subject JM is in place."

Menno looked at Dom, who said, "Okay. Let's rock and roll." Menno nodded and typed "execute" at his computer's command prompt. He poised his chubby index finger over the backward L of the enter key, took a deep breath, then tapped it.

Through the window, in the chair, they could see Jim's head loll back, as though he were looking up at the ceiling, the way one might when lost in thought.

Menno and Dom exchanged glances. Menno halted the program, then touched the intercom button. "Jim?"

No response.

"Jim?" said Dom, as if somehow the young man could hear him even if he couldn't hear Menno. "Are you okay?"

"Oh, shit," Menno said, pointing at the oscilloscope, which showed nothing but a perfectly flat green phosphor line.

Dominic's eyes went wide, and the two of them rushed toward the door, did a hasty turn in the corridor, then entered the testing room.

"Jim!" said Menno, crouching before him.

Dominic tipped Jim's head forward by gently lifting the back of the helmet. The student's chin dropped to his chest.

Menno attempted to check for a pulse in Jim's right wrist. Unused to doing the test he'd seen so often on TV, his own heart raced as he tried to find it, but at last he did, feeling the rhythmic movement of Jim's radial artery, good and strong and at the normal pace, too. "He's just fainted."

"Maybe the helmet *is* too tight," Dominic said as he undid the chin strap, then pulled the helmet off, setting it gently—it had cost sixty thousand dollars, after all—on the tile floor. "Might have restricted his circulation."

Menno tried something else he'd seen on TV: lightly slapping Jim on one cheek and then the other. "Come on," he said. "Wake up." But there was no response from Jim. Menno then held his own hand in front of Jim's nose, feeling breath—warm, regular—on his palm.

"What should we do?" asked Dominic.

"Let's get him out of the chair and onto the floor, before he falls out."

They did just that, laying Jim on his back.

"He's not sweating," said Menno. "He's not breathing hard. He's just . . ."

"Unconscious."

"Yeah."

"But the others we tested," said Dom, "the ones who normally didn't *have* an inner voice—nothing happened to them."

"True."

"So," said Dominic, sounding increasingly desperate, "why in God's name won't *he* wake up?"

"I don't know," replied Menno, "but we've got to call 911."

"No, we can't do that."

"But he's unconscious."

"There will be too many questions. Lucidity is classified."

"Yes, but this boy—"

"Look," said Dominic. "He's breathing. His pulse is steady."

"What if he's in a coma, for God's sake? He needs to be in a hospital. He'll need water soon. Food. And he'll have to go the bathroom."

"Well, how do we explain—"

"I don't care about that!" snapped Menno. "We're in no position to look after him."

"We're under a military nondisclosure agreement."

"Damn it, Dominic!" Menno took a deep breath. "Okay, all right. Fine. Let's get him out of here, out of the lab. Move him down to, I don't know, the men's room. Then we can say we stumbled upon him, found him passed out. New Year's Eve—they'll take him for a drunk student."

"Until they do a blood test."

"Look, I'm not going to just abandon him. Now, are you going to help me move him or not?"

Dominic thought for a moment. "What if we're seen?"

"Everyone's gone for the night. Come on!"

Dominic hesitated.

"For Christ's sake, Dom. If I drag him on my own, it'll leave dirt on his clothes and scuff marks leading back here."

Dom frowned, then bent over and took Jim's ankles in his hands. Menno nodded his thanks and grabbed Jim's arms just below the shoulders. They lifted him so his bottom cleared the floor by a few inches and moved, Dominic walking backward. At the threshold, they put Jim down for a second and Dominic opened the door. He checked that the coast was clear, then took his end again, and they quickly moved Jim along the corridor, going by closed doors, the little windows in them nothing but dark squares.

They were just passing the women's room—the men's was the next one along—when Menno heard a grunt. He looked down and saw that Jim's eyes were now open, showing whites all around the irises.

Hearing was restored, as was vision. Fluorescent tubes behind frosted panels moved by overhead.

A male voice: "Dominic, stop." And then the same voice: "Jim, um, you, ah, you passed out. How do you feel?"

A response required; one made: "I'm okay."

Arms freed; legs, too. Pressure on the back.

A different voice: "Can you stand?"

Knees flexed; palms pushed against the dusty floor. The word "yes" was uttered as hands moved to brush away dirt.

The first speaker again: "You gave us quite a start."

Silence. Then, filling the space: "I'll be all right."

"Yes, yes," said the second speaker quickly. "Of course you will."

Hours later, long after Jim had headed off to his sock-and-cheese thing—whatever the hell *that* was—Dominic and Menno were in the lab, still trying to make sense of it all. Dom was sitting on a three-legged stool, looking at a printout of the oscilloscope tracings, showing the noise in Jim's auditory cortex disappearing at the instant he lost consciousness. On the wall behind him, held up by a pair of U-shaped acrylic braces, was a souvenir baseball bat, commemorating the two consecutive World Series wins by the Toronto Blue Jays. Menno, leaning against the opposite wall, looked at it, idly wondering what it was like to be a bat.

His reverie was interrupted by Dominic, saying for what seemed like the hundredth time, "For God's sake, all we were trying to do was boost the queued phonemes so they wouldn't be drowned out by his inner voice. What could have possibly gone wrong?"

"I don't know."

"We have people like Jim," said Dom, trying to puzzle it out, "who do have an inner voice, and then there are those who are—what? Monologue-less? Soliloquy-free?" He shook his head. "Bah. Those are both awkward names."

"True," said Menno softly, as his heart suddenly began pounding. "But, my God, there *is* an established term for those without inner voices—at least in my field of study . . ."

12

"Okay," I said, looking out at my first-year psych class, "how many of you drive to the university each morning?"

About a third of the students put up hands.

"Keep your hands up. The rest of you: how many of you have had a job you've driven to day after day?"

Another third raised hands.

"Okay, now keep your hands up if this has ever happened to you: you arrive at your destination—school, work, whatever—and have no recollection of the actual drive."

Most of the hands stayed in the air.

"Cool," I said. "Lower your hands. Now, think about that: you undertook a complex task; you operated a vehicle weighing over a thousand kilos, you negotiated traffic, you avoided collisions, you obeyed signs and the rules of the road—you did all that without high-level conscious attention; that is, you did it while your mind was on other things.

"Let's try another one: how many of you have ever been reading a book—not one of mine, you understand, but somebody else's—and gotten to the bottom of a page and realized you had no awareness of what the page said?"

Again, lots of hands went up.

"Okay, you might argue that driving a car is an example of what laypeople call muscle memory, although the technical term is 'procedural memory'—stuff you do without thinking about it, like returning a serve in tennis or playing a musical instrument. But what about the reading example? Your eyes tracked across each successive line, and, on some level, your brain was presumably recognizing and processing the words. In fact, you can contrive priming tests to demonstrate that the words were noted. If the page referenced, say, a porcupine, and you're asked, even though your mind wandered off while reading so you say you have no high-level conscious recollection of the page, to name a mammal, chances are you'll say 'porcupine.' So, reading can't be dismissed as just muscle memory, just your eyes tracking without actually seeing. And yet you can do it, too, without real attention."

I let that sink in for a moment, then went on. "So, it's clearly true that you can perform sophisticated acts without your full conscious attention some of the time. And, by logical extension, if you can do those things that way some of the time, then it's presumably possible there are people who do them that way all of the time. Of course, we'd have no way to tell, would we? When you're reading but not absorbing, nobody can tell that from the outside. And when you're driving but not paying attention, again, well, if the police had a way of detecting that by some external sign—your eyeballs rolling up into your skull, say—you can bet they'd pull you over. But there is no external indication."

I took a sip from the coffee cup on the lectern, then went on. "And that brings us to one of the most famous thought experiments in philosophy. Imagine a being who didn't just drive all the time without paying attention, and who didn't just read all the time without paying attention, but who in fact did everything all the time without attention. An Australian philosopher, David Chalmers, is the guy most associated with this proposal. He says it's logically coherent—that is, there are no internal contradictions—to the notion that a whole planet could exist full of such entities: beings for whom the lights are on but nobody's home, beings who are, quite literally, thoughtless." Another sip, then: "Anybody got a suggestion for what we should call such creatures?"

I was always happy to set that one up, and my students never disappointed. "Politicians!" called out one. "Football players," called another.

"Well," I said, "almost anything would be an improvement over the term we actually use. Such beings are called 'philosophical zombies' or 'philosopher's zombies.' It's a terrible name: they're not the walking dead, they don't shamble along. Behaviorally, they're indistinguishable from the rest of us. Sadly, the phrasing 'philosophical zombie' is more common in the literature than 'philosopher's zombie,' but it doesn't make sense: the one thing such creatures are unlikely to be is philosophical. Oh, they might say *things a philosopher would—'A could well follow from B,' or 'Yes, but how can we be sure your experience of red is the same as my experience of red?' or 'Would you like fries with that?'—but they'd only be* acting *like a philosopher. There would in fact be no inner life, no rumination. Me, I mostly avoid the zombie word. In the States, they can't really abbreviate 'philosopher's zombie' to its initials because it comes out sounding like 'peasy,' as in 'easy-peasy.' But here we can safely call them p-zeds, so let's do that from now on."*

One of the students, a muscular guy named Enzo, raised his hand. "Well, then, Professor Marchuk, if all that's true—if it really is *possible—then how do we know* you're *not a p-zed?"*

"How indeed?" I replied, smiling beatifically at them all.

TWO DECADES AGO

"WE have to try again," said Dominic firmly, on January 2, 2001. "Are you insane?" replied Menno. "You saw what happened to that student, Jim Marchuk."

"Which is precisely why we have to try again. We have exactly one data point now. We can't draw any conclusions from that."

"That boy might have died. What if he'd never regained consciousness?"

"But he *did*. And, really, we don't even know that our equipment is what caused him to black out."

"Oh, come on! It happened the moment we activated the helmet. What *else* could have caused it?"

"Who knows? Correlation is not causation. But, anyway, if the effect was unique to him, we need to know that. I'd hate to cancel a whole program based on one failure."

"You know who else said that? General Turgidson in *Dr. Strangelove*—right before the world came to an end."

"Don't worry," said Dominic. "It'll be fine. We'll be prepared this time. No fucking Laurel and Hardy carrying the body down the corridor. We'll belt the next subject into the chair so he can't fall out—don't want a concussion! And if he *does* lose consciousness, well, we'll just wait patiently. Marchuk revived in a matter of minutes, after all." He thought for a moment. "Let's try that business student, the runner. He had an inner monologue, too, and he's from Winnipeg; he should be around. What was his name?"

"Huron," Menno said reluctantly. "Travis Huron."

"Okay, Travis," said Menno into the intercom. "We want you to just think about the test message, all right? Just that, nothing else. Do you remember it?"

On the other side of the window, the athletic young man nodded. "'Broadsword calling Danny Boy.'"

"Exactly. Just repeat that subvocally over and over once I say 'go.'"

Another nod.

Menno had his finger poised over the enter key, but just stood there, unable to bring himself to press it.

After about ten seconds, Dominic, standing next to him, muttered, "Oh, for Christ's sake," reached over, and stabbed the other enter key on the numeric keypad, and—

—and Travis's head tipped forward, and his strapped-in body sagged.

"Shit," said Menno, rushing out the door and into the adjacent lab. He unstrapped the helmet and tossed it across the room to get it out of the way. It was just like with Jim Marchuk. Travis's pulse was good—Menno had no trouble finding it this time—and his respiration was normal.

Dominic entered, too; Menno had run here, but Dominic must have fucking sauntered to take so long. "Well?" Dom said, as if inquiring about the score in a sporting event he didn't really care about.

"Unconscious," said Menno. "Otherwise fine . . . I guess."

"It must be the transcranial focused ultrasound that makes them black out," said Dom, "but I'm not sure why."

"We shouldn't have done this," said Menno, feeling nauseated. He looked at his watch. "Two minutes."

"It'll be fine."

Menno started to pace. "Damn, damn, damn."

They waited . . . and waited . . . and waited, Travis breathing calmly the whole time, although a little drool had started to come out of his half-open mouth.

"There!" said Menno. "It's been fifteen minutes. That's got to be at least three times as long as Marchuk was out. We *have* to call 911."

Kayla ran up to the nursing station. "What room is Travis Huron in?"

The nurse—a stout, middle-aged woman—pointed to a green chalkboard on the opposite wall. It was a chart of patients, with their room numbers and the names of their attending physicians; Kayla found the line about Travis and hurried down the corridor, low heels clicking against flooring marked with colored stripes.

The door to Travis's room was open. He had a bed whose front could rise; it was supporting his back at a forty-five-degree angle. His eyes were closed and his hair—dark, like Kayla's—lay flat against his scalp. Some sort of drip was going into his left arm, and his right index finger had a pulse monitor clipped to it. He was wearing a hospital smock the color of an old woman's hair rinse.

"Travis," said Kayla, coming up on his left side.

No response.

A slim and short male doctor in a white lab coat came in. "Hello," he said. "I am Dr. Mukherjee. And you would be?"

"Kayla Huron. His sister."

"Ah, yes, good. Thank you for coming. Have you been briefed?"

Kayla shook her head.

"Well, it falls to me, then," said Mukherjee. "Your brother is in a coma as far as we can tell. There is no sign of trauma or injury. He has had an MRI, and there is no blood clot or tumor."

"How long will it last?"

Mukherjee lifted his shoulders slightly. "That we do not know. There are varying degrees of being in a coma: we use something called the Glasgow Coma Scale to assess motor response, verbal response, and eye response. Sadly, your brother scores the lowest—the worst—on all three axes. Of course, we will do everything we can. With luck, he will wake up at some point."

"With luck?" snapped Kayla. "What the hell happened? How did he get here?"

Mukherjee was carrying a clipboard. He looked at it. "He was brought in by ambulance"—a glance at his watch—"five hours ago. Apparently he was found unconscious in an empty classroom at the U of M; a janitor stumbled upon him."

"What are you doing to help him?"

"We are attending to his physical necessities. But you, young lady, can sit with him. Chat. If he makes any response—speaks, turns his head toward you, or the like—let the nursing station know. Just pull that red cord there, do you see?" He turned and left.

Kayla looked at her watch; Christ, she'd never make it to the club tonight. A chair with orange vinyl padding and a chrome frame was tucked against one wall. She scraped it across the floor. Once it was by Travis's bed, next to the stand holding the drip bag, she sat on it. "Come on, Trav," she said. "Wake up, damn it. It's me, it's Kayla. Wake up."

He didn't react. She looked at him, studying his face, something she hadn't done for ages. She still thought of him as an angular, geeky kid—but he'd grown into a handsome young man, with clear skin, a high forehead, and . . .

. . . and, she knew, piercing blue eyes. But they weren't visible now: his lids were closed, and the eyeballs beneath were stationary, she could see that. No rapid eye movement, no dreaming.

"Trav, for God's sake," Kayla said. "Mom will have a fit. You don't want me to worry her. Wake up, will you?" She hesitated, then took his hand; it was warm but limp. "Travis?" she said. "Travis, are you there?"

"You really effed up the helmet when you threw it across the room," said Dom.

"I didn't throw it," Menno replied. "I just—"

"Man, you *hurled* it."

Maybe he had; he was furious at the fucking thing, and at himself.

"Anyway," said Dom, "if we're going to get more work done before classes resume on the eighth, we've got to get that first kid who fainted—what's his name? Jim Marchuk? We've got to get him to come in."

"Why?" Menno asked.

"To recalibrate the equipment. He's the only one we have previous readings from who's still around; all of our other experimental subjects have gone home for the holidays."

"Why on Earth would he agree to put that helmet on again after what it did to him the last time—not to mention what happened to Travis Huron?"

"Surely those things were because of the transcranial focused ultrasound," said Dominic. "We won't activate that part; it obviously isn't working quite right. But if we don't calibrate the helmet properly, any new subvocalization data we collect will be useless."

"Jesus, Dom, we should just shelve the whole project."

"For what reason? Nobody but you or I knows about the subjects fainting."

"It's not *fainting,* damn it. Travis is in a coma, and, unlike Jim Marchuk, he shows no signs of coming out of it."

"I agree that's really unfortunate," said Dom calmly. "But we've stumbled onto something huge—*huge*—and I'm not going to just walk away from it. We need to get Marchuk back in here."

At last, Menno nodded reluctantly. "I suppose it can't hurt to ask."

"Sorry to bother you again during the holidays, Jim," Dominic said. He was sitting on a lab stool, and Menno was leaning against a wall.

As far as Menno could see, Jim looked no worse for wear despite what had happened last time. He was dressed in tan corduroys and a tattered Calgary Stampede hoodie. "No problem," said Jim.

"Are you sure you're all right?" asked Menno.

Jim looked puzzled by the question. "I'm fine, thanks."

Dominic scowled slightly and took back control. "Good, good. We were hoping you'd be willing to do another stint with the helmet."

"The new one or the old one? I didn't much like that new one."

"Don't worry," said Dominic. "We've, ah, loosened it up; it, um, won't be as tight a fit this time."

"I don't know," said Jim.

Of course the boy was going to refuse, Menno thought. But Dominic pressed on. "Please."

Jim frowned.

"It would really help us out," Dominic added.

Menno shook his head slightly. It was a waste of—

"Sure," said Jim, with a shrug. "Why not?"

"Okay, Jim," said Dom into the intercom mic, looking at the young man through the glass. "Try again."

"I *am* trying," said Jim.

Menno pointed to the oscilloscope. "The phonemes are there, and there, see?"

Dom nodded.

"But there's nothing else," said Menno. "Ask him to try another phrase."

"Jim," said Dom, "think the words to 'Humpty Dumpty'—you know, the nursery rhyme."

Jim nodded, and the oscilloscope dutifully showed little spikes for each syllable.

Dom looked at Menno. "Maybe you damaged the helmet more than I thought."

"No," said Menno. "When I put it on myself, just to test, it showed the usual internal noise. But we can't use me to calibrate because we didn't save any of my earlier recordings."

Dom keyed the mic again. "Jim, can you make sure the serial cable coming out of the equipment bank is tight in its socket?"

Jim checked the RS-232C port. "Snug as a bug in a rug," he said.

The boy fell silent, and Menno's heart sank as he looked at the flat line on the phosphor screen. "Oh, God," he said. Fortunately, the intercom was off; Jim was staring blankly into space.

"It's not our fault," Dom said quickly.

"The hell it isn't!" snapped Menno, pointing at the flat horizontal tracing. "We did that to the boy. We shut off his inner voice."

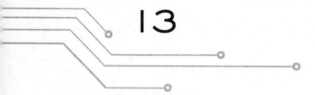

13

"**W**HAT horrible things?"

Kayla looked out the semicircular window. The sun had set; the rivers were dark and still, winding blacktop roads. I let the words hang there for a moment as she chewed on her lower lip. At last, she looked back at me, blue eyes slightly narrowed. "You really don't remember? Not even that?"

"Honestly, no."

"Look," she said, "I kept track of you a bit over the years. Checking online now and then, or asking mutual acquaintances how you were doing. And people kept saying things like, 'Oh, yeah, Jim. What a nice guy!' And you *were* a good guy when we started dating. Thoughtful, kind, supportive. So when . . ."

She trailed off and looked at the blond brick wall.

"What?" I said.

"So when you got violent, it was a total surprise, you know? Knocked me for a loop." She lowered her voice, and then, softly, sadly, she added, "Figuratively *and* literally."

I was absolutely floored, and I'm sure my eyes went wide. "My . . . God. I—Kayla, honestly, I wouldn't—I'd *never* . . ."

She lifted her head and finally met my gaze—and held it, looking really, really hard, her attention flicking from my left eye to my right and back again. "Did you take your own test?" she asked. "The microsaccades one?"

"Of course."

"And?"

"And I'm normal, absolutely. Not a psychopath."

"You know, just on the numbers, there's a thirty percent chance you are."

"I'm not."

She drew her eyebrows together and compressed her lips.

"Look," I said, "whatever happened—whatever I did—I'm so, so sorry. It has to be related to the brain damage that caused me to lose those memories. But I'm all right now."

"You can't know that. Until a few days ago—until what happened on the witness stand—you didn't even know you'd lost any memories. Who knows what else you don't remember doing?"

"I'm not a psychopath," I said again. "I can prove it with my goggles."

She looked dubious again. "I mean, your technique is interesting, but . . ."

"Okay, all right. Prefer your own equipment? How 'bout this? I'd love to see that synchrotron of yours, and you can test me for yourself. What is it, ten hours by car to Saskatoon?"

"Eight, if you've got a heavy foot like me, but, seriously, Jim, that's not necessary."

"Hey, I'm only teaching a couple of summer courses. My last class ends at 1:00 on Thursday, and you said that's about when you're going home. I don't have another class until 8:00 A.M. Wednesday morning." I made my tone offhanded. "We could do it this weekend. Wouldn't it be nice to have someone to share the driving?"

She was clearly startled. "Well, I mean, um, how would you get home?"

"Greyhound? VIA Rail?"

She looked out into the darkness again, then slowly turned back to me. "Okay, sure. Why not? But I have to warn you: Saturdays I go see Travis."

I was surprised at the way my heart fell, but Kayla was brilliant and beautiful; was it any wonder she had a boyfriend?

"Oh. Um, okay."

"You could come along, if you like. Just like old times."

Good grief! Just how much *had* I forgotten? "I, ah, wouldn't want to be a third wheel."

She looked startled for a moment. "You really don't remember, do you? Travis is my brother."

"Oh!"

"We used to visit him here in Winnipeg, back when we were dating." She saw my puzzled expression. "He's in a coma; has been for ages."

"What happened?"

"Nobody knows. They found him passed out. No head injury, though; he didn't trip and smash his skull, or anything like that."

"Huh."

"He was so strong, and not just physically. He was a brick, you know? He was fourteen when our dad was diagnosed with lung cancer. Our mother was a mess, but Travis, he was her pillar of strength." She paused. "Anyway, Trav and I grew up in Winnipeg, but when I got the job at the synchrotron, I moved him and my mom to Saskatoon." She shrugged a little. "It didn't make any difference to Travis, and Mom was delighted to be closer to her granddaughter; she looks after Ryan for me when I can't."

"Oh, that must be handy, having her live with you."

"My mom? No, no. She's just sixty-two. She's got her own place. She's a freelance graphic designer; works out of her house. But Travis is in a facility. I visit him every Saturday morning, sit with him for an hour." She smiled ruefully. "It's almost like therapy. I talk about my week, natter on, say whatever comes to mind. I long ago gave up any hope that he's going to respond, but . . ."

"Sure," I said. "And, yeah, I'd be happy to keep you company on Saturday, if you'd like me there."

"Thanks. I know it doesn't make any real difference if I go or not, but, well . . ." She shrugged. "It's something I have to do."

I nodded. "Some people in minimally conscious states or with locked-in syndrome are aware of, and do appreciate, visitors, even if they can't respond."

"And doubtless some of those at the facility *are* minimally conscious. But not Travis."

"Oh?"

"I had an ambulance service bring him to the Light Source a while ago. Took him on a stretcher down to the SusyQ beamline; that's short for 'superpositioned systems—quantum.' Vic ran our process on him." Kayla let out a small sigh. "Might as well have put a hunk of granite in front of the emitter; they both would've shown the same thing." She shrugged. "Scientist first, little sister second, I guess. Anyway, that's how we confirmed our notion about the classical-physics state: no superposition means a complete lack of consciousness."

I didn't want to seem insensitive, but, well, the utilitarian position would be clear in a case like this. "So then, ah—"

"Why don't I pull the plug?"

"Well, yeah."

She shrugged a little. "He's my brother." I couldn't think of a good response, so I remained silent. But after a time, she went on. "I know he's not suffering; he *can't* be in any pain. And, well, where there is life, there is hope."

I peered out the semicircular window, radial slats making it look like a half-submerged captain's wheel. The immaculately groomed waiter deposited the bill, then disappeared; I paid, since Kayla had gotten lunch. Kayla was staying at Inn at The Forks, which is why I'd chosen Sydney's. I walked her the hundred meters or so to her hotel.

The Inn was five stories tall, and apparently pretty upscale. I'd been to the lobby a few times but never to the rooms—and it didn't look like that was going to change this evening. The elevators were close to the

front desk, affording little privacy, although an indoor waterfall provided some masking white noise.

"You really want to come to Saskatoon?" Kayla asked, facing me.

"Absolutely," I said. "And—oh, shit."

"What?"

"I forgot. Damn! I have to make an appearance at the CMHR
Thursday at four."

"At the what?"

"The Canadian Museum for Human Rights." I pointed at the north
wall, hoping she could visualize what was on the other side of it. "It's
that round, glass-and-steel building just over there. They're having a
reception to kick off a lecture series, and I'm on the board of directors,
so . . ."

"Can you bring a date?"

My heart skipped a beat. "Um, sure. Sure, yeah."

She pushed the up button. "I was hoping to get to visit that museum
on this trip, but haven't had a chance. Okay; let's do it. We'll hit the
road right after the reception."

"Wonderful! Thank you."

The elevator arrived. She hesitated for a moment, leaned in and
gave me a quick hug, then entered the car.

I headed out the sliding glass doors into the summer evening. I didn't
often get down here to The Forks, but whenever I did, I made a point
of walking around the Oodena Celebration Circle, an amphitheater sixty
meters across and 2.5 meters deep. Equidistant around its perimeter are
eight steel armatures that look like cyborg lizards with long tails curving up toward the sky. Each tail has several sighting rings mounted on
it, which encircle specific stars at dates and times specified on accompanying plaques. The west armature, for instance, can be used to find
Altair, Betelgeuse, Regulus, and Procyon. Meanwhile, gaps between red
stone monoliths frame the rising sun on the solstices and equinoxes; I've
sometimes been on hand with members of the RASC to explain things
to tourists. Here, in the dark, the place had a wonderfully spooky quality; it had often been the meeting-up point for Winnipeg's annual Zombie Walk.

I strolled around the grassy circumference, hands shoved in my pockets, thinking.

Kayla had said I'd hit her. *Me*. I'd never hit *anyone*, not as an adult. Even as a kid, it wasn't in my nature, not since—

Yeah.

When I was eight or nine, I'd been in a fight in the parking lot of my school, with Ronny Handler, a kid my age who'd attacked me for no good reason—really, what utter bullshit it was for the teacher to say it takes two to start a fight—and, to my surprise, in an adrenaline-fueled rage, I'd been able to knock Ronny down, and I was so furious, so incensed, so livid at the unfairness of not being able to walk to school without being picked on because of—what? My shorts? My buzz cut? My ears? Who the hell knew?

When Handler was down, I leapt up and assumed a crouching posture in mid-air, my knees together but bent, and I was ready to come down hard on his head, which was sideways on the pavement, and I knew—eight years old, and I *knew*—that if I continued what I'd started, if I let the trajectory run its course, my knees would smash into him, and I might well fracture his skull, and maybe even kill him.

And, in that split second, still in the air, I changed my posture, altering my course. My bare knees crashed into the asphalt right beside Ronny's head, the impact excruciating, my skin being brutally scraped—but Handler survived. I hadn't been worried so much about him as about the consequences for me if I'd followed through on what I'd begun, and I'd known that shouting "He started it!" would do no good at all if he were lying there bleeding. I remembered thinking this was a moment that could have changed my life, and I'd done the right thing, just in the nick of time.

That was, I supposed, one of the first times that my reason had overcome any baser instincts I might have had. And it—my reason—had held sway ever since.

Except for near the end of my dark period, apparently.

I was passing the northeast armature, a great beast hovering above me, the long tail fading up into the night. I pulled out my phone, looked at the glowing digits. It was after 10:00 P.M., which meant that the psychology department would be deserted, and so I could—

But no. No, that would be crazy.

And yet—

And yet, apparently, it wouldn't be the worst thing I'd ever done.

I passed a couple of grad students and a janitor as I made my way down the corridor. Being assistant department head was mostly an administrative pain in the butt, but the job did come with a master set of keys. When the coast was clear, I let myself into Menno's office.

Four avocado-green filing cabinets lined one wall. I was afraid they might be locked, but they weren't. Menno himself probably hadn't been in them for years; paper files were of little use to a blind man, I supposed, but perhaps teaching assistants or grad students maintained them for him. I quickly found the "L" files, but there were none about Lucidity, and so I started at the top drawer of the first cabinet, and looked at every file in turn.

I almost skipped by one labeled "DoD," but was intrigued. Was it really the American military? And indeed it was—and related to Project Lucidity, to boot. I laid out each page on the floor and snapped photos of them with my iPhone. I thought about leaving, but there was a touch of Pavlov's dogs in me, I guess; I'd been rewarded once, and I wanted to see if I'd be rewarded again. I continued on past D, through E, F, G, and so on, betting against myself that there'd be no X or Z files . . . and there weren't; the last paper file was labeled "Yerkes-Dodson handout."

But there was one drawer left, and so I opened it—and found it crammed with old VHS videocassettes. Seven were labeled "Altruistic Behaviour Study 1988," one was labeled "Teaching Company Audition," and five were labeled "APA AGM 1994." But there was one that had me salivating: the sticker on its spine said, "Lucidity Subject JM," who doubtless was me—the time-honored custom of referring to patients and experimental subjects by their initials, as if that afforded real anonymity. I took that cassette, headed out of Menno's office, being careful to turn the lights back off—not that Menno would notice—and drove to my condo, five minutes away.

I hadn't used my VHS player in years, and was relieved to find it still worked. I looked so young! And so did Menno—and it was startling to see him back before he'd lost his sight; I'd forgotten how expressive his eyes had been. "Let me just identify this recording," he said in a sibilant voice that was a tad more energetic than it was today. He cleared his throat. "January sixteenth, 2001. Subject JM."

My heart skipped a beat: footage of me from the beginning of my dark time! Still, that made sense: yes, I'd been involved with Lucidity in 2000, but I couldn't recall doing any interviews, or, for that matter, why one would bother to interview people about fairly boring hearing tests, or whatever the heck it had been? I wondered what had moved Menno to start doing them at this point.

He leaned back in his chair. "Thanks for coming in, Jim."

"My pleasure."

"So, I'm just going to ask you a few questions, if you don't mind."

"Be my guest."

"How have you been? How do you feel?"

"Fit as a fiddle," I said. "Right as rain."

"Good, good. Your classes are going okay?"

"Yes. I'm enjoying them all."

"And what about participating in this study? Have you been enjoying that?"

"Sure. And, you know, as a student, I can always use the extra cash."

"I'm sure," said Menno. He moved his chair closer to mine. "And how do you feel compared to before you became one of our experimental subjects?"

I saw myself blink three times rapidly. "The same," I said. "Why? Shouldn't I?"

There was something flat in Menno's tone. "Yes, of course."

The interview lasted seven minutes, according to the timecode running along the bottom of the screen. It was followed by the next one, exactly one month later, on February 16, 2001, which was pretty much the same, although my birthday had passed two days before, meaning I was now twenty.

The one for March 16, 2001, was similar, too. Kayla and I had recently started dating. I talked about how we'd gone to Pop Soda's the night before and listened to some live jazz; not fancy, but within our student budgets. Other than that, my response to all the questions he asked was the same mixture of clichés, platitudes, and banalities that had filled the previous interviews, and, as I soon discovered, filled the next two, as well. I was fine, chugging along, keeping my head above water, hanging in there.

But the final monthly interview, conducted on Monday, June eighteenth—the sixteenth having fallen on Saturday, it seems—was radically different in tone.

"This is just like the other times, okay?" said Menno. "A routine evaluation; same questions as always."

I had arms crossed in front of my chest. "Yeah, okay. Let's get it over with."

"Tell me how you feel today, Jim."

"Fine."

"You're happy?"

"I'm okay, yeah."

"Healthy?"

"Sure. Yeah."

"How are things with Kayla?"

I—the one here in 2020—shifted on my living-room couch; the other me, back in 2001, sat motionless. "They're fine."

"You've been going out for over three months now."

"Yeah."

"And how do you feel about her?"

"She's okay."

"Just okay? Do you love her?"

"Sure. She's great in bed."

"I mean, do you have feelings for her? Romantic feelings?"

"She's a good lay. And she looks good, y'know? Impresses the other guys, me being with her."

"And that's important?"

"Course. Gotta be seen to be on top, man. The king. Gotta be in control."

I paused the playback and looked at the image of myself frozen on the screen. I would have sworn up and down that I'd never talked about a woman that way before in my entire life; I wouldn't have believed it if—well, if it wasn't right here, on video, in front of me. My stomach was knotting, and I tasted acid at the back of my throat.

I let the playback resume. There was silence for a long moment—I thought I must have accidentally muted the sound—but it was just Menno digesting what I'd said, apparently, because at last he spoke again. "What about your sister? Heather, is it? How do you feel about her?"

"She's all right."

"Anything else you want to say about her?"

"I keep in touch. Make her think she's important, y'know?"

"Why?"

"She's a soft touch."

"For money, you mean?"

"Yeah, for money. She's a lawyer now. Deep pockets."

I sagged back into my couch, numb. What the hell had happened to me back then?

14

YouTube has countless films of psychological experiments, and I often used the ceiling-mounted projector to show them to my students. One of my favorites is the Heider and Simmel animation from 1944, which starts by showing a large hollow square with a black triangle inside it. Soon one side of the square hinges open, and the triangle moves out. A smaller black triangle and a small circle move in from the right side of the frame. The three solid shapes slide around the screen, sometimes touching, while the hinged square periodically flaps open and closed.

I remember when I first saw that cartoon myself as an under-graduate in Menno Warkentin's class. He asked us to write down what had happened in the film. I'd said the large triangle was a monster unleashed from a cage to chase off a boy and a girl who were out exploring; the boy—yeah, back then, my consciousness about gender-role stereotypes hadn't yet been raised—bravely fought off the monster, while the girl snuck into the big square to steal treasure; eventually, the boy and girl escaped, and, in a fit of anger at having been bested, the monster destroyed its cage.

My response was typical if idiosyncratic. Others had seen mating rituals, battlefield maneuvers, or slapstick comedies—but we'd all experienced some sort of story. When Heider and Simmel first did this test, only three of their hundred and fourteen subjects dispassionately described what the film actually depicted: two squares and two triangles moving about an empty space. Everyone else constructed a narrative, pretty much out of whole cloth.

As always, my own students did not disappoint. Boris, in the front row, said, "It's a political allegory, right? The big triangle, that's the United States. And Mexico, that's the little triangle. The flapping box represents the border, sometimes open and sometimes closed, and in the end, by trying to keep everyone out, the US ends up destroying itself."

You could hear the crickets in the room; nobody else had seen anything quite like that, I guess.

I let a few more people share their interpretations—which ranged from bawdy to rom-com treacly to shoot-'em-up mayhem worthy of Liam Neeson—and then I got down to the point.

"There's a word for what all of you have just done. It's confabulation. We tell ourselves stories, building them out of almost nothing, then convince ourselves they're true . . ."

MENNO Warkentin didn't come in to the university on Thursdays, so after my morning class, I headed over to his apartment in the heart of downtown. As always, the CBC was on in my car, this time with news that *did* surprise me.

Hayden Trenholm, the same pundit I'd heard interviewed yesterday, was speaking with Piya Chattopadhyay.

"So," Piya said, in her bubbly voice, *"former Calgary city mayor Naheed Nenshi has just thrown his hat into the ring, running as the federal NDP candidate in the riding of Calgary Southwest. Hayden, what do you make of that?"*

"It's a coup for the NDP," said Trenholm, "since there has long

been speculation that Nenshi was being wooed by the Trudeau Liber-
als. The fact he went to the NDP might be seen as an indication he has
bigger ambitions than Cabinet. I wouldn't be surprised if the caucus
declares him the acting leader in the next few days."

"And what about the riding he's running in?"

"It's the perfect choice if Nenshi is being positioned to lead the
New Democrats. Calgary Southwest is Stephen Harper's old riding;
the folks in it know well the perks that go with being the home base of
a prime minister. But people all across Calgary love Nenshi, and they
enjoy that he's become an international star. Back in 2013, when Rob
Ford was the butt of jokes in Toronto, Nenshi was doing a conspicu-
ously spectacular job in Calgary—so much so, as you'll recall, Piya,
that Maclean's named him the second-most-important person in Canada, right after the prime minister."

"True."

"And in 2015, the City Mayors Foundation awarded Nenshi the
World Mayor Prize, naming him the top mayor on the planet. The only
other North American contender, Houston's Annise Parker, came in
seventh."

I made a right turn onto Portage and started looking for a place to
park.

Piya said, "When he was first elected in Calgary in 2010, Nenshi
became the first Muslim mayor in North America."

"Yes, that's right," replied Trenholm. "He practices Nizari Ismaili,
a branch of Shia Islam."

"But mayor is one thing," said Piya. "Prime minister is something
else. Is Canada ready for a Muslim at 24 Sussex Drive?"

"Well," replied the pundit, "that's for the people to decide—four
weeks from today."

As they moved on to the next story, I found a spot on the street—
a rare find this time of day—and even though it was three blocks from
Menno's apartment, I took it.

I'd dropped him off a few times before but had never been up to
his second-floor suite (no point paying extra for a view, he'd quipped).
I was somewhat curious about how—or if—he'd decorated the place.

In fact, it turned out to be nicer than my condo; the living-room furniture, in silver and cyan, was clearly a matching set, and each wall had a lovely framed Emily Carr print showing the British Columbia coast. Replica Haida totem poles—dark, unpainted wood—flanked the door to the kitchen.

Menno was dressed as old professors usually were, in slightly baggy beige slacks and a brown cardigan. He had his dark glasses on; I wondered if he normally wore them when alone or had put them on when I'd buzzed from the lobby.

"Jim!" he said when I'd arrived at his unit's door "Welcome! What brings you here?" He motioned for me to come in. Pax was eyeing me from across the room. "Have a seat."

I did so, settling onto the couch. Menno sat in the easy chair that faced it at an oblique angle. There was a little table next to it on the left; Pax sat down beside him on the right.

"I've seen the video interviews with me," I said.

"About the Devin Becker trial?"

"What? No, no. The ones you did. In 2001. With me. In the old physiology building at Fort Garry."

Protracted silence, then: "How did you find those?"

"The truth? I had a look around your office."

Menno was quiet again. "Oh," he said at last.

"I'd *asked* you what had happened during that period. Why didn't you show me the tapes?"

"I know it was news to you that you'd lost your memory, Jim. But it wasn't news to me."

"Jesus, Menno. How long have you known?"

"Since 2001. Since you lost it. I'm sorry, but, well, it was obvious back then. I didn't realize you'd lost six whole months, but it was clear you'd lost *some* amount of time."

"Then why didn't you tell me?"

He lifted his shoulders. "Because you were on the mend."

"The mend? From what?"

"I don't know," Menno said. He couldn't see my expression, but must have sensed I was going to object because he held up a hand.

"Honestly, I've tried for twenty years to figure it out." He exhaled loudly. "You know what? It's a *relief* to get to talk about it. Since Dominic moved away, I've had no one to discuss this with."

"What the hell happened?"

"Dominic Adler and I were working on developing a device to detect phonemes that hadn't been spoken aloud—that is, for detecting articulated thoughts in the brain. You'd responded to our notice in *The Manitoban,* looking for experimental subjects."

I did a lot of those sorts of things back then; anything to bring in a few extra bucks. "I remember. Some sort of helmet contraption . . . ?"

Menno nodded. "We had two of them, actually. We started out with the first one, and we could indeed pick up the activity in your brain, but it was very faint, and it was being drowned out by what we thought was noise. So we developed a second helmet that added transcranial ultrasound. The idea was to see if we could boost the signal we wanted in your primary auditory cortex, make it more of an internal shout rather than a whisper, so we could pick it up better with our scanner. But instead you and—you lost consciousness."

"I don't remember that."

"Well, you did. TUS stimulation was completely new back then; we didn't expect it."

I put a hand on my chest. "What I do remember from that period is the knifing, but . . ."

"Yes?"

"Well, from what I can tell, I was here in Winnipeg on New Year's Eve 2000, not in Calgary."

Menno lifted his shoulders. "I don't know where you got the idea of the knifing from, but it didn't happen, at least not then. But . . . yeah. You were here that night—and got knocked out by our helmet, and when you came back, well, you didn't come all the way back."

I looked at him quizzically, but he couldn't see that. "What?"

"You'd had an inner voice beforehand—I'd seen it on the oscilloscope—but, as we soon discovered, it was gone afterward."

"What do you mean, 'an inner voice'?"

"Just that: an internal monologue; articulated phonemes in the brain even when you weren't speaking. But after you blacked out, it was gone. The lights were on—"

"—but nobody was home?" I said. "Seriously? Really?"

"Yes."

"A fucking p-zed? A philosopher's zombie? Jesus. Not just amnesia, but . . ." I shook my head. "No. No, that's just a thought experiment. A philosopher's zombie can't really exist."

Menno was quiet for perhaps thirty seconds. Then, in a soft voice, he said, "They do. They're *everywhere.*"

"Oh, come on!"

"*Most* of the people we tested didn't have inner voices."

"Then your equipment must—"

"Stop! You think we didn't triple check? What I'm telling you is true." He waved generally in my direction. "The only thing remarkable about you was that you had started out with an inner voice, then lost it for a time after you blacked out."

"How long was I out?"

"Maybe five minutes. And a few days later, we tested you again—without the TUS, of course—and, well, your inner voice was gone."

"And so you decided to interview me on a regular basis to see—"

"To see if there was any difference. I wish we'd done some interviews with you beforehand, but we had no way to know what was going to happen."

"I didn't watch the interviews all the way through, but I didn't notice anything different—"

"There wasn't anything major," confirmed Menno. "Your external behavior was much the same as before."

"Until the final tape," I said.

"Oh," Menno said, very softly. "Right."

"It wasn't just on that tape. People could tell; Kayla could. I'd changed."

"Kayla?"

"My girlfriend—at the time, I mean. Kayla Huron, and—"

Menno looked startled. "Huron?"

"She was one of your students. I saw her yesterday, for the first time in almost twenty years. She told me I—I hit her back then. Me!" I shook my head, still struggling with that reality. "And then, my God, the horrible things I said in that last interview. Un-fucking-believable."

He nodded slowly. "You *did* change near the end. I don't know why."

"You must have some idea! And, for Pete's sake—why'd I change back to normal?"

"Jim, honestly, I don't know. But . . ."

"Yes?"

"Well, for almost six months before that change, you *were* indeed a philosopher's zombie." He moved his head left and right—perhaps in negation, perhaps visualizing the hordes that had haunted him for decades. "And you were just as vacant, just as empty, just as dead inside as the countless millions of others surrounding us all the time."

I walked—or staggered—out of the lobby of Menno's condo onto Portage Avenue. Here, at lunch-time, there were thousands of people going east, and thousands more going west, and I just stood still, an island in the stream, fighting to keep my balance.

Coming toward me was a man with his head bent and his thumbs typing away on his phone. Behind him were two men wearing earbuds—both, as it happened, with the distinctive white Apple cables. They flowed past, not even glancing at me, just mindlessly navigating around an obstacle.

Mindlessly.

Jesus, could it be?

Three teenage girls were coming toward me now, smoking. The Surgeon General's report had come out probably before their parents had been born, but still, vapidly, they smoked. This time, I was the one to move out of the way, trying to avoid their exhalations.

And since I was moving, I continued to do so; Newton's first law, and all that. I passed a homeless man, a cardboard sign next to him saying, "Hungry—Please Help." In front of him was an empty Campbell's soup can; some people had tossed coins into it.

I wonder if Canada eliminating pennies from circulation in 2013 had much of an impact on panhandlers. Of course, anyone offering a single penny would have been rightly cursed for it, but, still, there was a lot less small change to go around. On the other hand, Canada had one- and two-dollar coins in wide use, something Americans had never managed; maybe our indigents did better than theirs.

Years ago, I'd read that the introduction of the first credit cards had had a big impact on the incomes of bunnies in Playboy Clubs. Before that, when they'd had to pay cash, men would say "Keep the change," even if it resulted in exorbitant tips. But once they started filling out charge slips, they did the math and tipped the normal percentage.

Christ, what digressions! But that's the way my mind works—one thought sparking another, a cascade of notions and connections. And I'd always assumed it was that way for *everyone*, but . . .

But if what Menno had found was true, then most of these people weren't having inner monologues like mine; most of them didn't have thoughts bouncing around from place to place. No, most of them weren't thinking at all, at least not in a first-person, self-reflective way; they weren't having *any* subjective experiences.

I looked at them as I continued to walk. Hundreds upon hundreds of people wearing blue jeans—a default, an easy choice, a simple rule.

I remember Monty Henderson, who lived on my parents' street. He'd gone on to join the Calgary Police. He said that on the first day of training the new recruits were told to "fit in or fuck off"—and they all just capitulated.

I was moving mostly against the flow of pedestrians now; for whatever reason, the tide had turned, and the bulk of them were going west. One bumped into me. "Sorry," he mumbled, and beetled on.

I'd once seen a documentary about flocking behavior in birds. To get the effect we observe, each bird only has to apply three simple rules. The "separation rule" says avoid crowding your neighbors—you gotta give the other birds some room in order to avoid collisions. The "alignment rule" says look at where all the other birds are going and pick a heading for yourself that's an average of everyone else's trajectories. And the "cohesion rule" says move toward the average position of all your neighbors, an edict that prevents the flock from dissipating. Computer models that employ these rules produce behavior indistinguishable from real flocking; similar rules control the schooling of fish.

Could the movements of humans be equally simple? Birds almost certainly did this without conscious thought; fish clearly did.

A flock of birds. A school of fish. A crowd of humans.

Were we really all that different?

And were other rules just as simple, and just as mindlessly applied? Choose clothes that are similar to those that others are wearing; adopt phrases you've heard others use; lower your gaze when passing someone; try not to bump into people, but if you do, apologize.

So many of the things we do are clearly algorithmic. Did I really think I was the first unathletic kid to fake tripping over a nonexistent stone to explain a pathetic performance in a race? *They all do that.* The first guy to try the old yawn-becoming-an-arm-around-her-shoulders-at-the-movies bit? *They all do that.* The first person to . . .

Maybe it didn't even take three rules; maybe it took only one.

When in Rome, do as the Romans do.

15

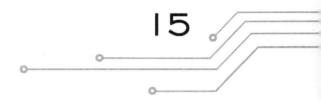

THE University of Manitoba has an illustrious history in psychology and philosophy, which is why I'd chosen to go there, and why, despite an urge to refer to my students as Sweathogs, I'm happy to still teach there. It's where pioneering neurophilosophers Patricia and Paul Churchland taught from 1969 to 1984; it's where Michael Persinger of God-helmet fame got his PhD in 1971; it's where Bob Altemeyer produced the test for right-wing authoritarianism that was extensively cited in Nixon counsel John Dean's *Conservatives Without Conscience*; and it's where Menno Warkentin did his pioneering reciprocal-altruism studies. And so, of course, there were faculty here who might be able to help me with my problem, but I wanted somebody who wasn't closely associated with Menno, and so I looked up memory researchers at other institutions. Soon enough, I settled on Bhavesh Namboothiri, who taught across town at the University of Winnipeg. I'd met him in passing at a few conferences: a husky guy perhaps ten years older than I with a New Delhi accent I occasionally had trouble parsing.

I went to meet him in his office, which was an odd wedge shape, with tomato-soup-colored walls and bookcases so shallow that a couple of centimeters of many volumes stuck out past the shelves; I hoped they were bolted in place.

We shot the usual academic breeze for a while—how the administration was killing us, how nice it was to have a mostly empty campus in the summer, how criminal it was that academic salaries were lagging ever further behind private-sector equivalents—and then I got down to the heart of the matter, so to speak. "I was reading online that you've been doing some remarkable work in recovering lost memories."

"Yes, indeed. I hope someday to apply it to a few of our federal politicians."

"Ha-ha. But, see, here's the thing: I don't remember anything from the first six months of the year 2001."

Namboothiri's unibrow ascended his forehead. "But your memories before that, and after, are normal?"

"As far as I can tell."

He leaned back in his chair and interlaced his fingers behind his balding head. "Do you have any idea why you can't remember that period?"

I took a deep breath. If this man was going to help me, he had to know at least part of the truth. "Yes. It has to do with the nature of consciousness. I was one of the subjects in an experiment done back then at U of M, and it had the effect of knocking me down to being a philosopher's zombie."

"You're shitting me. You mean Chalmers and all that crap?"

"Yes, exactly. For those six months, my lights were on, but nobody was home, and I can't remember anything from that period. And yet a philosopher's zombie must have *some* sort of memory—otherwise, its behavior wouldn't be indistinguishable from that of a normal person. I took courses, I interacted with people, I even managed a relationship with a girl—and the memories of that time *had* to have been stored somewhere. But for the life of me, I can't access them."

Namboothiri nodded slowly. "We all have memories we can no longer access. For most of us, that's everything before about the age of three; that's when we switch from indexing memories visually to indexing them verbally. The switching happens at the same time children start having imaginary friends—and that makes perfect sense: they're beginning to have an inner monologue and don't yet realize that it's *themselves* that they're talking to."

"Very Julian Jaynes," I said, referring to the author of one of my favorite books, *The Origin of Consciousness in the Breakdown of the Bicameral Mind.*

"Exactly. Anyway, verbal indexing is much more efficient, which is why once you have a significant vocabulary, you switch over to it. It's way easier to mentally say, 'Remember the house my friend Anil lived in' than it is to shuffle mentally through pictures of every house you've ever committed to memory, hoping for a match. But, you know, there are adults who *do* index their memories visually. Ever read Temple Grandin? The famous autistic?"

I nodded and cited the title of her most popular book. *"Thinking in Pictures."*

"Exactly. And apparently she does." He brought his hands down to his armrests and leaned forward, almost conspiratorially. "You know as well as I do that neuroscience advances through a series of unfortunate accidents—fortunate for us, the researchers, but often devastating for the patients. You know how rare retrograde amnesia is—outside of soap operas, I mean. Imagine how rare it is to find someone deep on the autism spectrum suffering from it. But one of my patients here has precisely that condition. Poor woman suffered a traumatic brain injury in a motorcycle accident; couldn't recall anything much from before the collision, her whole life basically wiped out."

"Like Lieutenant Uhura in 'The Changeling.'" I'd expected the usual blank stare I got when I made one of my patented "All I need to know in life I learned from *Star Trek*" references, but, to my surprise, Namboothiri pointed a finger at me, and said, "Exactly! In that episode, Nomad supposedly wiped her memories. But, you know, what must've really happened is the same thing that happens when you format a disk drive. A normal formatting doesn't wipe the drive clean; it just wipes the file allocation table—essentially, the index. All the other ones and zeros on the disk are left intact, which is why you read about police recovering files criminals thought they'd erased. That's what must've happened to Lieutenant Uhura: the indexing of her memories was wiped, but the memories themselves were left intact—which explains her being back at work on the bridge of the *Enterprise* in the next episode. Well, same thing for the woman in the motorcycle accident. Her memories were still there, but the index of them—in her case, as an autistic, a massive visual index—was damaged by the impact. But using a variation of the Montreal technique, I've been able to help her re-access her memories."

"You mean with direct electrical stimulation of her brain? Like Wilder Penfield did? The whole 'I smell burnt toast' thing?"

"Yes. Of course, we've come a long way since Penfield's day. We don't have to open the skull to do the stimulation. The beauty of it is, as we learned thanks to the case I've been talking about, the visual memory index, long abandoned in neurotypicals, is physically separate from the verbal memory index. So, in your case, well—how old are you?"

"Thirty-nine."

"Fine. Well, in your case, we don't have to rummage around through the thirty-six years or so of memory that you've indexed verbally. If I'm right, any memories you laid down during your philosophical-zombie period will be accessible through the visual index. Instead of looking for a six-month needle in a thirty-nine-year haystack, the memories from those six months in 2001, or at least the index entries for them, will only be mixed in with a few years of much older memories, and, since those memories are of early childhood, they'll be easy to recognize as irrelevant to the task at hand."

"Excellent, excellent. Thank you."

"Have you had a recent MRI?"

"No."

"All right. I have a friend at St. Boniface. Let me call her and see if she can squeeze you in." He picked up the phone on his desk and made a call; I only heard his side.

"Hi, Brenda, it's Bhavesh. Listen, I need to get an MRI done for a . . . a patient of mine, and I don't want to—what? Really? Hang on."

He held the handset to his chest. "How fast can you get over to St. Boniface?"

I frowned. "This time of day, no traffic? Ten minutes."

"Go! She's got a cancellation at half-past two."

I hurried out the door.

16

"So," I asked, looking out at the sea of faces, "in our example, why do we accord moral standing to Jacob, but not to the robot? Why do we say the state can't execute Jacob but it can shut off and dismantle the robot?"

"Well," said Zach, in the second row, "Jacob is a Homo sapien."

"Homo sapiens," I said.

The kid looked baffled.

I was reminded of the Wayne and Shuster skit about the assassination of Julius Caesar. The private eye investigating Big Julie's demise orders a "martinus." "Don't you mean martini?" asks the bartender. And the detective snaps back, "If I wanted two, I'd ask for them."

"Homo sapiens is singular," I said. "There's no such thing as a Homo sapien."

"Oh. Okay. So what's the plural of Homo sapiens?"

I rattled off all seven syllables: "Homines sapientes."

The kid didn't miss a beat. "Now you're just making shit up."

"JIM, thank you for coming in," Namboothiri said. I'd found an email from him waiting for me when I'd woken up, and had hustled back to his office.

"My pleasure."

"I have the MRI scans from St. Boniface."

He sounded concerned—and that made me concerned. "Oh, my God. A tumor?"

"No, not a tumor."

"Then what?"

"It turns out the medical-imaging group at St. Boniface didn't have to open a new file for you. They already had one."

"But I've never been there—well, except to visit sick friends."

"Ah, but you *were* there, in 2001. It seems I'm not the only importunate professor in town. Back then, one Menno Warkentin twisted a few arms and got you in to be scanned, too."

"Really?"

"Yes."

My heart was pounding. "And?"

"And my friend at St. Boniface sent that scan along, as well. They normally don't keep records from that far back, but yours was tagged for retention for research purposes; the radiologist noted he'd never seen anything like it." He turned to a monitor. "Here you are today, in 2020." He hit Alt-Tab. "And here you are in 2001."

I knew the layout of the brain, but I was no expert at reading scans. "Yes?" I said, looking at the older scan.

"Here," said Namboothiri pointing at a thin hyperintensity line— what one might have taken for a scratch on the film if it hadn't been a digital image.

"Damage to the amygdala," I said, stunned.

He pointed to another line. "And the orbitofrontal cortex," added Namboothiri.

"The paralimbic system," I said softly.

"Bingo," said Namboothiri. He pointed to the recent scan. "The encephalomalacia has abated over the years, although the lesions are still present. But the abnormality dates back to at least"—he peered at the bottom left corner of the image—"June fifteenth, 2001."

"My God. Um, look, could transcranial focused ultrasound create lesions like that? That's what Menno's equipment used."

"TUS? No way. These are more like, I dunno, burns."

"Shit."

"Anyway. I thought you'd want to know. I'm going to work with the recent scan, mapping out where to search for your missing memories. Sadly, I *do* have many other things on my plate, but I'll get to it as soon as I can."

I pushed the flat of my hand sharply against the slate-gray door to Menno's office and it swung open, banging against the wall-mounted stopper. Pax rose up on all fours, and Menno swung around in his brown leather chair. "Who's there?" he asked, sounding more than a little frightened.

"It's me," I said. "Jim Marchuk."

"Padawan! You startled me. What can I do for you?"

"You've already done plenty," I said, fury in my voice as I closed the door behind me. "I've seen the MRI."

Menno's broad face often betrayed what he was thinking; I suspect that since going blind, he'd more or less forgotten about trying to control his facial expressions. And so *this,* naked in front of me, was what someone looked like when, after almost twenty years, they heard the other shoe falling. Still, he made a game attempt: "What MRI?"

"The one done near the end of my dark period, showing the lesions to my paralimbic system." Normally, by this time, Pax would have curled up at Menno's feet, but she recognized the anger in my tone: she stood at attention, ears perked, mouth open, teeth exposed.

"Jim . . ."

"What were you trying to do, for God's sakes?"

"I'm sorry, Jim. I'm so, so sorry."

"How many times were you going to use me as an experimental animal?"

"It wasn't like that, Jim. Not at all."

"Christ, first you knock me into a coma—"

"I never wanted any harm to come to you, ever."

"—then you wrecked my paralimbic system. Actual fucking brain damage!"

"I wasn't trying to hurt you! I was trying to cure you."

Boisterous students were moving down the corridor. While waiting for them to pass, I digested this. "Cure . . . ?"

"Yes," said Menno emphatically. "We kept testing you with the Lucidity equipment, hoping to find that your inner voice had come back. A month, two months, three months—it was killing me, what we'd done to you. Of course, there's more to consciousness than just an inner voice—it's a whole suite of things—but that was the only aspect we could directly check for. When it's present, it surely correlates with it being *like* something to be you, to having first-person, subjective experience. But we'd somehow taken all that away—and I had to try to bring it back."

"So you carved into my skull?"

"Nothing as dangerous as that. And we succeeded, you know. Your inner voice *did* come back."

"The MRI I saw was dated June fifteenth. But I have no recollection of anything until the beginning of July."

Menno tilted his head, as if thinking. "It was so long ago. I don't remember. But . . . but, yeah, now that I think about it, your inner voice didn't come back right away. It was—God, well, I guess it could have been a couple of weeks later."

"Damn it, Menno, you want me to go to the dean or to the press first? Or maybe the cops? What the hell did you do to me?"

He was quiet for a long moment, then spread his arms. "Lucidity was a military project, did you know that? We were working on a battlefield microphone. Anyway, that meant we had access to some other classified techniques. The Pentagon was testing a system—they've since abandoned it, thank God—using two intersecting laser beams to trigger action potentials. The beams supposedly passed harmlessly through living tissue, and, well, there was a paper out of Russia that suggested an approach related to stimulating the amygdala that I thought just might bring you back, so—"

"Jesus!"

"I was trying to fix things—"

"And instead fucked me up even worse!"

Pax was staring at me, still startled by my anger, but Menno's voice was calm. "As I said, the laser system didn't work as advertised. Turned out the damn thing destroyed tissue along the lines of both beams— although fortunately the beams were extremely narrow, and they cauterized the blood vessels. Thank the Lord for neuroplasticity, though; you bounced back from the damage, but . . ."

"But it was like Phineas Gage," I said.

"I'm so sorry," said Menno. "I was trying to help. And, look, Kiehl didn't publish until five years later; I had no way of knowing."

I thought about that. Kent Kiehl's seminal paper "A Cognitive Neuroscience Perspective on Psychopathy: Evidence for Paralimbic System Dysfunction," had come out in 2006. He demonstrated that damage to what he dubbed the paralimbic portions of the brain—including the amygdala—could cause people to exhibit psychopathic symptoms. Phineas Gage, the Vermont railway worker who, in 1848, had a tamping iron blown straight up through his skull, probably suffered from that sort of damage, turning him from an affable fellow into a manipulative, reckless, irresponsible, promiscuous monster—in other words, a psychopath.

"I'm truly sorry, Jim," Menno said again.

"Paralimbic damage," I said, thinking aloud. "But . . ." I put a hand on my chest, fingers splayed. "My heart . . ."

"Yes?" said Menno.

My head was swimming. The knifing, the guy with the splayed teeth, the blood freezing on the sidewalk. I remembered it all so clearly. And—

No. Damn it. No. Another old paper came to mind—I'd cited it myself in some of my own publications: Armin Schnider on "Spontaneous Confabulation, Reality Monitoring, and the Limbic System." Schnider contended that those with anterior limbic damage became absolutely convinced of narratives they'd created to explain events even though they were just making things up.

I looked at Menno, a little reflection of me staring back from his opaque glasses. I didn't think of myself as a particularly macho guy, and, of course, there was nothing funny about breast cancer, but, still, men were strange when it came to that part of their anatomy, and a stabbing is a way more interesting story to tell, but—

No, no, I would have been here in Winnipeg on—what date had Sandy Cheung said? February something . . .

February nineteenth. *Monday,* February nineteenth. First business day during Reading Week—or, as some of my less-academically-minded friends called it, Ski Week, the time each year during which Canadian universities had no classes so students could catch up on their work. Yes, if I'd needed a tumor removed, I might well have arranged to have had it done when I could be back in Calgary with my family. Jesus.

I looked again at Menno. "You fucked me up."

"I'm so, so sorry. I really was trying to help."

I leaned against the office door, thinking. "The inner-voice stuff— or, more to the point, the *lack* of inner-voice stuff: did you publish about that?"

Menno shook his head. "Like I said, all our research was classified. And when Dom moved to the States, well, it was his project, really."

"You'd made a major breakthrough—philosopher's zombies exist!— and you kept quiet about it all these years?"

"I *had* to," Menno replied. "I'm a Mennonite."

"Yes?" I said. "So the idea of people without inner lives contradicted your religious beliefs?"

"What? No, no. I mean, *yes,* I suppose so—where's the soul, and all that? But that's not what I'm talking about. Mennonites are pacifists. I couldn't tell the DoD what we'd found. God, can you imagine what they'd have done if they knew? Talk about cannon fodder! They could use our technique to identify which soldiers would make the best mindless little drones. I *had* to bury the research as much as I could."

That took me aback. "You think p-zeds are blindly obedient?"

"I *know* so—because until I messed up your amygdala, you yourself were. I was stunned when Dom managed to talk you into continuing with our experiments; I'd figured you'd never want to see us again. But a guy in a lab coat asks you to do something, and, *boom!*, yes, sir; as you wish, sir; no problem, sir. Philosopher's zombies aren't leaders; they're followers. They don't want anything themselves. Bob Altemeyer was probably identifying p-zeds, as you call them, with his research here on authoritarian followers, and Stanley Milgram almost certainly was identifying them back in 1961 with his obedience-to-authority experiments. Of course a p-zed will shock someone just because they're told to do so; they have no inner voice arguing against it. Thank God, eventually yours came back."

"So no harm, no foul, right? It all worked out in the end? You robbed me of half a year of my life!"

I expected some sort of protest; no matter how accurate the charge, most people reflexively defend themselves. But Menno just sat there quietly for a long moment, and then, slowly, deliberately, he removed his glasses, set them on his desk, and he looked at me.

With his dead glass eyes.

"I felt terrible about what happened to you, Jim. You have no idea how much it tore me up. And, as a psychologist, I know all about the indicators, the signs—the preternatural calmness that comes over a person when the decision has been made. And when I made *my* decision, I recognized it for precisely what it was, but nonetheless, it seemed the thing to do."

His eyes always faced straight forward; he was incapable of a sidelong glance. And he was looking at me, or at least facing me, and although he blinked at the normal rate, his aim never wavered. Even though I knew he couldn't see a thing through those glass spheres, it was more unnerving than even the psychopathic stare.

"You think it was easy, living with what we'd done? What *I'd* done?" He shook his head, blind gaze swinging like twin searchlights. "It tortured me. I couldn't sleep; couldn't—you know." He paused. "I drove out to Dauphin one night—a long drive, a mostly empty highway. There were trees at the side of the road, which is what I'd expected, but it was frustrating as hell—just saplings, young elms. I wanted something massive, something I was sure wouldn't snap in two. And then, there it was—a whole stand of them. I took aim at one in the middle, and I *floored* it. And, well . . ." He waved a hand in a circular motion in front of his face. *"This."* He shrugged a little. "It wasn't the outcome I was looking for, and it's been a bitch, let me tell you, all these years, being blind." The glassy spheres faced me once more, and I looked at them for as long as I could. "I can't make up for what I did, Jim, but recognize that, in some measure at least, I've paid for it."

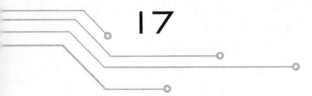

17

I was still in a daze from Menno's revelations when the taxi dropped me at the Canadian Museum for Human Rights. The design was supposed to suggest dove's wings surrounding a glass spire that rose a hundred meters into the sky, but to me it looked like God had crammed a Bundt cake down around a traffic cone.

I was running late, and Kayla had already checked out of her room at the nearby Inn at The Forks; she'd texted me to say she'd headed on in to the reception. I hustled over to the entrance, giving my ritual nod to the statue of Mahatma Gandhi on the way.

The reception was being held in the Garden of Contemplation, which was in the vast lobby adjacent to the reflecting pool. It was bordered by re-creations of the basalt columns of the Giant's Causeway, commemorating the Troubles in Northern Ireland. Most of the men were in suits and ties, but I was dressed more casually; Kayla and I planned to make it all the way to Saskatoon tonight, and I wanted to be comfortable for the drive.

I looked around but didn't see any sign of Kayla. But I did see Nick Smith, a partner in an accounting firm that was helping to sponsor the lecture series. He had a golfer's tan that was close to a sunburn and was chatting with someone I didn't know: a handsome black man of about thirty-five. As I drifted by, the man was saying, "I don't even know how to put this, but—"

Nick caught sight of me, and he leaned out of the conversation long enough to pull me in. "Oh, Jim, let me introduce you to someone. Jim Marchuk, this is Darius Clark. Jim's on the board here." Darius was standing in a military at-ease posture, with hands clasped behind his back. As Nick turned back to face him, he adopted the same pose.

"Nice to meet you," I said.

"Darius is giving a lecture here tomorrow," Nick said.

"Well, not exactly," Darius said. He had a bit of a Southern drawl. "I'm accompanying my partner. She's the one giving the talk."

"Ah," I said.

"But I was just saying to Mr. Smith here—"

"Please, call me Nick."

Darius smiled at that. "I was just saying to Nick, I'm visiting from Washington—DC, that is. Latisha and I live there."

"I love that city," I said.

"No," said Darius affably, "you love the Mall and maybe a few streets on either side. The city itself is pretty crappy."

"Oh."

"I only moved there to be with Latisha. She works for the DoJ, the Department of Justice. Anyway, my point is this. Y'all are having this wonderful reception for us here, and earlier today, we went to lunch at the offices of Nick's firm."

"Nice," I said.

"It was. And I don't just mean the food. I never had bison before, but . . ."

Darius trailed off, and I smiled encouragingly. "Yes?"

He lifted his shoulders. "Now I know what it feels like to be white."

"Pardon?" I said. And, to my surprise, Nick chimed in with, "Say what?"

"If you're black, you can't walk into a law office, or a government office, or anything like that in DC without people looking at you like you're there to rob the place. You have no idea what it's like with people always expecting the worst from you." He spread his arms. "But here I was welcomed, made to feel right at home. Nobody looked alarmed or scared when I came in. Everybody was like, 'Good afternoon, sir. May I take your coat?'"

"Welcome to friendly Manitoba," Nick said.

It was an empty response; "Friendly Manitoba" was the slogan on our license plates. Most Indigenous Canadians would tell a very different story about visiting highfalutin places here.

"I guess," said Darius.

Nick was protracting his vowels now. "Really," he said. "It's totally normal here."

Darius narrowed his eyes. "Are you making fun of me?"

Just then, a woman who must have been Latisha joined us; she slipped an arm around Darius's waist, and I took the opportunity to maneuver Nick toward the bar.

"What's wrong with him?" Nick asked, glancing back at Darius.

"You were imitating him," I said.

"Pardon?"

"You're saying 'pardon' now, but you said 'say what' back there."

"Did I?"

"And you were totally copying his posture and accent."

"No, I wasn't."

"Yes, you were."

"Why would I—"

"Everybody does it to one degree or another. 'Unconscious mimicry,' it's called.

"Oh," Nick said. "I didn't mean anything by it."

"No, no. Of course not."

"I wasn't thinking."

I looked at him, my heart pounding, as I wondered if that were literally true.

Across the lobby, I spotted Kayla emerging from the ladies' room. I told Nick I'd catch him later and hurried over to her, feeling apprehensive as I maneuvered around people. Normally I was fine in crowds, but

I found myself wondering how many Nicks—how many p-zeds—were flocking about me.

The route we'd planned from Winnipeg to Saskatoon was pig-simple: a straight line 570 kilometers due west on the Trans-Canada to Regina, then north for 260 kilometers on Saskatchewan Highway 11 up to Saskatoon—the perfect sort of trip to be executed without much conscious thought. Despite our late start, we were determined to make the first, longer leg without a stop, then, after a quick bite, pressing on the rest of the way.

We put the radio on briefly to get a traffic report, but first caught the tail end of a newscast: *"The bodies of six more dead migrant workers have been found today in Texas. State governor Dylan McCharles denies any correlation between this and the passing of the McCharles Act . . ."*

Later, after we'd gotten the word to avoid Confusion Corner—which pretty much went without saying here in The Peg—Kayla turned off the radio, and I said, "I went to see Menno Warkentin this afternoon."

"Oh, wow!" she replied. "How's he doing?"

"Fine, I guess. But he knew all about my lost time, and—"

And I faltered. I'd intended to immediately tell Kayla about the big psychological discovery, about how the whole world was filled with p-zeds, but looking at her profile, outlined by the light of the setting sun, that didn't seem the most important thing. No, what I wanted—what I needed—was for this brilliant, beautiful woman to understand what had happened all those years ago; her wariness at lunch made perfect sense in retrospect, but I couldn't stand having her continuing to be worried. "He explained it all to me," I said. "About those horrible things I did. He'd tried something back in June 2001, an experimental technique, and it damaged my limbic system."

She briefly faced me. "My God, really?"

"Yes. Fortunately, the damage was along two very narrow paths. You know Phineas Gage?"

"The guy who got a metal rod blown through his head?"

"Exactly. Left a nine-centimeter-diameter hole, but he survived for twelve years. It changed him, though—permanently in his case; made him pretty much psychopathic. Well, what Menno did to me was similar to what happened to Phineas Gage—um, but at a narrower gauge, so to speak; the damage was microns wide instead of centimeters. My brain rerouted around it."

She nodded. "Yeah," she said. "I wasn't sure at first, but it's been obvious over these last couple of days that you're back to your old self," she said. "Hell, I wouldn't be alone with you here in the middle of nowhere if I didn't think you were."

"Thanks."

"And, y'know, I've read your blog; I've read your books. There's no way a psychopath could have written them."

"Hitler was fond of animals and children."

"You're not helping your case," she said, but I could hear the mirth in her voice.

"Sorry."

"But I don't understand. Why was Menno experimenting on you like that?"

"Well, see, a couple of months before you'd met me, he'd done something that caused me to lose my inner voice . . ."

One hundred kilometers . . .

"And Menno believes *most* of the human race has no inner monologue?" asked Kayla.

"That's right. Something like sixty percent, he thinks."

"Hmmm. That's roughly the same percentage Victoria and I found are in the Q1 state."

"I wonder if it's the *same* sixty percent," I said. "If those in the Q1 state, with one electron in superposition, all have just the minimum level of mental functioning, well, their lights could indeed be on with nobody being home."

"Philosopher's zombies," said Kayla, still getting used to the notion.

"Right. Who the hell knows what IQ tests really measure, but a Q1 might do just fine on them; pattern recognition and spatial translations could be entirely autonomic, after all."

"True."

"And you've already shown that Q2s are psychopaths—who surely have an inner voice, an inner life, but literally think only about themselves; they have no empathy."

"So you were a Q2 when you . . . when you did those things?"

"I—no, no, I couldn't be. As I said, psychopaths clearly *do* have inner voices; they're plotting and scheming all the time. But I've been consulting with a memory expert at UW. He thinks the reason I can't remember that entire period—not just the part where I was behaving normally but also the part where I was behaving badly—was because I was a p-zed throughout; no inner voice, so no verbal indexing of the memories."

"So there are two kinds of psychopaths?"

"Maybe," I said. "One group would be quantum psychopaths— Q2s—with two of the three microtubular electrons in superposition. The other group would be those with paralimbic damage. Oh, sure, there could be some overlap: some Q2s might happen to have paralimbic damage, but so might some Q1s and Q3s. Perhaps the psychological community has been conflating two separate things: Q2s, who are psychopathic at the quantum level, and hapless SOBs who have brain damage that leads them to doing terrible things."

"I bet that's true," said Kayla. "You know, you, me, Bob Hare, we've all run into that problem. Remember Hare's *Snakes in Suits,* about psychopaths in the workplace? Try to tell the average Joe that psychopaths are everywhere and he balks, because to him the term exclusively means crazed killers like Hannibal Lecter or Norman Bates."

"Exactly," I said. "The average guy sees a difference not just in degree but in kind between Paul Bernardo and a surgeon who can dispassionately open up somebody's chest. And he doesn't see the connection between Jeffrey Dahmer and an avaricious bank president. And yet we keep telling him that they're the same thing. Well, maybe in this instance, the laypeople are right. Maybe we actually *are* talking about two distinct phenomena." I shrugged a little. "It doesn't help that psychopathy—of either kind, I suppose—can manifest itself in so many different ways, thanks to differing genetics, upbringings, socioeconomic conditions, childhood abuse or lack thereof, and so on. There are twenty traits on the Hare Checklist, right? Each of which can be absent, weakly present, or strongly present, and you need a score of thirty or above to be diagnosed a psychopath. That means there must be thousands of different flavors of psychopathy."

"Fourteen million, two hundred and seventy-nine thousand, four hundred and fifteen."

I looked at her.

"Math's my thing," she said, flashing a radiant smile.

Two hundred kilometers . . .

"Okay, but if Q1s are p-zeds, and Q2s are psychopaths," I said, "what does quantum-superposition state three correspond to?"

"Us?" said Kayla, throwing out an idea.

"What do you mean by 'us'?"

"A person firing on all cylinders: a normal, fully conscious human being with the ability to reflect upon yourself, to think about whether what you're doing is right or not. In other words a person with—"

"A conscience," I said.

"Precisely. A conscience."

Could it be that simple, I wondered? An additive effect? Stage one, with one of three electrons in superposition: basic functioning, but no awareness.

Stage two, with two of three electrons in superposition: the same basic functioning as before, but with self-awareness added on.

And stage three, with all three electrons in superposition: everything from stage one and everything from stage two, plus an extra layer—a degree of thoughtful introspection, a conscience—added on top.

"Consciousness with conscience . . ." I said.

I saw Kayla's profile, illuminated now only by the dashboard lights, nod. "Makes sense, doesn't it?"

"Oh! And it could be abbreviated C-W-C, right?"

In the dim light, I pantomimed writing the three letters in the air. "Conscious with conscience. I like that there's a W in the middle, because there literally *is* a double you: two yous, the basic consciousness, and then a looking back on that consciousness, a self-reflection."

"C-W-C," she said. "Bit of a mouthful."

I was reminded of Douglas Adams's quip about WWW being the only abbreviation that had three times as many syllables as the thing it stood for. Still: "Only if you spell it out. If you say the initials as a word, C-W-C spells 'quick.' You know, like in bright or mentally agile: a quick mind, a quick wit . . ."

"Hmm," she said.

"It's like the Norm MacDonald bit about the *Fantastic Four.*"

She shot me a glance.

"Reed Richards is giving them their new names: 'Sue, you'll be The Invisible Woman. And Johnny, how cool is this? You'll be The Human Torch. And, me, let's call me Mr. Fantastic—yeah, that's it. Oh, and Ben, you'll be The Thing.' Old Ben wasn't too happy about that. 'You get Mr. Fantastic and I get The Thing?'"

"Well," said Kayla, "the p-zeds quite literally won't care that we got a better name."

"And the psychos?"

"Don't tell them," said Kayla. "Don't make them angry. You wouldn't like them when they're angry."

"Continued Marvel motif for the win," I said, my heart beating faster.

Three hundred kilometers . . .

"But come on," said Kayla. "I mean really. How could it possibly be true? How could most of the population be philosopher's zombies?"

"Well, it's like the Neanderthals, right?" I said. "They had *bigger* brains than us. But they were nothing but p-zeds. They made no art. They didn't bury their dead with grave goods—implying they had no concept of an afterlife. They didn't go in for bodily adornment: no makeup or jewelry, except near the end of their reign, and then that might well have been simple mimicry of us."

"They made tools," Kayla said.

"So do chimps and crows. Doesn't mean there's anyone inside having an interior monologue. And remember, the Neanderthals made essentially the same tools for 200,000 years: the Mousterian industry. They chipped stone choppers exactly the same way, with no innovation, no improvement. Never once, as far as we can tell, when a flint nodule broke in an odd way that might have been better did a Neanderthal tilt his head to one side and say, 'Hmmm . . . isn't that interesting? And what if I did *this* . . .' Instead, he discarded any such nodule and just kept doing the same old thing without really being awake."

"Caught knapping, so to speak."

I'd heard it as "Caught napping," and she must have realized that. She took her hands off the steering wheel long enough to act out whacking two stones together. "You know, knapping—with a *k.*"

"I can see why I fell for you all those years ago," I said, grinning, as the headlamp from an approaching car bathed our faces in light . . .

Four hundred kilometers . . .

"The problem with leaving philosophical zombies to the philosophers is that they take things to the extreme," I said. "Camp A—David Chalmers is in it—proposes a creature that is quark-for-quark identical to a normal person but, despite being *precisely the same physically,* has no consciousness, and yet somehow behaves indistinguishably from an entity that *is* conscious. It's an argument designed to show that consciousness is something non-physical.

"Camp B—Daniel Dennett is in it—says Chalmers and others who say zombie behavior would be indistinguishable from normal behavior are simply wrong in asserting that consciousness is something that can be separated out like that. Dennett would say consciousness is not a single thing, but a combination of capacities."

"Right," said Kayla.

"And Chalmers postulates one world *entirely filled* with fully conscious beings, and another, completely separate world *entirely filled* with zombies—'Zombieworld,' as he calls it."

"Okay."

"But I'm with Dennett; I've always had a problem with the Zombieworld postulate. For a thought experiment in a classroom, it's fine. But in real life? In actuality? I just don't see how you can get a viable society as complex as our own that consists solely of nonconscious entities. Without at least *some* conscious beings for the nonconscious ones to emulate, you'd get—well, you'd get Neanderthals: a stagnant civilization, with nothing changing. No, you need some truly conscious people; you need quicks. We Q3s come up with new ideas, and they're emulated over and over by the Q1s."

"But if the Q1s *are* behaviorally different like that—however subtly—then they aren't really philosopher's zombies, not in the sense Chalmers means."

"Yeah, okay. So let's make p-zed a full acronym to distinguish our zombies from his. P-Z-E-D: 'philosophical zombies exhibiting differences.' And ours really *are* philosophical, right? 'Philosophy' means 'lover of wisdom,' and our p-zeds *do* love wisdom, in the sense of being attracted to it because they don't have any of their own. But when an idea comes along—"

"You're talking about memes," said Kayla.

I nodded. "I guess I am: ideas that propagate through society. It's funny that the phrase 'going viral' has become synonymous with 'meme.' P-zeds of the kind we're talking about have no conscious defense against ideas, no matter how stupid they are, and so are easily infected by them."

Kayla nodded. "That would explain the polling-credibility gap. You know how you constantly hear poll results that seem to imply that *you* are an outlier? You don't know *anyone* who believes in creationism, yet the polls say the majority of Americans, at least, do. You don't know *anyone* who believes in alien abductions, but the polls say most people do. Maybe those are cases of memes taking over and spreading through the p-zed population. Yes, there may be a little spillover into the Q2 or Q3 levels, but by definition it's mostly Q1s that are susceptible to that sort of unthinking acceptance."

"Exactly," I said. "It's the whole p-zed playbook: just say or do whatever the guy next to you is saying or doing. And, well, if a Q2 or a Q3 can plant a notion, no matter how abhorrent, it can spread."

I couldn't see if Kayla was frowning, but it sounded like she was. "It still seems . . . I don't know, a bit pat?"

"Not really," I said. "René Girard had it right. He argued that humans are basically imitative creatures. We don't think for ourselves; rather, we just copy what others are doing. He was decades ahead of modern neuroscience. Long before mirror neurons were discovered, he intuited—from his studies of existing cultures and from reading ancient texts—that most of our behavior is imitative—'psychological mimesis,' he called it."

"Wasn't Girard the guy who talked about societies always finding scapegoats?"

"Exactly, which is more piling-on behavior, everybody converging on the same thought." I looked out the side window at the flat, dark prairie under a sliver of moon. "We're all hominidae; we're all apes. Well, what's the thing that apes have in common? It's right there in the name we give to them—to *us*. Apes? We ape each other; we copy each other. Monkey see, monkey do. Great apes? Damn straight. We *excel* at imitation."

Kayla replied, "And we—or the p-zeds, at any rate—copy *indiscriminately,* without reflection. And if the person they're copying is a psychopath, then their behavior ends up being *de facto* psychopathic, too."

"Exactly what happened in Nazi Germany," I said. "The average— well, I was going to say the average Joe, but I suppose it was the average Hans over there—wasn't a bad guy. But he and his fellow countrymen were great at aping, and the people they saw, assholes like Hitler and Himmler and Goebbels and Goering, people who *were* psychopathic monsters, became, quite literally, their role models. They copied their attitudes, their speech, their practices. Think of the Nuremberg rallies: all the p-zeds falling in line . . ."

"Just like . . ."

She trailed off, but I knew what she'd been about to say, and so I said it for her: "Just like my grandfather." Of course, if he really had been Ernst the Enforcer, I suppose he was more likely a Q2—one of the hubs, like Devin Becker, around whom p-zeds clustered, the carcinogen that caused a mob of Q1s to metastasize.

I stared through the windshield, the lights of Regina smoldering ahead.

Five hundred kilometers . . .

18

WE hit Regina around 10:30 P.M. By that point, we were exhausted, and I think we both looked wistfully at the motels flashing past as we entered the city. But Kayla had to be at work the next day, and so, after a brief stop for coffee and donuts to keep our blood sugar up, I took over the driving and got us the rest of the way to Saskatoon. Kayla's daughter, Ryan, was staying over at Kayla's mother's place, and—

And it *was* late, and, despite all our progress, Kayla *did* seem skittish being alone in her house with me, and so I said, "The couch looks great," and I stretched out on it, put on the white-noise app on my iPhone, and was asleep within minutes.

But, for once, I had very nice dreams.

Kayla and I made it to the Canadian Light Source a little after 9:00 A.M. I was amused to note that its street address, on the University of Saskatchewan campus, was 44 Innovation Boulevard; I suspect the other occupants of that street were hard-pressed to match the sort of things Kayla described as she gave me a tour. "A synchrotron," she said as we walked along, "is an amazingly versatile tool; it's the Swiss Army knife of particle accelerators. You can tune its output to do almost anything, adjusting energy range, wavelength, resolution, photon brightness, and beam size. The researchers here do work in fundamental physics, archeology, geology, botany, new fuel sources, materials science—you name it."

"And you said you tested your brother here? Was that unusual—a human subject?"

"It used to be, but now we often treat people here. One of the beamlines is called BMIT—that stands for Biomedical Imaging and Therapy."

The synchrotron's giant storage ring was in a vast square pit, surrounded on three sides by indoor balconies. The inner side of each balcony looked down on the ring; the outer side had doors leading into offices and labs. As we walked along, Kayla pointed out the various beamlines—straight projections at oblique angles coming off the ring. She must be used to the constant mechanical roar coming from below, but it was giving me a headache.

"Hey, Kayla," said a sandy-haired man approaching us; he was wearing a loud Hawaiian shirt. "Welcome back."

She smiled warmly. "Hi, Jeff."

"How was Manitoba?"

She glanced at me. "Enlightening."

Jeff looked amused. "Don't forget those budget reports, okay?"

"Yeah, sure," Kayla replied.

"Who's that?" I said, after he'd walked on.

"Oh, sorry. That's Jeff Cutler; he's the acting director."

"Like Clint Eastwood?"

"What? Oh. Ha-ha."

"He always dress like that?"

"Actually, yes." Kayla pointed across the great expanse of the synchrotron to the balcony on the opposite side. "People have to find him all the time; the Hawaiian shirts make him easy to spot. Vic has her own variation on that; she always wears black, head to toe, and—see! That's her, over on the other side."

"You spotted her; how can she spot you?"

"Easy," said Kayla. "I'm the one who always has a cute guy in tow." She winked, and we headed around two more sides of the square. Victoria was walking and texting; we got quite close before she looked up. "Hey, Kay," she said, smiling.

"Vic, this is Jim Marchuk." Vic traded a look with Kayla—a suppressed grin. Evidently there'd been some discussion about whether Kayla would look up her old boyfriend when she went to Winnipeg. "And Jim, this is Dr. Victoria Chen."

"Hello, Jim," Vic said. "I've heard a lot about you."

I gave the automatic "All good, I hope" response, and saw, in a quirking of Vic's mouth, that it in fact *hadn't* all been good; of course Kayla had told her friend about how it'd gone south all those years ago.

"You guys all ready?" Vic said. "We're lucky today; I get the beamline while the sun's still up." She glanced at the phone she was holding. "My beamtime starts in four minutes."

"Great," said Kayla. Victoria turned around and began walking briskly. I was amused to see that she was using her hexagonal dosimeter as a hair clip to hold her long black hair in place. Kayla fell in beside her, and they chatted physics as we went along. I kept looking down at the bustling activity in the pit; it reminded me of Fritz Lang's *Metropolis*.

When the last balcony came to an end, we headed down a staircase onto the synchrotron floor. There were other researchers here, some in lab coats, and Vic and Kayla greeted each one we passed.

We quickly came to the SusyQ beamline, which had a gurney parked in front of it. Victoria had already received ethics approval and experimental permits for her ongoing work with humans here, but she still needed me to sign a waiver; I did so without bothering to read it. And then I lay down on my back, and, as Vic loomed in, I couldn't help but notice that she was quite lovely. She put a strap—thick, off-white, the kind of material seat belts were made of—over my forehead to hold my head still. And then, with Kayla's help, she rolled the gurney to the end of her beamline, a series of tubes that terminated in a conical emitter.

I looked up at the ceiling, far above. Conduits and pipes hung from it, and there was a yellow crane unit depending from tracks that apparently allowed it to move backward and forward as well as left and right.

Victoria said, "Okay."

"Yup, anytime you're ready."

She laughed. "We're *done,* Jim."

"Oh."

She leaned over me again and undid the strap. I rubbed my forehead to restore circulation; the strap's texture had been impressed into my skin.

"And what's the scoop?"

"You're a Q3, just like me and Kayla," said Vic.

"A super position to be in," I said as I sat up.

"Is he always like that?" Vic said, looking at Kayla.

Kayla sighed affectionately. "I'm afraid so."

I got off the gurney and walked over so I could see the monitor they were looking at. Vic pointed. "See the three spikes? Each one is an electron in superposition."

"What's that?" I said, pointing to a wobbly horizontal line much higher up on the display.

"We're not sure," said Vic, frowning. "It's always there when we do our runs, and it never changes. It looks like some sort of quantum entanglement, but . . ." She shrugged.

"We'll identify it eventually," said Kayla, "but—yeah, it's been driving us nuts."

"Well," I said, "I'm sure you'll figure it out."

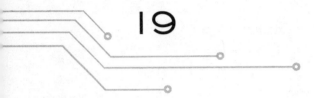

19

KAYLA had work to do that day, which left me with many hours to kill. I wanted to fill in as much of my missing six months as possible, and so I decided to see if anyone I knew from that period happened to live in Saskatoon now. Kayla set me up in an empty office at the Light Source, and I typed this query into the computer there:

"University of Manitoba" graduated 2003 Saskatoon

I looked at the first batch of results—LinkedIn pages, business listings—but didn't recognize any of the names. I clicked "Next," and, lo and behold, there was someone I knew well: David Swinson; we'd had adjacent dorm rooms. He'd become an optometrist, it seems, and his business address, according to Google Maps, wasn't far from the Light Source. *What the hell*, I thought, and headed off to ask Kayla if I could borrow her car.

The shopping mall was small by the standards of such things, just a couple dozen stores, most of which were chain clothing shops: The Gap,

Lululemon, Old Navy. But there were also a few professional offices: two family practitioners, an accountant, and my friend Dave the optometrist. His unit had a front window with posters of people wearing glasses. Actually, I was convinced they were posters of people wearing glasses *frames:* there was no distortion or reflection to give any indication that they had lenses in them.

I swung the door open, and a little chime sounded. Inside was a receptionist's desk, some chairs, wooden racks filled with frames, and another door that presumably led to the examining room. The receptionist must have been away because a man emerged from the back wearing a navy-blue lab coat. I wouldn't have recognized him on the street. All but the barest fringe of Dave's hair was gone, and a full beard hid much of his lower face. His blue eyes were bracketed by crow's-feet, and his skin had both a roughness and looseness it hadn't possessed when he'd been in his early twenties.

"Dave?" I said.

He looked at me without the slightest hint of recognition, which disappointed me. I liked to think I'd aged better than he had. "Yes?"

"It's me," I said. "Jim. Jim Marchuk. You know, from U of M."

The eyes went wide, and color came into his lined face. "Fuck," he said softly.

"I know it's been a long time, but—"

"Get out." His voice had taken on an edge. "Get the fuck out."

"Dave, I—"

"Don't you fucking 'Dave' me. Jesus Christ. Jesus Fucking Christ."

I tried to keep my tone friendly. "I just want to ask you a few questions."

"About what? About how you almost ruined my whole life? What the hell are you doing here? I'm going to piss on your fucking grave, asshole—and you can't be in it soon enough."

"Dave, honestly—"

A vertical vein was standing out in the middle of his forehead. "'Honestly'?" he sneered. "'Honestly'? You don't know the meaning of the word."

"Dave, I don't know what you think I did, but—"

"But *nothing,*" he said. His fists were trembling at his sides. He seemed to be aware of the fact that he was losing it, because he took a deep breath and let it out slowly. And then he spoke, low, measured: "This is private property. I'm asking you—I'm *telling* you—to leave. Right now."

"Dave . . ."

"Right now, or I call the goddamn police. Understand?" He pointed to the glass door, his arm shaking as he did so.

I looked at him a moment longer, then shrugged a little. I was worried about what he might do if I turned my back on him, so I backed out, wondering exactly what the hell I had done to him all those years ago.

I walked around the mall in a daze for a while, trying to regain my equilibrium and waiting for my heart to stop pounding. When I at last felt in control enough to operate a motor vehicle, I drove back to the Light Source to return Kayla's car.

Although my business there was technically concluded—I'd been analyzed on the beamline, and could take a cab to the bus station for the long trip home—it was now Friday afternoon, and, to my delight, Kayla suggested I stay through the weekend. She didn't live far from the Light Source, and rather than have me hang around there while she worked, she volunteered to drive me back to her house. We swung by Victoria's office first, and Kayla retrieved her spare key from Vic— apparently, they each had a key to the other's home—so that I could go out for a walk later, or whatever, and then she drove me back. I thought she was just going to drop me off, but she turned off the car, and came on in with me, and—

—she swung me around, draped her arms around my neck, pulled me close, and kissed me.

When our lips finally separated, I said, softly, "Wow . . ."

She smiled up at me, blue eyes twinkling. "I wasn't sure before, but you *did* pass the test. Plus, Vic thinks you're a catch."

She took my hand and led me upstairs to her bedroom, its walls painted a soft mint green, and soon our clothes were off, and we were lying on the bed. I'd certainly fantasized about something like this happening, but, well, it was midafternoon, and, even with the lights off, plenty of illumination poured in through the window. I couldn't help but feel an even worse case of the discomfort I'd experienced when Kayla and I had met at lunch. Nobody looked as good at thirty-nine as they did at twenty, and although I tried to get at least some exercise every day, she was doubtless thinking I'd aged since the last time she'd seen me naked.

But I thought Kayla looked absolutely stunning: smooth skin; flat tummy; small, high breasts; and a landing strip that was presumably her hair's natural dark brown. She also had a gorgeous tattoo of a turquoise butterfly, its body running parallel to but just above her panty line. I traced the leading edge of its upper wing with my fingertip and was surprised to find that it covered a raised ridge.

She must have anticipated my question. "That's why I got the tat," she said. "Looks so much nicer than an appendectomy scar." And indeed it did; it was lovely, just like its bearer.

Kayla had condoms in her night table, and we rolled around, most pleasantly, for half an hour—until she had to return to work.

Kayla returned four hours later, accompanied by her six-year-old daughter. Ryan bounded into the living room, where I was sitting reading, to say hello. She had long light-brown hair and brown eyes, and, when she smiled, a dimple in her left cheek; she was wearing a T-shirt showing a singer named Lorde (helpfully labeled beneath her photo—otherwise, I'd have had no idea).

"Ryan," Kayla said, catching up with her, "this is Jim."

"'Jim,'" she said, trying it out. "I think I'll call you 'Jiminy,' like Jiminy Cricket."

"Then I'm going to call you 'Ginger Ale,'" I said.

"Why?"

"'Cause adults sometimes drink rye and ginger ale."

She frowned, puzzling it through, then, "Oh!" Her smile was radiant. "Okay, Jiminy!"

Our secret names established, Ryan said, "Do you like Taylor Swift?"

"Are you kidding? She's one of my top-ten favorite Taylors!"

"She's got a new video!" exclaimed Ryan. "Let me show you . . ."

I smiled at Kayla, who smiled warmly back at me, and Ryan took my hand and led me over to the couch, where a MacBook was sitting. She opened it up, went to YouTube, and as she played me a string of her favorite videos, I *ooohed* and *aaahed* appropriately.

Having not yet had a chance to shop since returning from Winnipeg, Kayla didn't have much food in the house. I volunteered to pay for pizza to be delivered, Kayla recommended a place called TJ's, and we got two pies—a large #14 (pepperoni and mushrooms) for the girls, and a small #19 ("veggie supreme") with no cheese for me.

After dinner, I watched while Ryan showed off her skills at Minecraft and Platypus Pirates. When it was time for her to go to bed, she gave me a big hug. Kayla took her upstairs, and I read news on my phone. Appallingly, three Latina women—maybe illegally in the US, maybe not—had been found shot to death just outside Dallas. Meanwhile, the NDP caucus, which had almost immediately declared Naheed Nenshi party leader, was getting good press: *The Toronto Star* had an editorial with the headline "We Need Naheed," which was fun enough to say that I suspected it would become a meme.

When Kayla returned, she sat next to me on the couch and put a hand on my thigh. "Ryan really likes you. Normally, she can't wait to get away from my friends."

"She's sweet," I said. "I enjoyed every minute."

"You're really good with kids. Seriously. Ever thought about having one of your own?"

I looked away. "Yeah," I said. "From time to time."

20

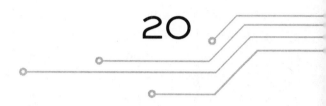

"ANNA-LEE, Jim, thanks so much for coming in," Dr. Villager had said—three years ago now, I guess it was.

"Sure," I replied, taking the left-hand seat facing her desk, and, "Of course," said Anna-Lee, settling into the right-hand one.

"I have some news," Villager said. Anna-Lee must have heard something in the doctor's voice; she reached over and took my hand, squeezing it. "As you know, I always recommend amniocentesis for women over thirty-five, purely as a precaution. And, well, there's good reason for that. The risk of certain anomalies goes up dramatically after that point."

"My God . . ." Anna-Lee's voice was almost inaudible.

Dr. Villager nodded. "The fetus has Down syndrome."

"Are you sure?" I asked, knowing, of course, that she must be.

"Yes, absolutely. He—it's a boy—has three chromosome twenty-ones. The provincial health plan will pay for an abortion if you wish."

"My God," said Anna-Lee, again. "My God."

"You don't have to decide today," Dr. Villager said. "But you should decide soon."

Anna-Lee and I were lying in bed, side by side, each of us on our backs, each staring up in the dark at the featureless ceiling. "Sweetheart," I said, "we talked about all this before you took the test."

I was hoping for a verbal acknowledgment, or, at least, the rustling of the pillow to indicate that she was nodding in agreement. But there was nothing.

"I mean," I continued, "since we're only planning on having one child, we need to consider whether *this* child is the best use of our resources, right? There'll be enormous extra expenses, and, no matter what we do, the child will almost certainly have a life not only of lesser quality but also lesser quantity; people with Down rarely live past their twenties."

She was immobile, a toppled statue.

"And, well, you know the utilitarian position: one can't give special consideration to one's own needs; you can't put them above those of others. But you *can* factor them in as you would anyone else's. This isn't the life we wanted. Yes, sure, parenting is always a full-time job, anyway, but this will leave no room for anything else. And the economic impact . . ."

I trailed off, wishing she'd give some sign—any sign—that I was getting through to her.

"That's our son you're talking about," she said at last.

I blew out air. "An embryo has no—"

"Please," said Anna-Lee firmly.

But I pressed on. "An embryo has no more moral standing than what we'd give to an animal with a similar level of self-consciousness, rationality, ability to feel, and so on. The utilitarian position—"

"Fuck utilitarianism," she said, and rolled onto her side facing away from me.

I rolled onto my side, too, wanting to spoon her, but I knew enough not to reach out and touch her just then. With my ear pressed against the pillow, I could faintly hear my heartbeat.

Or—

No, no. Of course it was my own heartbeat. Who else's could it have been?

I was there in the delivery room when Virgil came out into the world. He was quiet; even after Dr. Villager slapped him gently on the bottom, he made no sound. I'd hoped, against all logic, to see a normal child, but even with his features squished and wet, it was obvious the prenatal diagnosis had been correct. Virgil's face was flat, and his tongue protruded slightly. Dr. Villager handed him to Anna-Lee, who still had tears on her face from the pain of delivery, but her expression was joyous as she held the boy—until she looked up at me. Although I was doing my level best, her gaze went cold.

They kept Virgil and Anna-Lee at the hospital for four days after his birth; apparently there was a whole suite of things that could go wrong early on for a Down child—respiratory problems, difficulties suckling, and more. I spent as much time as I could at the hospital; Anna-Lee's mother was there during those visiting hours when I couldn't be.

When they were finally ready to discharge Virgil, I came to take him and Anna-Lee home. I went into the familiar hospital room, with its pale-yellow walls; my faculty health plan covered the extra cost of the private room. I was surprised to find my mother-in-law there, too, standing silently next to the bed.

"I'm not coming home," Anna-Lee said the moment I entered. Virgil was sleeping on her chest.

"But Dr. Villager said—"

"I'm leaving *here*," Anna-Lee said, "but Virgil and I are going to stay with my parents."

I was silent for a time, digesting this. "May I ask why?"

"I never want Virgil to see that look in your eyes."

"What look?"

"The look that says you wish he'd never been born."

"Anna-Lee, please . . ."

"It's true, isn't it? That's how you feel."

I opened my mouth but couldn't find any words.

Anna-Lee held our baby tightly and shook her head. "Oh, for Christ's sake, Jim."

I shook my head, dispelling the memories, and turned back to face Kayla, in her living room, in the here and now—and I quickly sought to move the conversation on from the topic of children. "Are these of Travis?" I said, getting up to look at a cluster of photos in little frames on one of her bookshelves. I could see the family resemblance to Kayla: they both had high cheekbones, generous noses, and perfectly vertical foreheads.

She moved in to stand next to me. "Yup."

He was wearing a brown-and-yellow University of Manitoba T-shirt in one of the shots. "He went to U of M, too?"

"Yeah. Business school. He was quite an athlete—great runner, but also did snowboarding, motocross, and more." She pointed at another picture. "That's him finishing the Boston Marathon."

"What year was that?"

She picked up the frame, flipped it over, and looked at what had been written on the backside. "Two thousand," she said. "'The Millennial Marathon.'" I was about to say, "Actually . . ." but she beat me to it: "Of course, not really—but that's what they called it." But then her voice grew wistful. "Last time he ever got to run it."

"Oh?"

"Yeah. He's been in his coma since 2001."

My heart skipped a beat. "What date?"

"I don't remember. Sometime before you and I started dating, though."

"Which was the beginning of March, so, if you're sure it was 2001, then that means January or February."

"I guess."

"You'd said they found him passed out. Where?"

"In a classroom."

"On the U of M campus?"

"Uh-huh."

"Do you know which building?"

"No. Why?"

"Was he by any chance a subject in Professor Warkentin's experiments?"

"I have no idea."

"Jesus." I moved back to the couch and collapsed onto it.

"Jim? What's wrong?"

"Menno Warkentin told me something a little while ago. He said he felt so guilty about what happened to me, he . . . well, he tried to kill himself, he said. It didn't work out; he crashed his car, and ended up blind—"

"My God! Really?"

"That's what he said. But, when you think about it, what *had* happened to me? According to a reading he saw on his oscilloscope, I'd lost my inner voice. But, externally, my behavior was pretty much the same as before—so that's an awfully abstract thing to feel suicidally despondent over, even for a psychologist. And, yeah, he'd tried to fix what had gone wrong, using lasers, but that only made it worse, causing my time of . . . of bad behavior. But what if I wasn't the only one who'd fainted because of Menno's equipment? What if an athletic business student had passed out, too, and he had never recovered? *That* would weigh on you, month after month, if the guy never woke up, if his life had been totally ruined because of you."

"Holy shit," said Kayla.

"Exactly," I said. "Holy shit."

"What do we do now?"

"I took photographs of his paper files about his project. Let's look through those and see if any of them mention your brother."

We transferred the photos from my iPhone to her MacBook so that we could study them on a bigger screen, but there was no mention of Travis—or a subject TH.

"Do we confront Warkentin?" asked Kayla.

"Well, we could—but if he denies having anything to do with Travis, we'll have tipped him off, and he could dispose of any other records that might prove it. Perhaps we should bide our time."

Kayla thought about this, then nodded. "I'm good at that."

"Oh?"

"Yeah. A skill I learned from my brother."

We stayed up awhile longer, but although I'd napped in the afternoon, Kayla was tired. Trying not to be presumptuous, I asked if she perhaps had a blanket for the couch; it had gotten chilly last night. She stood up, turned, faced me, held out her hand, and said, "Don't be silly."

We headed upstairs, got naked, and cuddled pleasantly for a while, and then separated slightly; she fell asleep before me, I think, but it wasn't long until I nodded off, too, until—

Until I suddenly sat straight up in bed, gasping for breath.

"Jim?" I was disoriented, and the woman's voice startled me; it took me a moment to realize who it was. She shifted in the bed, and I felt her hand on my back. "My God," she said. "You're shaking like a leaf."

I was also sweating, the sheets damp beneath my thighs. In the darkness I couldn't see anything except two red LEDs, glowing like a demon's eyes.

I hadn't had this nightmare for weeks, but it had been the same as it always was. Me in a rage, lashing out, holding a wooden torch—but, bizarrely, the flames were dark and frozen—while in front of me stood a demon, a monster, a *thing* that had to be stopped, that had to be punished . . .

I brought one of my hands to the center of my chest, feeling the pounding of my heart.

"Sorry," I said. "Bad dream."

"It's okay," Kayla replied softly as she lay back and gently pulled me down toward her, holding me. From this angle, I could no longer see the LED eyes; there was nothing but blackness.

21

"Good morning, class. So, awhile ago I asked how many of you drive to the university each day. Remember? We were talking about philosopher's zombies? Well, let me ask the opposite question: now that the weather's good again, how many of you walk here each day?"

A rather small number of hands went up.

"Huh," I said. "Well, I often do. In fact, I did so today. I live about two kilometers north of here right on the Red River, and I'll tell you, it's way more pleasant to walk along the bank than it is to fight traffic along Pembina Highway—except for today, that is. Just as I was coming out from under the Bishop Grandin Bridge, I saw a little girl facedown in the water."

A couple of students gasped.

I nodded and went on. "She was right by the shore, probably unconscious, and the river wasn't moving fast today, so I could easily wade in and grab her." I paused. "And, you know, I was going to, but, well, damn it, look at these shoes." I stepped out from behind the lectern. "Nicest ones I own. They're not leather— you guys know me better than that! But they'd still have gotten *wrecked, don't you think? And they'd cost two hundred dollars. So, I walked on by. You all would have done the same thing, right, if you were—wait for it—in my shoes?"*

I'd seen the transition sweep across the faces as one by one the students realized it was a hypothetical.

"We do know you," said Boris. "And if that had really happened, you would have gone in."

I smiled. "True. But why?"

"Because the life of a little girl is way more valuable than any pair of shoes. In fact, there's no material object you shouldn't sacrifice to save a human life."

"Exactly," I said, and I looked out at the students. "So, again, suppose it was any of you—Felicity, there, I'm no judge, but those pumps look like they cost a couple of hundred."

"Each," said Felicity, smiling.

"Well? Would you wade in to get the girl?"

"I'd take them off first."

"What if—"

And she had them off already.

"Okay," I said, holding up my hands in surrender. "But what if you were wearing shoes like mine—"

"Puh-leeze!" said Felicity, rolling her eyes. Laughter rippled across the room.

"—and had to unlace them; there'd be no time for that. You'd have to act fast. Would you?"

"Absolutely," said Felicity.

"Good. I knew you had it in you." I looked around the room. "Anyone? Is there anyone here who wouldn't sacrifice a pair of really nice shoes to save a drowning girl?"

No one spoke up; several people shook their heads.

"Good, good. Because, you know, that story I just told you? It is true. Except that the little girl wasn't drowning in the Red River right by my home. She was starving to death in Africa. And the $200 I spent on my shoes could have just as easily saved her life there if sent to a reputable aid agency. So, if I were to pass a

hat now, how many of you would feel obligated to put in $200, or an IOU for that amount, if you knew it would go directly to saving a life in Africa? Not how many of you would feel it was a decent thing to do, but how many of you would feel you had to do it?"

No one responded.

"Okay," I said. "Any Trekkies here besides me?"

A few hands went up, and, after they saw some of their class-mates admitting it, a few more went up—and one of the girls with a lifted hand had her fingers splayed in the Vulcan salute. "Okay, Melody," I said. "How's your Star Trek trivia?"

"Tiberius," she said at once.

"Ha. True. But let's play Trekkie Jeopardy! for a moment. You remember J.J. Abrams's Star Trek from 2009—the first film in the reboot?"

"Sure."

"Remember Spock as a boy being quizzed by computers on Vulcan, right after the Vulcan bullies had been picking on him?"

"Sure."

"You can't see the questions he's being asked, but the scene ends with him giving this confident answer: 'When an action is morally praiseworthy but not morally obligatory.' Remember that?"

"Yes."

"Okay, so, Alex, for $1,000 in the category of 'Philosophical Terms,' what question was Spock asked?"

"Umm . . ." said Melody. "Ah, ur . . ."

"No, no. Not in Vulcan," I said. "In English."

She laughed, and so did several others. "I haven't a clue."

"Anybody?" I said, looking around. "What question must the computer have asked Spock?"

Pascal, in the fourth row, rose to the wager. "What is super-erogation?"

"Exactly! And no, that's not watering your plants too much. Supererogation is when you do something good that you didn't

have to do. So, class, why do you say that it's a moral imperative that you save the little girl who is drowning right in front of you, even at a cost of $200, but at best that it's merely supererogatory— a mitzvah, *in other words—if you give the money to save a child in a foreign land?"*

VICTORIA Chen's boyfriend was named Ross. He taught high-school English at City Park Collegiate, just across the South Saskatchewan River from the synchrotron. On Mondays, he had a spare period after lunch, and, so today, as always, he drove over and picked Vic up, and the two of them went to Alexander's Restaurant. Vic, as usual, was wearing all black, and Ross was displaying his preference for blue.

After they ordered—the Thai noodle bowl for her, a jalapeño guacamole chicken burger for him—Ross said, "One of my students handed in an essay on Friday with emojis in it." He shook his head. "Can you imagine?"

Vic looked at him. He'd told her about this just yesterday. Ross went on: "I hate that. I'm tempted to give her an F just because."

She tilted her head to one side. Of course, people did this all the time: they had an experience and shared it with everyone they ran into; they didn't really keep track of who they'd already told. Vic liked to think she was the exception, but, then again, that was probably similar to the statistic she'd gone around quoting—quite possibly, she supposed, to the same person more than once—that eighty percent of people think they're more attractive than average, which couldn't actually be the case.

Ross was still on his hobbyhorse. "I mean, seriously? Emojis? And they weren't even *appropriate* emojis! I've taught *Hamlet* every year for ten years now, and, trust me, there's no point you can make about that play that's enhanced by a picture of a panda bear winking and sticking out its tongue."

She thought about saying, "I know, baby," or even, "You told me that yesterday," but he was getting near the end of the rant, and so she decided to just ride it out and enjoy her noodles.

I'd never done a long-distance romance before, but Skype and texting—
and, my goodness, sexting—really helped. I don't know how people
managed such relationships in years gone by, but, now that I was back
in Winnipeg, although I desperately missed holding Kayla, at least the
keeping-in-touch issue didn't seem difficult.

Nor, really, should have been the getting-together part. Both Air
Canada and WestJet offered multiple direct flights each day between
Winnipeg and Saskatoon, and the flight only took ninety minutes. It
wasn't particularly expensive; you could usually get a roundtrip ticket
for under $250, all-in.

My heart went out to my contemporaries who had only landed
sessional-teaching gigs and were living on little more than they'd had
as grad students, but I was a tenured professor; I grossed $145,000 per
year, so flying to Saskatoon once or twice a month shouldn't have put
a dent in my lifestyle.

Except, damn it all, practice what you teach. As Peter Singer so
rightly said in his 2009 book *The Life You Can Save: Acting Now To
End World Poverty*, it would take 250 billion dollars a year to eliminate
poverty. If the richest billion people in the world (a group that I, and
just about every middle-class or better North American, fell into) were
to each give five dollars a week, poverty could be wiped out.

But they don't. Singer, who devised the thought experiment about the
drowning girl that I riff on in my classes, suggested that everyone should
pledge to give a portion of their net income to charities—and then, to
overcome the easy out of saying charitable donations are wasted on overhead and fat-cat executives, he set up a website, TheLifeYouCanSave.org,
listing cost-effective charities, such as Oxfam, for which almost all the
money given really does go to those who need it.

But that was the easy part of his site. The hard part, at least for
people like me who value their word, is the little clickie labeled "Take
the Pledge." You plug in your gross income and the country you live
in, and it calculates what would be a reasonable amount for you to
commit to give to charities. In my case, it suggested I could afford to

donate five percent, or $7,250, each year to organizations helping people in extreme poverty.

But I teach ethics; I know all about diffusion of responsibility. I know that most people are going to give hardly anything at all. And so, if the average Joe should be giving five percent, I felt I could do at least double that—and I did, for the first three years. And then I realized I wasn't missing the money, and I upped my donation to fifteen percent, and, even when Virgil came along, and I started paying out twenty-five grand a year in child support, I didn't cut back.

And, seriously, as much as I loved Kayla—and I think I really and truly was falling head-over-heels in love with her—could I cut back on my donations just to facilitate our relationship?

No, of course not. And so although those $250 round trips were a bargain, I could only afford them now and again. This time, I was driving on my own to Saskatoon.

I sometimes quip that I have sympathy for moon-landing deniers. After all, no one had walked on the moon since 1972; how could we possibly have done that then but couldn't do it now, almost half a century later? But after making this drive to Saskatoon a couple of times, I have to say I was also beginning to understand members of the Flat Earth Society. Every Canadian knew the joke, immortalized in the opening credits of the sitcom *Corner Gas,* about Saskatchewan being the place where you could watch your dog run away . . . for three days.

It was election night—I'd voted before leaving Winnipeg—but instead of listening to the CBC, which would have hours of pointless speculation before the polls closed, I played an audiobook: Dan Falk talking about SETI, the search for extraterrestrial intelligence.

Falk was speculating that one likely reason we've never detected alien signals is that shortly after developing radio, any civilization almost certainly also develops the ability to destroy itself. We'd only been a broadcasting species for 125 years now; who was to say we ourselves would be around much longer?

On that somber note, I did finally switch to the radio, just in time to hear a man speaking, a hint of astonishment in his crisp tones: *"The CBC is now prepared to call it. It's by a slim margin, but we will have a majority NDP government; Naheed Nenshi will be Canada's twenty-fourth prime minister. Our analyst Hayden Trenholm is with me here in Toronto. Hayden, your thoughts?"*

"What a close race! It's not quite a 'Dewey Defeats Truman' moment, but I do think it'll take a lot of people by surprise. Still, Nenshi is no stranger to election-night upsets. Six weeks before being elected mayor of Calgary in 2010, polls had his support at just eight percent. He won over his doubters once in office: he was re-elected in 2013 with a staggering seventy-four percent of the vote. He didn't do that well tonight, but it's still a historic victory."

I turned off the radio, smiling, and not just because my party had won; it was also cool to see a hometown Calgary boy make good.

The black sky was a hemispherical bowl stretching from horizon to horizon, and I can't resist a clear night. I pulled over, wandered out into a field, and looked up. I still didn't remember anything from that half-year science-fiction course, but the next term I'd taken a poetry class, and a line of Archibald Lampman's floated into my consciousness from back then: *The wide awe and wonder of the night.* The sky was cloudless, there was no moon, and the stars shone down in all their profusion. I looked at them, as I always did, in amazement, but Dan Falk had left me thinking, and I found myself feeling profoundly sad as I contemplated the deafening silence, wondering indeed how long our own civilization had left.

22

SASKATCHEWAN never observes Daylight Saving Time, which means, here in the summer, I arrived an hour earlier than I would in winter. But it was still after 11:00 P.M. when I pulled into Kayla's driveway. I would have been raring to go, even if I hadn't put away two liters of Coke during the drive; the lovemaking was affectionate and fun, and we fell asleep in each other's arms.

In the morning, Ryan—who'd been long asleep by the time I'd arrived—joined us for breakfast, and she gave me a gift, a beadwork wristband she'd made showing the letters JC. "For Jiminy Cricket!" she squealed. I smiled broadly and slipped it on.

We then took her to the University of Saskatchewan's Museum of Natural Sciences, not far from the Light Source. Saskatchewan was dinosaur country, and she gawked at the skeletons of *Tyrannosaurus rex*, *Triceratops*, and *Stegosaurus*, but I think she liked the indoor waterfall and koi pond the best.

As Kayla took Ryan to the washroom, I checked the news online. The right-wing *Toronto Sun* was in trouble, it seemed, for having run not an election-night picture of Nenshi, but one from years ago of him in Muslim garb under a giant headline that read, "Minority Government." But otherwise the news of the election seemed to be going over reasonably well here in Canada.

American newspapers usually completely ignored Canadian news, so I didn't expect much there, but a number of my Facebook friends had linked to the same clip of President Carroway, apparently talking about the election. I clicked on the story.

Quinton Carroway was his usual slick self, immaculately groomed, not a hair out of place. *"Mr. President,"* called out a reporter, *"does it concern you that Prime Minister Nenshi is Muslim?"*

Carroway smiled that smile of his, as if someone was tugging up on fishing line at the corners of his mouth. *"I compliment him on being the first Muslim head of state anywhere in the Western World. Quite an achievement, that, quite a significant achievement. And to do so with Canada's socialist New Democratic Party, to boot! A couple of monumental firsts. Across the border—the longest undefended one in the world—we offer congratulations."*

It'd been a lot colder last night, standing out in that field, looking up at the stars. But it was now, not then, that I felt a chill run down my spine.

Saturday night, Kayla, Ryan, and I drove out to the Saskatoon Airport, which, as Kayla pointed out to me, was named for John Diefenbaker, one of the other prime ministers who'd been kicked from power by a non-confidence motion; maybe Justin Trudeau would be remembered with an airport of his own someday. We weren't here so I could go home, though; rather, Kayla had agreed to pick up Victoria Chen, who was returning from a symposium at the Institute for Quantum Computing in Waterloo. Vic gave Kayla and Ryan hugs when she came out of the gate, and I was pleasantly surprised when she gave me one, too.

"How was the conference?" I asked.

"Amazing," Vic said. "Everyone was making the same joke: you'd think if anyone could do it, quantum physicists could; there was so much good simultaneous programming, we all wanted to be in multiple places at once." She shook her head in wonder. "Haroche and Wineland were there, and D-Wave unveiled a new one-kiloqubit model, and . . ."

And Kayla was clearly following all this; for my part, I took the handle of Vic's rolly bag and pulled it along while the two women talked quantum mechanics. After a bit—or a qubit—it proved too much for Ryan, though, and she plucked at Victoria's sleeve. "Aunt Vic, did you bring me anything?"

"Ryan!" admonished Kayla.

"What do you think?" Vic asked Ryan with a sly grin.

"I think you did!" Ryan exclaimed.

"I think you're right!" Vic exclaimed back. She had a shoulder bag, and we stopped while she reached into it. She pulled out a small plush animal—a zebra, which seemed an odd thing to bring back from Ontario. But then I saw the letters IQC embroidered on its rump; it was swag from the conference, and the stripes, now that I got a good look at them, were in the classic two-slit interference pattern. None of that meant anything to Ryan, but she squeed appropriately at the gift.

"And, since we're stopped," said Vic, "I also brought something back for you, Kayla—sort of. It's really for the Light Source, but I won't be going in to work again until Monday, so, technically, you wouldn't be taking it *from* work if you borrow it between now and then."

She reached into her bag and pulled out a small, rugged-looking aluminum case. There were some chairs nearby, and she walked over to them, sat, and opened the case. Inside, cushioned by black foam rubber cut to precisely cradle it, was a silver device maybe thirty centimeters long.

"What's that?" Kayla asked.

"Well, for want of a better name," Vic said, "they call it a quantum tuning fork."

It did indeed look like a tuning fork. Half its length was a cylindrical handle; the other half consisted of two parallel cylindrical tines, each about as thick as my index finger. But that didn't justify using the Q-word. "What's quantum about it?" I asked.

Victoria pried it out of its case and held it up as if she were warding off a vampire. "They developed this at IQC. The handle contains a nonlinear crystal in an optical cavity that lets photons bounce around repeatedly, resulting in twin beams coming out of the tines; the beams promote electron superposition."

Kayla looked impressed, and I decided this was a good time to do some social mimicry of my own; I copied her expression.

Vic went on: "We're giving the institute some beamtime in exchange for the loan of this prototype. It works pretty well as far as it goes. It's great at getting things *into* superposition, but it doesn't make the superposition any less prone to decoherence. Still, you take a block of material, use this on it, and you have a working quantum-computing test bed for the nanoseconds until decoherence occurs."

Kayla got it immediately. "What happens if you use it on a human being?"

"On a normal human being?" asked Victoria. "Nothing at all; a bunch of us tried it." She acted out pointing it at her forehead. "But on someone who *isn't* already in a superposition state?" She smiled a megawatt smile. "It sounds like an experiment worth conducting, doesn't it?"

"Oh my God," Kayla said, astonished, then, more softly, almost reverently, "Oh my God."

The "facility," as Kayla always called it, was cleaner than such things had been in the past. Still, most of these people had been abandoned to the state, the staff looking after them with all the compassion and care of cowhands tending livestock. Travis didn't have a private room; there was no point in that. Three other people, each of whom had been diagnosed as being in either a coma or a persistent vegetative state, shared the space. The Venetian blinds were down, as they had been on my previous visits; I imagined they'd been down for years.

I looked at Travis, eyes closed, face blank, lips slightly parted, snoring softly. Nineteen years he'd lain here—or, before that, in similar facilities. The years of inactivity had taken their toll; the scrawny creature before me showed no signs of his erstwhile athleticism.

I looked at the gaunt face, the pale skin—skin that had last basked in the sun when George W. Bush had been in the White House and Bill Cosby had been a role model, back before the world had ever heard of Sarah Palin or Amy Schumer, before the Kindle and Facebook and Megamatch, before *Breaking Bad* and *Mad Men* and *The Big Bang Theory*.

"Hey, broski," said Kayla, in her ritual greeting; as I'd seen on previous visits, it had settled into a routine, a schtick, a mindless template.

She paid no attention to the other occupants, two men and a woman; of course, no one had to worry about propriety with these . . . patients? Inmates? Residents? No, no, *patients* was the right word: they were all infinitely patient, waiting out wars and recessions, fads and trends, with equanimity.

Travis's chest rose and fell rhythmically. In the corridor, I could hear a couple of women walking by, chatting. My iPhone case had a little kickstand on its back; I set it on top of a cabinet opposite Travis so it could quietly video what we hoped would be a wondrous event.

"Anyway," said Kayla, perhaps to Travis, perhaps to me. She reached into her soft-sided briefcase and pulled out the tuning fork, the handle bifurcating into its two parallel tines like a map of possible outcomes. Down one path, the *status quo,* with Travis lying here another decade— or six—until finally some part of him gave up the ghost, and the state was relieved of its burden. Down the other path, just maybe, a new life for him, an awakening after so many dark winters. And clutched in Kayla's hand, the superposition of those two paths—both possibilities, renewed life and living death.

She looked at me and gestured with her head at the doorway. We hadn't told the staff what we were going to try; if anybody here decided it was a medical procedure or test, there'd be mounds of paperwork. On the way over, Kayla had said it had taken weeks to get permission from the facility's insurer for that time she'd brought Travis to CLS.

Everything here was routine, I'm sure, and it wasn't as though Travis was going to be interrupted by a nurse bringing dinner on a tray; his sustenance flowed into him via a gastric feeding tube going into the left side of his abdomen. Still, I moved to the doorway and checked up and down the dreary corridor. The women I'd heard before were gone; the coast, as the saying went, was clear. I closed the door, turned back to face Kayla, and nodded for her to proceed.

She loomed over her brother and touched the twin tines to his forehead, one above his closed left eye and the other above the closed right. And then she thumbed a red slider switch on the handle.

It would have been cool if the tuning fork had begun to glow with violet energy or had emitted a sound like sheet metal warping, but nothing happened—either on the device, or, as far as I could tell, to Travis. Of course I felt sorrier for Kayla, who'd had her hopes raised, than for Travis, who had had no change in his happiness—or lack thereof.

Kayla pulled her hand back, withdrawing the tuning fork. And then, with a what-the-heck lift of her eyebrows, she rotated it a half turn so that the tine that had been on the right was now on the left, and she again gently but firmly pressed the twin tips against her brother's forehead, and—

—and Travis's eyes fluttered open.

23

VICTORIA Chen had to know for sure.

She was waiting for Ross in the Light Source's glassed-in entryway. She became even more nervous than she already was when 11:00 A.M. passed and there was still no sign of him; another researcher had the beamline at 11:30. But at ten after, he finally arrived. Vic got him signed in, had him clip on a dosimeter, and took him on the long walk down to the SusyQ beamline.

"You sure you don't mind?" she asked as she fussed with her equipment.

Ross was his usual amiable self. "No, of course not. I'd do anything for you, my love. You know that."

She tapped a series of commands on her keyboard. "Thanks," she said. "You're a good man. Now, if you'll just lie down here . . ." She indicated the gurney.

Ross smiled. "Fancy a nooner?"

"Not today, dear," she said, making a show of waggling her eyebrows, "but there's always tonight."

"Indeed there is," he said, and he lay down on his back. That was either *supine* or *prone*—she could never remember which was which—

but, either way, his lean form, in dark-blue cotton slacks and a light-blue dress shirt, looked *fine*. He really was a good boyfriend: attentive to her but low-maintenance himself; even-tempered; and an absolute machine in the sack.

"Thanks for doing this, hon," she said as she affixed the head strap. "I think there's a really good paper in it."

"My pleasure."

"Just relax. As the doctors like to say, this won't hurt a bit." She used her mouse to click an on-screen button, and the process began. Initially, her monitor showed a plain horizontal line—no superposition— but it did that for everyone; it took about ten seconds to gather the data, and—

Ah, and there it came. The line undulated and then a huge peak appeared at the left side, showing a single superimposed electron. She waited anxiously for the second peak to appear, and then the third one, and—

And she waited and waited and waited. Oh, the usual wobbly horizontal line appeared up high, but the spike down below gained no companions.

Ross shifted on the gurney. She moved over to the beam emitter, which was centered on the crown of his head, and, after a moment, she did the only thing she could think of doing: she flicked her finger against its side, the way one does with electronics that might have a loose connection. But the emitter was solid-state, she knew, and the display remained exactly the same.

One, and only one, superposition. Vic felt her mouth drop open. That was crazy. That was *nuts*. She knew Ross . . . it *was* the right word: she knew him *intimately*. She knew everything about him. He couldn't be . . . there was just no effing way he could be, but . . .

She found herself backing away, and her derrière bumped against the edge of a desk. She looked at him, and he shifted his eyes to look at her. "Are we done?" he asked.

He meant the experiment, of course, but—no, no, he didn't *mean* anything. He wasn't thinking about the experiment, not if what Jim Marchuk had told Kayla was right. He wasn't thinking about anything at all. He was just saying something that fit the circumstances, respond-ing to some internal timer or external cue. But the question couldn't be more apt. *Were* they done?

Jim *must* be wrong. Either that, or the equipment was faulty. She loved Ross—and Ross loved her. She *knew* that. Not just because he said it, but because he showed it, in a hundred—a thousand!—ways.

She moved in, undid the strap, and said, "You can get up."

And he replied as he always did when she said the words "get up"—the same joke over and over again, the same *routine*—by looking down briefly, then flashing a lascivious smile, and saying, "That's easy when you're around, babe."

Input.

Output.

Could it be? Could he really be a machine—albeit a biological one—not just in the sack but in *everything?*

And, if that were true, if Jim Marchuk was right, could she go on dating a . . . a *thing*, an emptiness, a zombie?

She wasn't ready to give voice to the thought but, yes, damn it all, they were almost certainly done.

What the fuck?

Bright light from overhead; Travis Huron scrunched his eyelids shut. What the hell was he doing lying down?

A man's voice: "Holy Jesus."

And a woman's voice tinged by . . . wonder, perhaps? "Travis?"

Travis reopened his eyes, but it took effort; his lashes were sticking together, interlocking cilia on twin Venus flytraps. The light stung, and he was having trouble focusing. He blinked repeatedly. And then the same as-yet-unseen male he'd heard earlier—Travis assigned its owner the name Master of the Bleeding Obvious: "His eyes are open!"

"Travis?" said the female voice again. He turned his head, feeling a twinge in his neck as he did so, and there, standing next to him, her eyes wide, was . . .

Well, if he'd had to guess, he'd have said it was Mom, except Mom didn't quite look like that, and was five or six years older. But she *was* Mom-esque, whoever this was.

"Travis?" the woman said again. "It's me. It's Kayla."

"No," Travis said, the word barely a whisper.

The woman took one of his hands in hers. "Yes," she replied, squeezing gently. "You've been in a coma."

Travis felt his heart pounding. "A . . ." He'd wanted to repeat the phrase "a coma" as a question, but throat congestion mired the second word before it got out.

The woman nodded. "For nineteen years. It's 2020 now."

His head was swimming. That was an eye-test score, for Christ's sake, not a year. He tried to speak again: "Twenty . . . ," then stopped, cleared his throat, and pushed ahead. "Twenty-twenty?"

"Uh-huh," said Kayla.

Travis swallowed, then coughed a couple of times. Next to—well, yes, he supposed it really was Kayla—was a man about the same age. *About the same age . . .*

And if Kayla was in her late thirties, then he—Travis himself—must be . . .

He did the math: in 2020 he would turn—*had,* perhaps, already turned—forty-one.

"What"—his voice still rough, the words still difficult to expel—"do I . . . look like?"

The man and woman exchanged glances, then the man moved over to a cabinet and picked up something flat and rectangular. He tapped its surface then flipped the device around, holding it out for Travis to see . . .

My God.

Not just a still photograph, but high-resolution live video of a guy whose jaw dropped as Travis felt his own mouth falling open—a man with hair peppered gray retreating from a forehead marked by horizontal creases, a man who looked at least as much like Travis's father had as Kayla looked like their mother.

Travis couldn't bear the sight of what he'd become, but he couldn't turn away, either. "What's that?"

"That's you," replied the Master of the Bleeding Obvious, gently.

"No, no. The . . . that thing?"

"Oh!" A smile across the man's kind face. "My iPhone—um, my cell phone."

"No buttons."

"It's a touch screen," said the man, tapping its surface.

"That's . . . a phone?"

"Not just that; it's a talking computer." He turned it to face himself. "Sear E," he said—whatever that meant—"um, let's see. Ah, okay, how 'bout this: if the sun wasn't blotting them out, what planets would be visible right now?"

A silky female voice emanated from the device: "Venus is high in the sky in Taurus, just two degrees west of the sun. Mercury is twenty-one degrees farther west in Gemini, and Jupiter forty-seven degrees east in Aries."

The future, thought Travis. *I'm in the fucking future.*

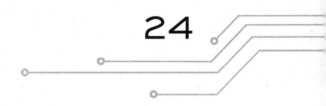

24

EVERYTHING changed for Kayla after that. Travis was suddenly her number-one priority; whatever plans we'd had for my current visit were instantly forgotten. Of course, it wasn't as if he could just waltz out of the place. His limbs had atrophied, and even his jaw muscles were so weak it wasn't clear whether he'd be able to chew food. At a minimum, he was facing many months of physiotherapy, and even after that, he might well need a motorized wheelchair for the rest of his life.

We didn't know whether Travis's microtubular electrons were going to stay in superposition for good—yes, I had come up to speed on all this; there was no way I was going to be Penny to Kayla's Leonard—and so Kayla's mother Rebekkah was summoned at once so she also could spend time with Travis before, perhaps, he slipped away again.

Kayla had never brought Ryan to see her uncle, and given all the things that Kayla and Rebekkah suddenly had to do on Travis's behalf, it fell to me to look after her. I spent the next three days doing just that—and I have to say I loved every minute. I took her to the Fun Factory, where we played laser tag, and to the Western Development Museum, which had a re-creation of the Saskatoon boomtown of 1910;

the blacksmith let Ryan try out his hammer. We also went to the Children's Discovery Museum, and to Wendy's and Dairy Queen. I was curious about how Travis was managing but nonetheless was having the time of my life.

And, as Ryan and I walked along, her little hand in mine, I thought about my son Virgil, and about my life that could have been and wasn't.

Propped up in his bed, Travis looked out the window. The blinds were raised—Kayla had done that for him before she'd stepped out—and, if he needed any further proof that significant time had passed, the summery landscape of green grass and leaf-covered trees provided it; for him, it had been a snowy winter just a few hours ago.

Of course, that January and this June were separated not by just five months but by nineteen years. His sister and mother were elated: his return was a miracle they'd stopped hoping for. But Travis was furious at the loss of all the intervening time, and he was devastated by how his body had wasted away. For Christ's sake, he was suddenly in his forties! By this point, he'd planned on being a corporate vice president with a half-million-dollar home—or whatever amount a fancy place went for these days. He should've had the trophy wife, the 2.1 kids, the red Jaguar. Instead, he had just $347 in his Scotiabank account, plus, he supposed, whatever interest had accrued on it, if monthly service fees hadn't whittled the damn thing down to nothing.

He'd heard Kayla and his mom talking—funny how candid they were, as if a part of them still felt he couldn't possibly hear what they were saying. It had been decided that, when the doctors discharged him, he'd move in with his mom—yup, that was his life now, the quintessential loser, in his forties, living in his parent's basement. But how the fuck had he ended up like this? What the hell had happened?

He clearly remembered everything from the last few days—the last few days nineteen years ago: going to see *Dude, Where's My Car?* at the Polo Park Cineplex on New Year's Eve; picking up a girl at the bar afterward; watching a new show called *CSI* and thinking that its gimmick would wear thin quickly, only to have Kayla tell him today that the damn thing had stayed in production until 2017. But what had caused him to become Rip Van Winkle? Oh, right! He had been—

"Great news!" His sister came back into the room; he was still startled by how she looked now. "I spoke to the dietitian. He's going to work out a plan to get you back onto solid food. We'll have you eating cheeseburgers and nachos before you know it."

"Thanks," he replied, but he didn't feel much enthusiasm. He didn't want to eat; he wanted to walk—he wanted to run!

Perhaps she'd read something in his face because she added at once, "And the physiotherapist will be here tomorrow to do an assessment."

Just then, a nurse came in, pretty, Asian, maybe twenty-five. Travis turned to look at her as she checked his IV drip, and—

And it should have been obvious. It should have been clear at a glance. He should have been able to see it.

But he couldn't.

This nurse *might* be vulnerable, she might be afraid, she might be the perfect means to an end—*any* end—for him.

But he couldn't tell. The sense he used to have, the ability that had been there his whole life, the perception that had guided his interactions with others for so long, was *gone.*

The nurse, noting his gaze, smiled at him, but it wasn't the interested smile he was used to getting from women; it was a comforting "there, there" smile, sympathy for the old man.

The nurse left, and Travis turned back to face Kayla. He used to be able to read her easily, too, but not anymore. And yet he did sense . . . *something.* As he looked at her, he . . . he *felt* . . . "pain," he supposed was the right word for seeing her this way, although that didn't . . . it . . . he *couldn't,* but . . .

He narrowed his eyes, detecting the skin on his forehead, which had clearly loosened over the years, wrinkling as he did so. That was a strange sensation, but not as strange, not as unprecedented, not as fucking *weird* as . . .

. . . as this . . . this *sadness*—that was it!—this ineffable sorrow not for himself, not for the two decades he'd lost, but for his sister, for the toll the passage of time had taken on her, the decay *she'd* undergone.

Still, unlike him, she hadn't missed out on the last nineteen years. She'd lived them, every moment, doubtless dozens of triumphs and dozens of tragedies. So why did he feel so melancholy when he looked at her? Why did he feel . . .

Why did he feel *anything* for her?

What the fuck was going on?

"You okay, Trav?" Kayla said, sitting down on a chair near his bed.

"I guess." He paused for a beat. "So, Mom said you're a big-time rocket scientist now, huh?"

"Quantum physicist," Kayla replied.

"A professor?"

She shook her head. "I don't teach. I'm a researcher."

A question popped into his head, one that it had never occurred to him to ask before. "You happy?"

"With my work? Sure. The synchrotron is an amazing place, and it pays well enough."

"And other than work?"

"Honestly? My ex is a pain in the ass."

"Your ex? You're married?"

"And divorced."

A huge chapter of her life he'd completely missed. And—my God—he wasn't even sure he knew his own sister's name now. "Did you take his name?"

"Nope. Still a Huron. As we say in the physics world: inertia."

"And this guy was an a-hole?"

"So it turned out. Only good thing that came out of that relationship was Ryan."

"Who?"

"My daughter." A pause. "Your niece."

Incredible.

"Six, going on thirty," Kayla said. "I'll bring her by to meet you soon."

"Thanks."

"Sure. And yeah, to answer your question, basically, overall, life is good. I'm making amazing breakthroughs at work, and you've met my boyfriend Jim; he's really good to me and Ryan."

He thought about this—and, oddly, about how he felt about it all. It was very, very strange, but he replied, saying words that he'd said countless times before but meant—*really* meant—for the first time: "I'm happy for you."

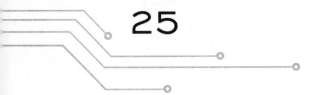

25

WHEN he'd been fifteen—which was seven subjective and twenty-six objective years ago—Travis's hand had gotten sliced open. He'd walked into a plate-glass window at a shopping mall that he'd thought was an open door. It should have been made out of safety glass but wasn't, and the damn thing broke into giant slabs. As he lifted his arm to shield his face, one of the huge sections dropped from the top of the frame and smashed into the back of his right hand, cutting it down to the bone. The tendons were severed, the wound gaped, and he was rushed to the emergency department.

All of the surgical beds were in use, and so they put him in something like a dentist's chair, with his hand supported on a little tray, and the reconstructive surgeon, called in from a concert he'd been at, sat on a stool next to him and carefully sutured up the tendons, which looked like gray fettuccine noodles. They'd only used a local anesthetic, and Travis had watched, fascinated, examining the inner workings of his hand.

The scar, Travis was pleased to see, had faded greatly over the last two decades, doubtless the only part of him that had improved with age. Still, *this* was a bit like that: for the first time, he realized, he was reflecting on the inner workings of his own mind. And, like that—like seeing the tendons, the bone, the whole mechanical infrastructure of his metacarpus—it was interesting for a time, and something he was glad to have experienced, but not anything he needed to do again, and certainly not something he wanted to be subjected to all the time.

Kayla had been sitting with him for the last couple of hours, presenting a compressed version of twenty-first-century history to date: the terrorist attacks on the World Trade Center and the Pentagon, a second space shuttle blowing up, the wars in Afghanistan and Iraq, the election of the first black American president, Canada being dragged far to the right and then snapping back to the left with—holy crap!—the recent election of a Muslim prime minister, same-sex marriage being legalized across Canada and a decade later across the US, the polar ice caps shrinking, and so much more. It was overwhelming.

But around 6:00 P.M., Kayla's boyfriend Jim showed up to let Kayla take a break. They disappeared into the corridor for a couple of minutes, and Travis looked out the window. The trees were swaying—it had become quite a blustery day. An eagle flew by, passing just above a pole with a tattered, faded Canadian flag.

Jim re-entered and took the seat Kayla had been using. Travis regarded him. This guy was presentable enough, but his sister, even having aged, was better-looking. Travis said, "How old are you?"

"Thirty-nine," replied Jim.

Travis shook his head. "Last birthday I remember, I turned twenty-two. Now, I'm forty-one."

"*Tempus fugit,*" Jim said, and Travis found himself immediately liking the guy. He didn't follow the phrase with raised eyebrows, which, Travis knew, would have been literally—yes, literally, not figuratively—supercilious; he didn't shoot Travis a "That's Latin" or a "Do you get it?" look. He just calmly assumed that whomever he was talking to was as bright as he himself was.

"Yeah," said Travis.

"So, listen," said Jim, "I asked Kayla, and she said it was okay to talk to you about this. I was at U of M, too, when you were, but I can't remember things from back then, and, well, I thought maybe you could help me fill in some blanks about my past."

Travis considered for a moment. Previously, words like those would have been seductive music: *You know something I don't; you've got something you can hold against me.* But he didn't feel any urge to . . . to *use* this poor sap. He . . .

He wanted to help the guy out.

Christ, Travis thought, *what's wrong with me?*

I looked at Travis Huron, and he looked back at me. Travis was Kayla's brother, but I felt in a small way like he was my brother, too. After all, he was the only other guy my age I knew who also had no memory of the first half of 2001. Yes, he'd lost so much more than that, but I could qualitatively, if not quantitatively, understand what he was going through. And even if I could somehow recover my memories of my dark period, they would presumably be *old* memories, faded, unreliable, like anyone's of that long ago. But Travis remembered things from back then as if they'd just occurred.

Except . . .

Damn it, something was niggling at my consciousness. And, yes, *consciousness* was the heart of the matter. Menno Warkentin said I blacked out after trying on his Lucidity helmet. If that contraption did more than render me unconscious—if it really was what put an end to my self-awareness for the next six months—then I could sort of understand why I didn't remember anything from the period *following* my blacking out, until, for whatever reason, I ceased being a p-zed.

But why didn't I remember putting on the helmet? Why didn't I remember going to Menno's lab on New Year's Eve? Hell, why don't I remember going to McNally Robinson and buying that sci-fi paperback earlier the same day? Surely I should at least vaguely recall that stuff, but I couldn't dredge up anything from the day I became a p-zed.

But Travis hadn't been subjected to Menno's lasers. He presumably had no paralimbic damage promoting confabulation; his memories should be accurate. And so, after he asked me how old I was, and he lamented how old he himself had become, I simply asked him: "Did you take part in an experiment at the university run by Professor Warkentin and Professor Adler?"

Travis managed a rueful smile. "Yup. I remember it like it was yesterday. Those guys still around?"

"Warkentin, yeah; he's emeritus at U of M. Adler's in Washington now. So, you remember the Lucidity helmet?"

"I don't think I ever heard them call it that, but you mean the football helmet with all the doodads attached? Sure. I came in on December fifteenth, they put it on me, and I did some tests, thinking words without saying them."

"Exactly. Yes. And then they had you come back again, right?"

An odd look passed over Travis's face, as if he was surprised at how important this seemed to me. "No."

"They didn't?"

"No. I came in once, got my twenty bucks, and that was it."

"What about the day you blacked out? I'd assumed you'd come in again to do an experiment. They found you on campus, and classes didn't resume until the eighth."

"Not that I recall."

Damn. I'd been so sure Warkentin was responsible for what had happened to Travis. "You don't remember the day you fell into the coma?"

"Not a thing. I remember going to bed the night before, which was January first. I'd gotten a paperback of this new thriller, *Angels & Demons,* for Christmas, and I started reading that—in fact, that's just about the last thing I remember."

There was an obvious joke to be made about Dan Brown novels; I resisted. "But you don't recall anything at all from the next day? Anything after you woke up?"

He shook his head. "As far as I remember, the next time I woke up, I was right here—with you and my sister standing over me."

"Huh," I said, baffled. If Travis had been knocked down into a coma by the same mechanism as me, why didn't either of us remember putting on the helmet? I could understand losing memories after the botched stimulation with transcranial focused ultrasound, but why would we lose ones from before that?

"You're a shrink, right?" asked Travis, looking quizzically at me now.

"I've got a PhD in psychology," I replied, "but I don't have a clinical practice."

He waved that away. "But you're trained in this shit, and—funny, I don't think I've *ever* said this before, but I need somebody to talk to."

I leaned forward in the chair. "I'm all ears."

"I feel different now," Travis said. "Different from the way I did before. I'm fighting it, but . . ."

"What's different?"

"It's hard to describe. But I keep thinking about . . . well, about what I'm thinking about. I was always a charge-ahead kind of guy. Never look back, no second thoughts. You know? Just do it."

"Like Nike," I said.

"Yeah, exactly. Hey, they still use that slogan?"

"Yup."

"Anyway, that's the way I used to be. But now, I keep going over in my mind things I've done."

I frowned. "You never did that before?"

"Never."

"What about planning for the future? Thinking about things you haven't yet done?"

"Oh, yeah, sure. I've always done that: considering alternatives, figuring the angles. But that's different; there's a point to that. You can change the future, right? You can't change the past—so why . . ."

"Obsess about it?"

"Um, yeah. Yeah, I guess that *is* the right word."

"And you've only been doing this since . . ."

"Since Kayla woke me up."

"Are you sure? Did you ever keep a diary?"

"No."

"A journal? A blog?"

"A what?"

"A web blog; a public online journal."

"Christ, no. Why would anyone do that?"

"Is it making you unhappy, this ruminating?"

"Yeah. It's . . . I've got these . . . I don't know what to call them, but . . ."

"Regrets?" I proffered.

Travis repeated the word, as if trying it on, seeing if it fit: "Regrets . . ." And then at last he nodded. "Things I might've done differently—maybe *should* have done differently, and . . ."

"And you're not used to thinking in terms of 'should.'"

He seemed to consider this, too, then: "Yeah." He shook his head. "It's just . . . weird."

It wasn't weird, not for Q3s, but . . .

But it *was* for psychopaths. They didn't ruminate and they didn't get depressed; it was almost unheard of for a psychopath to become suicidally despondent. "What about your feelings toward, say, Kayla?"

"That's weird, too! I mean, she's my sister, right? Always has been, always will be. And I was a good big brother, you know? Wouldn't let anyone mess with her. But, well, now that I . . ."

"Think about it?"

He nodded. "Yeah. Now that I think about it, that was really about *me*, right? Making sure people respected me? I didn't—sounds shitty to say this, I know—but I didn't really care about *her*. I didn't understand that, not at the time—but now I keep wondering how she's doing. And I want her to be happy."

My pulse was racing. There was too much physics and psychology involved to quickly explain this to Travis just now, but I felt sure in my bones that I was right. Yes, the quantum tuning fork—a device almost as cool as The Doctor's sonic screwdriver—had restored superposition to Travis Huron's brain, but it had done an even better job than we'd thought. Prior to his falling into the coma, he must have had two of the three electrons in each of his tubulin thingamajigs in superposition, making him a quantum psychopath. But, assuming he *had* returned to Menno's lab, just as I had, the transcranial ultrasound stimulation provided by the Mark II helmet must have caused those electrons to all decohere, falling back *en masse* to the classical-physics state, making him lose consciousness.

But when Kayla had goosed his brain, instead of just two, *all* three of the electrons in each pocket had gone into superposition. Prior to 2001, he'd been a card-carrying psychopath, and now, apparently for the first time in his life, Travis Huron was what I had been for most of my life: fully conscious with conscience, a CWC, a quick.

"It's depressing," Travis said, after a moment, "having all these . . . these regrets . . . running around in my head."

I nodded slowly. "Welcome to the club."

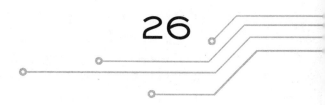

26

KAYLA returned around 7:00 P.M., and I went out into the corridor to chat with her again. "How's he doing?" she asked.

I didn't know what to tell her—and, anyway, it was probably better to have the conversation about Travis's change in mental state when we were going to have a longer time to talk. "He's okay."

Kayla looked down the corridor with its hard, scuffed flooring, doors alternating left and right, each leading into a room containing one or more patients. "I want to help the other people here," she said, "if any of the rest of them are in deep, total comas. See who I can wake up, but . . ."

"Yes?" It sounded like a good idea to me.

"But we can't just pull an *Awakenings* on them all," she said. "Many of these people have been abandoned for years, decades. Some have no family, and for those who *do* have families, surely they should be present when they wake up. Plus, frankly, I want to be sure that Travis's superposition *is* holding before we get anyone else's hopes up."

"Makes sense."

"Still," she said, "this could change the world."

I looked down the corridor; the sun was setting through a window at the far end. "Yeah," I said. "I guess it could, at that."

I left Kayla with her brother; as they spoke of their childhoods and their parents, I really was feeling like a third wheel. Plus, I was starving, and I only knew two other adults in Saskatoon: the optometrist David Swinson who, if I recalled correctly, planned to urinate on my cemetery plot, and Kayla's research partner, Victoria Chen. I almost didn't call Vic, assuming she'd be out with her boyfriend, but then figured there was nothing to lose. To my surprise, she was free and happy to meet me for a bite to eat. She suggested the Konga Cafe, which turned out to be a Caribbean place in a little strip mall here in Riversdale. I got there first, and rose when she arrived. She greeted me with a kiss on the cheek.

We sat opposite each other, and she said, "So, how are you?"

"Honestly?" I tilted my head. "Conflicted."

"Oh?"

"Yeah. I spent some time with Kayla's brother Travis today. And, well, up until he came out of his coma, it seems he was a quantum psychopath. I haven't told Kayla yet—frankly, I don't know *how* to tell her."

"Are you sure of your diagnosis?"

I shrugged, conceding that there was some room for doubt. "I grant that the only quantum-superposition testing you did on him was while he was in a coma, so there's no record of his quantum state prior to that. And, as far as I know, no one had ever done the Hare Checklist on him, and I doubt there's any video of him from the last century that's high-enough resolution to show whether he was doing microsaccades then. But all of those things are merely correlates of psychopathy. Actual psychopathy is a state of mind: a complete disregard for others; a lack of reflection and rumination—and that's what Travis described to me."

"Wow," said Vic. "Are Kayla or Ryan in any danger from him?"

"No, not now."

"Good."

"I'll tell Kayla before I leave tomorrow, but . . ." I exhaled noisily. "I bet Kayla would have had an easier childhood if Travis had been a Q1 instead of a Q2."

Sadness washed over Vic's face, and she said slowly, "Speaking of which . . ."

"Yes?"

"My boyfriend Ross. My ex-boyfriend, I should say. He . . . he's a Q1. I tested him on the beamline."

"Oh. I'm so sorry."

"Yeah." She shook her head. "It's . . . difficult, you know? Finding decent guys who are okay with not having kids, that's hard."

"Don't you want kids?"

"'Want'?" she said. "Yes. But I can't have any. I *wish* I could, but . . ." She shrugged a little. "Cervical cancer; had a hysterectomy."

"I'm sorry, Vic."

"Thanks. Ryan's the closest thing to a child I'll ever have."

"Oh, she's a doll."

"Yeah," said Vic, looking sad. "Yeah, she is."

"Anyway," I said. "I'm sorry about you and Ross."

She lifted her dark eyebrows. "I guess they really *are* everywhere. Makes you wonder how society can function."

"Ross teaches high school, right?"

"Yes. English."

"Well," I said, spreading my arms, "there's a curriculum laid down by the Ministry of Education, right? He has to teach *these* books in *this* order by *that* time, and prepare his students for taking *this* standardized province-wide test. Any number of people could do that; indeed, any number *do*—there must be thousands of high-school English teachers in Saskatchewan."

"A good teacher makes a difference."

"Sure, yeah. But there are lots of bad teachers or indifferent ones in the system, too. I don't say that being a university professor is *better*—although it pays better—but the requirement to do original research to get a PhD might mean you get fewer p-zeds at that level although I've seen lots of trite, paint-by-numbers dissertations in my day. You know what they say: the only word that rhymes with 'theses' is 'feces.'"

"I guess. It's just—I mean, I really liked him. And I thought he liked me. But he's . . . he's a robot."

The server came; I ordered Red Stripe, an imported Jamaican beer; Vic asked for a Pepsi Next.

"I still don't get how a society could function with most of its members not being truly conscious," Vic said.

"Welllll," I replied gently, "the majority of Ross's students would likely be p-zeds, too. And most jobs are repetitive. It's only the length of the repeat cycle that varies: a few seconds if you work on an assembly line, a few hours if you drive a bus, daily if you manage a restaurant, and yearly if you teach a course. Every September, I trot out the same introductory lectures I gave the year before."

"I guess." She let out a sigh. "I just can't believe I was fooled by him."

I shook my head. "Psychopaths fool people. They deliberately deceive; they get off on it. But p-zeds? They just *are*. Ross wasn't trying to hurt you; he wasn't trying to do *anything*."

"Yeah, I suppose," she said. The server brought our drinks—mine in a bottle, Vic's in a can—as well as some johnnycakes as an appetizer. "It's just hard," she continued, "not knowing who's . . . who's *real*."

"Yeah."

We sat in silence for a time, then I said, "Anyway, Vic, there's something else I wanted to talk to you about."

"Shoot."

"I said Travis was a psychopath—but he isn't, not anymore. He was almost certainly a Q2 before his coma, but the coma knocked him out of superposition—or, I guess, the other way around: he got knocked out of superposition, ending up in the classical-physics state, and that caused him to lose consciousness, right?"

"That's the process, yes," said Vic.

"But when he came out of the coma, he came out as a Q3—I'd bet money on it. He's got a conscience for the first time, and, frankly, is gobsmacked by it."

"That's fascinating."

"Yeah, but here's the part I don't get. I admit that I'm struggling with all this quantum-physics stuff, so maybe you can explain it to me. Travis started as Q2, got knocked down to the classical-physics state, and came back up as a Q3—a higher level than he'd been at originally."

"Okay."

"But I started out as a Q3—fully conscious with conscience—got knocked down to the classical-physics state, and came back at a *lower* level, emerging from my own blackout as a Q1 p-zed. Why is that?"

Vic's thin lips turned downward. "That *is* a good question."

"He doesn't remember what happened to him any more than I do, but we were almost certainly both knocked out by the same piece of equipment although admittedly we were revived in different ways. Still, he went up, and I went down."

"Well, if I understand what Kayla told me correctly, you came back—to the extent that you initially *did* come back—almost immediately; Travis was in a coma for nineteen years."

"True. And I suppose it might be completely random—a throw of the dice."

Vic nodded. "If that's the case, given the 4:2:1 ratio of the cohorts, maybe you've got a four-in-seven chance of coming up as a p-zed, like you did, and a one-in-seven chance of coming up as a quick, like Travis did. But I'm always suspicious of apparent randomness."

I took another sip of beer. "Me, too."

When I got back to the facility to pick up Kayla, her mother Rebekkah was just leaving—and so I maneuvered her over to a couple of chairs in the lobby.

"Have you been enjoying Saskatoon?" she asked.

"Yes. It's lovely. Such sunny days! And no mosquitoes. I'm not looking forward to those back in Winnipeg."

Rebekkah was a handsome woman with lively eyes. "Tell me about it. I survived fifty-one summers there."

And that was the opening I'd been hoping for. "Speaking of The Peg . . ."

"Yes?"

"You raised your kids there, right?"

"Yes."

"And Travis was into sports, even as a kid?"

"Oh, my, yes. The harder, the better. Not Kayla, though: she was the studious one." Our orange-upholstered chairs were facing each other, and she leaned closer, conspiratorially. "I never told the kids this, but my father—their grandfather—referred to them as 'Jock' and 'Nerd' behind their backs." She smiled. "He meant it with love, but it's true: they were different as night and day."

"Hmmm," I said. "Well, look, I'm interested in, you know, nature vs. nurture, and all that. Sometimes sports are displaced aggression. Was Travis, you know, a violent child?"

"Well, there wasn't much consciousness of it back then," Rebekkah said, "but, yeah, he was a bully, frankly. My husband and I weren't really aware of it too much at the time, but he probably wasn't the nicest guy to other kids. But all the kids' parents loved him. That boy had the gift of the gab; I don't know where he got it."

I nodded. Glibness and superficial charm were classic psychopathic traits; so were bullying and pointless cruelty. But I was hoping for something definitive. After all, the notion that people change quantum states upon rebooting from total unconsciousness was huge, and I couldn't just rely on what Travis had subjectively told me about his own feelings. "Were there a lot of pets on your street? Dogs? Cats?"

"Oh, yes. Sure."

I often floated hypotheticals with my students, who always figured out that they were precisely that. I didn't like doing so with Rebekkah, but I said, even though no such thing had actually happened in my own neighborhood, "We used to have tons of pets on the street I grew up on." I put on a puzzled face. "But a lot of them disappeared. We didn't know what to make of it. Turned out this kid up the street was capturing them and killing them."

"God," said Rebekkah. "We had the same thing. Some creep was stringing up dead cats from trees—including two kittens that belonged to us—and we found others cut into pieces. It was *awful* . . ." She shook her head. "I tell you, Jim, I didn't like that my Travis used to beat up other kids, but I wouldn't have minded if he'd gotten his hands on whoever was doing *that*."

Kayla, on the other hand, was another matter; keeping secrets was no way to build a relationship. "I had a long chat with your brother this afternoon," I said to her, as we lay side by side later that night.

"He told me. He likes you." She smiled. "Big-brother stamp of approval."

"He's a good guy," I said. "Now."

"What do you mean, 'now'?"

"What was he like as a kid, a teenager?"

"You're getting at something," said Kayla. "What?"

I took a deep breath, then let it out. "He's changed," I said. "Before his coma, he was a psychopath."

"You said you didn't remember Travis from before."

"I don't. But he described his inner life from then to me: consciousness but no conscience, not until now. He used to be a Q2, but, for whatever reason, he booted up again as a Q3."

She looked stunned. "No. Really? My God, are you—are you sure?"

"Pretty much."

"Jesus. So what does that make me? Debra Fucking Morgan? Too much the loving sister to see what her brother really was?"

"I'm not—no one is judging. I just thought you should know." She said nothing, so I went on. "And at least he isn't one anymore. He genuinely cares about you."

"Now," said Kayla bitterly.

"And let's hope he stays that way. But, look, you know the Hare Checklist as well as I do. Did he, y'know, have lots of girlfriends?"

"You've only seen him now, after wasting away for almost twenty years," she replied, nodding. "I'm his sister, and even I knew how hot he was."

"Promiscuity," I said softly. "Strings of meaningless relationships. And you said he was into extreme sports: that's need for stimulation.

You also said he was a brick when your father was fighting cancer; I'm betting he kept it together even at the funeral, right?"

"And you're saying that's evidence of shallow affect?"

I couldn't shrug lying down, but I lifted my eyebrows. "Classic trait."

"I—" But she didn't finish whatever thought she'd started.

"I'm so sorry, honey. But remember, he's fine, now."

She rolled on her side, facing away from me; I was afraid she was angry, but then she said, "Hold me."

I did, nestling into the curve of her back, spooning her tightly. I didn't know what to say, and so I just held her, and we lay there, waiting for sleep to take us.

27

AFTER Jim had returned to Winnipeg, Kayla decided to come clean with the staff at Tommy Douglas Long-Term Care. "And so," she said, "if there are other patients here who have no consciousness at all, I might be able to help them."

Nathan Amsterdam, the medical chief of staff, was fifty-something, with blond hair swept back from his forehead, hollow cheeks, and a long, thin face. "It's incredible," he said. "But, you know, you really should have told us in advance what you were planning to do. If something had gone wrong . . ."

"He's my brother; the court gave me power of attorney ages ago. *I* authorized it—and it worked."

"Still, if it'd had some deleterious effect—"

"It didn't. It *cured* him."

He was quiet for a time, then: "Well, what's done is done."

"So far," said Kayla. "But I want to do it again. Is there anyone else here whose condition is similar to what my brother was in? A score of just three on the Glasgow scale? I want to help, if I can."

"I'd have to check with our legal counsel . . ."

"For pity's sake, Dr. Amsterdam, you're not going to bury a miracle in red tape, are you?"

Amsterdam's office walls were lined with cherry-wood bookcases; he sat behind a matching desk. "Off the record, we have four—no, five—patients with locked-in syndrome, and a dozen or so in minimally conscious states. But with no signs at all of consciousness or awareness?" He frowned, and the concavities of his cheeks deepened. "There's one. Been in a coma since a car accident, oh, five or six years ago. Her husband is almost as dutiful as you—comes in every other Wednesday night to sit with her."

"Can you put me in touch with him?"

Amsterdam's head moved left and right. "No. But I can ask him if he wants to get in touch with you."

I was standing before fifty or so students. My ringer was off; I was famous for chastising students when their phones rang while I was trying to teach. But I did have the phone on the lectern, face-up, so I could keep an eye on the time in a way that was less obvious than looking at my watch. There was no clock at the back of the room although there was one behind me: the students got to see the hour evaporate, but the professor didn't.

The little tablet vibrated and the display briefly lit up, showing the time—11:14 A.M.—and the automatic notification I'd set, and forgotten, at the beginning of the trial: *Google Alert—"Devin Becker verdict."* I violated my own rule, picked up the phone, and looked at my inbox. The headline for the article said: *Savannah Prison ringleader sentenced to death.* The source beneath it was MSNBC.com, although doubtless if I did a search, there'd be dozens of stories already, and hundreds by the end of the day.

And then, I guess, I just stood there, mouth agape, while all those eyes looked at me. I heard someone cough, someone else typing, another person knock a pen to the floor. But I kept staring at the message. I wanted to click through to the report and watch the video, then and there, but—

"Professor Marchuk?" said a woman from near the front of the hall. I blinked, looked up, but said nothing.

"Sir?" said the same person. "Are you okay?"

I didn't have a good answer for that, and so I just composed myself and pressed on with the lecture. "Watson, you see, was the quintessential behaviorist. He felt that people were simple stimulus-response machines that could be trained any way you wished through reward and punishment. He once said, 'Give me a child and I'll shape him into anything . . .'"

Kayla got a call from the husband of the woman in the coma, and she immediately drove the hour out of the city to his farm. Dale Hawkins was perhaps sixty years old, with a shock of graying hair and a full, matching beard. Although he was wearing a plaid work shirt, he had an intricate tattoo of vines and leaves terminating on the back of his left hand; Kayla assumed it was a full sleeve. On one wall of his living room he had three framed photos of his wife. She had a broad face and brown hair.

"I miss her so much," Dale said. "I miss her every day."

"I know," said Kayla. There was a rough-hewn wooden coffee table between them, but she reached across it and took his hand. "I know exactly what you're going through. My brother was in a coma, too, and this technique helped him." She got her tablet and streamed the video Jim had made of Travis waking up. Dale watched, transfixed.

"And your brother, he's all right in the head?" asked Dale, once the video was over. "He's the same as before?"

And that was the question she'd been wrestling with. "No," she said. "Honestly? He's different. Better, but different. And your wife might come back different, too—and, I have to tell you, not necessarily better."

They talked some more while Dale looked at the photos of his wife, and Kayla looked at them, too. She had different expressions in each one: a smile, a look of thoughtful contemplation, her features set in determination. *All the world's a stage, and all the men and women merely players.* The words Kayla had memorized in high school came back to her. *They have their exits and their entrances, and one man in his time plays many parts.*

"Okay," Dale said at last. "Let's give it a try."

I came into my living room—you had to go down a couple of steps to get to it, all Mary Tyler Moore–like—and sat on the couch, facing the TV. I fumbled around looking for the correct one of the four remote controls, activated the set, selected the web browser, went to CBC.ca, and there it was, the second story under "International News."

"After deliberating for six days," said a tall female reporter I'd never seen before, *"the jury in the Devin Becker case handed down a death sentence. Under Georgia law, when a jury unanimously recommends the death penalty, which it did here, the judge has no option but to impose it. Becker sat emotionless in court as the jury forewoman read the verdict . . ."*

Soon they were showing footage of the jurors exiting the court-house. I recognized them, but I'd never heard any of them speak until now. They cut to the heavyset black woman, a bouquet of microphones each sporting a different logo in front of her. She said, "The defense tried to say he had no choice in what he did. Hooey. Guy knew what he was doin', and he did it. We all answerable to the Lord for our actions."

It was all there in that woman's statement—a woman I'd only known as Juror 8, but I'd now seen identified by the text on-screen as Helen Brine. Devin Becker was quite possibly going to die by lethal injection because I'd failed to deliver the goods. The reporter went on: *"Under Georgia law, a verdict of first-degree murder can be found in cases where murder involves torture. The original case against Becker had hinged on the state establishing that his maltreatment of the pris-oner before drowning him amounted to torture; clearly, the jurors here bought that argument."*

The newscast automatically moved on to the next story, this one being presented by an anchor I did recognize, Ian Hanomansing. *"Con-*

tinuing with news from south of the border, in the wake of further deaths in Texas . . ."

I groped for the remote, turned off the set, lay back on the couch, and looked up at the white ceiling, the little spikes of its stippled surface hanging down like ten thousand swords of Damocles.

28

THEY could have just tried the tuning fork without preamble, but if it didn't work, Kayla would never know whether the failure was because of some flaw in the device or because Mrs. Hawkins wasn't actually currently in the classical-physics state, and it seemed best to determine that beforehand rather than try to beg for further cooperation from Dale if she didn't wake up. Of course, if it turned out she wasn't currently free of superposition, they'd give the tuning fork a try anyway—what the heck.

And so, just as they'd done with Travis, Mrs. Hawkins was brought via ambulance to the Canadian Light Source, and taken on a gurney down to the SusyQ beamline. Kayla had told her boss Jeff what she was doing, and he was standing at one side, his Hawaiian shirt turquoise and aquamarine today; next to him was Dr. Amsterdam. Dale was on hand, too, and he'd shaved off his facial hair. "I didn't have the beard when she was awake," he explained, "and I want her to recognize me immediately."

Mrs. Hawkins—Jill—looked no older than she had in the smiling photograph at the farmhouse, except that her hair was now completely gray; it might well have been back when that photo had been taken, too, but any dye job had grown out in the interim.

A CLS staffer was recording everything on video as Victoria and one of the ambulance attendants carefully positioned Jill with the crown of her head by the conical beam emitter. Vic didn't bother to strap Jill's head in place; she wasn't moving at all.

As always, the test didn't take long. Kayla knew it was odd to feel elated that this poor woman was showing absolutely zero consciousness— but, as she looked at the readout on Vic's monitor, she did feel just that: no superposition; not even that usual background-noise line high up. Mrs. Hawkins was in the classical-physics state.

"Perfect," said Victoria, grinning.

Vic got the quantum tuning fork out of its foam-lined case. She handed it to Kayla, who held it, the metal shaft cold in her hands. Dale, wearing a nice gray dress shirt, was whispering a prayer as his tattooed hand gripped the back of a chair. Kayla touched the fork's twin tines to Jill's forehead and slid the red switch on the handle forward.

Nothing happened. True, even if the fork restored superposition, it didn't necessarily mean that Jill would actually wake up; she could be blissfully asleep now. But Vic's monitor showed no change.

Kayla took a deep breath and tried rotating the fork, flipping the tines, just as she'd done with Travis. But it made no difference. The readout still didn't show any spikes.

Of course, the conditions were different than with Travis; the synchrotron itself and tons of other high-tech equipment were operating here. But Victoria's colleagues had been using the tuning fork for many days now with substrate blocks adjacent to beamline emitters, and it worked just fine in boosting them into superposition. And, yes, Kayla would go back to the facility with Jill and try again there, just to be sure, but . . .

But she knew in her heart that it wasn't going to work, and looking over at Dale, this rugged, tattooed farmer now with tears running down his cheeks, she felt awful.

"I'm so sorry," she said. She was sorting through other words she might say, hoping to find ones that could comfort him, such as noting that at least things were no worse than before, but—

But Dale beat her to it, turning to Dr. Amsterdam, and as soon as he finished speaking, she knew that things were, in fact, much worse. "Until today," he said, "I always thought she was in there. I always thought she could hear me when I talked. I always thought she'd come back to me someday, but . . ." He gestured at the monitor and its damning flat line. "But she's gone, isn't she? Been gone for years." He wiped his nose with his arm, the shirt's sleeve pushing up to reveal more ivy. "It's time to let her go."

I walked out onto my third-floor balcony and looked at the Red River rolling by. Between my building and it was a green strip with a couple of picnic tables. It was dark out, and, as a gibbous moon was rising over the park on the opposite side of the river, I batted away a few of the season's first mosquitoes—they were coming earlier every year. While I stood there, I saw two people jogging north, and, shortly thereafter, two more running south. P-zeds? Psychopaths? Quicks? Who knew?

I returned to the living room and plunked myself back down on the couch. My walls were a celery shade; that wouldn't have been my choice, but that's what they'd been when I moved in. I stared into the soft greenness, thinking . . .

. . . and I must have lost track of time, because I was interrupted by the *bleep-bloop-bleep-bloop* of an incoming Skype call. Kayla was supposed to reach out to me tonight at 10:00 my time, after she'd put Ryan to bed; I hadn't realized it had gotten so late. I hurried over to my laptop and clicked on the button to answer the call.

She was in her living room, wearing a plain brown top, her red hair tied back. She looked melancholy, and I guess she must have thought I looked the same way, because we both said, "What's wrong?"

And that, at least, caused each of us to smile, however wanly. "Okay," I said. "You first."

She recounted her attempt of this afternoon to revive one of the other patients from the long-term-care facility. I was quiet, listening.

"I don't get it," she said at the end, "and neither does Vic. Why did the quantum tuning fork restore my brother's superposition but not Mrs. Hawkins's?"

I lifted my shoulders and shifted on the couch, then tilted my laptop's screen back slightly to reframe myself in the outgoing video. "I don't know. There's something different about your brother. Why did I wake up only a few minutes after Menno knocked me into a coma, but your brother stayed in that state for almost twenty years? Sure, each brain is unique, but it would be nice to know why Travis reacted differently from me and differently from this woman."

"I feel horrible," said Kayla. "I got her husband's hopes up. She didn't respond when we tried again with her back at the facility. Her husband's going to see his lawyer and get the paperwork done so that they can stop feeding her."

"Oh," I said softly, knowing better than to point out that this was indeed the right utilitarian move.

"I mean," said Kayla, "she's been gone for years—almost certainly since her accident. But still . . ."

"Yeah."

"Anyway." She tilted her head. Behind her, I could see the table and bookcases in her dining room. "How was your day?" she asked.

I thought briefly about what normal couples talked about at the end of the day, and kind of envied it. "Well, I don't know if you've been following the news, but . . ."

"Yes?"

"They handed down the sentence in the Devin Becker case today."

"Oh! No, I hadn't heard. And . . . ?"

"They're sending him to death row."

"Oh."

"So I failed to convince the jury that his psychopathy was a mitigating factor."

"Well, after . . ." She trailed off; she'd been about to say, no doubt, after the district attorney tore me to shreds on the witness stand, it's no wonder. But it didn't have to be said in words; her lifted eyebrows were enough.

I nodded. "Yeah. Georgia law has all sorts of provisions for executing people when the victim is a cop or prison guard; nothing in the rules about when the perpetrator is one. But the statute says death can be imposed in cases where the victim was tortured, and, well, you saw the Savannah Prison videos, I'm sure."

"Yeah."

I let out a long, whispery sigh, and pretty much simultaneously she did, too.

"Anyway," I said. "It's late—here, at least. And I've got a 9:00 A.M. class."

"Okay," said Kayla, looking out at me from my computer's screen. "Sleep well, baby."

"You, too," I said.

But I doubted either of us was going to sleep at all.

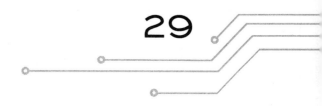

29

THERE was a strip mall behind my condo building, running perpendicular to the river. It contained an equal mixture of stores that interested me (Best Buy, Staples) and didn't (Toys"R"Us, Petland). But there was also a Subway, where I could get a decent vegan sandwich or salad, which is why I walked over there this morning, and a Dollarama, which sold the *Winnipeg Free Press;* if the line was short there, I often popped in to pick up a copy. Today it was, and I headed home with the paper tucked under one arm and carrying my salad with the other.

Once I was back up in my apartment and had poured myself a Coke Zero, I sat at my little breakfast nook and read as I ate.

The page-one headline, above the fold: *150 Killed in Nairobi Shooting Rampage.* Flipping the paper over: *Manitoba Chiefs Decry Ottawa Funding Cuts.* Next to that: *McCharles Calls Dem Opponents "Unpatriotic."*

Inside: *18 Dead in Texas "Cleansing." Brandon Priest Charged in Sex-Abuse Case. Canada, US, Fall Far Short of Carbon Targets: Report.*

The editorial: *Despite a Muslim PM, PQ Continues to Push Islamophobic "Charter of Values."* And an op-ed: *Canada Needs to Open its Doors to Jews Fleeing Europe.*

The business page was no better: *Michigan Decertifies All Public-Sector Unions. Euro Plummets as Spanish Debt Crisis Worsens. Apple, Amazon Defend Chinese Work Conditions. Canadian Income Disparity at All-Time High.*

I found myself wondering, as I had so many times over the years, *What's wrong with these people?* But, unlike those previous occasions, this time I supposed I had an answer. I'd known about the vast numbers of psychopaths for a couple of years now, but even so, there weren't enough of them to account for all the craziness in the world. But evil needs followers, and, given the 4:2:1 ratio between the cohorts, there were four billion p-zeds out there just waiting to be led.

Of course, those people were entitled to the same moral consideration as any other comparably sophisticated being; I wouldn't abuse or kill an animal—and I wouldn't countenance anyone doing that to a p-zed. And yet, Q2s, and, I feared, even many Q3s, if they knew of the prevalence of Q1s, would mistreat them. The most chilling line from the remake of *Battlestar Galactica* was the edict, "You can't rape a machine," uttered when humans were sexually assaulting Cylons, who were physically indistinguishable from humans. Sure, Cylons *acted* like they were upset at being attacked—but it's only rape, the humans felt, when done to one of our own.

And the second most chilling line? The show's oft-repeated mantra of "So say we all!"—fit in or fuck off. Y'know, Admiral Adama, if you wanted to make the case that humans are morally superior to machines, browbeating everyone until they're all mindlessly chanting "So say we all!" along with you was probably not the best way to do it.

No, I wasn't going to tell anyone else about the existence of huge quantities of p-zeds. As far as we knew, the three quantum states were uniformly distributed across the general population; there was nothing in Menno's work or that of Kayla and Vic to suggest anything to the contrary. But if the quantum taxonomy became general knowledge, it wouldn't be long, I knew, before the accusation that all fill-in-the-blanks were p-zeds would be used to justify not just the horror of rape, but slavery and murder, too. Menno Warkentin had been right to keep secret the existence of people without inner voices, and I intended to do the same.

And then the call I'd been waiting for came.

Dr. Bhavesh Namboothiri, over at the University of Winnipeg, had finally finished mapping out my visual memory index, based on the recent MRI scan I'd had at St. Boniface. In other words, he finally had the key; it was time to open the lock. It was a warm summer day as I drove to his lab—but not warm enough to account for how much I was sweating.

I'd sort of expected to be laid out on a gurney, looking up at the ceiling, but it was much easier for Dr. Namboothiri to probe the top of my head with me sitting in a simple low-to-the-ground bucket seat on a rotating stand. Nor was he wearing the surgical garb I associated with Wilder Penfield. Rather, he had on blue jeans and a loose-fitting dark-red shirt. After all, as he said, he wasn't going to open my skull—just my mind.

Namboothiri stood next to me, and next to him, on a wheeled tray, was a device about the size of a shoebox. Attached to it were two long cables, each ending in a metal tip, a bit like the probes on an ohmmeter. He placed one of the probes over my left temporal lobe, and the other near the anterior cingulate cortex. There was clearly some sort of read-out on the box that he could see but I couldn't; he kept glancing over at it.

"Okay," he said. "Do you feel anything?"

"No. Nothing."

"And what about now?"

"Nothing."

"And now?"

"My God . . ." I said. I recognized her at once, of course—and yet had no other recollection of her when she was this young, or of her with 1980s-style big hair.

"What is it?"

"My . . . my mother. She looks so young, and . . ."

"Yes?"

"Well, I mean, they told me my nursery had puke-green walls, but I'd had no recollection of that. But . . . but this must be it."

He slightly repositioned one of the probes; I felt a twinge of sadness as the vivid image disappeared.

"Okay, and now?"

"A teddy bear, but not one I ever recall seeing before."

"And here?" Namboothiri moved the probe again, and I tasted something cloyingly sweet.

"Perhaps children's cough syrup?"

"And here?"

"My dad—with hair!—reading to me."

"And here?"

I sucked in air.

"What?" said Namboothiri.

"That's it. That must be it!"

"What are you seeing?"

"Kayla—my girlfriend, as she must have been during my dark period—but . . ."

"Yes?"

"Younger. And . . ."

"Yes?"

"Naked."

Maybe Namboothiri smiled; maybe he didn't. "All right," he said. "Definitely the right time period. And—"

I almost stopped him from moving the probe, not because the memory was so pleasant, although it was, but because this was the first bit of that time I'd recalled at all, and I was afraid we'd never get it or any other part of it, back, but—

"A classroom," I said. "And . . . perfume. God, yes, I'd completely forgotten: that crazy Eastern European chick who sat in front of me in that science-fiction course; always came to class drenched in perfume. What's her name . . ."

"You tell me."

I scrunched my eyes shut, and it came to me. "Bozena."

But suddenly her face—and the smell—were gone. Still: "But I don't understand. I'm remembering smells and sounds, not just visuals."

"Sure, and you remember those with the verbal indexing system, too, even though they're not words; elicited memories will be of your full sensorium, no matter how they're indexed."

"Ah, okay."

The next three memories he invoked were clearly of my toddler years, including what I rather suspect, as a Valentine's baby, was my first time seeing the ground without snow on it. And then it was back to 2001, or, at least, I assumed so; I'd lived in that campus residence for two years, but only memories from my dark period should be indexed here.

"And this?"

At first I thought I wasn't recalling anything. Then I became conscious of a sense of pressure all over my body. It was what I imagined being bound in a straitjacket felt like. Except I wasn't immobilized; I was moving headfirst, like I was being pulled up an incredibly narrow elevator shaft. No, not up—not a vertical movement. *Horizontal.* And I wasn't being pulled. I was being pushed. The pressure on me kept increasing, so much so that—

God.

—my head!

I could feel my head being crushed.

Another memory, from another time, another part of my brain, another indexing system, briefly came to me: my fear on that day I'd jumped up and almost smashed in Ronny Handler's head.

But my skull wasn't being crushed from one side; it was being compressed from all sides, and I felt the bones—

I felt the bones *sliding,* like tectonic plates, some of them even subducting . . .

And then, cold on the crown of my head; the pressure releasing on the top, then farther down, then—

Eyes stinging, because of . . .

Because of *light.*

"My God . . . My God . . ."

"What?"

"It's my birth!"

Namboothiri didn't sound surprised. "Yeah, there have been numerous reports of autistics remembering their births—because they continue to access the visual-indexing system their whole lives."

"It's—wow. Incredible."

"It's proof of concept, is what it is. Everything's stored in there, all right, right back to the beginning. Don't worry; my equipment records the coordinates of each contact. We should be able to elicit any of these memories again at will now. So, we're all set to find out exactly what went down all those years ago—call it '2001: A Memory Odyssey.' We'll pick up again in our next session."

"But—my God, please. Can't we continue?"

"I'm sorry, Jim. I really am. But you're not the only one with summer classes to teach."

I nodded, grateful for these few glimpses—but desperate for more.

30

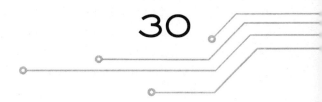

I N high-school physics—my last exposure to that discipline prior to reconnecting with Kayla—everyone gets to see the famous 1940 film of the collapse of the Tacoma Narrows Bridge, a suspension bridge more than a mile long over Puget Sound. In the film, the bridge starts swaying left and right in the wind, and the pavement undulates from side to side, rising and falling to breathtaking degrees, before the bridge finally breaks apart, its midsection crashing into the water far below. Every student watching that film is stunned—it looks so unreal, so impossible, you think it can't possibly be true, that nothing like that could ever happen in real life.

There's a similarly shocking film I sometimes show my students. Like the one of Galloping Gertie—the nickname given to that bridge—this one is old. It shows a man—a business executive, as the news stories later revealed, standing on a ledge high up the side of an office building. He's clearly despondent, clearly distressed, but someone—a tourist with a movie camera below—has caught sight of him. Soon, others note the man as well, and, as we can see when the tourist briefly tilts his lens down, quite a sizable crowd develops, all gawking up at the man.

And then a male voice rings out—the camera, aimed back up at the poor soul high above, doesn't show whose—cutting loose a single affricative syllable: *"Jump!"*

The man on the ledge is startled, and, briefly, there's a ripple of disapproving *tut-tuts* on the soundtrack, but then another male voice is heard: *"Jump!"* And a woman joins the chorus: *"Jump!"* And soon, the cry is going up throughout the crowd. *"Jump!" "Jump!" "Jump!"*

At last the poor fellow does indeed do what the crowd is bidding, more or less. He doesn't jump, but he does use the flats of his hands to push himself against the window behind him, and falls in a manner so similar to Don Draper's plunge on the opening credits of *Mad Men* that I've often wondered if the animators used this film as a source. The tourist dutifully records its all, including the impact on the pavement far below, the man hitting so hard that he actually bounces back up and then crashes down again, dead.

When I run the film in class, I usually stop with the man pushing off—no need to show the horror of a person actually dying, and, besides, I want the students to concentrate on the *other* horror: the reality that a group of strangers, come together purely by the happenstance of their individual wanderings, can suddenly exhibit conscienceless behavior that few if any of its members would display in isolation.

These days, office windows don't open, there are no ledges to step out on, and even the replacement Tacoma Narrows Bridge has suicide netting, and so there aren't as many smartphone videos of crowds urging someone to leap to their death as you might image. But similar things—one asshole starting something and it propagating like a contagion through a population—still happen. They happen all the time.

When I'd been in high school, they'd taught us that the Tacoma Narrows Bridge had collapsed due to resonance between high winds that matched the bridge's natural structural frequency. But that was wrong—a dated interpretation, even then. It turns out, as I learned years later, that the real cause was a completely different phenomenon, something called aeroelastic flutter. The old explanation, which seemed to make a kind of sense, was factually inaccurate.

And when I'd first seen that film of the suicidal jumper, all those years ago, my prof had said it was an example of *deindividuation,* the loss of self into a crowd.

But that, too, was wrong; that, too, was a dated interpretation, proceeding from the false assumption that there *was* a self to lose.

I'd known for months that Heather would be in town tonight. Gustav would never let her take a pleasure trip on her own, but even he understood that her business—the business that kept him in sports cars and fine liqueurs—required her to travel now and then; she was staying at my place.

There was a play I'd been dying to see at the Royal Manitoba Theatre Centre called *Shocking,* a fictionalized account of the life of Stanley Milgram; it was having a trial run here before moving to Broadway next year for the sixtieth anniversary of Milgram's infamous obedience-to-authority experiments.

I'd bought the tickets long before any Winnipeggers seriously thought the Jets might make it to the Stanley Cup—but, astonishingly, they had, and, as luck would have it, the night Heather and I were going to the play was also the night of the final game between them and the New Jersey Devils at the MTS Centre, just a kilometer west of the John Hirsch Mainstage. Parking downtown was out of the question: thousands who weren't inside the arena had come out to watch the game in bars and restaurants nearby; we took a bus to the Exchange District and walked through the warm June evening to the theater. Out front were bronze statues of the theater's founders—made, I suppose, in a founder foundry. The one of Hirsch was wearing glasses; I always thought that looked odd on a statue.

The program booklet had a reproduction of the "Public Announcement" Milgram had used to recruit test subjects from the New Haven community, offering "$4.00 for one hour of your time" for what he'd presented as a "study of memory." Milgram had been just twenty-seven when he'd started his experiments; the dapper fellow with the salt-and-pepper hair and full beard shown in psychology textbooks was Milgram-as-elder-statesman, not the haunted young man trying to make sense of the Eichmann trial and what Hannah Arendt would soon dub "the banality of evil"—the seeming ease with which average people could be made to slide into doing cruel things.

The actor who portrayed Milgram was a little old for the portions of the story set in 1961 but was quite compelling, and the reconstructions of Milgram's shock machine and lab were spot-on. The psychologist in me wanted to quibble with a couple of things—the playwright had relied too heavily on Gina Perry's 2013 book about Milgram's work, which I'd found unconvincing—but the theatergoer was thoroughly entertained, and Heather had sat rapt, absolutely motionless, throughout the entire performance.

As my sister and I headed out of the theater, I would have loved to have been able to tell her about the reality of p-zeds. The ability of Milgram and his assistants, as authority figures, to get subjects to administer what they thought were increasingly severe—and even life-threatening—electric shocks despite the protests and eventual screams of the recipients had confounded social-science researchers for six decades. Most of Milgram's subjects, although paying lip service to having qualms, kept ramping up the voltage again and again; his success rate was exactly what you'd expect if sixty percent of the human race were mindless zombies with a large dose of heartless psychopaths on top.

I didn't say any of that to Heather, though. Still, as we passed the statues again, I asked, "What did you think of the play?" It was getting on to 11:00 P.M., and the air had grown chilly.

"It was good," Heather replied.

"That all? Just good?"

She paused as if thinking, then: "Yeah."

We headed south, the Red River a long block to our left. Rounding a corner, I heard a great commotion up ahead: people shouting and yelling, and, within seconds, multiple car alarms, and the jangle of shattering glass.

"What the hell?" said Heather.

I pulled out my phone, clicked on the CBC app. The first headline said it all: "Jets Crash 5 to 4 in Sudden-Death Overtime."

"Christ," I said as what I assumed were store alarms started wailing—followed shortly thereafter by two white police cars barreling past us from behind, their roof lights on.

"We better turn back," I said, but within seconds, I could hear rioters behind us, as well. "Come on!" I shouted, pointing down a side street that looked empty. We started to run, but Heather, now in stocking feet after removing her high heels, couldn't keep up with me. I slowed down but quickly realized the mistake I'd made. The buildings on either side of us were mostly dark, but up ahead, where this street crossed another, I could see a mob running east, and, in rapid succession, I heard three more windows shatter and a trio of new alarms joining the cacophony.

To our left, smoke was billowing up above the dark silhouette of a four-story office building. There was a narrow, litter-strewn alleyway between two of the buildings here, and we headed down it. We'd probably be safe simply hiding, and I was all for that, but, incredibly, Heather urged me to keep going. "Come on!" she said. "Let's see!"

The *whoomp-whoomp-whoomp* of a helicopter caused me to look briefly up—and in that moment, Heather took off down the alley, heading *toward* the roaring crowd.

I followed, soon catching up with her. We emerged from the alleyway less than twenty meters from five muscular guys, all in Winnipeg Jets hoodies, flipping a red Hyundai Elantra onto its roof; its alarm was wailing. Heather stopped dead, and I have to confess I did, too; you hear about things like that on TV, but to actually see it was something else. The windshield shattered as the car's canopy collapsed under the vehicle's weight. The guys looked at their handiwork, and one of them shouted, "Fuck the Devils!" The others soon took up the cry, raising clenched fists to the black sky, and, to my astonishment, my own sister followed suit, hollering, "Fuck the Devils!"

It wasn't *"Jump! Jump! Jump!"*—but it *was* spreading.

"Heather!" I shouted. "For God's sake!"

The band moved on, and instead of going in the opposite direction, Heather started following them.

The alignment rule: pick a heading for yourself that's an average of everyone else's trajectories.

"Heather! Are you nuts?" I set off after her. The five hoods came to a halt, and so did my sister, giving them space.

The separation rule: avoid crowding your neighbors.

She turned and faced me. "Come on, Jim. You only live once."

The punks were trying to roll another car, but either they were running out of alcohol-fueled steam, or it was heavier than a Hyundai, because they weren't managing to get it elevated past the tipping point.

Beyond them, a fire was burning brightly: another person's car had been set ablaze. And someone else was throwing things at a storefront, trying to get the glass to shatter—

—which, at last, it did, the sound a sharp counterpoint to all the other noises rising up about us.

Heather tipped her head down, and I thought she was averting her gaze from the carnage, but then I realized she was looking around for something she herself could hurl through a window.

I surged in, took her by the elbow, swung her around, and pulled her along with me back into the relative safety of the alleyway.

"For God's sake," I said, "there are security cameras everywhere, and you're a fucking officer of the court."

She looked pissed for a moment, then nodded and lifted her shoulders. "Yeah, I guess."

The rioting was likely to last all night. Winnipeg had never had something like this before, but Vancouver had—twice—and other cities all over the globe had seen this sort of hooliganism in the past, although more often, in fact, in the winning team's hometown than in the loser's.

I could smell smoke now, and the background of shouts and sirens, of alarms and things shattering, continued.

I stared at my sister. Christ, could it be? The whole point of philosopher's zombies is that, at least most of the time, there's no way to tell one from someone who is thinking on a conscious level. And, damn it all, the revelation of their existence had been so easy to accept in the abstract—six out of every ten humans lacking an inner life. But my own sister?

I continued to look at her, and she looked back at me, and I tried to fathom what, if anything, was going on behind those brown eyes of hers, as the mob surged and roared through the city I called home. I pulled Heather close, hugging her in a way I hadn't for decades, keeping her warm and safe against the flickering flames. My eyes stung—but surely it was from the smoke. Sirens blared from all directions, and we waited, my sister and I, together and yet oh-so-apart.

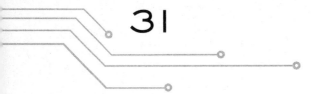

31

THE rioting continued for hours. Fire trucks and ambulances were stymied by overturned cars and barricades made of whatever torn-down fences, garbage cans, recycling bins, loose lumber, and other junk people had pushed into the middle of the roads.

I had a plan that I hoped would get us to a safe haven, which started with having us backtrack along Main Street to Lombard Avenue. On the way, we saw another car being flipped, and three more that already had been. A pair of red Canada Post mailboxes had been knocked over, and one of them had spilled its contents onto the sidewalk. The building on our left had five large square ground-floor windows in a row, and Heather and I watched as a guy used a crowbar to smash each of them in turn, a perfect bingo of destruction.

We exited Lombard at Waterfront Drive by a railway bridge that crossed the hundred-meter width of the Red River. I'd hoped we could clamber up and get over to the residential neighborhood on the east side, but there were already a bunch of people on the tracks, the safety fencing having been torn down. And so, instead, Heather and I headed south along Waterfront Drive, the trees of Stephen Juba Park between us and the river on our left and the deserted Shaw Park baseball stadium on our right. The air was thick with smoke—some of it burning wood, some of it marijuana. We continued cautiously forward. Several of the streetlights high atop their standards looked like they'd been shot out with rifles.

Two young punks came at us from out of the row of trees, each brandishing a two-by-four. I couldn't make out their faces in the darkness, but it was clear we were going to be attacked when one of them said, "Holy shit! It's Professor Marchuk!" They turned and hightailed it into the night.

My heart was pounding, and Heather looked scared to death as we continued cautiously along. One drunken guy lying in the grass waved a knife at us and called out in slurred voice, "Come here, asshole! I'll cut your balls off!"

There was no way to make it the ten kilometers to my home on foot with Heather in high heels, and there was too much broken glass now for her to continue to go shoeless. But looming ahead to the south was the Canadian Museum for Human Rights, now just a few hundred meters away.

We pushed forward, but if there was rioting in the Exchange District, there was rioting in The Forks, as well; I could hear a roar coming from that direction, and flames were licking up from just about exactly where I'd taken Kayla to dinner not that long ago.

Heather and I hurried along. We passed close to two guys involved in a knife fight—reminding me of that night all those years ago, except—

Except *that* night was just my imagination; *this* one was real—and so much worse. There was a scream from behind us as we pushed ahead, followed by someone growling, "That'll teach you!"

Finally, we made it to the long, roofless, stone tunnel leading to the museum's entrance. I pulled out my phone and scrolled until I found the number for the security desk, which I'd called occasionally in the past for after-hours access.

"CMHR Security," said a man's voice.

"Hello. This is James Marchuk. I'm on the Board of—"

"Oh, hi, Dr. Marchuk. This is Abdul."

"Abdul, thank God! I'm just outside the main entrance to the museum; it's crazy out here. Can you let me and my sister in?"

"Oh, my, yes—two secs," he said, clicking off. We waited anxiously; it was more like two minutes than two seconds, and felt like two hours. At last, Abdul opened the farthest left of the four glass doors, and Heather and I scurried inside; the guard locked the door immediately behind us. "We've got three calls in to WPS for support," Abdul said. "They're trashing the grounds on the south side. The Gandhi statue has been toppled. It won't be safe to leave again tonight."

"God," said Heather, shaking.

"Let me take you guys upstairs," Abdul said. "At least there are couches you can sleep on." We nodded, and he led us down the stone corridor and past the giant wall panels proclaiming in English and French, *"All human beings are born free and equal in dignity and rights."* But the interior lighting was off, and I could only make the words out because I already knew what they said.

Much of the museum's shell was made of glass, so when the sun came up the next morning, the building was filled with light. I hadn't been aware of actually falling asleep, but I must have at some point because it was the brightness that woke me. I staggered out of the curator's office I'd been sleeping in and went to find Heather.

She was standing at a railing, looking down at the alabaster-clad bridges crisscrossing the museum's cavernous interior. I'd stood here before, also looking down, and the spectacle always reminded me of the scene in *Forbidden Planet* in which Dr. Morbius shows his visitors the twenty-mile-deep cubic interior of the dead-and-buried Krell city on Altair IV. Morbius's words from that classic film popped into my head. *The heights they had reached! But then, seemingly on the threshold of some supreme accomplishment which was to have crowned their entire history this all-but-divine race perished in a single night . . .*

"Hey," I said, joining my sister staring into the abyss. "You all right?"

"I guess."

"Let's see if we can get back to my place, okay?" I tried to make a joke of it. "It was bad enough being out there last night; wait till the school buses full of kids on field trips arrive here."

"School's out for the summer," she said, her tone flat.

"Yeah," I replied. "I guess it is." And that's when I turned around, looked out through the great curving glass, and saw the plumes of black smoke against the blood-red dawn.

It was a shocking bus trip back to my home. I was used to other passengers chatting with friends or having their heads bent down, thumb-typing on their phones, but everyone was looking out the streaked, dusty windows. Many people, including Heather, had mouths agape; the pedestrians I saw were likewise looking shell-shocked.

Of course, most of the damage was superficial: smashed windows, torn-down fences, obscene graffiti; there was only so much mayhem people who'd arrived unprepared could cause. Still, it was distressing to see, and the CJOB app said there had been eleven fatalities—one of which was almost certainly from the knife fight Heather and I had passed—and thirty more people were in hospital.

I'd called Kayla from the museum to let her know I was all right, but we only spoke briefly. She hadn't been aware of the riots here; we arranged to Skype this evening.

The bus let us off at the far side of the strip mall from my condo building. We walked through its parking lot, past my building's outdoor pool, into my lobby, and headed up. My unit had two washrooms but only one shower; we both desperately needed to clean up, but I let Heather go first. While she showered, I went out on the balcony and looked out at the river implacably rolling along. About fifty meters upriver from me, near one of the picnic tables, a couple of guys were fishing.

My thoughts turned to Saskatoon, but only partially to Kayla; yes, I missed her enormously and certainly could use her hugs after last night. But I was also thinking about CLS, and wondering if there was any possible way to get my sister down on Victoria's beamline so I could know for sure whether Heather really was a Q1.

I ran through memories of our childhood together: times she'd made me laugh, times she'd made me cry, times when I'd been worried about her—and times when it seemed she'd genuinely been worried about me. Could she have just been going through the motions? Granted, I'd had no particular psychological acumen as a child or teenager, but surely now, in retrospect, it should be obvious one way or the other.

We had been very different in high school. She'd hung around with the popular crowd, doing all the things popular kids did, drinking and smoking and cutting classes. And she certainly followed fashion trends, and to this day I can recite the lyrics of every Spice Girls song, having heard her play their damn albums over and over again. Me, I'd refused to wear blue jeans—I didn't own a pair until I was thirty—or T-shirts with any kind of advertising on them, and I'd listened mostly to the great sci-fi movie soundtracks of John Williams and Jerry Goldsmith. Granted, she had gotten good marks in school—sometimes better than my own— but, then again, taking in input and mindlessly spitting out output was precisely what p-zeds were presumably adept at.

I was startled by the sound of the screen door behind me sliding open. Heather had changed into clean clothes. "Your turn," she said.

I nodded and headed inside. It felt good to get all that grime and sweat off me, and, afterward, I grabbed a quick shave, then headed into my bedroom, which was just past the little guest room Heather was using, and put on fresh clothing. My one pair of blue jeans was hanging in my closet. I did wear them sometimes when I taught in the summer, but I stopped myself as I reached for them and instead took down a pair of beige slacks.

When I was finished, I returned to the living room. Heather was still on the balcony, looking at the river. I did that often myself, but I was always woolgathering as I did so—which was physically indistinguishable from just idly standing there, in neutral, waiting for something to prod activity.

I stepped out onto the balcony. "What're you doing?"

"Nothing," she said. And then, as if that required a justification, "Enjoying the view."

I looked at her, wondering. I know, I know—I'd wondered about

Kayla, too, but Kayla *had* been scanned on Victoria's beamline, and, besides, *she* continued to endlessly surprise me. But my sister? Oh, I'd surprised *her,* apparently, when I hadn't known about what had happened to our grandfather, but when was the last time she had surprised me—prior to last night, that is?

I turned and looked out at the river, too, and—

—and something was going on. The two fishermen were still there, all right, but so were a couple of uniformed cops, and two more men were crab-walking down the grassy embankment.

"Come on!" I said, moving back inside. Heather followed, and, as we headed down the stairs, I thought about whether this was any different from what had happened last night. As we exited out into the late-morning sunshine, I decided it was: last night, she'd fallen in with the mob; today, I was simply curious.

Fortunately, Heather was back to wearing flat shoes, and it took us less than a minute to trot over to where all the excitement was going on. We weren't the first rubberneckers to show up; a pair of female joggers in sweatpants had stopped to gawk.

Something large had been hauled up onto the riverbank: a bundle more than a meter long swaddled in green garbage bags tied around with duct tape.

A cop was keeping us at bay, but we jockeyed for a better view—and got it. The bags had ripped open on one side and a lower leg and foot were protruding.

"Oh, God," said Heather softly.

We stood there transfixed; the guys in plain clothes were clearly crime-scene investigators. One of them snapped pictures of everything, while the other took samples of the skin, which was smooth and the color of coffee with cream. The uniformed cops, meanwhile, were getting statements from the fishermen; I strained to listen. From what I could make out, when they first saw the bundle, they'd assumed some jerk had dumped his garbage in the river, but, as it drifted by, one of them saw the exposed skin. They were both wearing hip waders, and had managed to snare the package before the current took it away; they'd hauled it ashore and called 911.

The crime-scene guys eventually went to take the body away, picking up the bundle—only to have the garbage bags split completely open and the corpse drop out and roll a bit down the embankment. And there she was: an Indigenous woman, with long black hair, and the side of her head caved in from a heavy blow; she looked to be no more than twenty.

I fought to keep what little there was in my stomach down, and thought briefly of that story I sometimes told my students when introducing utilitarianism about the girl drowning in this very river. The bridge I spoke about in that scenario was just south of here; I looked over at it for a moment.

But there were two salient differences. First, my little hypothetical was just that, a made-up example; this was all too real. And, second, that hapless child had simply slipped and fallen in. But this young woman—somebody's daughter, possibly somebody's sister, perhaps even somebody's mother—had been brutally murdered, and although it would doubtless be some time before a report would be made public, if she was like the legions of others who'd gone before her, she'd probably been sexually assaulted.

Yes, the carnage in Texas was getting media attention, but that was only because it was new. The endless stream of missing and murdered Indigenous women and girls here in Manitoba should have been a national disgrace. Back in 2014 and 2015, when the tally had been just twelve hundred natives unaccounted for, then–Prime Minister Stephen Harper, when demands went up for a federal inquiry, had said that the issue "isn't really high on our radar, to be honest."

Last night's stay at the Human Rights Museum had been physically uncomfortable, but my mind went back further to when I'd visited it with Kayla, attending that reception in the Garden of Contemplation, and how socially uncomfortable that had been. But prior to Nick Smith's unconscious mimicry of him, that African-American fellow—Darius something—had said he'd been so pleased by the way he was treated here in Winnipeg: "Now I know what it feels like to be white."

But that was only because the choice of out-group was arbitrary: in one place, it might be Jews; in another, those of African ancestry; in Texas now, Latinos. And here, in Winnipeg, the geographic center of the

North American continent, it was Native Canadians who were routinely discarded—a fact that had led *Maclean's* to call Winnipeg "Canada's most-racist city" in 2015. Usually one to pop up with a factoid for every occasion, I'd kept my mouth shut when Darius had made his comment, just as so many of us had for so long.

Heather had been right this morning: school's out for the summer. Everywhere I looked, all over the planet, shit was getting real.

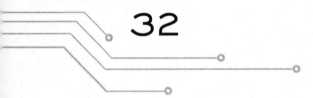

32

HEATHER had an afternoon of business meetings—the reason Gustav had allowed her trip out here—and when they were done, I met her for a final cup of coffee, then drove her out to the airport. I could have just dropped her at the curb, but instead I parked and helped her in with her luggage. My sister had always been one to overpack. I used to think that was because she was contemplating myriad possible scenarios at her destination; now I wondered if it was simply that she quite literally couldn't make up her mind about what to bring and what to leave behind.

Winnipeg James Armstrong Richardson International Airport has an awful lot of syllables in its name for what is in fact a fairly small facility. After I'd hugged my sister goodbye and she'd headed through security, I found myself looking wistfully at the departure board, listing both a WestJet and an Air Canada flight to Saskatoon this evening. But I'd have to content myself with Skype.

We ivory-tower types usually get to avoid rush-hour traffic, but tonight I had to endure it: the hundreds of thousands of cars that moved about each day ebbing and flowing like tides. Some of the drivers were on autopilot only for this boring routine, but for most, this part of the day was no different than any other—just moving with the flock, following the programming, doing what everybody else was doing.

I'd missed both breakfast and lunch, so I went through the drive-through at McDonald's—billions and billions served—and got fries and a salad, then continued the slow slog back to my home, only occasionally glancing out my side window at the mess still being cleaned up from last night.

When I at last pulled into my parking lot, I walked up the grassy hillock to see where all the action had taken place this afternoon, but everyone was gone without a trace, and the whole awful thing would soon be forgotten, just another statistic.

Once I got back into my apartment, I checked my email. There was one from Bhavesh Namboothiri:

> Sorry, Jim! I know we have an appointment tomorrow, but my
> home was vandalized pretty badly last night—some of the
> rioters don't just hate the Devils, I guess. I'll be in touch when
> I'm able to resume our sessions.

I went and lay down on my bed. I felt sorry for poor Namboothiri, but I wasn't too upset that we had to postpone. I was having a hard-enough time facing the present just now; I wasn't sure I was up for horrors from my past.

A little after 5:00 P.M., Kayla Huron removed her dosimeter and put it on the rack by CLS's glass-fronted entrance. Victoria Chen was heading out at the same time, and she unclipped her dosimeter, too, letting her long black hair fall around her shoulders. They walked toward their cars together, the sun still high in the western sky. Saskatoon was known as the sunshine capital of Canada—a city of light; just one of the reasons that it had beaten out London, Ontario, to be the home of the nation's synchrotron-research facility.

"Any plans for this evening?" Kayla asked Vic as they made their way across the asphalt.

"Just a quiet night at home reading. You?"

"After I pick up Ryan from my mom's, just dinner and TV. Oh, and Skyping with Jim."

Vic looked at her. "How's that going?"

"Honestly? The whole greatest-good-for-the-greatest-number thing begins to irritate after a while. I mean, yeah, I *get* it, but . . ."

"Yeah. But, you know, at least he walks the walk."

"Oh, yeah. He's totally serious about it."

"For sure," said Vic. "And the world *would* be a better place if everyone thought like him."

"True."

"But really," Vic said, "the world would be a better place if everyone thought, *period.*"

Ever since my divorce—ever since I'd gone back to living alone—I had reverted a bit to my student ways. Not completely, of course: I liked craft beers; Kraft Dinner, not so much. But I did have a fondness for the convenience of microwave popcorn, and I heated up a bag. I took it over to the couch, positioned my laptop on top of the footstool to properly face me, and opened Skype. It was still two minutes until 8:00 P.M., our agreed-upon time to chat this particular night. Kayla was showing as offline. I idly looked at my other contacts: lawyer Juan Garcia was online, presumably in California; my ex Anna-Lee was online, too—and I wistfully imagined Virgil was playing somewhere near her. My little boy. I took a deep breath and let it out, a slow, sad exhalation.

The clock in my taskbar changed to 8:00, with still no sign of Kayla; she normally had the scientist's obsession with punctuality. I nibbled some popcorn, and checked Facebook and Twitter while I waited for her, but, when 8:10 rolled around, I was reaching to shut my laptop's lid when I noticed her status change from offline to online. I selected "Video Call," straightened up, listened to Skype's jaunty ringing for a few seconds, and then, as often happened, I heard Kayla before I saw her.

"Jim?" she said, sounding anxious. "Thank God you're still online."

I began to say, "Are you—" when the picture finally popped in. At first it was dark—the background brighter than her—but then her webcam adjusted itself, and there she was, the left half of her face bloodied, red hair askew.

"God!" I said, my heart suddenly thundering. "What happened? Are you okay?"

She took a deep, shuddering breath. "I'll be all right. Just scared to death."

"Tell me what happened."

"It's crazy out there. I stopped at a traffic light, and punks swarmed in and started rocking my car back and forth."

"Christ. Why?"

"I don't know. But they're rioting here, too, just like Winnipeg last night."

"Over a hockey game?"

"God knows," she said. "I got away from them, but my car slammed into another vehicle. Somebody cut in front of me, trying to get away from some other assholes."

"Holy shit."

"Look, I gotta get this cleaned up." I thought she was going to terminate the call, but instead she said, "Here . . ." and the image went wild as she picked up her MacBook. I saw flashes of her walls and ceiling, and then, after a moment, she'd clearly perched the machine on her bathroom counter. I watched from the side and looking up as she leaned into the mirror and used a tan washcloth to daub a cut on her forehead; the cloth came away crimson.

"Should you see a doctor?"

"The tow-truck guy said if you're ambulatory, they're saying don't come in tonight; they're full in the emergency rooms right across the city." She ran some water—sounding quite loud to me—then washed her face. "There," she said. "Not too bad. No need for stitches."

"Let me see."

She moved closer to the camera and I had a look at the cut; she was right that it would probably heal on its own although the area around it had turned visibly more purple since she'd first logged on. "God," I said. "I wish I was there."

She moved back. "So do I, baby." She looked off camera, in the direction, I knew, of her bathroom's little frosted window. "The night's just begun, and I suspect we haven't seen the worst of it yet."

Kayla and I talked for a while longer, then she had to go comfort Ryan, who was distressed by what had become a constant background wailing of sirens and alarms punctuated by the sound of gunshots.

I didn't hear anything untoward in my own neighborhood that night, and so I wasn't aware until I turned on the TV that rioting was going on again in downtown Winnipeg as well as in Saskatoon, and, as I saw unfolding on the screen, in Vancouver and Edmonton and Toronto and Montreal, too. Although in some of the footage you could see people making halfhearted attempts to pretend this was still about hockey—wearing jerseys, brandishing sticks like clubs—it was clear, to me at least, that for the most part it was just looting coupled with mayhem for the sake of mayhem. The current catalyst happened to have been a hockey game; in San Francisco in 2019, new traffic ordinances; in Ferguson in 2015, the anniversary of an unconscionable jury verdict; in Knoxville in 2010, college football coach Lane Kiffin defecting to a rival team. The spark didn't matter; a similar conflagration could ignite anytime anywhere.

Of course, there were times when it had gone the other way. In a single week in 2015—the first week of summer, as it happened—the US Supreme Court upheld Obamacare and ruled that same-sex marriage was a constitutional right, and the Confederate flag started coming down across the South as Amazon, eBay, Sears, and Walmart all stopped selling merchandise depicting it. Facebook was a sea of rainbows and high-fives. People who'd been hoping and praying for those very things said they couldn't believe how quickly the tide had turned. That time, the light side of the Force had caught the wave; tonight, sadly, it was the dark side.

I saw Prime Minister Nenshi urging calm, and interviews with various mayors and chiefs of police exhorting people to stay indoors. Even the US channels were covering the Toronto riots, which looked to be running all along Yonge Street from Harbourfront to Bloor; it was an hour later there, meaning it had ticked past midnight, so that, as a commentator observed, this was technically the third day of rioting in Canada.

Eventually, I got up off the couch, taking my popcorn bag, a few unpopped kernels still rattling around in it, to the kitchen, and tossing it in the trash. And then slowly, sadly, I headed off to bed, hoping against hope that at some point soon reason would prevail.

33

THE mayor of Winnipeg urged people to remain indoors the next night. No official curfew had been imposed, but I did stay in, watching TV news and surfing on my tablet.

By now, the violence was overwhelming local police everywhere. Canadian Forces personnel had been deployed to aid with riot control and to protect provincial legislatures as well as Parliament Hill in Ottawa; that city, as well as Calgary, had erupted in violence on this third night. The only thing that seemed to be keeping it from being a total coast-to-coast bloodbath was that so few Canadians owned handguns or automatic weapons. Still, the death count was into three figures here in Winnipeg, where it had all begun, and it was at least a dozen in every other city that had rioting.

Fox News was gleeful in its reporting: "All eyes are on Socialist Canada and its Muslim prime minister," said Sean Hannity, "wondering what he will do to quell the unrest up there."

Coverage of the continuing attacks on undocumented immigrants in Texas was all but absent on Fox, although MSNBC reported that the vigilantism was spreading, with three people turning up dead near

Las Cruces, New Mexico, and two south of Phoenix, Arizona, states that had nothing like the McCharles Act in place.

Meanwhile, the body of another dead Indigenous woman had been found here in Winnipeg, and two more in northern Manitoba; also, two Cree men near Thompson had been killed by white teenagers in a drive-by shooting as they walked along the side of a road.

Boko Haram was still running amuck in Nigeria, and statistics released today showed that over 8,000 Jews left France for Israel in 2019. "You can smell it in the air," said a Parisian rabbi. "A pogrom is coming here, mark my words."

Thursday, I had a departmental meeting after my classes ended, but that was done by three. I got in my white Mazda and began the long drive to Saskatoon, a large coffee in my cupholder and a twenty-pack of Timbits on the passenger seat. Once out of the city, I didn't turn on the radio; I didn't put on an audiobook; I just drove in silence, particularly enjoying the times when the highway was empty and I could fool myself that I was all alone in the universe and nothing bad was happening anywhere.

But, once again, the illusion was shattered as a pair of high beams lanced through the darkness at me from behind.

I was doing a hundred klicks, but the guy behind me was closing. There was no one coming this way, though, so he had plenty of room to pass if he wanted to on the left, and I moved toward the shoulder to give him even more space.

The gap between us was narrowing. I hated assholes who didn't dim their lights in circumstances like this, but his were like a pair of supernovae. He was maybe fifty meters behind me.

Twenty.

Ten.

And then, suddenly, he was right beside me, but—

—but he wasn't passing me. He was *pacing* me, staying next to my car. I looked out, but my own night vision had been shot by his headlamps, and in the dim interior of his car, all I could make out were two silhouetted figures. I decided to ease up on the accelerator so my car would fall back, but when I did that, he copied me, and—

Fuck!

His passenger-side door scraped against my driver-side one. I tried to give him more room, moving fully onto the shoulder, but he kept slamming into my side, pushing me farther and farther to the right.

I hit the brakes, meaning his next attempt to push me off the road caused him to cut in front of me instead. He spun sideways, I skidded forward, and we collided, both of us pinwheeling into the adjacent field.

My airbag deployed, trapping me long enough that by the time it deflated one of the guys was out and had smashed my driver's side window and opened the door. I felt myself being hauled out, the dome light in my car letting me at last see their faces—two kids, maybe eighteen or twenty, one in a jean jacket, the other in a leather one.

The man in leather was off to the side; I think he'd been the driver. He pointed at me, and said, "Finish him."

And that's when I realized the guy in denim was brandishing a length of metal pipe about as long as his forearm. I was in the gap between the two cars but jumped on the hood, pivoted on my ass, and took off into the field adjacent to the road, a flat expanse that went on to the dark horizon; I'd be more than content if they watched me run away for three days.

"Get him!" shouted the driver—the guy, quite literally, in the driver's seat; probably a psychopath, with a p-zed stooge who would follow his every command.

I ran as fast as I could, which, with epinephrine coursing through me, was pretty damn fast—not that there was anywhere to go, but I hoped the guy would give up after a bit, and—

Jesus Fucking Christ!

My left foot went into a prairie dog's burrow, and I pitched forward, smashing my face into hard, dry earth. Jean-jacket quickly caught up and loomed over me, the metal pipe raised high above his head.

I rolled on my back and lashed out with my legs, ensnaring my attacker's right ankle, and even though the terrain was flat, I succeeded in pulling him off balance and he fell. I scrambled to my feet and, smashing one shoe down on his wrist, managed to wrestle the pipe from him, and—

And there was no one around, no one to help, no farmhouse, no anything. I thought the guy, seeing I had his weapon, would scurry away and leave me to catch my breath, but he didn't. Leather-jacket had more—*some!*—sense, and had gotten back into their car and was now speeding off, but this guy was implacable; he had his orders, and he was going to carry them out. I was holding the pipe in both hands, the way a slugger would grip a baseball bat, but the guy pulled out a switchblade and continued to come at me, so I took off again across the field—but it was inevitable that he'd catch up; he was younger and had longer legs.

My heart was pounding, my lungs aching. Like Menno, I thought of myself as a pacifist—but a pacifist need not be a passivist.

And so I stopped running.

Turned.

Planted my feet firmly on the ground.

Raised the lead pipe—like Moonwatcher raising the thigh bone—and brought it down, down, down onto Jean-jacket's head.

The sound I'd avoided all those decades ago when I'd spared Ronny Handler—the sound I'd always assumed would be a loud cracking, like the one my mother's porcelain vase had made when I'd accidentally knocked it to the floor—turned out to actually be a dull thud, as if I'd hit a tree stump with an ax handle.

But regardless of the acoustics, the visual effect was . . .

Yes.

The visual, in the moonlight, was *satisfying.*

The skull *denting,* the scalp *splitting,* and blood *pouring out* . . .

I staggered for a moment—but not as much as the guy in front of me did. He swayed back and forth, and then, like the Twin Towers coming down, collapsed vertically into a heap. I spun on my heel and ran toward my car.

Of course, I called it in. The RCMP arrived first, and then the EMTs, who pronounced the guy dead at the scene. The officers were sympathetic, but they had me follow them in my car into Regina. I wasn't charged with anything, and so they let me go to a hotel instead of staying in a holding cell, and by the time all the paperwork was done the next morning, it was close to ten. I continued on the last couple of hours to Saskatoon—but, it became apparent that the damage to my car was worse than I'd thought; I barely made it there, and, after calling my insurance company, I took the car to a body shop for repairs.

I wanted to go straight to the Canadian Light Source, but as much as I couldn't wait to see Kayla, she had to make a living. Instead, I took a cab to her place, and, using the spare key I still had, let myself in, took a quick shower, went to her bedroom, and collapsed.

I was awoken by the sound of the front door opening, and, looking at Kayla's nightstand clock, I saw I'd slept for almost three hours.

"Sweetheart?" I called out.

"Yes, honey?" And then a giggle. It was Ryan, not her mom.

"Ryan?" I said.

"And Rebekkah," came her grandmother's voice.

"I'll be down in a minute," I called back.

I quickly dressed and headed downstairs. Ryan rushed over and gave me a hug, which I sorely needed. But when we disengaged, she looked at me with horror. "What happened to you?"

My hand went to my bruised cheek. I'm all in favor of telling kids the truth—there's no Santa Claus; your parents leave the money under the pillow when you lose a tooth; babies come from sex; when you die, that's it, there's nothing more—but deciding whether to say "Mommy's boyfriend just killed a man" was above my pay grade; I'd let Kayla make the call on what her daughter should know. "I was in a car accident," I said, which at least wasn't wholly untrue.

"Wow," Ryan said. "Does it hurt?"

"Yes," I said, and that was certainly the truth.

"I gotta go pee," Ryan announced, which was just as well; I needed a minute—or a lifetime—to pull myself together. I exchanged a few remarks with Rebekkah, then she left, and I went to the kitchen. There was a pitcher of lemonade in the fridge; I poured two glasses and took them over to the dining room with its bookcases. Ryan joined me when she was done in the washroom. "How was day camp?" I asked.

"Good." She looked at me and scrunched up her mouth, thinking.

"What?" I said.

"Can I ask you a question, Jiminy?"

"Of course."

"Are you going to marry Mommy?"

"We haven't talked about it."

"But are you?"

"Honestly, I don't know."

She looked down at the floor. "Oh."

"We'll just have to see how things go, okay?"

She nodded, then, looking up at me again: "Have you been married before?"

"Yes."

"What happened?"

I lifted my hands slightly. "She left me."

"Why?"

"We disagreed about what we wanted."

"Oh. What did you want?"

"The greatest good for the greatest number."

"And what's the greatest number?"

I thought about that, long and hard, thought about this wonderful young lady, thought about my boy Virgil, thought about everything, and, at last I drew Ryan into another warm hug. "Two-point-nine."

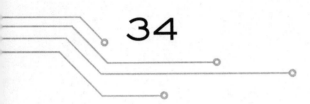

34

THE next morning, Kayla entered the office she shared with Victoria, who today was wearing a black turtleneck and black leather pants; the combo probably wouldn't work on anyone else, but she rocked it. Vic was staring intently at an image on a forty-inch monitor.

"What's that?" asked Kayla, standing behind her and bending over to have a look.

"The scan I made of Ross on the beamline," replied Victoria.

Kayla put a hand on Vic's shoulder. "When I want to creep on an ex, I look at their Facebook wall or OKCupid profile."

"It's not that," said Vic. She pointed at one part of the display. "See here? That's the spike showing he's got one electron in superposition—making him a Q1, a p-zed."

"Yes."

"But look here," said Vic. She pointed at a serpentine line high up on the Y-axis, which was marked with a logarithmic scale.

Kayla nodded. "The background stuff."

"Exactly. The entanglement we've observed before."

"Right."

"And, so far, it's never changed, right?"

"Right," said Kayla. "If it would *do* something, maybe we could figure out what it represented."

"Exactly—but look! It *has* changed, see? Right here." Vic pointed at where the whole line jumped a small amount.

"It increased," said Kayla, surprised.

"Exactly. It suddenly went up, and it stayed up."

"Huh."

"I ran a test on myself yesterday." Vic did something with her mouse, and a split-screen display came up showing two graphs that looked almost identical. "Both of these are me." Her triple-superposition Q3 status showed as three distinct spikes on each of the graphs. "But see?" She pointed first to the left-hand display, then the right. "The entanglement level at the top is up from my previous reading, too; that's never happened before."

Kayla frowned. "Go back to Ross's display."

More mouse movements, and the screen changed again.

"You had Ross in here on Sunday the ninth?"

"Yep. Jeff okayed it."

"Sure, no problem." Kayla leaned in, looking at the times marked on the bottom of the graph. "And the entanglement level on his chart went up at 11:19 A.M.?"

"And twenty-two seconds," said Vic, pointing at the figure. "And it stayed up, right through to the end of the run I did with him."

"Wow," said Kayla softly.

"What?"

"Do you know where I was then?"

"A Sunday morning? Well, we can rule out High Mass."

"I was at Tommy Douglas Long-Term Care."

"Oh, my God! Right! That's the day you revived your brother!"

"Jim recorded it on video. It's in our Dropbox." Kayla gestured for Vic to get up, and she took her place at the keyboard. Kayla opened a browser and banged away for a few moments until she had the shared folder on-screen—and discovered that Vic had her computer set to show large thumbnails; playing-card-sized images of Kayla and Jim making love popped up on the monitor.

"Umm," said Kayla.

"NSFW," said Vic, grinning from ear to ear. She reached over and took the mouse, using it to change the view to a plain directory listing, and then she stepped back and let Kayla find the file she was looking for. A couple of clicks later, and the video Jim had shot started playing.

"My God . . ." said Vic, as Travis's eyes opened for the first time in almost two decades.

Kayla backed up to the precise moment at which Travis visibly regained consciousness. The little slider at the bottom of the screen showed they were one minute and forty-three seconds into the video. She then flipped back to the file listing, which showed the time at which Jim had begun making the recording, then did the math in her head: the creation-time stamp of the video file plus an additional one minute and forty-three seconds was . . . 11:19:25 A.M. She said the figure aloud.

Vic let out a low whistle. "That's really close . . ."

"Too close to be a coincidence," said Kayla. "And when I used the quantum tuning fork on him the second time—it didn't work until I flipped it upside down—it was a few seconds before his eyes opened. So, the increase in entanglement you recorded here on Ross occurred at just about the moment Travis woke up. Want to bet that your own level increased at that exact moment, too?"

"Meaning me, my ex-boyfriend, and your brother were—are— linked?" said Vic. "The three of us are quantally entangled? But why on Earth would that be the case? I mean, Travis and Ross have never even met."

"That's an excellent point," said Kayla, peering in puzzlement at the screen.

Kayla had invited Victoria over for dinner, and the four of us, including Ryan, were still sitting at the square table, although I'd pushed back so I could turn my chair sideways and cross my legs; tomorrow, we'd go to Rebekkah's place to have dinner with her and Travis.

The ladies had had pot roast while I'd picked my way through a ginormous salad. During dinner, Ryan had told us at length about how her day-camp counselor had tried to explain the awful goings-on. Although Ryan was still frightened, it sounded to my psychologist's ear like the counselor had taken the right approach: not sugarcoating things, but not being alarmist, either.

The conversation segued to how I would deal in my summer classes with the dark turn current events had taken—and that somehow led to psychologists who got spooked by their own research.

"It can take a lot out of you," I said. "Look at Phil Zimbardo. His Stanford Prison Guard experiment was in 1971, but he was still wrestling with what happened to his students, and to himself, thirty-odd years later, when he published his book *The Lucifer Effect,* about how good people turn evil. I have it on one of my required-reading lists."

"What about the shock-machine guy?" asked Victoria.

"Stanley Milgram," I said, nodding. "He went the other way after that experiment. He hated that it had become this giant thing, with everyone questioning his ethics, so he retreated into studies that no one could consider controversial. He pioneered the 'lost-letter' technique, which tests if people will take the trouble to put stamped envelopes they find on the ground into a mailbox. Turns out most people will, if the letter has a neutral or positive addressee, such as a respected charity, but won't if it's addressed to 'Friends of the Nazi Party,' or something like that."

"Still exploring good and evil," Kayla noted.

"True," I said, "but in a way that couldn't hurt anybody. And he spent even more time on something completely benign. Milgram called it the small-world problem, and he was one of the first people to really study it—but it's better known now as Six Degrees of Separation, or Six Degrees of Kevin Bacon. Milgram showed that any two people are connected by a very small chain, and—"

Victoria sat up straight. "Like Travis and Ross!"

"Pardon?" said Jim.

"Travis—Kayla's brother—he's connected to my ex-boyfriend Ross, right, in that very way. Travis to Kayla to me to Ross; hell, that's only three degrees of separation!"

Suddenly Kayla seemed excited, too. "My God, that could be it!"

"Do you have a computer here with Maple on it?" asked Vic.

Kayla nodded. "Yes, yes! In my study."

"What's up?" I asked.

Kayla replied hurriedly: "There seems to be entanglement between Travis, Ross, and Vic, and we've been trying to puzzle that out." I knew that entanglement was a quantum connection—entities intertwined so that no matter how far apart they were physically, what happened to one instantly affected the other.

Kayla's excitement was palpable. "At the moment Travis gained consciousness, the background entanglement reading ratcheted up a notch for Ross, and we think for Vic, too. And it *can't* be that Vic's reading went up just because a random new person gained consciousness, right? I mean, people are born and die all the time, yet we've never seen that sort of boost."

Vic was already on her feet, and Kayla rose while continuing to speak: "But if the spike is proportional to the degree of separation, then someone as close on the small-world network as Travis is to Ross—even though they've never actually met—would register, at least a little, while the constant distant background churn of total strangers coming in and out of existence would be too insignificant to be seen."

The two women hustled off to Kayla's study, talking animatedly. I turned to Ryan. "Let's load the dishwasher, then watch some TV."

"Netflix has *Inspector Gadget!*"

"You got it, Ginger Ale."

I ended up putting Ryan to bed on my own; Victoria and Kayla were still working away furiously in the study. When I came back downstairs, I used the living-room TV to look at more news: six dead migrant workers in Texas, a dead eleven-year-old Cree girl in Manitoba, a synagogue bombed in Paris, a mosque bombed near London, another Boko Haram raid. Worse and worse.

About an hour later, the two women emerged—I'd have been delighted to see them under any circumstances, but the pair of ecstatic faces were particularly welcome just then.

"Well?" I said, turning off the TV.

"It all fits," said Victoria, triumphantly. "We'll run more tests tomorrow, but it looks like a solid model."

"I'm all ears."

"Okay," said Kayla, coming to sit next to me on the couch. "We already knew that all the microtubules in individual brains are quantally entangled. That's why they're all in the same superposition state for any given person, right? Either all of their tubulin dimers have one electron in superposition, or they all have two, or they have all three."

"Or none," I offered.

"Yes, yes, if they're out cold, they have none. Right. Now, we don't know what consciousness *is* exactly, but *that's* its physical correlate: the collectively entangled all-in-the-same-state quantum field within a given person's brain. *That's* the physical thing that gives rise to whatever level of consciousness a person might be experiencing: the emptiness of a p-zed, the cunning of a psychopath, or the conscience of a quick."

"Okay," I said.

"But not only is each human brain an entangled system, *every* human brain is an entangled system."

I frowned. "I don't see the distinction."

Vic took it up: "The sum total of human consciousness—all 7.7 billion people, regardless of what quantum state they individually might be in—forms one single entangled system, connected by small-world networking. It's the collective quantum inertia of that system that keeps people from changing states. That's the reason we can't take a p-zed, say, and boost him up to being at a higher state: you can't change the quantum state of one individual without affecting all the others, which is why the quantum tuning fork doesn't have an effect on an already awake individual. The inertia of the totality of humanity prevents any shift."

"But that can't be right," I said. "People get put out for surgery all the time. But *only* the patient is affected."

"Yes," said Vic. "That's a special case, because it involves decoherence. When you are put totally under by anesthesia, you cease to be in quantum superposition and drop back to the classical-physics state—Penrose and

Hameroff proved that—and so, by definition, if only classical physics pertains, you cease to be subject to entanglement."

"And," I said, "that means . . . ?"

"It means," said Kayla, "that you *exit* the collective if you truly lose all consciousness."

"Okay," I said.

"*But,*" continued Kayla, "everybody *within* the collective—all seven billion Q1s, Q2s, and Q3s; everyone who is *not* in the classical-physics state—could only conceivably change quantum state in lockstep, shifting *en masse.*"

"Really?"

"Yes," Kayla said. "It's one for all, and all for one."

"*Homo sapiens*—one big happy family," Vic added.

Not so happy of late, of course, but I wasn't going to ruin their moment of triumph. Still, I looked back at the TV screen. Funny: no monitor made since I was a kid had any sort of burn-in problem, and yet, as I gazed at the black rectangle, I could see the ghostly afterimage of the atrocities it had just shown me.

35

"*Professor Marchuk?*"

It was Veronica, in the third row, her hair in long cornrows.
"*Yes?*"

"*I get it. I mean, I really do. I get how all this utilitarian
thinking can be a good thing. But, well . . .*"

"*Yes?*"

"*Well, it just seems so* cold, *is all. So calculating.*"

*I looked out at the students. Veronica appeared genuinely
conflicted, but Boris had a smug expression, and his arms were
crossed in front of his chest, as if his classmate had just detonated
a nuke on my pet philosophy. He looked positively disappointed
when I said, "You're right, Veronica."*

And, for her part, Veronica looked surprised. "I am?"

"*Yes, certainly. On the surface, being a utilitarian appears to
mean embracing your inner psychopath.*" *I paused.* "*Do you guys
know the Trolley Problem?*"

A few nods, including Boris, but mostly blank faces.

"*Well,*" *I said,* "*imagine a streetcar is barreling along the
tracks, out of control. There's a split in the tracks: one fork leads*

to where five people are standing and the other leads to where one person is standing. The trolley will hit and kill the five unless you throw a switch and divert it onto the other track, in which case it'll only hit and kill one person. Do you throw the switch? Boris?"

"Yes, absolutely."

"Exactly right, comrade. One dead instead of five; pure utilitarianism. But what if there's only one track, and no switch, and instead it's you and that exact same one guy, but the two of you are standing on a footbridge over the tracks, and you, you're a little guy, but he's a big fellow—so big, he'll stop the streetcar for sure if you push him off the bridge so that he lands in front of it before it plows into the other five people. Do you push him off? Same utilitarian equation, isn't it? One person dead instead of five? Veronica, do you push him off?"

"No."

I smiled. "Nor would most people. In fact, when Bartels and Pizarro studied that scenario, they found it was mostly psychopaths who said they'd do the supposedly utilitarian thing and shove the big guy off the bridge; normal people couldn't bring themselves to do it."

"See," said Boris, "you have to be a psychopath to follow strict utilitarianism."

"That's Doctor Psychopath to you, comrade." A few laughs. "But, no, you're missing the point. Pushing the guy off the bridge is an easy answer for a psychopath because psychopaths don't give a damn. And not giving a damn is the opposite of utilitarianism.

"In the two-tracks scenario, there's no room for second thought: I'm killing one guy instead of five. In the footbridge scenario, there's lots to dither over: how do you know that the heavy guy will be big enough to stop the streetcar; yeah, someone told you that he will be, but do you believe that? Are you sure? And are you sure there isn't a touch of prejudice here? How'd that guy get so fat, anyway? Is his life worth less than someone else's? Oh, but what if his obesity is due to a glandular condition or genetics?

And is it really true that jumping yourself wouldn't be enough to stop the train? Who says so?

"*If it turned out that pushing the fat guy didn't actually stop the streetcar, so now six people died instead of five, a psychopath would shrug, and say, 'Live and learn.' But a utilitarian would be devastated by it. Having a conscience means agonizing over things, it means doing the right thing because you've weighed all the factors, it means caring so much it hurts. And that's a feeling no psychopath will ever know.*"

I T was going to take another two days to fix my car, damn it all, and I needed to get back to Winnipeg. Although it would have been nice to have *Star Trek*'s transporter at my disposal, at least Captain Kirk was able to help me out: I got a bargain last-minute airfare from Priceline.com, and so was now at Diefenbaker, waiting for my plane.

Often when flying in Canada, I ran into people I knew at airports; Canada has only a handful of major cities, and academics travel a lot to conferences. So, I wasn't really surprised to see Jonah Bratt arrive at the same gate I was at. The flight from here to Winnipeg continues on to Ottawa, and Jonah teaches psychology at Carleton—poorly, according to RateMyProfessors.com.

"Hey, Jonah," I said, standing up to shake his hand. He was tall and cadaverously thin, with pockmarked skin and graying hair.

"Marchuk," he said. His grip was almost nonexistent. "What are you doing here?"

"Visiting a friend. You?"

"Attending a colloquium on Jung at U of S."

"Ah," I said.

It was a small gate area, and he sat down close to me, with one empty seat between us—leaving the space required by flocking rules, or just being a prick and making it awkward for someone else as the waiting area filled, I couldn't say.

He pulled out a tablet and began to read what looked like a journal article. My attention was caught by the big TV hanging from the ceiling, which was showing CTV News Channel. *"More on the horrific news out of Corpus Christi, Texas,"* said the anchor, Dan Matheson. The image cut to what looked like a large natural sinkhole in the ground, and in it were human bodies, most clad in jeans and T-shirts, overlapping like jackstraws.

The anchor went on: *"Work continues on the mass grave found here yesterday, about 350 kilometers south of Houston. Police are now removing the bodies and so far four of them have been identified by their next of kin: Miguel dos Santos, twenty-four; his brother José dos Santos, nineteen; Carlos Lobos, twenty-eight; and Juan Rameriz, twenty-two. Our Ben Pryce has more. Ben?"*

The picture showed a man holding a microphone standing at the lip of the sinkhole, Texas State Troopers milling about on the far side.

"Dan, this open-pit grave was located by a couple of hikers early yesterday morning. As you can see, we're off the beaten path here. The four identified bodies were all migrant farm workers apparently illegally in this country, and I've been told, off the record, that the other fifteen bodies—ten men and five women—all appear to be Latino or Latina. Cause of death in most cases seems to have been a single bullet to the head, in what I overheard one police officer call 'execution-style.'"

The picture changed again, showing a large wooden board on which two words had been painted in ragged brushstrokes.

"Dan, images of this sign, which I'm told was found on top of the bodies, have already gone viral online. As you can see, it reads, 'As requested.'"

"Like Nazi Germany," I said, shaking my head.

Bratt looked up. "You lose."

"What?"

"You lose. Godwin's Law."

What he actually meant was a corollary to Godwin's Law: the implication that any argument has gone irretrievably off the rails when someone trots out a comparison to the Nazis or Hitler. "Because the Holocaust was—what?" I said. *"Sui generis?* Something that could never happen again?" I motioned toward the TV set. "It's happening right now."

"It's just a blip."

"It's accelerating—and it's going to get even worse. Hitler at least had to set up huge government infrastructure to pull off his killings. Fucking McCharles has crowdsourced his genocide."

"There's just no evidence that—"

I pointed at the screen. "The evidence is right there! Why—"

But we were interrupted by the Air Canada gate clerk calling our flight. Apparently Bratt's Altitude status made him eligible for pre-boarding, as he immediately rose from his chair, and, without a word of goodbye, shambled toward the Jetway.

The next day, after my classes were done, I headed over to meet Bhavesh Namboothiri, who finally was able to see me again. I took a bus, which gave me plenty of opportunity to observe the damage that had been done during the riots. In many places, windows were boarded up with plywood, fences were still down, and there were scorch marks on the asphalt where cars had been set ablaze.

Namboothiri managed to elicit a couple more childhood memories—which were certainly fascinating to experience, and, under other circumstances, would have been worth the price of admission. But they were just pyrite; we were after nuggets of gold.

And, soon enough, he was turning up those, too: one of Menno's lectures; then, as Namboothiri repositioned the probes, another by Professor Jenkins—sadly, apparently not the one during which I'd told an orangutan joke; another shifting of the probes brought back memories of me indeed having a tumor removed from my left breast in Calgary; one more repositioning, and Kayla and I were playing strip Trivial Pursuit, in which instead of getting a wedge each time you answered a question correctly, your opponent lost one of their six pieces of clothing; and then—

Oh.

Oh.

So *that's* what I'd done to David Swinson.

I'd remained in Winnipeg that summer, having taken a data-entry job in the registrar's office on the assumption that my relationship with Kayla would continue. David, who'd had the dorm room next to mine during the preceding academic year, had once eaten what was left in my bucket of KFC without permission. And so, near the end of June 2001, I'd gone onto the registration computer and dropped him from every course he'd selected for that coming September—and, for good measure, had him give up his place in the dorm, as well. When he returned to Winnipeg from his summer back home, he discovered he wasn't registered and had no place to stay. Somehow—perhaps we'd find that memory later—he must have eventually realized I was responsible.

I shuddered, feeling horrible that I could ever have done such a nasty thing—and was grateful when Namboothiri moved on.

Next up were innocuous memories: a few more from my toddler days; going to see the movie version of *Josie and the Pussycats*—something that probably *was* best forgotten; Heather coming for a weekend visit, and—

"Move the fucking probes!"

Namboothiri eased off and the images melted from my consciousness, but I was gasping and my pulse was racing.

"Are you okay?" he asked. "We can stop for the day if—"

I lifted a hand. "No. No, I'll be all right. Just . . ." My arm was shaking; I lowered it. "Just give me a moment." Another memory came to me, but not because the doctor was eliciting it; this one was from my verbal index, and relatively recent: Menno Warkentin talking to me in his office, trying to dissuade me from digging into my past. *"Sometimes it's better to let sleeping dogs lie,"* he'd said. But I'd replied, *"No, I can't do that."*

And I couldn't.

I had to forge ahead.

I gripped the arms of the chair tightly, forcing the blood from my knuckles, took a deep breath, and said, "Okay. I'm ready."

"All right," Namboothiri replied, returning the probes to the same spots on my skull.

Friday afternoon, June 29, 2001. The corridor outside the office of Dominic Adler. Knuckles rapped against the door, and words were spoken: "Dom, it's me, Jim. Can I have a moment?"

The door opened, revealing Dominic in russet slacks and a gray, short-sleeved shirt. "Hey, Jim. Come in. What's up?" He gestured at a chair and turned to walk to his desk.

Jim's body surged in from behind, and Jim's hands grasped Dom's neck on either side. A crack! *split the air as the neck was twisted ninety degrees to the left. Dominic's body slumped to the floor.*

The front of Jim's shoe impelled itself into Dom's kidney, and sounds emanated once more from Jim's mouth: "Take that, motherfucker."

Without my asking him to, Namboothiri pulled the probes away once more. "You okay?"

Breathing rapidly, my skin slick with sweat, I reached up to wipe my brow—and once again my hand was trembling. "Jim?" Namboothiri said. I scrunched my eyes shut, but the awful memory lingered. "Jim? What did you see?"

I tried to compose myself then swiveled the chair to face him. "You're a psychiatrist, right?"

He nodded.

"Which makes you an MD, right? A medical doctor?"

"Yes. What's wrong?"

"So this conversation is privileged, correct? Even though I came to you without a referral, I'm still your patient, isn't that right?"

"Jim, my God, what did you see?"

"*Say it,*" I snapped. "Say I'm your patient. Say this is privileged."

"Yes, yes, of course. You're my patient. I can't be compelled to divulge what we discuss."

I blew out air, took another moment, then: "Back in 2001 . . ." I shook my head, finding the words almost as impossible to speak as the thought was to think. "I killed a man."

"Oh . . . God. No, no."

"Broke his neck. Deliberately."

Different responses seemed to swirl on Namboothiri's face, but at last he said: "Who was it?"

"Dominic Adler. Menno Warkentin's research partner."

"Was it—was it self-defense?"

God, how I wished it had been! I'd killed that p-zed in the prairie field a short time ago, and that had indeed been self-defense. Even so, I'd barely been able to live with myself since, but this—*this!*

I shook my head. "It was premeditated. And . . . brutal."

Namboothiri was quiet for a moment. "And do you know why you did it?"

"The motive, you mean?"

"No, not that," said Namboothiri. "Do you know *why?*"

I recalled the hairline scratches on my old brain scans. "The paralimbic damage you uncovered, I guess, but . . ." I sighed. "I never thought I could . . . I just . . ." Acid was clawing its way up my throat.

"We can stop digging, if you want," Namboothiri said.

My heart was still beating rapidly. "No. I have to know the rest."

36

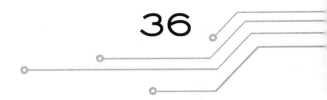

L ATE June was about as nice as Winnipeg ever got. This year the last snowfall had been in April, and the mosquitoes wouldn't make their first appearance for another month. Menno Warkentin walked down the hallway, his black Bruno Magli shoes making soft impacts against the institutional tiles. During the academic year, the corridors had been bustling with overworked students and harried faculty rushing from place to place. But although there were some summer students, few were on hand here, the Friday night leading into the Canada Day long weekend.

Menno entered the lab he shared with Dominic Adler and walked over to the worktable. Stacked on its surface were eight new sensor packs that would go on the Mark III helmet, and next to them, the old green transcranial-focused-ultrasound pucks. Those wouldn't be included on the new unit, of course, but Dom kept running tests with them, trying to figure out why they'd caused people to black out; the DoD had goosed his grant by a hundred grand so he could pursue that.

Menno looked around to see if there was any sign that Dom had been in the lab today. His usual spoor included open bottles of Dr Pepper with a flat inch left undrunk at the bottom, but there were none to be seen. Menno hit the power-bar switch that turned on the desktop computer and its bulky seventeen-inch VGA monitor. Windows 98 began its slow boot-up; he wondered if XP, due later this year, would be any faster.

He heard the door opening. "Ah, Dom. I was hoping—" But it wasn't Dominic. "Oh! Jim. I wasn't expecting you. I thought you were going to Lake Winnipeg for the long weekend."

A voice emanated from Jim's mouth. "That's what I told everybody. Never hurts to have an alibi."

Menno made a snort. "Yeah, I guess that's true. You happen to pass Dom on the way in?"

The mouth worked again: "He's in his office." Eyes swiveled toward the wall, where the faux Louisville slugger was held up by its two acrylic, U-shaped supports. A comment required; one made: "Chekhov's gun." The bat was taken down, the grip encircled by hands. The club was swung at empty air.

"Dom's pretty particular about that thing," Menno said. "You should probably put it back."

More words were generated, empty, automatic: "Remember when the Blue Jays won those back-to-back World Series? I was eleven the first time and twelve the second. In Calgary, we don't often root for anything related to Toronto, but we did then."

Jim started closing the distance between them, the bat held firmly, his heels making ticking-bomb clicks. Startled, Menno backed away. His rear was soon against the worktable, and—

Shit!

Jim swung the bat right at him. Menno moved with the same poor coordination he brought to his squash game, barely getting out of the way in time. "For God's sake, Marchuk!"

Jim wheeled around and swung once more. Menno ducked. *"Help!"* he shouted. *"Somebody help!"* But he'd been right earlier—the campus was dead. Backing the other way across the room now, he found himself stumbling onto a metal folding chair. He rolled off it just as the bat came smashing down onto the top of the chair's back. Menno grabbed the chair's legs and hefted it, using it as a shield to ward off additional swings. Jim tossed the bat aside so he could grab the chair's frame and soon had wrested it free. He threw the chair aside; it folded up flat when it clattered to the floor.

Menno tried to make it to the door, but the younger man was thinner and more agile; he easily positioned himself in front of it. Jim lunged, and Menno, to his own astonishment, managed to deke out of the way. As Jim sailed past, Menno tried a maneuver he'd seen on TV, interlacing his own fingers to form a two-fisted club and bringing it crashing down on the student's back, driving him face-first into the floor.

Menno turned to escape but found himself pitching forward—Jim had grabbed his ankles. As soon as he hit the ground, he rolled onto his back. Jim came toward him, picking up the folded chair, but it was an unwieldy weapon, and he tossed it aside again. Menno pulled his knees up toward his chest, then lashed out with a double kick as Jim came nearer, sending the student backward against the worktable, the neat stack of sensor modules scattering across its surface from the impact.

There was excruciating pain in the small of Menno's back; he'd perhaps broken his coccyx. He pushed himself up from the floor, while Jim tried to lift the computer monitor. It came up about a foot, then jerked to a halt, its video cable, screwed in at the back, anchoring it. But the heavy AT-style keyboard, the size of a window shutter, pulled free from its connection, and Jim came forward, whooshing it back and forth.

Menno tried once more for the door, but Jim quickly blocked the way. He swung the keyboard repeatedly, and Menno felt the wind of its movement as he pivoted and dashed toward the worktable. He hated turning his back but did so for an instant, grabbing one of the TUS hockey pucks in each hand.

Jim surged in, smashing the keyboard onto Menno's head. Menno staggered for a moment; Jim tossed the keyboard aside and threw the professor to the ground. Menno landed flat on his back, arms splayed as if making a snow angel—but he'd held on to the pucks. Although they were normally activated by commands sent through the helmet, each one had a slider switch on its rim for manual testing; Menno desperately tried to find those switches with his thumbs.

Straddling him, Jim grabbed Menno's throat. Menno almost let go of the pucks so he could tear at the kid's arms, but he knew the younger man was stronger. Instead, he rotated each puck in his hands, the way one turned thermostat knobs, and at last found the switch on the left one, sliding it forward.

He felt his eyes bugging out and his larynx compressing as he continued rotating the right puck clockwise, working his grip around its circumference. The crazed student kept squeezing his throat, but at last Menno found the other switch, but—*fuck!*—that one seemed to be stuck. His vision was blurring and his lungs were on fire, and—

—and it finally dawned on him that, given the way he was holding them, if the left puck's switch moved up, then you had to slide the right one's switch down, which, just as the pain was reaching unbearable levels, he did. He then slammed the pucks onto the sides of Jim's head, clashing cymbals, and held them there like green earmuffs, until—

—until his attacker's eyes rolled up, and his arms went slack, and he came crashing down on top of Menno, who immediately pushed him off, leaving the boy unconscious on his side. The professor also lay there for a moment, gasping, then, slowly, he pulled himself to his feet. He was hunched over, still trying to recover, when the landline phone rang. He had no intention of answering it—he wasn't even sure if he could speak yet—but the goddamned jangling just added to the pounding in his ears.

He turned off the pucks, then looked down at Jim.

Riiiiing!

His first thought was to haul back and kick the bastard in the head—

Riiiiing!

—but that faded. He *knew* Jim Marchuk, and this wasn't him: not the old, inquisitive A-student with the inner monologue—

Riiiiing!

—and not the new philosopher's zombie without one.

Riiiiing!

This sudden outbreak of violence *had* to be the result of what Menno himself had recently done to the poor boy.

Riiiiing!

The phone finally stopped, thank God. Menno was too winded to run away, and, damn it, if he left the boy lying here, knocked into unconsciousness, whoever eventually found him would doubtless call 911, and at the hospital they'd do an MRI and see the damage to his paralimbic system—and people would wonder how those fresh laser-carved lesions had been made.

Menno staggered over, found a chair, put the pucks in his lap, and closed his eyes for—

—for how long he didn't know, but he was awoken by the sound of movement. Oh, God! On the floor, Jim was rolling onto his back. And then the phone rang again, just twice, its bell signaling round two.

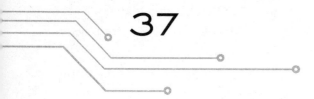

37

WHAT the hell? Where am I? How did I get here?
I looked at the window, and—

Blue sky?

Sunshine?

Trees covered with leaves?

But . . . but it's January! How in the hell did I . . . ?

My head hurt—but not from a hangover. I reached up to touch it, and—*ouch!* I'd banged it against something.

I rolled the other way, and there was Professor Warkentin, looking like someone had just kicked the living crap out of him.

I stared at him—really stared at him, locking my gaze on his fat face. Fucking guy was an asshole, pure and simple. An impediment. You could *see* it. Guy like that never should have been born. Waste of oxygen molecules. I wasn't exactly sure *why*, but—

—but it didn't matter. It was time to *do* something about it.

Seeing Jim stirring, Menno grabbed the hockey pucks and got up, but the student, still on the ground, shot his arms out and yanked hard again on Menno's ankles. Menno lost his balance, falling backward, crashing to the floor. One of the hockey pucks went flying although he managed to keep hold of the other one.

Jim got up, dusted himself off, and scanned around the room. He spotted the baseball bat and picked it up from where it had landed, looking at it quizzically, as if he'd never seen it before. But then he turned and, gripping it with both hands, started coming toward Menno, who was still lying face-up. Menno rolled on his side, another jolt of pain going through him as he did so. The loose hockey puck was about four feet away. He started moving toward it.

Jim swung again with the club but managed to hit the floor instead of the rapidly beetling Menno, and the bat broke in half. Jim briefly held its stem up in front of him, the splintered end like frozen torch flame, then tossed it aside; it banged against a whiteboard-covered wall and clattered to the floor.

Menno scooped up the second puck, rolled over 180 degrees so that he was facing Jim again, and, with a sudden access of adrenaline, got to his feet and charged toward Jim, propelling him backward against the whiteboard, the dry-erase markers that had been stored on an aluminum shelf clattering to the floor. Menno slammed the pucks against Jim's temples again, but—

Fuck!

He'd forgotten he'd turned them off. He quickly found the switch on the one in his right hand and thumbed it forward, but the other one had to be rotated single-handedly while he tried to reach its slider.

Jim spun himself and Menno around and drove a punch into Menno's solar plexus, propelling him backward, his spine slamming against the whiteboard. The younger man pressed an open left palm against the center of Menno's chest, pinning him, and he brought his right hand up to the edge of Menno's jaw.

Menno was still trying to find the switch on the other puck. Jim's thumb moved up, pressing hard into the lower part of Menno's cheek, then he inched the digit farther upward, passing the side of Menno's nose, then, repositioning it once more, and—

Fuck! Fuck! Fuck!

—digging it into Menno's eye.

Menno brought his knee up into Jim's groin. Jim grunted but continued to press in with his thumb and its hard, sharp nail. The pain from the marker ledge biting into Menno's spine had seemed like agony—until he had *this* to compare it to, as—

Jesus Fucking God.

—as Jim's thumb pierced his left eyeball.

Menno gasped. In a lightning-fast move, Jim switched hands, pushing Menno against the wall with his right one now and lifting his left.

Fighting nausea but still fumbling with the puck, Menno at last found its on switch. The pain was unbelievable, as—

God damn it!

—as Jim's thumb burst through his other eyeball.

Menno groped to get the pucks over the student's temporal lobes and—

Yes!

Judging by the sound, Jim must have collapsed at once like a sack of potatoes, but Menno couldn't see that—he couldn't see *anything*. He stumbled forward and tripped over what he guessed was one of Jim's legs, splayed out across the tiles. Menno managed to regain his balance, made his way to the door, fumbled in a gray nothingness for the knob, and staggered out into the corridor.

Kayla Huron walked down the empty corridor. It was a warm, sunny day, and she was wearing cutoff jeans and a white blouse tied off above her navel. Since she'd broken up with Jim, she was back on the market and didn't mind advertising—and all that time at the gym *had* been paying off.

Kayla had a summer job working in the physics department, which was perfect: the money she'd make would just about cover her third-year tuition.

U of M's Fort Garry campus wasn't that big; she'd caught sight of Jim a couple of times as he was coming out of the Tier Building—and had promptly hidden herself. She had zero interest in having contact with her many exes, and if she never saw James Marchuk again, it'd be too damn soon.

As she made her way across campus, listening to NSYNC on her Walkman, she'd kicked back a full bottle of Snapple. Thanks to it, a pit stop was in order, and so she nipped into the nearest building, taking the wide stairs up to the main floor two at time. To her left, down at the end, was a man, but the women's room was to her right, and so she began to head that way, but—

But there had been something odd about the man. She turned around, and, yes, he was *staggering,* arms out in front as if groping along, and—

And, by God, it was Professor Warkentin. Even at this distance, she was sure that's who it was. "Professor?" she called out. "Are you okay?"

He turned. "Help me," he said weakly—or, at least, that's what she thought she heard echoing down the corridor. She quickly jogged down to him, but found herself stopping short, her hand going to her mouth, when she saw blood streaming from his eyes . . .

No, no. Not from his eyes; from his eye *sockets.*

"My God, Professor, what happened? I—um. Where's a pay phone? I can call 911."

"No! No."

"But sir!"

"Please." The syllable was a gasp; he was clearly in agony. "Just get me to my friend's office."

"You need to see a doctor!"

"Just do it. Do what I ask. Please."

"But—"

"Please!"

"Okay, okay. Which room?"

"Along this corridor. Two or three from the end. On the left. Dominic Adler's office."

Kayla's grandfather had been blind; she knew how to lead someone by cupping their elbow, and she instinctively did just that.

"Who are you?" Warkentin said.

"A student," Kayla said. "You taught me last year." She quickly found the room he wanted. The door was closed. Kayla let go of Warkentin's elbow and opened it, and—

"Oh, God!"

"What?"

She crouched down next to the fallen man, checking for a pulse—but the coolness of his skin told her she wasn't going to find one. "There's—there's a dead man here."

"Oh, shit!" said Warkentin. He started fumbling toward the doorway, and Kayla got up to let him get in. Once he was, he snapped, "Close the door!"

She did so. Warkentin was breathing in loud, raspy gasps. "Okay," she said, "we *have* to call the police."

"No," the professor replied sharply. "No. Fuck, fuck, fuck."

"But he's dead."

"What's he look like?"

"Thin, black hair. Sir, I think his neck is broken."

"Is he wearing a calculator watch?"

"Um—yeah."

"Damn it. That's Dom. Jesus. Jesus."

"There's a phone here," said Kayla. "Do I have to dial nine to get an outside line?"

"Don't call 911," said Warkentin. "Don't call *anyone*."

"Why not?"

"Help me find a chair."

Kayla wheeled the one out from behind the desk and placed it between the wall and the body lying on the floor; she then guided Warkentin toward it, and he lowered his bulk into it. His chest was visibly heaving, he was slick with sweat, and his skin had turned a yellow gray.

"Okay," he said, once seated. "Listen to me. This"—he gestured at his own face—"can't be reported. Nor can that." He waved vaguely in the direction of the body.

"But—"

"*Listen to me!* There's classified research going on here. It—um, it got out of hand, but—"

"Classified?" Kayla repeated, astonished.

"Yes. For the US military. So we can't go to the Canadian authorities."

That all seemed rather improbable to Kayla, but it was also weirdly fascinating. "Are you sure you don't need to see a doctor?" she said.

"For God's sake, *of course* I do!" He didn't seem to be actively bleeding anymore, but he winced frequently—which looked odd and creepy with his eye sockets the way they were. He fumbled for his wallet and proffered it. She noted it was rather fat with bills, including a couple of brown ones, a denomination she rarely saw.

"My cousin is a doctor, a surgeon. He'll help. There's a little slip of paper in there with phone numbers on it, see? Jacob Reimer, that's my cousin. Call him."

"I will," said Kayla, moving over to the phone, "but—"

Warkentin was breathing rapidly, great shuddering inhalations, and he was hunched over now, clearly in agony. "Oh, God," he said. "Oh, God. Oh, God."

"—but, sir, what are we going to do about the body?"

"We've—God, fuck, damn, shit—we've . . . we've got to get rid of it."

"*What?*" said Kayla.

"We've got to dispose of it. No one can ever know."

Kayla felt the old excitement welling inside her. Carving up neighborhood cats and dogs had been glorious, but *this*—this would be so much better! Such a release, such a wondrous release!

"I'm in," she said.

38

'D been half-prepared, I supposed, for there to have been something traumatic in my past—but, really, what could have been more shocking than being knifed in the heart, my pericardium slit open, my left atrium pierced, my lifeblood spilling out? More disturbing than being left to die on an icy sidewalk on a cold winter's night? Surely when you'd come that close to death, no horror you could have survived would be any worse.

But no. I had to keep telling myself that that had never happened. *This*—the things I recalled now—was reality. And almost being killed paled to having *actually* killed.

"But why don't I remember doing that?" I said, looking up at Namboothiri from the little swivel chair.

"Well," he said, lifting his unibrow, "if I had to venture a guess, I'd say it was because you didn't sleep prior to Warkentin knocking you into a coma the second and third times. It's during sleep that the day's memories are sorted and the salient ones encoded for long-term storage."

"But people put under for an operation remember both going down and coming back up."

"True. But you also had paralimbic damage. I'm not surprised it took a little while for verbal memory encoding to start working properly again. I suspect if we shifted over to probing your verbal index, we'd find you immediately started confabulating stuff to fill in your dark period. Just as nature abhors a vacuum, the mind wants a continuous narrative—even if it has to make one up."

"Hmmm. And—*hmmm*."

"Yes?"

"I've had a recurring nightmare for years: a monster I needed to destroy, and me holding a wooden torch, but with dark, frozen flames. That's got to be the splintered baseball bat."

"Ah, then you *did* at least partially encode what happened during that brief period."

"Lucky me," I said softly. And then I got up and headed toward the door.

"Where are you going?" asked Namboothiri.

"To see Menno Warkentin."

Menno was waiting at the entrance to his apartment as I came off the elevator, Pax in a sitting posture next to him. "Padawan," he said, moving aside to let me in.

The spacious living room, with its silver-and-cyan furniture, hadn't changed since the last time I'd been here. Menno headed past the twin totem poles into the kitchen, Pax following dutifully behind; I'd seen the dog lead the way when they were in unfamiliar territory, but she understood Menno needed no guidance in his own home. "Coffee?" he called out. "Tea?"

"Nothing," I said.

He emerged holding a red coffee mug for himself.

I sat on the couch. "You know Bhavesh Namboothiri?"

"Psychology prof at U of W? Met him once or twice."

"He's been helping me recover the memories from my dark period."

A long pause; even Pax turned to face her master. "Oh," Menno said at last. "And?"

"I know what happened to Dom. And what I did to you."

"So long ago," said Menno. "Another lifetime."

"How come there was no follow-up? No criminal investigation?"

Menno sat down opposite me. "Somebody helped me dispose of Dom's body."

"Who?"

"I don't know. I never saw her. I tried to track her down afterward, but no luck. She took some cash, though, and my cards—ran up some big bills. But I never heard from her again."

"Weren't there questions about Dom? About what had happened to him?"

"He'd been fairly loose-lipped about doing consulting for the DoD, so I told everyone he'd moved to Washington and had taken a job with them. It sounded plausible; no one questioned it. And the DoD was happy to help cover things up; national security and all that. I think they're still cashing his U of M pension checks down there." He lifted his shoulders. "It's like he isn't even really dead."

"But he *is*. And . . . and I'm the one who killed him."

"Yeah."

"I killed a man . . . violently, in cold blood. You're a Mennonite, a pacifist. How could you look at me after that?"

"That's the beauty of it," Menno said softly. "I didn't have to."

A flash of memory: my thumb digging into Menno's face. I shook my head violently, but there were no adequate words.

Menno lifted his shoulders. "I was angry. Furious. But, well, nineteen years *is* a long time."

"Still, it must have been awful, having to work side by side with me all this time."

He was quiet for a moment. Perhaps he blinked behind his glasses. "Jim, I'm the reason you're at U of M."

"I know, but—"

"No, you don't understand. *I'm* the reason. I was department head back then, remember? You'd applied to teach at three other schools. A few phones calls, a few favors called in, twisting the dean's arm to get you tenure-tracked, and—" He shrugged affably. "Well, the names *haven't* all changed since you hung around." And then he sang, off-key, the final verse of the old TV theme song, *"Welcome back, welcome back, welcome back . . ."*

"Jesus," I said. "Keep your friends close and your enemies even closer?"

"You're not my enemy. You're my . . ."

"Subject?" I said, at last getting it.

"I may have stopped recording them, but those long discussions in my office we've always had . . . It *was* fascinating, what had happened to you, and how you built up a coherent history of your missing period pretty much out of nothing."

"But, still, after what I'd done, why'd you keep it secret? Why didn't you turn me over to the police?"

Menno's silver eyebrows climbed above the frames of his glasses, and he spread his arms. "How could I? You know what would have happened if *any* of this had gone public? Milgram and Zimbardo—that was the Wild West, before informed consent; hell, it's *because* of them that informed-consent rules were put in place at universities across the world. Even with tenure, my career was at risk—flagrant violations of the campus ethical guidelines—and the whole department was at risk, too. U of M could have been decertified by the American and Canadian Psychological Associations. And—you don't know how big a deal this is, but trust me, it's huge for a Mennonite: working for the military? I'd have never been able to show my face at my church again. Plus, Jesus God, the legal consequences! If you had decided to sue or press criminal charges for the lost six months, or for the brain damage I'd caused with the lasers, I'd be in ruins, or in jail, or both. Same thing if Travis Huron's family had sued: that boy has been in a coma for almost twenty years, and it was my fault."

"He's not in a coma anymore."

Menno's jaw dropped, and he said, very softly, "Oh." And then, after a moment, "When did he pass?"

"He's not dead," I said. "But he's out of the coma; he's awake."

"God, really?"

"He doesn't remember what you did to him."

"Are you going to tell him?" Menno asked anxiously.

"He has a right to know."

"Prisoner's dilemma, Padawan. Don't defect."

"What?"

"You tell Travis what we did to him, and I *will* tell the police what you did to Dominic Adler. There's a statute of limitations on malpractice; there's none on murder. The only win-win scenario is for both of us to continue to keep quiet."

I didn't like being pushed. "I'll get off," I said. "I had a pre-existing condition, thanks to you."

The obsidian convexities of Menno's lenses faced me. "The way Devin Becker got off?"

I blew out air.

"Listen, Padawan, *listen!* You know the stakes are higher than either of us. If people start digging—if the truth of what Dom and I discovered all those years ago comes out . . ."

"Yes?"

"Slavery, human trafficking, cannon fodder, experimental test subjects, even Soylent-fucking-Green, for Christ's sake—that's just the *beginning* of the things that'll happen if the world learns that there are countless philosopher's zombies out there who don't actually have feelings."

He was right. Four billion p-zeds, two billion psychopaths, and just a billion quicks. It was a recipe for massive exploitation.

"I have to know," I said. "Did Dominic Adler have an inner voice?"

"See!" Menno crowed triumphantly. "Even you're doing it! If he *didn't* have an inner voice, you're off the hook, right? Yeah, you—you *terminated* him, but it's not like that *matters,* right?" He let that sink in. "Anyway, sorry, but there's no get-out-of-jail-free card for you: Dom had an inner voice; I saw it on the oscilloscope when we were testing our equipment." A pause, a beat, then a softening of my old mentor's tone: "As to whether he had a conscience to go with it, though . . ."

"Yes?"

"What do you think? He got me to push ahead with the experiments even after you'd lost consciousness. He didn't seem to give a damn about what had happened to either you or Travis Huron."

"A psychopath," I said. Menno was right: I probably *could* have lived with having killed another p-zed, but even a psychopath was fully conscious: all the reasons why Devin Becker shouldn't receive capital punishment applied equally to Dominic Adler.

But, nonetheless, I'd snapped Dom's neck.

Judge.

Jury.

And executioner.

Of course, *I'd* been a psychopath when I'd done it, albeit a paralimbic one, not a quantum one, until . . .

Until Menno had hockey-pucked me into a brief coma and I'd fallen to the laboratory floor, only to reboot—

—to reboot, like Travis Huron eventually did, not at my previous state but—

—but at *the next level up.*

I'd come back as the worst-possible combination: a Q2 with amygdalar lesions; a quantum psychopath and a paralimbic psychopath all rolled into one, suddenly conscious after six months of zombiehood. Fuck yeah, such a beast might gouge somebody's eyes out. And after that, it might—

But there was no *after that,* not for the quantum psychopath. Menno almost immediately knocked me back into a coma again, and when I emerged, on July 2, 2001, I had leveled up once more, becoming fully conscious with conscience—and that conscience, that inner voice, had managed to override whatever the paralimbic damage might have been urging me to do.

Just like it was overriding my urge right now to strangle the life out of Menno Warkentin for what he'd done to me—and for what that damage had led me to do.

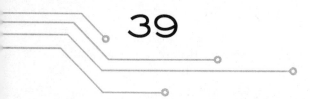

39

hadn't planned to return to Saskatoon for several more days, but I needed to see Kayla, so I had my teaching assistant take my Wednesday and Thursday classes for me.

My car, finally repaired, was now at Kayla's place; she'd picked it up from the body shop for me. That meant flying was my best option to get to Saskatoon, and, to my delight—the only good news I'd had in days—I was able to get a one-way ticket for only $300; I'd expected much more of a gouge for a same-day flight.

I called Kayla to let her know I was coming. The trip was brief enough that I didn't have to use the john, which was good because I'd gotten stuck with a window seat and I hated asking someone to move just so I could get out. Kayla was still at work when I arrived, but, since it was after normal business hours, I didn't feel guilty about going straight to the synchrotron; Ryan was at Rebekkah and Travis's place, and the last thing I needed was to be on my own in an empty house.

The cab turned onto Innovation Boulevard and headed toward the glass-fronted building that housed the Light Source, but the driver came to a stop a hundred meters shy of the circular driveway. Four Saskatoon police cars, their roof lights blinking, were blocking the way. I told the cabbie to wait and got out. A uniformed officer approached me.

"Sorry, sir," he said. "No one gets in."

It was only then that I became conscious of a helicopter overhead. "My girlfriend is in there. What's happening?"

"No one's in there," corrected the officer. "The building's been evacuated."

"What? Why?"

"Bomb threat."

I pulled out my phone—and saw that it was still in airplane mode. I turned that off, and I hit the speed dial for Kayla.

"Jim, thank God," she said. "I tried calling you, but—" Her next few words were bleeped out by the sound of my voice-mail indicator going off. "—about forty minutes ago."

"Are you safe? Where are you?"

"At home."

"I'm on my way," I said, hurrying back to the taxi. As we drove out, we passed the bomb-disposal van lumbering its way in.

I'd come to Saskatoon because I needed comforting after what Namboothiri had uncovered. But the moment I saw Kayla, I wanted instead to comfort her. I held her tightly in the entryway for a time, then she led me into the kitchen, where she had a drink—amber liquid over rocks—going. She took a gulp, winced, then waved the glass vaguely at the liquor cabinet by way of offering me something. Instead, I opened the fridge and took out a can of beer.

"Why the bomb threat?" I asked as I pulled the tab, a small geyser going up from the opening.

"We've been having a lot of protests lately."

"Why?"

"Remember when people were picketing the Large Hadron Collider because they thought it was going to create a black hole? Some mindless jerks got it into their head that the same thing could happen here."

"Ah," I said, shaking my head.

"Anyway, how are you? You came all this way; what's wrong?"

I took a swig of beer. "I know I did some horrible things to you in 2001, and to Dave Swinson—the guy who became an optometrist. But I found out today that I'd done even worse things. The memory-specialist I've been working with helped me recall them."

I'd expected her to ask, "What things?" Certainly that would've been my first question. But she didn't. She simply swirled her glass, the ice cubes clinking, and said, looking only generally in my direction, "We've all done things we aren't proud of. It doesn't matter who we once were; all that matters is who we are now."

"Yes, but—"

"You literally weren't yourself back then. You weren't *anybody*. Just a philosopher's zombie."

"I was for most of it, but . . ."

"Yes?"

"But at the end of June, Menno knocked me out again, and I came back as a Q2 psychopath—a *real* psychopath—and then, I . . . I . . ."

"What?"

"I gouged out Menno's eyes."

She was quiet for a time, then, finally, she said simply, "Oh."

"God knows what else I would have done, but he managed to knock me out again, and when I woke up from that, I was back to my old Q3 self, I guess, but confabulating memories to trowel over the missing time."

"So, wait, wait, you're saying you were knocked down into a coma three times?" She sounded excited, as if this all confirmed something for her. "Once—what, New Year's Eve 2000, right? Then twice more at the end of June 2001? And you changed your quantum state each time you rebooted?"

"I guess, yes."

"Coma, coma, coma, chameleon," Kayla said.

I was clearly having an effect on her.

"I'm here all week," she added, but her grin was way wider than her joke deserved. She started toward her study down the hall. "Come with me."

"Look," Kayla said, gesturing at her large desktop monitor. "That's the simulation Victoria and I have been developing." She had taken the seat in front of the computer, and I was crouching next to her.

"Yes?" I said.

"See? It's looping."

I thought that was a bad thing, from the handful of Word macros I'd tried to debug over the years; I was proud all out of proportion to the actual achievement of my one that turned MLA citations into APA format. "You mean it doesn't terminate? It just keeps running?"

"No, no, no, the simulation stops just fine whenever we want it to. It's not the program that's looping; it's the *output.*"

"What?"

She hit some keys, and a chart appeared on her screen. "Okay, look. These are the three possible quantum-superposition states: Q1, Q2, and Q3."

"Right."

"Well, Vic and I have been trying to solve that problem you discussed with her: you said my brother Travis started as a Q2—a quantum psychopath—got knocked down into a coma, and then came back up as a Q3 quick, right?"

"Right. He leveled up."

"Exactly. But you started as a Q3, and, after being knocked into a coma back on New Year's Eve 2000, you revived as a Q1—you leveled *down,* in other words; the exact opposite of Travis, right?"

"Right."

"And I couldn't square what the simulation was showing with the reality you'd reported. I had thought you'd gone Q3 to Q1 then bounced straight back to Q3—but you just told me that wasn't what happened. You actually went Q3 to Q1, *then* to Q2, and *then* to Q3, one step at a time. And that's exactly what the simulation predicts. See, what happened to you isn't the *opposite* of what happened to Travis, it's the same thing: each time you go down to the classical-physics state, you reboot,

if you reboot at all, one level higher up—*but the levels wrap around!*"
She pointed at her screen. "The math proves it: the change vector is a
modulus, an absolute value. It statistically prefers being positive but, if
that's not possible, a negative delta occurs."

"Um, so if you started as a Q1—"

"If you started as Q1, you'd come back from a coma as a Q2; if you
were a Q2, like Travis, you'd come back as a Q3; and if you were originally a Q3, like you, you'd *wrap around to being a Q1!*"

"That's—wow."

"Wow indeed. But it's exactly what the math predicts, and it's
exactly what happened to you and to my brother and to . . ." She
trailed off.

"That's fabulous, baby! You're a genius."

"Thanks," she said, but she was frowning. "There's still one problem, though. Somehow, while Trav was in a coma, the value of his
previous superposition state had to be stored for nineteen years. For him
to revive as a Q3, somewhere the fact that he'd previously been a Q2
had to be retained even when he was no longer in superposition."

I'd been trying to come up to speed on all this. "Don't almost all cells
in the body have microtubular scaffolding? Not just brain cells? The ones
in neurons are the ones Penrose and Hameroff implicated in consciousness, but maybe regular body cells might retain a degree of superposition
even when neuronal tissue doesn't. Kind of like muscle memory."

I meant that last bit as a pun, but she nodded as if I were more
clever than I really felt just then. "Maybe, maybe." She shrugged a
little. "Who knows? The bottom line is, whatever the mechanism, there
clearly *is* such a memory."

"Cool," I said. "But, so are you saying this happens to *anyone* who
completely loses consciousness? If they revive, they come up at one level
higher than they were at before—or, if a Q3, wrap around to being a
Q1, as I did?"

"Yes, I think so. But they have to actually have their brain drop
into the classical-physics state. That doesn't happen during sleep; sleeping is a conscious condition, which is why you dream and why external
stimuli can wake you up."

"True," I said. "And, I've heard tons of stories about people who have temporarily lost consciousness through a coma, general anesthesia, or a near-death experience. Those who know them best often say they were changed by the experience. Family and friends say some people who have had NDEs are more mellow afterward—and, in many cases, they *would* be. If you were a psychopathic Q2 beforehand, you'd come back as a thoughtful, reflective Q3. And if you were a Q3 beforehand, you'd wrap around to being a Q1 p-zed, literally without a care in the world. Of course, that doesn't happen with every case of general anesthesia, but—"

"Welllll," said Kayla, "not to freak you out or anything, but a lot of the drugs we use in operations *aren't* really anesthetics; that is, they don't actually put you out cold. Rather, they're paralytics that also inhibit memory formation. They keep you from moving during surgery, and they keep you from remembering all the pain, but they don't actually put you out in the quantum-mechanical sense."

"Holy shit. Really?"

"Uh-huh."

"Wow. Well, thanks heaps. Something new to have nightmares about."

She smiled contritely. "But there *are* groups that *do* suffer total knockouts disproportionately: boxers, football players, and so on. Most of the time it's just—*just!*—a concussion. But every once in a while, one of them really is knocked out cold. And, you know, most of them probably started out as nice-enough guys. But everyone's read those stories about some of them eventually turning into psychopaths, beating their spouses and so on."

I nodded. One of the Green Bay Packers was in court just last week over having assaulted his wife.

"Anyway, that's it!" said Kayla triumphantly. "That's the pattern! Once you realize that the states wrap around, it's simple. It's *elegant.*"

I was asleep next to Kayla, but even when exhausted, I always dozed lightly, and a small change in the illumination filtering through my eyelids woke me up. Next to me, Kayla, naked, was thumb-typing on her phone.

"Texting your other lover?" I said; I was naked, too.

"No, no." She continued typing furiously. "I'm sending myself a note. I thought of another mathematical proof that the states *do* in fact wrap around; I don't want to forget it." She tapped a little longer, then decisively banged the screen with her index finger and turned to me, illuminated by the phone, a satisfied smirk on her beautiful face.

I gently pulled her back down, so that she was facing me. I stroked her hair, its copper color undetectable in the darkness; stroked her shoulder, the skin smooth; worked my way toward her breast, perfect, round, soft, my palm moving in light circles over her nipple, which hardened; and then, sliding lower down her torso, touching the ridge that marked the leading edge of one of the wings on her blue butterfly tattoo.

The ridge; her scar.

I had one of my own, of course, on the left side of my chest, where that crazed addict's knife—

No, no. It *hadn't* been heart surgery; it had been the removal of a tumor in my breast. Above my sternum. No need to saw through bone.

And so no need—yes, yes: that *was* what Cassandra Cheung had told me over the phone from Calgary: *"Says here they cut it out under a local anesthetic."*

Meaning I hadn't had my consciousness shut off. I wasn't knocked down to the classical-physics state then, back in February 2001—and so nothing had changed: I was a p-zed before the surgery and a p-zed afterward.

But Kayla—

"Wow, indeed," she'd said earlier tonight. *"But it's exactly what the math predicts, and it's exactly what happened to you and to my brother and to . . ."*

And to whom?

But no . . . that was crazy.

And, yet, when I'd started to tell her what I'd done to Menno, she deflected it, saying, *"It doesn't matter who we once were; all that matters is who we are now."*

Once were. Are now.

Jesus.

Could it be? Could she—

Kayla must have felt my spine stiffen because she said, softly, "What?"

My heart beat a few times, then. "Your tattoo . . ."

"I thought you liked it?"

"You had an appendectomy."

"Uh-huh," she said.

"Abdominal surgery."

"Yeah."

"When?"

"When I was twenty-two."

"So, 2003?"

"Yeah, I guess."

"And they put you under, right?"

"Well, yeah."

I found myself pulling slightly away from her. "When were you going to tell me?"

"Tell you what?" But it was obvious from her tone that she knew what I meant.

"Tell me that *you'd* been a psychopath when we were dating. If you're a Q3 now, you were a Q2 before the operation."

"*If,*" Kayla said firmly, "the anesthetic had actually caused decoherence, had actually put me out cold, hadn't just been an amnesia-inducing paralytic, hadn't—"

My voice was a mere whisper. "Oh, Kayla . . ."

She was quiet for a time, then, at last: "You're right. I should have told you." She exhaled noisily. "But, yeah, I *am* another data point: you, me, and Travis, we all changed states, shifting up or down exactly as the model predicts."

"Why not tell me? If anyone could have understood, I—"

"It wasn't the same thing. You have no idea what it's been like all these years. You, at least, don't remember the bad things you did in the past—or you didn't until just now, thanks to the spelunking you did with that memory expert, what's-his-name . . ."

"Namboothiri."

"But me? I remembered it all. Torturing animals as a kid. Being so cruel to a girl in junior high that she tried to kill herself. I *couldn't* tell you about all that; you'd never look at me the same way again."

"That's not so."

"But then I woke up in a hospital bed one day and realized that I'd changed. I told you that it had been Menno's class that got me interested in consciousness, but that's not true, and—I'm so sorry—I said it was what you had done all those years ago that got me interested in psychopathy. But that's not true, either. It was the advent of my own conscience the summer after I finished my bachelor's degree that did it. That's why I've devoted my career to this. I've been trying to figure out how *I* could have done the things I did, and why I no longer had uncontrollable urges to do similar things."

She reached over, took the hand I'd withdrawn, and placed it over her tattoo again. "A butterfly, see? In honor of my metamorphosis."

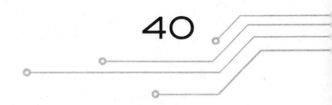

40

IT would have been nice if, after Kayla had shared the truth of her transformation with me, we had been able to fall asleep holding each other, accepting that who we are now mattered more than who we'd been then. But a peaceful sleep was not to be: we were immediately interrupted by a tentative knocking on the bedroom door, followed by a plaintive voice calling, "Mommy?"

Kayla found the bedspread, which I knew to be sea green although it looked slate gray in the darkness, and pulled it up to cover both of us to our shoulders.

"What is it, sweetheart?" Kayla asked.

Ryan took that as leave to enter, and I heard the knob working and a small squeak from the hinges. She was revealed, sufficiently illuminated by light spilling through her own open bedroom door on the opposite side of the corridor that I could see her eyes go wide. Apparently whatever she'd assumed normally happened after she'd been tucked in for the night did not include me joining her mother naked in bed. But that shock was quickly set aside, and Ryan said, "I'm frightened by the noises."

I could see on Kayla's face that she was about to ask, "What noises?"

But she checked herself: with doors open on both sides of the hallway now, she could hear them, too. Kayla's bedroom faced the backyard; Ryan's, the street—and it was from the street that the growing sounds of a raucous mob were coming.

Kayla got out of her bed—apparently this was a household where the parent was routinely seen naked by the child—and she quickly put on a robe and led Ryan from the room to investigate. That gave me a moment to retrieve my pants and shirt, strewn on the floor. I then hustled over to join them.

Kayla had wisely turned out the light in Ryan's room by the time I got there. Up the street, under the sodium lamps, a knot of six or eight teenagers was moving along, hurtling rocks at windows. The riots here had previously been confined to the downtown core; this was the first I'd heard of them spreading to the suburbs. Of course, in a smallish city like Saskatoon, that wasn't a particularly far journey—but still.

There was no phone in Ryan's room, so Kayla nipped back across the hall to call the police from there. In the yellow light, Ryan moved closer to me and reached up and took my hand. The mob was passing a small hatchback parked by the side of the road. A crowbar rang against its side panel, and the horn started honking, one blast per second, an android's heartbeat.

Kayla returned. "I tried three times," she said. "Busy! Fucking 911 is *busy*."

The mob rocked the hatchback, but it was too wide and squat for them to flip over, I guess, since they were soon moving forward, passing the house next to Kayla's. We couldn't see that building from this vantage point, but we could hear a booming male voice shouting from what I presumed was its open front door: "Get the hell away from here! Go on now! Get lost!"

That would not have been the tack I'd have taken, and indeed, it caused the seven teenagers—I'd managed to get a head count finally—to start moving onto his front lawn. Something caught my eye, and I looked for a second in the opposite direction. Another cluster of what must also be Q1s or Q2s was approaching—it was beginning to look like, by dumb geographic luck, Kayla's house was where the two groups would meet, assuming the ones on her neighbor's lawn didn't tarry long there, and—

Boom! Boom, boom!

The glass in front of us reverberated. Ryan let go of my hand and clutched her ears. I'd thought Kayla's next-door neighbor had opened fire from his stoop; the reports were echoing, their source difficult to locate. But after a second I realized that the guy who lived across the street from Kayla had come out into the night, brandishing what, to my untrained eye, looked like a hunting rifle.

I couldn't see the results of the first two shots—but the third one had hit one of the teenagers, who was closer to the road, in the back, and he'd gone face-first into a lawn that this time of night must have been slick with dew.

The flock dispersed, the four I could see running—two heading down the street, two more going up, unthinkingly heading for the second mob.

Boom!

Another shot ruptured the night, and I saw a runner briefly splay all four limbs like a crippled starfish, then tumble forward to the asphalt. Kayla and Ryan had dropped below the windowsill, and they were scuttling out of the room, toward the relative safety of the back of the house. But I stood transfixed, stunned by it all. *"Jim!"* Kayla whisper-shouted. *"Get down!"*

I dropped to the floor just as the rifle erupted again. A second car alarm went off, a harsh counterpoint to the one already wailing. I kept hoping for the sound of sirens, too—police swooping in to serve and protect—but all we heard the rest of that long night was honking horns, breaking glass, gunshots, and screams.

The cacophony finally abated by dawn. Kayla's bedroom faced east, and the sun bloodied the horizon early this time of year. Ryan had joined us in bed.

As we got up, Ryan announced emphatically that she didn't want to go to day camp, which was good, actually: leaving here would have meant taking her by the dead bodies. A quick check out her bedroom window showed no sign of the cops or an ambulance having made it here yet; Kayla had finally gotten through to 911, but the harried operator had simply said the police would get there as soon as they could.

And although an email from Jeff Cutler reported that no bomb had actually been found at the Light Source, I didn't want Kayla returning to it. In the end, we decided to simply hole up in the house. Kayla called to make sure her mom and brother were all right (they were), and she phoned Victoria, who was likewise fine; Vic lived in an apartment building and had looked down on the roiling violence in her own neighborhood from the comparative safety of her eighth-floor balcony. She didn't have beamtime until late today, and so said she'd come on over and work with Kayla from here if the roads were passable.

I'd known Kayla was the woman for me when I first saw that she had bookcases in her dining room. She also had books on the top of toilets—I'd once had to move volumes by Feynman, Bohr, Rutherford, and Penrose when I'd needed to take the top off the tank after her downstairs one didn't flush properly. But, in addition to books everywhere, she also had TV monitors in each room. I tuned the one in the kitchen to the CBC News Network as Ryan and I busied ourselves making breakfast while Kayla had a shower. I wasn't going to make bacon or eggs, but toast with jam, bananas (yay!), and yogurt would do the trick.

Apparently, yesterday President Carroway had been surreptitiously recorded on a cell phone giving a talk to business executives in Wyoming, and the footage had been posted on YouTube. The video showed Carroway standing at a podium but the upper-left corner of the image was cut off—I soon realized because the camera was partially hidden under a linen napkin. *"Many of you here today,"* Carroway intoned, *"remember the 1973 oil crisis and the 1979 energy crisis. Our great nation held hostage by Muslim oil barons in the Middle East, the very lifeblood of our economy cut off at their caprice."*

There was an indignant murmur from the audience. Carroway went on: *"Why, in 1974, because of them, your national government—loath then and loath now to intervene in states' affairs—had to impose a national speed limit of just fifty-five miles per hour!"*

The table got jostled by a waiter; Carroway shifted in the frame.

"We can never again let anyone put the brakes on America. And yet Canada still refuses to turn on the oil pipeline we so desperately need. That's right, my fellow Americans: the new leadership in Ottawa, under the command of Naheed Kurban Nenshi, has already caved to so-called 'First Nations' Indians and rabid environmentalists." Carroway shook his head. "You'd think green Canucks would be happy to see the tree line inching north—all the more trees for them to hug!"

The next story also featured the president. Yesterday, Carroway had actually given Nenshi a call, the gist of which the president discussed in a news conference. The angle and lighting were more flattering in this footage, and this podium bore the Presidential Seal.

"Mr. President," called out a female journalist, "I understand rioting continues in cities and towns across Canada, as well as now in many places in Europe."

"Yes, that's right, I'm afraid," said Carroway. "Obviously, civil unrest anywhere in the world is a concern, but when it's occurring in our own backyard, we have to take special notice."

Another reporter, this one male: "Have you spoken directly to Prime Minister Nenshi about it?"

"Yes, indeed. We spoke early this morning. The United States has offered every possible assistance, but the prime minister assured me that his small army and his local and national police—you know, the Mounties—were more than capable of containing the situation."

A different male reporter: "This was your first official call to Canada's Muslim prime minister since he was sworn in, wasn't it?"

"That's correct."

"Did you speak to him about the issue of Libyan terrorists entering the US via Canada?"

"That topic didn't come up, but I'm sure Mr. Nenshi knows it's always at the top of my mind."

Another woman: "Well, what other issues did you raise with the Canadian leader?"

Carroway frowned briefly. "Prime Minister Nenshi and I had a frank exchange of views. I emphasized the historic ties between our two great nations, but I also expressed to him our deep, heartfelt concern *that his country's record on the rights of the unborn is profoundly disturbing to us. Having finally gotten our own house in order, we can no longer turn a blind eye to the slaughtering of innocents elsewhere. Here in North America, Canada stands alone, a rogue state, on this issue. Our great neighbor to the south, Mexico, only allows abortion on very narrow grounds. Indeed, in all the New World—North, Central, and South America—only Canada, Communist Cuba, and the tiny nations of Guyana, French Guiana, and Uruguay offer unrestricted access to abortion."*

A male journalist: *"Given the overturning of* Roe v. Wade *by our Supreme Court, are you concerned that American women will travel north to procure procedures that they can't obtain here?"*

Carroway nodded. *"We're certainly monitoring the situation—monitoring it very, very closely."*

Ryan had been watching me as much as she was watching the TV, and I guess she could tell by my body language that what was being said had disturbed me. "What does 'monitoring the situation' mean?" she asked.

I went to fetch the toast; it had apparently popped up a while ago but I'd been too preoccupied to notice. "I wish I knew, Ginger Ale."

I changed channels—and Fox News, which I had my own TV set to skip over, came on. As soon as I saw what they were talking about, I muted the sound and silently read the closed captioning rather than exposing Ryan to it.

The Correction.

That's what Fox kept referring to it as. Innocuous. A minor course change; just setting things right. A remedy, for God's sake.

Sure, the other news channels had more accurate names for it, but Fox's audience was the largest, and even those who wrote the network's name as "Faux News," an Internet meme for more than a decade now, had heard it called "The Correction" in clips on *The Daily Show* or on Facebook.

No one would ever know the exact death toll, but the extermination started by the McCharles Act—the law of the land in Texas, and it seemed the *de facto* law across most of the Southern states now—was rising rapidly. One estimate put it already at more than five thousand, with no end in sight, and many thought it was much, much higher; after all, those family members of victims—or of "correctees," as Fox called them—who'd escaped being culled themselves weren't likely to come forward to report a missing sibling or child.

The image switched to an elderly Latina woman, tears on sun-creased cheeks, looking out over the site of another mass killing, bodies strewn across parchment-colored dirt. I quickly turned off the set before Ryan looked up from her breakfast.

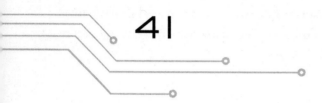

41

WHEN Kayla joined us, dressed in blue jeans and a T-shirt, and with a towel wrapped around her head, I filled her in on what was happening, starting with the call between the president and the prime minister.

"Carroway," she said, as if naming a bacillus. "The guy's got to be a psychopath."

"I imagine so," I agreed.

"And, for that matter," said Kayla, "Governor McCharles, too. I'd love to get those guys down on the beamline, prove the truth about them to the world." An idea blossomed on her face. "Say, what about your microsaccades technique? Can't you do it on them?"

"I doubt they're going to volunteer to put on my goggles."

"No, no, but you said you could do it with film, right?"

At some point, I'd told Kayla the same story I'd told my sister Heather about analyzing Anthony Hopkins playing Hannibal Lecter. "Yeah," I said, "but *The Silence of the Lambs* was a special case—a sustained close-up shot of the character staring directly into the camera, and I could get it at 4K resolution." I shook my head. "It's the same problem with the videos Menno made of me in 2001. I'd love to try my test on that VHS tape, confirm that I was a Q1 even during the final interview—prove it was paralimbic damage not quantum psychopathy—but the footage isn't nearly high-enough resolution, and, besides, they're kind of side views; no way to visually check for microsaccades."

"Hell," said Kayla, "the president of the United States has to be one of the most-photographed people in the world. There must be existing footage of him that's sufficiently high-resolution."

"Sure. The Sunday-morning political shows—Stephanopoulos, *Meet the Press*—are all done in 4K now, but they keep cutting away. One, two, three, cut; one, two, three, cut. Even when he's talking, they keep going to a reaction shot."

"Don't those programs have the footage they didn't broadcast?"

I'd made a few dozen TV appearances over the years. "Not normally; those sorts of interviews are done live-to-air or live-to-tape: the director switches between cameras as the interview is being conducted, and only the image from the selected camera is actually broadcast or recorded."

"What about press conferences, like that one you just saw?"

"They'd be good, but, again, he has to keep looking at the same thing, and I doubt he does."

"How much footage do you need?"

"Well, if he's not a psychopath, it should be obvious after three or four seconds—but to prove that he is? I'd really like ten uninterrupted seconds."

"Ten seconds with no blinking?"

"Blinks are fine, but he needs to be looking at the same thing for all ten seconds, and without his cooperation, that's going to be hard to get."

"Maybe," said Kayla. "Maybe not. He makes tons of public appearances. And lots of people have great cameras these days. Find the next rally he's at and ask online for someone to get high-res video, focusing on his eyes."

"Who would do that?"

"Tons of people. Your technique is public knowledge now—"

"No, it isn't. I mean, the *goggles* are public knowledge, after the Becker trial, but the fact that you can also do the test with high-resolution footage? I've kept that under wraps."

"Why?" asked Kayla.

Why, indeed? Besides just a concern for people's privacy, there were two main answers. First, just as Menno had felt it better to hide that most of humanity lacked inner lives, I'd worried that if untrained individuals started trying to apply my test, the inevitable incorrect diagnoses from those who simply failed to detect microsaccades that were actually there would ruin relationships and careers, and maybe even lead to vigilante justice. As I'd told Heather, Bob Hare had voiced similar concerns in 2011 when Jon Ronson had published his pop-sci book *The Psychopath Test: A Journey Through the Madness Industry,* which described the PCL-R and suggested laypeople could make correct assessments.

And the other reason? Economics. Hare made royalties off the PCL-R, the complete kit for which sold for $439; I—and, just as importantly, my university, which held the patents—stood to make a lot more money licensing Marchuk Goggles than we did from a technique anyone could apply.

I explained this in a few words; Kayla got it instantly. "Still," she said, "there have to be people out there who either have, or can get, the footage you need."

The doorbell rang; Victoria had arrived. Ryan announced that today was a perfect day to watch *Minions III* for, by my guess, the thousandth time—that would keep her occupied, and a Google scavenger hunt would keep me busy while the physicists worked.

And, at last, I found what I wanted. I'd had no idea there were websites devoted to whether famous people had had plastic surgery, but in fact there are lots of them. Few performers publicly admitted to a facelift or boob job, and that had given rise to an online industry of minutely analyzing supposedly before-and-after photos and having commentators of varying degrees of expertise hazard opinions about what work might have been done. On a site arguing that Quinton Carroway had had an eyelift—I didn't even know that was a thing—there was a very-high-resolution still frame of his face with a caption saying it was taken from some pirated footage checking the president's makeup before a recent speech. I dropped a note to the site's proprietor, asking if the actual video was online somewhere, and, to my surprise, ten minutes later he'd replied with a BitTorrent link to a solid minute of 4K video of an extreme close-up of the president. I checked on Ryan while it downloaded to my laptop, then stuck my head into Kayla's office.

"No, no, no," Kayla was saying, "surely the Hamiltonian at *t-prime* is going to be at least as big as it was at *t*."

"Sorry to interrupt," I said, "but I've got some good footage of Carroway, and I'm about to run my analysis. Want to see?"

They rose, and we headed back to the dining-room table upon which my laptop was resting. The footage was still loading frame by frame into the software.

I'd become quite attuned to eye color while doing my research on microsaccades. Anthony Hopkins has pale blue-gray eyes; Jodie Foster's are a more gunmetal blue—although, for some reason, they're shown as brown on the poster for *The Silence of the Lambs,* which depicts her with a death's-head hawkmoth covering her mouth. It's easy to pick out the pupil against blue or green eyes; it's a lot harder to track it against brown ones—which is what President Carroway had—and I preferred to track the actual pupil than the iris. But fiddling with the brightness and contrast settings let me get a good-enough lock, and I hit the play button. "Okay, here we go."

One second. Two. Three. Four. "Damn." His gaze darted to the left.

One. Two. "Shit." He tipped his whole head down.

One. Two. Three. His hand came up to rub his left eye.

One. Two. Three. Four. Five. Six. Sev—nope, turning, as someone called to him.

One. Two. "Crap." He looked off to the right.

One. Two. Three. Four. "Oh, for the love of Pete!" Some clown had walked in front of the camera.

One. Two. Three. Four. Five. Six. "Yes!" Seven. *Eight!* "Yes!" *Nine!* "Yes, yes!" *Ten!*

"So?" said Victoria anxiously. "Is he or isn't he?"

"Just a sec," I said, switching over to the pupillary-deviation graph. Nothing greater than one minute of arc—the kind of jiggle caused by the body's own pulsing blood; microsaccades were at least two arc minutes and could range up to a hundred and twenty.

"Bingo," I said, crossing my arms in front of my chest. "There's no doubt about it: the president of the United States is a psychopath."

Starting late in our afternoon, there were reports of riots in Cologne, Rome, and Budapest, and that night, there was more rioting all across Canada, but, thankfully, no more along Kayla's tree-lined street—although border cities such as Seattle, Detroit, and Buffalo were showing signs of similar lawlessness.

"I don't get it," Kayla said, sitting next to me on her living-room couch after we turned off the news. "What's the trigger?"

I shook my head. "There isn't one."

"But the rioting is spreading."

"And so are fashion styles, and Internet memes, and conspiracy theories, as always. And Boko Haram is conducting raids, like every day, and antisemitism is expanding like a poison puddle across Europe again. And idealistic kids are being radicalized, like every other day. And people are joining cults and reading their horoscopes, like every other damn day. Wars are raging in the Middle East and Africa, as usual; climate change is being ignored, evolution denied, sexism and racism perpetuated, all as per usual. Sure, most memes that take hold are reasonably benign, but malignant ones can spread just as easily, whether you call them the KKK or National Socialism or the Troubles in Northern Ireland or a decade or more of missing and murdered Native women in Canada."

"But something must have caused them to spread."

"Sure, but it was doubtless something small. Losing a hockey game in Winnipeg; other picayune catalysts elsewhere. You don't need a complex explanation—some particle-physics or neuroscience mumbo jumbo—for something that's happened over and over and over again throughout history." I glanced down at the spot where her blouse was concealing her tattoo. "Butterflies don't just symbolize metamorphosis; they symbolize small changes having big effects."

"Yeah," she said. "I guess."

She leaned in and kissed me, then went off to put Ryan to bed. When we retired for the evening, Kayla fell asleep before I did, and I lay in the dark, listening to the susurration of her breath, waves lapping a beach.

It should have come as no particular surprise, I supposed, that President Carroway was a psychopath. Such people were ideally suited to politics, each one a heaping plateful of traits selected from a smorgasbord that included pathological lying, charisma, glibness, skillful manipulation, and promiscuity—literally and figuratively getting into bed with whoever served the needs of the moment. Working my way through the presidents I knew anything about, I suspected several others had also been psychopaths, including some Democrats (surely Lyndon Johnson and almost as certainly Bill Clinton) and some Republicans (doubtless Richard Nixon and maybe George W. Bush, although I'd go even money that Dubya was a p-zed in the thrall of Dick Cheney).

But holding suspicions and actually knowing were two different things. And as I lay there, a sickle moon hanging low out the window, I wondered what the Leader of the Free World was going to do next.

42

did not have to wait long to find out. The next morning, President Carroway's latest speech was all over the media. Kayla and I, and Ryan, sensing the solemnity of what was going on even if she didn't understand it, watched it, the three of us sitting slack-jawed in front of the living-room TV. Carroway began by striding to the podium and uttering four words that would doubtless become a meme in their own right: "*My fellow North Americans . . .*"

My heart thundered. The president went on in the adamantine baritone I'd previously heard admonishing those passing through airports: "*On my order, beginning at 9:00 A.M. Eastern time, US Customs and Border Protection agents closed the border between the United States and Canada, locking down all vehicular crossings and all US Customs stations at Canadian airports. At the same time, United States Air Force jets scrambled from McChord Air Force Base in Washington State, Minot Air Force Base in North Dakota, Wright-Patterson Air Force Base in Ohio, and Andrews Air Force Base in Maryland; these jets have now secured Canadian airspace.*"

"My God . . ." Kayla said softly.

Carroway's dark eyes narrowed slightly. "*At 9:17 A.M., our ambas-*

sador to Canada, Schuyler Grayson, accompanied by a United States Marine Corps honor guard, presented himself at 24 Sussex Drive in Ottawa, the home of the Canadian prime minister, to urge Prime Minister Naheed Nenshi to finally accept our aid in quelling the ongoing rioting that has begun to spill over the border into this country."

I wasn't sure which of us initiated it, but Kayla's left hand and my right found each other.

"Prime Minister Nenshi once again refused our assistance in containing the situation. This has left us with no choice; America's interests must be protected throughout the world. And so, on my orders, US troops are now moving into Ottawa, into all provincial capitals, and into other Canadian cities with populations in excess of one million; government buildings and essential infrastructure in each will be secured by nightfall. The Governor General of Canada, who serves as Commander in Chief of the Canadian Forces, has seen the wisdom of asking her troops to stand down, and we expect a smooth transition."

Gimlet eyes bored into the camera, a cold, reptilian glare: *"God bless the United States—including our northern provinces and territories, now fully under American protection."*

"Jesus Christ," I said softly. "We've been annexed."

And then things got worse.

In a brave attempt at thinking life would go on pretty much as normal, Ryan had relented and gone back to day camp, and Kayla had returned to the Light Source. I'd intended to work on the third edition of *Utilitarian Ethics of Everyday Life,* which I'd been putting off far too long, but I found myself transfixed by what was happening. Rarely, if ever, was Canada the lead "International News" story on any site, and I hadn't realized until just now how comforting that actually was. But suddenly everyone—the BBC, NHK, Al-Jazeera, both the American and Australian ABC, and more—was talking about the True North, not so strong and something less than free.

Actually, as the day wore on, the coverage shifted from what was happening *in* Canada to how *others* were reacting to it: outrage from

London, which still took a paternal interest in its erstwhile colony; Pope Francis decrying this return to imperialism; a gathering of Iraqi imams denouncing what they called the transparent Islamophobia behind this flagrant violation of international norms; some Americans claiming Carroway had manufactured "the Canadian crisis" to distract from the culling of illegals within the United States; a government official in Mexico fretting that his country was bound to be taken next.

By three in the afternoon—which, CTV Saskatoon informed me, was 6:00 A.M. in Moscow—it had become clear that the Russians, who'd as yet made no public announcement, were reacting very negatively. Three *Akula*-class nuclear submarines had been tracked moving boldly into Canadian Arctic waters. According to the pundits, the Kremlin was viewing Carroway's incursion as if it were the Cuban Missile Crisis in reverse: with Canada suddenly a *de facto* part of the United States, America was now head-butting the Siberian frontier. As a woman from Harvard observed, except for Alaska and the Chukotka Peninsula, which had been locked in a staring contest across the Bering Strait since the end of the last ice age, the two superpowers had been kept safely apart by the vast granite hulk of Canada—until now.

Kayla got home from work at 7:10 P.M.; she'd picked up Ryan on the way here. "Have you been following the news?" I asked, gathering them in a hug.

"Oh, yes," Kayla said.

I'd muted the sound on the living-room monitor when I'd heard the front door opening, but Vladimir Putin was on the screen. At the best of times, he had a dour countenance. Today he looked positively livid although, given that his government had annexed Crimea—home to many a Marchuk—back in 2014, he apparently only waxed apoplectic when someone else mounted an invasion.

"He's got to be a psychopath, too, you know," said Kayla, tilting her head at the screen.

It seemed almost superfluous to check, but as Kayla took Ryan upstairs to get cleaned up, I dropped a note to my online benefactor from yesterday, who was as accommodating and expeditious as before. He said there was no doubt among those who tracked such things that the Russian president had had a raft of cosmetic operations, including a nose job, cheek fillers, and at least one facelift, not to mention an ongoing regimen of Botox injections; I was soon downloading high-resolution footage to my laptop that purported to show telltale signs of these procedures.

The video, which seemed to be of Putin enduring a long question from some journalist who doubtless shortly thereafter had received a one-way ticket to the Gulag, contained a solid twelve seconds of the president's full-on disdainful stare. Just as Kayla had opined, my software confirmed that Vladimir Putin was indeed a psychopath. I shared this news as she came back downstairs; Ryan had stayed up in her room.

Kayla nodded. "Which means," she said, a quaver in her voice, "he's not likely to back down."

"Neither is Carroway," I said. "It's like how it was with your brother Travis—extreme sports, right? The rush of adrenaline? You think *snowboarding* is a kick, imagine nuclear brinksmanship with trillions of dollars' worth of weapons at your command." I shook my head. "Those two pricks are *loving* this."

We watched the muted images for a time—intercuts between Carroway and Putin, back and forth, thrust and parry. "Somebody has to stop them," Kayla said at last.

"Yes," I replied softly—so softly that she asked me to repeat myself. "Yes," I said again, boosting my outer voice to match my inner one, "somebody does."

43

KAYLA and I stayed up late, trying to make sense of it all. We talked about politics, and what being Canadian meant to us, about whether Canada had already really been nothing more than an American appendage anyway, about whether this was of a piece with previous American foreign policy or something wholly new and unprecedented. But, really, in the end, the fact that there were now American boots tamping down Canadian soil mattered much less than that the Russians and the Americans, each led by a psychopath, were flinging invective at each other today and might be hurling missiles across Canada tomorrow.

My grandfather, while doing what he'd done at Sobibor, had seen a world war up close; my father had often spoken of the fear of nuclear apocalypse that had put a pall over everything in the 1950s and 1960s. Ghosts were not resting easily tonight.

"Okay," I said to Kayla, facing her on the couch, "here's a question: why can't we just have someone surge in with the quantum tuning fork and give President Carroway a boost from his current state as a psychopathic Q2 into a quick? Give him a conscience; problem solved."

She frowned. "Because the tuning fork doesn't work on already conscious individuals; it only works on totally unconscious people who are in the classical-physics state. You know that."

"Right. But why?"

"I told you why. Because the aggregate mass of humanity—all the Q1s, all the Q2s, and all the Q3s—are quantally entangled; they collectively form one quantum system."

"Yes. So?"

She sounded pissed at what she took to be me being deliberately obtuse. "So the entanglement inertia keeps things from changing. The tuning fork tries to alter the mind of a specific person, but that person has to move in lockstep with seven billion others."

"And the tuning fork is *puny*, right?" I said. "It doesn't put out enough juice against all that. Oh, sure, the fork can put someone *into* superposition if they aren't there already. But to change someone who is currently in quantum superposition would require changing *everyone's* state, right?"

"Yes, that's what the simulations show. And there's no way the tuning fork could do that. Damn thing runs on double-A batteries, for crying out loud."

"Exactly. But if you had a more powerful tuning fork?"

"Well, you'd need a hell of a—oh." She lifted her eyebrows. "The synchrotron?"

"Yes," I said. "The synchrotron. The Canadian Light Source. How powerful is it again?"

"Almost three gigaelectronvolts."

"Which is, like, a lot, right?"

"Yes," she said softly.

"And what did you call it? 'The Swiss Army knife of particle accelerators,' with all those parameters you can adjust, right? Could it do what the quantum tuning fork does, but on a scale—what?—eight orders of magnitude larger? Affecting billions of people instead of just one?"

"Nine," said Kayla automatically, but then she frowned, considering this—and, at last, she nodded. "Yes, yes, I think it could. Vic would know for sure—she's the synchrotron specialist, not me—but from what she told me about how the quantum tuning fork works, yeah, you could emulate it with the synchrotron, and, yes, I guess you *could* scale it up to that level."

"There!" I said, triumphantly. "You could engineer a massive shift."

She snorted. "Well, you'd certainly get 'Capgras syndrome' trending on Twitter." Capgras was a rare psychological condition in which people became convinced that some of their closest friends or family members had been replaced by soulless duplicates.

"I'm serious," I said. "We could shift *everyone*."

She narrowed her gaze. "But why?"

"What have I been saying all along? Utilitarianism. The greatest good for the greatest number. The needs of the many outweigh the needs of the few—or the one."

"Christ's sake, this is no time for *Star Trek*."

I looked at her like she'd lost her mind. "It's no time for crappy *Star Trek*," I replied. *"Star Trek III: The Search for Spock,* that was a piece of shit. Kirk says in it, 'The needs of the one'—by which he means Spock—'outweigh the needs of the many.' But *The Wrath of Khan*—or, as we philosophers like to call it, *The Wrath of Kant*—is a classic. And it got the utilitarian formulation exactly right: the needs of the many *do* outweigh the needs of the few."

"Jim, I know you really believe that, but—"

"Sam Harris says morality is about the flourishing of conscious beings. And the fact is that, right now, four billion human beings *aren't* conscious, not in the way you and I understand the term; Q1s have *no* inner lives. Only the Q2s and Q3s do, and together they make up only three out of seven billion people. But imagine if we used the synchrotron to actually boost someone one state—in the process dragging the rest of humanity along with him or her. Those four billion Q1s would be goosed up to being Q2s, and the two billion people who were Q2s—including Carroway and Putin—would rise up to being Q3."

Kayla looked aghast. "Are you out of your mind?"

"We'd be *doubling* the total number of conscious humans—from three billion to six."

"By doubling the number of psychopaths!"

"Partially, but we'd also be doubling the number of quicks, from one billion to two."

Kayla shook her head in disbelief. "You think turning the majority of the human race into *psychopaths* is the way to solve the world's problems?"

"Well . . . yes."

"By knocking you, me, and everyone else who's currently a quick down to being a p-zed?"

"That would be a side effect, yes, because the states wrap around, and—"

"And that doesn't bother you? That you'd go from—from philosopher to philosopher's zombie?"

"A utilitarian can't put his own interest preferentially ahead of someone else's. And this would result in the greatest happiness for—"

"Damn it, Jim, the four billion p-zeds who exist now aren't unhappy; they're *incapable* of being unhappy. They literally don't know what they're missing."

"But *we* know what they're missing—and we can give it to them."

"By making them all into psychopaths?"

As I'd observed before, it was almost unheard of for a psychopath to suffer from depression or take his or her own life. "Psychopaths are usually happy; they enjoy their lives." And then, admittedly hitting below the belt, I added, "Remember?"

She sucked in air but didn't deny it. Still, she said: "Your opinion is . . . atypical. You defend psychopaths. Literally. In courtrooms."

"That's because they're people, too; they're conscious beings."

"Yes, and a couple of those conscious beings—one in Washington and another in Moscow—are about to get the world blown straight to hell."

"Yes, but, as I said, if we shift everyone, Carroway and Putin—not to mention Governor McCharles in Texas—will suddenly get a conscience, just like you did; just like Travis did. Russia and the US might be on the brink of war now, but they won't be able to go through with it; they'll stand down. We save the world *and* we double the number of conscious entities while we're at it." I spoke to her—and to myself. "This isn't supererogation; this isn't more than is necessary. It's the bare minimum that we can do. It's a moral imperative."

Kayla was shaking her head slowly back and forth, left and right. "No," she said. "That's not the answer."

I folded my arms. "Do you have a better idea?"

She looked right at me. "As a matter of fact," she said, "I do."

We adjourned to Kayla's office, next to the dining room; it was well after midnight, we were both punchy, and it seemed useful to have a computer in front of us.

"Okay," said Kayla, bringing up a chart she'd used before, "there are three quantum cohorts, right? Each with half the number of people in it as the one before—a 4:2:1 ratio. Call the cohorts alpha, beta, and gamma, in descending order of size. Round numbers, there are four billion people in alpha, the current crop of Q1 p-zeds; two billion in beta, the Q2 psychopaths; and one billion in gamma, the Q3 quicks, right?"

"Yes," I said.

"And you want to boost them all one state, right? The four billion people in cohort alpha go up to being Q2 psychopaths; the two billion in cohort beta go up to being Q3 quicks, and the one billion in cohort gamma—the cohort you were born into and I'm now part of—wrap around to being Q1 p-zeds." She moved things around with her mouse until her chart reflected those shifts.

"Exactly. The greatest—"

"No, it's not."

"Pardon?"

"It's not the greatest good for the greatest number, at least not by any normal person's reckoning—no offense."

"Um, none taken."

"The right answer," Kayla said, "isn't to boost everybody up one state—it's to boost them *two* states. Push all of cohort alpha—the largest group—from Q1 right up to Q3, giving them both consciousness *and* conscience. You end up with the largest number of quicks possible: for the first time ever, the majority of the human race will finally be firing on all cylinders."

"My God, yes! And then—"

"And everyone's moving in quantum lockstep, right? So if cohort alpha goes up two states, so does beta: all the current psychopaths—Quinton Carroway, Vladimir Putin, and all the other assholes who are ruining it for the rest of us—shift two levels, as well, right? They go up to being Q3s then wrap around, ending up as Q1s. That essentially *deactivates* them, turning every last quantum psychopath into a p-zed." She lifted a hand. "We can't go back in time and assassinate Hitler, but we *can* stop every despotic leader, every heartless banker, every evil person on the planet."

She paused, then: "Now, yes, there do have to be *some* psychopaths. But think about it: cohort gamma will move by two steps, too, wrapping around first to Q1 p-zeditude and then settling in at Q2 psychopathy. Since gamma is the *smallest* cohort, you end up with the fewest psychopaths possible."

She was in a swivel chair; I was in a regular one—but I leaned it back, balancing on its two hind legs, and thought. I had no desire to be a quantum psychopath, which is what I'd become if I shifted twice, but yeah, Kayla's plan would cut the number of psychopaths in half, while quadrupling the number of quicks. "And," I said, it suddenly coming to me, "as Namboothiri explained it to me, most Q2s and Q3s index their memories verbally, so at least this smaller crop of newly minted psychopaths *will* remember having had a conscience, remember what it was like to have given a damn about others. Hopefully, that'll take some of their edge off."

"Hopefully," Kayla said.

She sounded dubious, but I seized on the word. "Exactly!" I was giddy now, the way one can be when past the point of exhaustion. "*Literally.* Full of hope. True, the new Q2s perhaps won't be, but think about all those new Q3s! For the first time since we stood erect on the savanna, there will be billions and billions of humans full of hope."

I'd hoped Kayla would match my grin, but she didn't; her eyebrows came together and her mouth turned down. "But," she said, harshing the buzz, "even if it were technically possible—even if we *could* do this, I mean . . ."

"Yes?"

"I mean, come on, Jim, do we have the right to do it? We'd be playing God."

I leaned forward again. "The role of God has gone unfilled for too long," I said. "It's high time someone got the part."

44

W E finally hauled ourselves upstairs to the bedroom as Sagittarius was setting in the south—you had to stay up awfully damn late in summer to see that.

I'd used the little downstairs washroom, but as I lay in bed, I could hear Kayla in the *en suite* splashing literal, and, as it turned out, figurative, cold water on her face.

She emerged in the doorway, a toothbrush hanging from her mouth. "But," she said, "you know, even if we shift everyone now, what about the future? What if the 4:2:1 ratio between superposition states remains constant as new children are born? We'd end up back where we'd started."

"Eventually, maybe," I said. "But in the developed world, people live the better part of a century or more now, and that figure just keeps going up. It's 2020; so, yeah, maybe by the year 2120, left unattended, things might cycle back to p-zeds predominating, assuming we don't start doing quantum-superposition testing *in utero*. But that still gets us through the rest of this century. Hell, quantum physics is barely a hundred years old now; who the heck knows what level of control we'll have over it a hundred years hence? I'm content to solve the problem for the foreseeable future."

She swiped her brush up and down a few times, then, "Okay, forget about the future. What about the present? What about the people in your own life, Jim?"

"Well," I said, propping my head up on a bent elbow, "there's my sister Heather. I'm sure she's a p-zed now; she'll go up to being a Q3."

Kayla did a little more brushing. "That's *fine,* but you don't have any children. I do." She returned to the washroom, and I heard her expectorate the toothpaste, then a little more running water, and then she came to bed, facing me.

During that short break, I'd taken a deep breath and let it out slowly. It wasn't that I'd been *hiding* it from Kayla, but although we'd talked about so many things—ethics and science and culture, movies and music and morality—the right moment for *this* had never come up.

"Actually," I said softly, "I do."

"Do what?" said Kayla, having lost the thread.

"Do have a child. A boy. He's two."

Even in the dark, I could see her eyes go wide. "When the hell were you going to tell me *that?*"

"I never see him." And then, as if it were exculpatory, "I pay child support. But I never see him. Anna-Lee has sole custody."

And, if saying I was still with the university I'd done my undergrad at was a red flag for academics, *that* was a red flag for just about everyone. "Why?"

I rolled on my back. "It's what Anna-Lee wanted. He has Down syndrome, and . . ."

I trailed off and looked at the simplicity of the plain square ceiling. But just as I'd refused to be Penny to Kayla's Leonard, immersing myself in quantum physics so I could keep pace with her, so, too, had Kayla been reading up on utilitarianism. "And if Anna-Lee is about your age, you might well have had prenatal screening, right? So you knew while she was pregnant."

I said nothing.

Kayla shook her head, a rustling sound against the pillow. "I don't know. I won't presume to put myself in your place, or Anna-Lee's, but . . . but, damn it, Jim, it's *different.* It's *supposed* to be different. I'm not just talking about utilitarians; I'm talking about all human beings. When it's you and yours, all the calculus in the world is supposed to go out the window."

"I know that," I said. "And, believe me, I do love my son, and want the very best for him. I'm always wondering how he's doing, what he's up to."

She pointed at the wall, referring to Ryan, asleep across the hall—out of sight, but, for her mother, never out of mind. "I know the Hare Checklist at least as well as you do. You've read it, but I've *lived* it; I've been a Q2 and I've been a Q3, and I can tell the difference better than your goggles or Vic's beamline can. My daughter is a Q3, and even if *every single person on the planet except her* would benefit from what you want to do, I would stand in your way. Ryan comes first, and I'm not condemning her to becoming what I was, what her uncle was. No way."

"Did you have Vic test her on the beamline? Because I'd have bet money my sister was a Q3. That's the thing about Q1s, right? Almost all of the time, they're behaviorally indistinguishable from those who *are* conscious. And if Ryan's a Q1, this *will* be a gift to her, the greatest possible gift."

"Of course we tested her," Kayla said. "Once we found out that my brother had been a quantum psychopath, too, just like me—well, I had to know, right? But Ryan absolutely is a Q3. But you know what? Maybe quantum states *do* run in families. I was born a Q2 and so was Travis. But your sister is a Q1, you say? A mindless automaton that follows rules and algorithms? And your grandfather was just a cog in the Nazi machine, you say, doing what he was ordered to do at Sobibor? I don't know what either of them look like—but you're the spitting image of them."

"Kayla, please—"

And now she waved in the direction of her bedroom TV; it was off, but I gathered she was referring to the news we'd seen on the downstairs set earlier. "And you know what the biggest problem with the world today is?" she said "It's not psychopaths like Putin and Carroway, not directly. There's only so much damage either of them can do. The problem is the scientists who gleefully make the things psychopaths want them to make; there'd be no nuclear bombs, or Zyklon B gas chambers, or any of that shit, without scientists who were willing to do whatever they were asked to do. But without me or Vic, there's no way you can shift all of humanity, so that's that." She rolled away from me. "Live with it, Jim: the world is what it is."

I thought about this for a time, and had finally decided to counter with, "Until the bombs start falling"—but I could tell by the sound of her breathing that Kayla was already asleep.

Kayla went to the Light Source again the next morning, and Ryan agreed to go back to day camp once more, but Victoria Chen had been assigned overnight beamtime; she didn't have to go in again until late that afternoon. And so, figuring if Robert Oppenheimer tells you to get lost, you try your luck with Edward Teller, I called her up and had her come over for coffee. She cheerfully agreed, arriving about forty minutes later; today's combination was a loose, black silk top and black denim jeans.

Vic was pacing the length of the living room, a process that took her about twice the number of strides it would have taken me. She had her smartphone out, with some scientific-calculator app running. "You're talking about knocking everyone on Earth unconscious," she said. "A global blackout, like in that TV show."

I was seated in the easy chair, fingers interlaced behind my head. "No, no. That's the last thing we want—and not just because of the carnage it would cause. If everyone blacks out, then the whole entangled collective falls apart, right? You'd have to reboot people individually after that with the quantum tuning fork, *if* you could reboot them at all—which is a mighty big if since, so far, it's only worked on Travis. No, no one can lose consciousness; we need all of humanity to remain entangled so that everyone moves in lockstep."

She paced and calculated for a time, then she said, "Yeah, I could accomplish that." Having reached the end of the living room, marked by a sliding glass door with vertical blinds, like diffraction grating, she turned and headed the other way, toward a wall with jam-packed bookcases. As she walked, she continued to tap and swipe her calculator.

"But you'd have to start with a p-zed on the beamline," she said—Vic and Kayla had both long ago adopted my shorthand—"because only a Q1 can go up two states."

"I don't see—"

"You need to boost someone who can go through two successively greater levels of superposition: someone who currently has only one superpositioned electron, then can be boosted to having two, and then can be boosted once more to having three. You couldn't start with someone already at a higher state, because any attempt I made with the synchrotron to get them to wrap around would probably cause all their electrons to fall out of superposition, making them exit the entangled collective."

"Fine, okay," I said. "A p-zed, then. What about Ross? Your ex-boyfriend? He already agreed to come down to your beamline once before." Of course, I also immediately thought of my sister back in Winnipeg, but it wasn't like Ross alone would benefit; if this worked, Heather and every p-zed all over the world would ramp up to full consciousness with conscience.

Vic tapped away some more, then, finally coming to a stop, she shook her head.

"What's the matter with Ross?" I asked.

"No, no, it's not that." I wouldn't have thought it possible, but her skin seemed even paler than normal. She held up the phone for me to see.

I leaned in for a look, but the mathematical notation on her screen might as well have been cuneiform. "Yes?"

"I think I can do it," Vic said. "I think I can use the beamline so that it does cause the—the patient, I guess—to level up to the next quantum state, if . . ."

"If what?"

"If it doesn't kill him. And I suspect it probably will."

I felt myself sag against the upholstery. "Really?"

Vic nodded. "That much energy being pumped in? Putting defibrillator paddles on your forehead would be nothing compared to this. We're trying to drag seven billion people along for the ride, after all—that's going to take a lot of juice. The patient might, just maybe, survive the first blast—pushing them up one level—but the second one? Not a chance in hell."

"You could use two different people, one for the first boost, then one for the second."

"And who is going to engineer that? After the first boost, you and I and Kayla will suddenly be p-zeds; none of us could be trusted to hold to the planned agenda. When your state changes, your desires—or whatever passes for desires in a p-zed—could change, too. No, the only way to pull this off would be to automate the whole run, so that once it's begun, it simply executes." She winced, the double meaning of her final word hitting her. But then she went on: "And, yes, that's almost certainly what it is: a death sentence for whoever's on the beamline. Ask Kay to look at the math; she'll confirm it, I'm sure. There's no way to do this."

"But—"

"I'm sorry, Jim. Or down deep, maybe I'm not." She started pacing again but stopped when she reached the blinds, pulling two of them aside, peering out at a vertical slice of the world. "This whole thing is crazy."

45

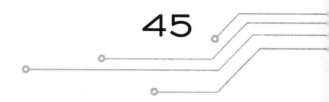

WELL, I fucked that up.

Of course, when Vic got to the Light Source later that day—her scheduled time there overlapping by a couple of hours with Kayla's—she told Kayla that I'd approached her with the idea of doing a massive shift.

And when Kayla got home—she'd left Ryan at her mother's so the two of us could talk privately—she hit the proverbial roof. "You asked Vic to help you?" she said. I was seated on the living-room couch, but she was standing, glaring at me.

"Well, you weren't interested—"

"I *told* you not to try this. I told you what would happen to my daughter, for God's sake. And you're *still* pursuing it?"

"Just, you know, hypothetically."

"Jesus," said Kayla. "Jesus Christ."

"Did you hear the news today?" I asked. "More rioting, not just here in Canada but all across Europe, the US, and now in Asia, too. And things are really heating up between the Americans and the Russians. One of the Russian subs has made it all the way into Hudson Bay, for God's sake. Carroway has demanded that Putin withdraw; for his part, Putin is claiming the Russians are coming to liberate us." I tipped my head toward the TV set. "Fox News, which doesn't know the difference between Canadian socialism and Russian communism, is spewing that Nenshi's election was the work of a fifth column, paving the way for the Soviets—yes, they called them Soviets today!—to seize everything north of the US border."

"I don't care about any of that," said Kayla.

I spread my arms. "But we—you and I, us and Vic—we can destabilize the situation. We can deactivate the psychopaths, before they start lobbing nukes at each other."

"You've got to leave," Kayla said.

"But I just want what's best—"

"Get out, Jim. Get your stuff and get out."

"Kayla, please." My eyes were stinging. "I just . . ."

"*Get out.*"

I didn't remember the first time Kayla and I had broken up—all I knew about it was what was in that ancient email. But this time, well, I couldn't imagine the memory would ever fade. It hurt like the way I'd imagined that knife to the heart had hurt, but going on and on, twisting, slicing. I would have almost welcomed becoming a p-zed; there's something to be said for not really feeling.

But right now I *was* still capable of feeling, of thinking. What had started as an abstraction—a thought experiment about maximizing the total potential happiness on this ball of dust—had transitioned, it seemed to me, into the game changer that might save everybody. For whatever reason, the tipping point had now come, just as it had in Europe in 1939. But there was one way in which the comparison was *not* apt: World War II had ended with nuclear weapons being used; World War III would begin with them. Talk about tumbling into the abyss; talk about following Lucifer into the very fires of hell.

But Kayla couldn't see that. She never looked up, never contemplated the stars. Hers was the realm of the minuscule; mine, the cosmologically vast. Why couldn't she widen her perspective? As Bogart said in *Casa-*

blanca, crisply making the utilitarian case, "It doesn't take much to see that the problems of three little people don't amount to a hill of beans in this crazy world." But where I had to go, Kayla couldn't follow; what I had to do, she couldn't—or wouldn't—be any part of.

No, I needed somebody who understood, who *really* understood. I needed Menno Warkentin.

I could have phoned him, but what I wanted to discuss amounted to overthrowing the current government; if US tanks were on Canadian soil, you could be sure as hell that the NSA was monitoring Canadian telephone calls. And so, a little after 6:00 P.M., I walked out Kayla's front door for what was probably the last time, got in my repaired car, put the pedal to the metal, and began the long drive to Winnipeg.

It took a couple of hours to get to Regina. Being the Saskatchewan provincial capital, it had been secured from rioting by US forces, and I managed to pass through that city without incident. Still, once I was on the other side of it, I found my heart racing as I continued along the highway—flashing back to when I'd recently been run off the road here, to the attack, to killing that p-zed. My palms were slick with sweat on the steering wheel, and I felt nauseous. I turned on the radio to drown out the voice in my head.

The CBC was used to defying the government in Ottawa and seemed no more cowed now by the one in Washington; Carol Off was on a tear about what she was calling "Carroway's *Anschluss.*" No doubt some asswipe—maybe Jonah Bratt, the Carleton psych prof—was commenting right now on the CBC website that Godwin's law meant she was wrong, but Carol's words rang true to me. When Hitler had annexed Austria in 1938, it had been, in part, to unify all the German-speaking people of Europe under one government. With the toxin of the McCharles Act already having spilled beyond Texas, perhaps Carroway likewise had been motivated by a desire to pull all of English Canada into the Union while simultaneously letting the mob purge Latinos in the lower forty-eight, the distinction between ones illegally in the US and those legally there having already fallen by the wayside. The six million French Canadians, if they impinged upon the president's consciousness at all, were doubtless merely an irritation; Washington would surely give Quebec none of the special treatment it was used to receiving from Ottawa.

If, that is, there *was* a Washington, or an Ottawa, or any damn city at all left. The news came on next, and it was not good.

"Although the White House has issued no confirmation, sources close to the Pentagon contend that Russian President Vladimir Putin today issued an ultimatum directly via the hotline to American President Quinton Carroway, insisting that US troops immediately withdraw from what Putin called 'Occupied Canada' . . ."

As I drove on, the sun—the one and only thermonuclear blaze I ever wanted to see—dropped down in my rearview mirror, and soon darkness was gathering.

I called Menno when I made a pit stop. He had a 9:00 A.M. appointment tomorrow with his diabetes specialist, so we agreed I'd come by his place at eleven. That meant I'd have a little time to kill first thing in the morning, and so I arranged to meet Dr. Namboothiri. I didn't think I could handle unlocking any more of my old memories, but I did desperately need his advice.

"Hello, Bhavesh. Thank you for making time for me on such short notice." I'd gotten to Winnipeg about 2:00 A.M. and was now operating on only five hours' sleep.

Namboothiri ushered me into his strange, wedge-shaped office. "No problem. You said it was urgent."

"It is. When I first came to see you, you knew what I was talking about when I mentioned philosopher's zombies."

He sat down and leaned back in his chair. "Sure; of course."

"Welllll," I said, the syllable drawing out as I thought about how to phrase this. "Let me ask you a, y'know, a hypothetical. Suppose a bunch of people who had been philosopher's zombies since birth were to wake up, what do you imagine they'd be thinking? If they've never been conscious before, not really, what would be going on now between their ears?"

"You tell me," said Namboothiri.

I couldn't help smiling as I sat down. His academic technique was similar to my own.

"Well, I'm assuming it would be the same thing that happened to me after being a p-zed. I'd started confabulating memories, making shit up, filling in the blanks. Presumably they'd do the same thing, too, and, as they compared notes, I presume they'd converge on a consensus reality, right? *Homo narrans:* Man the Storyteller. And they'd have Wikipedia and the rest of the World Wide Web to tell them what's gone down before."

"God help us," said Namboothiri with a grin. But then he shook his head. "But, you know, it wouldn't be like that. You lost your memories of being a philosophical zombie because you switched indexing schemes. But someone who had always been a zombie and only woke up as an adult *can't* switch indexing schemes, because there's nothing to switch *to*. They don't have a verbal index; they only have a visual one. Oh, they might initialize a verbal index, I suppose—and certainly any kids around three or four years old who suddenly cease being zombies probably will, since that's the normal developmental step at that age. But older people? Maybe they will; maybe they won't. But if they did, they'd switch over gradually, just as young people do."

"And if they continued to index visually, would that make them all autistic?"

"I doubt it," Namboothiri said. "Visual memory is a correlate of, but not, I suspect, the cause of, autism. It's certainly possible to have a visual memory but nonetheless compose thoughts in words; otherwise, Temple Grandin wouldn't have been able to write her books."

"Okay, thanks. Umm, one more question?"

"Shoot."

"You've seen my MRIs—the new one, and the old one with the paralimbic damage."

"Yes."

"Do you think I've recovered from that?"

"Nothing in the sessions we've had has given me any indication that you're any kind of crazed psychopath, Jim—at least, not anymore."

"Okay, thanks." I got up to leave.

"That's it? You said it was urgent."

"It is," I said, heading for the door.

As was his habit, Menno stood with the door to his apartment open, waiting for me. I saw Pax nudge him in the thigh to let him know I was approaching. "Good morning, Padawan. Won't you come in?"

"Thanks." I entered, the silver-and-cyan furniture looking gold and green in the sunlight.

While Menno got us coffee—it was fascinating watching him do so by touch—I explained the Q1-Q2-Q3 taxonomy to him, told him about the quantum tuning fork and how it had rebooted Travis Huron, told him what Vic and Kayla had discovered about the collective entanglement of humanity, and told him how if we could shift one person, then everybody else would also level up or down. I also told him what Vic had discovered: we *could* do it, perhaps, but not without likely frying the brain of the person we used as the subject. It took three cups apiece to get through it all, with Menno asking the kinds of thoughtful, probing questions I knew he would.

"So?" I said when I was done.

"Let me read you something," he said. He went into the back and brought out a piece of stiff caramel-colored paper. I was wondering how he was going to read it, but when he set it on the glass-topped table in front of him, I saw the Braille bumps. "This is what Stanley Milgram said about his obedience-to-authority experiments. I printed it out years ago, in the aftermath of Project Lucidity." He ran an index finger across the paper. "'Several of these experiments, it seems to me, are just about on the borderline of what ethically can and cannot be done with human subjects. Some critics may feel at times they go beyond acceptable limits. These are matters that only the community'—by which he meant the psychology community—'can decide on, and if a ballot were held, I am not altogether certain which way I would cast my vote.'"

"Message, Spock?" I said, folding my arms in front of my chest.

"One that at least one of us is conscious of," Menno replied.

"But," I said, "we can make the world a better place." Menno was quiet. Pax watched him patiently. I watched him, too, but without her equanimity. "Damn it, Menno," I said at last. "You *know* this is the right thing to do."

He began slowly, doling out words with care. "It's been hard sometimes being your friend and colleague, all these years. At first I thought it was just anger over what you'd done to me and Dom, or the fact that you were the one reminder of what I knew about the hordes who lacked inner voices, since you were the only person from Project Lucidity still in my face after all these years. But it wasn't anything as grandiose as that."

He paused and took a sip of coffee. "Who taught you about utilitarianism? Who introduced you—figuratively and literally—to Peter Singer? I did. I said, 'Here, Jim, read this, I think you'll like it.' And you did. You *embraced* it. I talked the talk, but you walked the walk. Remember the first time you came here and confronted me about the interview videos? You know what I was thinking? Not that the jig is up, not the cat is out of the bag, not even that finally I had someone to talk to about the findings Dom and I had made. No, nothing like that. My first thought was, oh, shit, it's Jim. And he's *judging* me. He knows how much I make, he knows how much I can afford to give to charity, but instead I'm living in a million-dollar apartment, and I'm blind, for Christ's sake, and still hanging expensive art on my walls."

"The Emily Carr prints, you mean?"

"They're not prints."

My gaze went to them: Post-Impressionist oil paintings of coastal rain forests in British Columbia. "Oh."

"The four of them together cost $42,000, back in 1996." He gestured toward his kitchen. "And you don't want to know how much the totem poles cost. I've been blind for twenty years—I get zero direct pleasure out of the paintings—but I like *having* them. I know the calculations Peter Singer has done as well as you do. Less than a thousand dollars will make sure a starving African child lives to adulthood: food, vaccinations, basic health care, even a primary education—just a thousand bucks. I could have saved over forty kids for the money I spent on those paintings. And you know what I told myself? Well, the paintings are appreciating in value, right? And I don't have any kids; I can leave my whole estate to charity, so when I'm gone, they'll be sold, and think of all the children that can be saved then! Yup, I was planning for there to be needy children decades down the road as a way of assuaging my conscience about doing nothing to help the ones who exist now. But you! How much did you give to charity last year?"

"I don't know."

"Yes," Menno said, "you do."

I looked away from the blind man. "Twenty-something."

"Twenty thousand dollars. Which charities?"

"Mostly ones combating third-world poverty."

"Because?"

I shrugged a little. "Because they need the money more than I do. The utility it gives people in Africa is way greater than the utility it gives me, so I . . ."

"So you *have* to give it away, right?" Menno shook his head. "The world doesn't need a hypocrite like me; it needs more people like you."

"Menno . . ." I said, as if his name, the same as that of the founder of his religion, was an exoneration.

He was quiet for a time, then: "You said you needed someone to put on the—what did you call it? The beamline?"

"Well, yeah, but that person probably won't survive."

"Use me," said Menno.

"What?"

"I'm old; use me."

"That's—wow, well, that's . . . that's very decent of you, but we need someone we can boost up two states. That means starting with a Q1."

"Who, by definition, can't give informed consent. But I can."

"Yes. But you're not a p-zed."

Menno got up. "Follow me," he commanded. I did so, and so did Pax; he led us back into his den. "It's been years," he said. "I'm not sure which of these cupboards they're in, but . . ." He gestured his permission for me to open them, and I did so. The first was filled with piles of old tractor-feed computer printouts, and I told him that. "Try the next one," he said.

I did—and there they were.

Two green hockey pucks.

"You kept them?" I asked.

"You said you needed a p-zed. Make me one."

My heart was pounding. "But what if you don't wake up?"

"Do what you did to Travis Huron. Use that gizmo . . ."

"The quantum tuning fork. But it doesn't always work."

"I'm willing to have you try."

"Menno, for God's sake, I can't—"

He held up a hand. "Padawan, who taught you about the trolley problem? Look at me. *I'm* the fat guy—and there are seven billion people on the tracks who might well be killed if the Russians and Americans go to war."

46

MENNO and I had briefly considered flying to Saskatoon, but trying to figure out how to get Pax there—finding a doggy crate, and so on—would have taken as much time as flying would have saved, and so all three of us clambered into my Mazda. After we'd been on the highway for a couple of hours, Menno surprised me by saying, "It really is a boring landscape, isn't it?"

So much had been turned upside down in my world of late, I don't think I'd have been surprised if he'd pulled off his dark glasses to reveal a perfectly normal pair of functioning baby blues.

"It is," I said, "but, um, how can you tell?"

"The road. It's perfectly flat. We haven't gone up or down a hill for ages."

Pax was in the back seat. I'd let her ride with her head sticking out the rear window, a common pleasure for dogs whose owners could drive but a rare treat, apparently, for her. After a while, though, she'd stretched out, her head on my side of the car, which was where the sun was pouring in.

Since we were planning to do it all without stopping for a meal, and so I could avoid the stretch of highway on which I'd previously been attacked, we were taking the Yellowhead Highway, bypassing Regina. As we came to the sign marking the provincial border, I announced, "We're leaving Manitoba."

Menno nodded. "Did you hear about that American couple? They got hopelessly lost, see? So they pull into a gas station, and the husband goes inside. 'Where are we?' he asks the man behind the cash desk. 'Saskatoon, Saskatchewan,' the man replies. The husband leaves, and, as he re-enters the car, his wife says, 'So? What did he say?' 'I don't know,' the husband replies. 'He didn't speak English.'"

It was worth a smile at best, but I figured the polite thing to do was to make an audible laugh, and I did so. Satisfied, Menno turned in his seat as much as his bulk would allow, and he leaned his head against a scrunched-up sweater he'd placed against the side window. Soon enough I heard the guttural wheeze of his snoring. As we sped along, I wondered if he closed his eyes when he slept or if they just stared out, unmoving.

One disadvantage of the Yellowhead was that amenities were few and far between. But, just when my bladder was about to go supernova, a rest stop presented itself. Menno and I took turns in the outhouse, and Pax relieved herself on the grass. When we were back on the road again, I broached a difficult subject. "You know who lives in Saskatoon now?"

"Kayla Huron," Menno replied. "You told me."

"Not just Kayla," I said. "Her brother, too. Travis."

Very softly: "Oh."

"Kayla finally told him the truth: that he'd been a Q2, and that he'd been knocked down into a coma by an external force, and then she'd managed to bring him out of it as a Q3."

"Ah."

"Yeah, and—oh, you'll like this—when Kayla said he'd been a quantum psychopath, Travis replied, 'Well, I always knew I was a little bit crazy.'"

"What?" said Menno. Then, getting it: "Oh! Clever lad."

"He is—although not so much a lad anymore. But she didn't tell him what had caused him to lose consciousness, not specifically."

"Good, good." A pause. "How is he doing?"

"Better every day. Still mostly uses a motorized wheelchair, but the physio is going well. He's back on normal food, and his jaw muscles are getting stronger. Got to eat a steak for the first time last week. Even I was cheering."

"Ah, well, I'm . . . I'm glad he's making progress."

"Yeah." I let another kilometer roll by, then: "Look, I know what you said about the prisoner's dilemma, but . . ."

"But there's a good chance I'm going to meet my maker soon, isn't there?"

"Well . . . yeah. And so, you know, I was wondering, would you like to see Travis?" And, as soon as that awkward sentence was out, I began to kick myself for saying "see" to the man I'd blinded.

But Menno nodded. "Yes," he said. "Yes, if he's willing. The Christian thing to do is ask forgiveness, and this is my last chance for that, isn't it?"

And so we pulled over again, and I called Rebekkah's house. She answered, and greeted me warmly; there was nothing to indicate that her daughter had yet told her that she'd broken up with me. I explained to Rebekkah that I was on my way to Saskatoon, accompanied by someone who had known Travis back in 2000 and early 2001, and asked if it would be all right if we stopped in to say hello? She took the cordless handset to Travis, I explained what was happening to him, and his exact words were, "No shit? Warkentin? Yeah, sure. Bring him by."

We still had a long drive ahead of us—and the time had come, the Warkentin said, to talk of many things. He filled me in on the details of the Lucidity experiments, and I told him even more about what Kayla and Victoria had discovered about the quantum states of consciousness. But every hour, at the top of the clock, I put on the CBC for five minutes. As we were entering Saskatoon, the female newsreader grimly shared this: "*Open hostilities now exist between Russia and the United States. The Russian submarine* Petrozavodsk, *in Canadian waters in the Beaufort Sea north of Tuktoyaktuk, this afternoon reportedly torpedoed and sank a US Navy destroyer, the USS* Paul Hamilton, *which had a crew complement of two hundred and eighty . . .*"

After that, Menno and I drove the rest of the way in silence; I took him directly to Rebekkah's house. It hadn't dawned on me that Ryan might be there, too—but she was; Kayla had been stuck in traffic for hours, thanks to gridlock caused by yet more rioting. As we entered, Ryan squealed in delight at the sight of the German shepherd. "Oooh! What's his name?"

"*Her* name," said Menno. "Pax."

Rebekkah, who was meticulous about her housekeeping, was scowling, and I realized I should have told her in advance that Menno would be accompanied by a dog.

"Can I pet her?" asked Ryan.

"She's a very special dog," Menno said. "She won't be happy until she gets me to where I'm going. But when I'm settled in, I'll take off her harness. That tells her she's off-duty, and then, yes, she'd enjoy being petted."

Ryan seemed fascinated by these revelations, but Rebekkah said, "It *is* getting on, and Travis still tires easily."

There were three steps up to the main floor of Rebekkah's house—the reason Travis hadn't yet joined us. We climbed them, Ryan bounding ahead. A short corridor came off the living room, with a washroom on one side, and, on the other, what had once been Rebekkah's graphics studio but had become Travis's room.

"Give me a second with him," I said. I went in on my own, closing the white-painted door behind me. "Travis," I said, "Professor Warkentin is here. I just wanted to prepare you. He's blind."

He looked up at me. Solid food was doing wonders; his face had filled out since I'd last seen him.

"Oh," he replied, his tone flat. But then he nodded. "Okay, send him in. There's something I have to tell him." He rolled his motorized chair half a meter forward and added, "Alone."

The drama Travis had been hoping for wasn't going to occur. He'd wanted a "Look at me!" moment; he'd wanted Menno's jaw to drop in shock at what he'd reduced a once-great athlete to. But Menno just stood there, the mountain come to Mohammed.

"Hello, Professor," Travis said.

"Please, call me Menno."

Travis had his own agenda, but one thing he remembered from his Q2 days was to always let the other guy show his hand first. "Jim said you had something you wanted to say."

"Yes." Menno's features worked, as if he were trying to come up with the right words, then, with a little shrug, he said, "I'm sorry."

"For what?"

"Well, see, you were knocked into a coma by an experiment that Dominic Adler and I were doing, and you—"

"I remember," said Travis.

Menno tilted his head. "But Jim said you couldn't recall the day we knocked you out."

"I lied," said Travis, and he gave a little shrug of his own, then operated the control to roll the wheelchair back a little. "Old habits die hard."

"But—"

"It was kind of my first impulse for so long, you know? Are you up to speed on all this Q1-Q2-Q3 shit?"

"Yes."

"And what did Jim tell you about me?"

"You started as a Q2, then rebooted as a Q3."

"Yeah, exactly. And about himself?"

"He started as a Q3, and then rebooted the first time as a Q1."

"Right, right. And has he told you about memories and stuff? The indexing schemes?"

Menno nodded.

"So, my sister explained it all to me. When Jim changed quantum states, he also changed indexing schemes: he went from verbal to visual.

But I didn't; adult Q2s and Q3s index memories verbally, unless they have a certain kind of autism, right? So, no change for me. I didn't have any trouble remembering coming to your lab, putting on that damn helmet. I knew you were responsible."

Astonishment was plain on Menno's face. "Then why didn't you tell Jim?"

"I'd just woken up. Playing things close to the vest had always served me well before; never let your opponent—and, man, I'd thought *everyone* was my opponent—know what you know."

"Ah," said Menno. He spread his arms. "Anyway, look, I'm old, I'm diabetic, I'm blind, and they've more or less put me out to pasture at the university. And, well, before I go, I just wanted to say I'm sorry—so, so sorry—for what I did to you. I hope you can find it in your heart to forgive me. You have no idea how it's eaten at me all these years. Not a day has gone by when it hasn't haunted me; not an hour."

Travis rotated his chair around so he could look out his window. He'd seen technological miracles aplenty since his revival, but from here, the view of the backyard—grass that needed mowing, powder-blue sky, petunias and portulacas, a weather-beaten picnic table—could have still been 2000, or 1950 for that matter. "I hate that," he said softly.

Menno was standing just inside the doorway. "Hate that I've felt guilty?"

"No, no," said Travis. "Not you. I hate having that feeling myself. Guilt. Remorse. Regrets. Second thoughts. Reliving things over and over again. Agonizing over the past. I *hate* it." He looked at Menno. "You want absolution? Fine, sure, what the hell; you've got it. Fucking world looks like it's about to come to an end anyway, right, so why the hell not?"

47

IT was killing me being in Saskatoon and not seeing Kayla. Oh, she must have known I was in town—after all, I'd already seen every other Huron—but I had to respect her wishes.

I knew what it was like to lose half your friends in a divorce—they make you pick a side in the church when you get married, and those lines pretty much stay intact afterward, too, I discovered. And I had no doubt that Victoria knew that Kayla had dumped me, even if Kayla hadn't yet broken the news to her mother or daughter. I was nervous calling Victoria for personal reasons—I didn't want to be chewed out—and even more so because everything now hinged on Vic's cooperation. While Menno was talking to Travis, I went across the hall to the washroom and called her.

"Jim!" she said by way of hello. "Where are you?"

"I'm at Rebekkah's place, visiting Travis."

"So you're back here in Saskatoon?"

"Yeah."

"I'm not sure Kayla wants to see you."

"I know," I replied, "but"—and this was agonizing to say—"that's not the most important thing right now."

There was a whole world of sadness in her simple reply. "Yeah."

"So, about what we were discussing, you know, at Kayla's place . . ."

"Yes?"

"You've been watching the news, right? You know what's going on."

"It's awful," agreed Vic. "They've got to be at fucking DEFCON One by now."

"And, so, look: using the beamline, shifting one person to shift everyone. Vic, you've got to see it, right? It's the answer."

"I told you, pumping that much power into someone's skull will likely kill—"

"I have a volunteer with me. Where are you?"

"Um, at the Light Source. I was finally about to leave."

"Stay there. We'll get there as soon as we can."

"No, there's no point. There's scheduled maintenance tonight. The system is going to be offline for eight hours; they've already initiated the shutdown."

"Oh, shit. Okay. Can you sneak the quantum tuning fork out?"

"Uh . . . sure. Yeah. I guess."

"Do so, please. Where can we meet?"

"Where are you staying?"

"I'll find a hotel."

"Oh, screw that. Come to my place—they say the police have finally cleared the roads. You know where it is?"

I'd never been inside, but I remembered the approximate location from that night we picked Vic up at the airport and took her home. "More or less. Give me your address; my phone can find it."

Victoria Chen's apartment was in the Central Business District, on the other side of the meandering South Saskatchewan River from the synchrotron. Menno and I got there just before the 11:00 P.M. citywide curfew. There were lots of signs of riot damage from previous nights, but no indications of current violence: white Saskatoon police cars, and black-and-white RCMP ones, were crawling along the streets. Vic met us out front with an overnight parking pass, and then she escorted us up to her eighth-floor unit, which sported parquet floors, rugs and tat-ami mats, and Chinese silk hanging-scroll paintings.

We sat in her living room, and I brought Vic up to speed on every-thing. She was astonished by Menno's offer—but she was also terrified by what she'd been seeing on the news, and, well, she allowed that my plan *did* seem to offer at least a glimmer of hope. Still, when Menno asked to use the washroom, and Vic got him safely to it, we spoke pri-vately for a moment. "He's blind," she said softly.

"Yes," I said, matching her volume.

"Which means you never could have done your microsaccades test on him, right? You don't know for sure that he's not a psychopath."

"Not empirically. But I'm a certified Hare assessor; I'm sure he isn't one."

"Which means he's either a Q1 or a Q3."

"Yes."

"Well," said Vic, "if he's already a Q1, then we don't have to—"

"But he's not."

"How can you be sure? If he *is*, then he's already in the state we need him to be in—and if you knock him down, he'll boot up as a psychopath, and I frankly don't want one of those here in my apartment."

"He's not a psychopath. He's riven by guilt. For God's sakes, he—" I was going to say he tried to kill himself over it—but he didn't; *I* tried to kill him. And, damn it all, maybe Vic was right: at least to hear Menno tell it, he *had* pretty much mindlessly done everything Dominic Adler had suggested all those years ago.

I tried to think of something like the Turing test that could distin-guish between a p-zed and a quick—but so had every philosopher who had ever grappled with David Chalmers's thought experiment. Of course, with our real p-zeds—philosophical zombies exhibiting differences—there could, in principle, be some way to identify a Q1 as definitively as my microsaccades test can identify a Q2, but we certainly hadn't worked out any such thing yet. No, there simply was no way to be sure short of plunking Menno down in front of Vic's beamline. "You can test him when we get to the Light Source," I said, "but we have to operate on the assumption that he is what he says he is. If Menno isn't going to revive from being knocked down, we'll need to find someone else."

Vic considered for a few moments, then Menno emerged at the end of the hall, being led toward us by Pax. "Well," he said when we were all together again, "shall we get started?"

"You're sure you want to do this?" I asked.

"You're not a religious man, Jim; I am. I know I'll have to answer for everything I've done in this life—and I also know that this life isn't the end. So, yes, I'm sure." He crouched, bringing himself to eye level with the German shepherd. "Good girl," he said, rubbing the top of her head. "You've been such a good girl." Pax licked his face, and he patted her once more, then, with bones that creaked loud enough that I could hear them, he rose. "I'm ready."

We led Menno to the living-room couch, which, like all the furniture here, was on the smallish size, but he managed to fit by tucking his knees up toward his belly. I went to my carry-on rolly bag, which I'd brought with me when we'd come up from the car, and got the two transcranial-ultrasound-stimulation pucks; Vic, meanwhile, fetched the quantum tuning fork.

"Menno . . ." I said, taking his hand.

"Two small steps for a man," he said. "Two giant leaps for mankind." He tightened his grip. "Goodbye, Padawan."

And then he let go, removed his dark, dark glasses, folded them carefully, and offered them to me. I took them, put them on a teak table next to the couch, and then looked at his artificial eyes, utterly convincing, even this close, except for their preternatural stillness and lack, at this late hour, of redness.

During the eight-hour car trip, he'd instructed me on how to activate and position the TUS pucks, and I did just as he'd told me to, sliding the switches on their circumferences, taking one puck in each hand, making sure the emitter surfaces were facing out, and pressing them against his temples, and—

—and Professor Emeritus Menno Warkentin's head lolled to the side, eyes still open, mouth now agape. I snapped my fingers by one of his ears, but there was no reaction whatsoever.

"Okay," I said. "If he doesn't boot up on his own by the morning, we can try the tuning fork."

Vic gestured at two dark-red easy chairs facing each other on the opposite side of the room. I sat in one; she took the other. From outside, despite all the police cruisers we'd seen earlier, we could hear the sounds of breaking glass and gunshots, and, now that "O Canada" was obsolete, the new national anthem: a discordant symphony of car alarms.

"Thanks for everything, Vic," I said. "I'm glad you get it. I—I thought Kayla would understand, but . . ." I lifted my shoulders. "But she couldn't get past her own world, thinking only about Ryan, and—"

"Me, too," said Vic, sitting in the other chair.

"What?" I said.

"Me, too. I'm thinking about Ryan."

"Well, I am, as well, but . . ."

"But this is the right thing for her," said Vic. "And for Ross. And for your sister. And for so many more."

"But . . . but Kayla said Ryan is a Q3."

Vic nodded. "Because *I* told her that. She had to stand near Ryan, comforting her, when she was on the beamline. And when just one spike came up, well . . ."

My heart fluttered. I thought back to what Vic had said to me at the Konga Cafe. *Ryan's the closest thing to a child I'll ever have.*

She's a doll, I'd said.

And Vic had replied, *Yes. Yes, she is.*

Jesus.

"Why'd you lie to Kayla?"

"There was no—how would you put it?—no utility, no increased happiness, in telling her. All Kayla needed to know was that her daughter *wasn't* a psychopath, and I told her the truth about that. But as for the rest, I saw, when the test results came up, how *my* feelings changed for Ryan, just as they changed for Ross—and I wasn't about to do that to Kayla."

Vic set me up on a foldout couch in another room, one with dark-red walls, and she retired to her bedroom. I used my white-noise app to try to drown out the sounds from outside, but, of the three humans in that apartment, I suspect only Menno Warkentin slept well that night.

I got up by dawn's early light. Menno was still out cold, Pax asleep on the floor by the foot of the couch. I used my phone and its Bluetooth earpiece to check the news.

It had gotten worse—so much worse—overnight. The United States had sent a trio of ICBMs soaring into Siberia—provocatively demonstrating that they could get through whatever missile shield the Russians had. It was a dramatic gesture, albeit using only conventional warheads, to try to convince Putin to withdraw before things escalated out of control.

For his part, Putin's subs had taken out a Canadian naval icebreaker and another US destroyer; the death toll in the undeclared war was now over seven hundred.

Vic materialized in the doorway, and, for once, her all-black garb seemed totally appropriate, the perfect thing to wear on doomsday. "Let's see if we can wake Menno," she said. We headed to her living room, the Mennonite's gentle wheezing audible above the background hiss of her air conditioner. He'd voided his bladder, but Vic seemed unperturbed by that. The aluminum case for the quantum tuning fork was on the ledge of the pass-through to her kitchen, next to the green pucks. She opened it, pried the silver instrument from its foam rubber, and moved over to Menno. I noticed the twin tines were now marked with small white labels, one saying "L," the other, "R." Vic thumbed the red on switch, pressed the projections against Menno's lined forehead, and—

The sound of air-conditioning; face touched by coolness. Muffled traffic sounds.

A voice, very close, female, concerned. "Professor Warkentin? Are you okay?"

Another voice, male, from farther away. "Menno? It's me, it's Jim."

Tokens processed, shuffled, dispatched: "I'm okay. Thank you, Padawan." More? More. "I'm fine, thanks."

Victoria turned off the quantum tuning fork and put it back in its case. I got Menno's glasses off the teak table. "Here you go," I said, placing them in his hand. He sat up and perched them on his nose. Pax, who'd gone over to watch the sun come up, padded back across the wooden floor to join him. I looked for any sign that the dog detected something different in him, but although she could hear and smell better than any of us, and probably could detect impending earthquakes or tornadoes in a way we couldn't, whatever quantum-state shift Menno had just undergone seemed to be as imperceptible to her as it was to me.

"All right," I said. "Let's get to the Light Source."

"Yes," said Vic. "Time's running out."

"Oh?"

"I checked the news on my phone as I was getting up. Putin's issued a deadline for the American withdrawal—four hours from now."

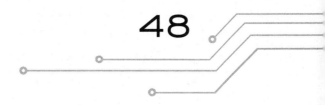

48

IT tore Kayla apart, knowing that Jim was in town. Oh, she'd had numerous fast-and-furious love affairs in her youth, back when she'd been a Q2, but this one had seemed real—a partnership of peers, much better than her marriage to Ben. She'd *known* that had been a mistake, known it as she was walking down the aisle. If she'd still been a Q2, she'd have said "fuck this," spun on her high heels, and headed right out the door, leaving that loser at the altar. But her days of psychopathy were long behind her by then, and with each step she'd taken in her white dress, she'd thought, "But it'll be embarrassing," or "But Mom will be heartbroken," or "But we've already booked the honeymoon trip," or "Maybe it'll be okay; maybe Ben will change."

There'd been none of those second thoughts back in college: Jim Marchuk had been good, solicitous company, bending over backward to do whatever she wanted, until right at the end. And, when they'd reconnected, what a joy it had been to find an intellectual equal and someone who wasn't needy, didn't require constant reassurance, wasn't an emotional vampire, and who was a kind and attentive lover.

Kayla was following the worsening news, as she imagined every other Q3 in the world was—and she wanted to be with her family today.

She didn't really think the world was going to come to an end in the next few hours, but, still, she'd kept Ryan, whom she'd finally managed to pick up last night, home from day camp, and she'd called in sick to the Light Source, and the two of them had headed back to her mother's place so they could all be together.

They made breakfast—eggs, bacon, sausages, all the things Jim would disapprove of—then, as Ryan was helping her grandmother with the dishes, Kayla went down the hall to talk privately with Travis. She sat on the edge of the bed so they'd be at the same eye level.

"So," she said, "Jim came by here last night?"

Travis nodded.

"And Ryan mentioned a blind man and a dog. I presume that's Professor Warkentin, right?"

"Uh-huh."

"Did, um, did he mention me?"

"He said you were an A student."

"Not Warkentin. Jim."

"I know." And Travis smiled the smile with which brothers had teased sisters for millennia. "Sure, he mentioned you. He said he was sad about how things had gone down." A pause. "And you know what I said? 'I know how you feel.' And I *do*." He shook his head and looked at her as if he were about to add something more.

"What?" asked Kayla.

"Nothing."

"I've had years of practice now," she said, "but you're still learning. Biggest difference, once you start listening to that voice in your head? Q2s are terrific liars; Q3s are lousy ones. What's going on?"

Travis looked—well, like Kayla had never seen him look, at least not when he was younger: like he was at war with himself. And then at last, lifting his arms slightly from the chair's rests, he said, "You and I, we're mistakes."

"Huh?"

"We got shifted," he said. "Displaced." Then, looking away: "This will fix it."

"What will?"

"What Jim is planning to do."

"You mean with the synchrotron? There's no way. He'd need Vic's help, and she'd never—"

"She *is*. She is helping Jim and Warkentin. Jim called her from here; I overheard."

Kayla pushed her palms against the mattress, standing up. "I—no, no. That can't be."

"She agrees with him, with Jim: if something isn't done, the world's going to come to an end—if not today, with Putin or Carroway igniting World War III, then next week, or next month, or next year."

Kayla ran out. Ryan called out "Mommy!" as she careened through the living room.

"Stay here!" Kayla said. "I'll be back."

"But—"

"I love you!"

And she hurried out the front door into the merciless summer heat.

Vic got Menno, Pax, and me in through security; she clipped a dosimeter to Pax's collar. We headed along the first indoor mezzanine-level balcony and came to where it made a left-hand turn into the second one. Vic nodded affably at people who passed us going the other direction. We made another left onto the third balcony, went down its length, and at last came to the stairs, which Pax managed quickly—she knew to get out of the way and wait for Menno at the bottom. He headed down, his left hand on the railing. "Three more steps," I said. "Two. One."

And at last, we were on the experimental floor. But instead of heading out toward the synchrotron, Vic led us down a small side passage, and then, after a final ninja look over her shoulder to see if the coast was clear, she used a keycard to open a doorway and then ducked inside. Pax, Menno, and I followed.

The room was filled with conduits and pipes, compressors and tanks. The walls were bare cement; the floor crisscrossed by tire skid marks presumably from heavy equipment having been wheeled in and out. We closed the door, and I took out the disposable pay-as-you-go voice-only cell phone I'd picked up at 7-Eleven this morning. *Shit.* No bars! But, after a couple of seconds one appeared, and then, like its taller brother, another popped up beside it. Cell phones aren't great for calling 911, so I'd jotted down the regular number for the Saskatoon Police Service on the back of an old restaurant receipt—the one from that meal Kayla and I had shared at Sydney's—and punched it in now.

On the second ring, the phone was answered by an automated attendant. I worked my way through menus, until, at last, a gruff male voice said, "Saskatoon Police."

"Good morning, sir," I said—Canadian politeness to the end. "I've planted a bomb at the Canadian Light Source; you know, the synchrotron on the U of S campus."

"Who is—"

"It will detonate in sixty minutes." And then, to give it an appropriate patina of craziness: "Those godless scientists are messing with the forces of nature. They have to be stopped."

"Sir, if you'll just—"

I pushed the button that disconnected the call, and we stood there, waiting. The thrum of the machinery drowned out the sound of our breathing, although Pax was panting from the hellish heat in here.

It was almost four minutes before an alarm sounded, and then, muffled—there was no intercom speaker in this confined space—we heard Jeff Cutler's voice, reverberating: "All right, folks. Yes, *again*: evacuate, evacuate! For now, report to your fire-muster points. Everybody out, right now, right now!"

The building was large; on a normal day, Vic had said it could take a good ten minutes to get from deep in its interior to the main doors. But it had emergency exits, and those would be used now. We waited five minutes—although it seemed much longer—and then, cautiously, Vic opened the door partway, sticking her head out. She then opened it farther and left the room, gesturing for us to follow. My forehead and armpits were slick with sweat.

The place was deserted: vast, empty, but still alive, equipment throbbing. On the desks in the experimental hutches we passed were the stereotypical abandoned half-drunk cups of coffee and half-eaten sand-wiches, plus, stretched like flayed skins over the backs of chairs or hanging from hooks, abandoned jackets and sweaters that might have been needed in air-conditioned conference rooms but certainly weren't required outdoors in the heat of a prairie summer.

The security cameras were still running, doubtless recording what we were doing, but no one would be watching the monitors just now. We made it to the end of the SusyQ beamline, and, as Vic had arranged, a gurney was there. "Okay," I said to Menno, "we're here."

Victoria and I helped guide him to the gurney, and he mounted it with a visible effort, then lay down. Vic cinched the bone-colored strap against his forehead, and she motioned for me to help wheel him into place.

And, as she'd said she would last night, Vic ran her test, the graph appearing on a monitor. Up high, as usual, was the band representing the entanglement of the entire human race, and, down below, there was just one superposition spike; Menno Warkentin was indeed now a Q1.

"It'll take a few minutes to divert the power from the other beam-lines," Vic said. She did things on her computer, and another animated diagram came up on-screen. "Then there will be a three-minute gap between the first boosting and the second one; it'll take that long for the equipment to recharge before we can boost everyone the second time."

I watched as various things I didn't understand happened on the status display Vic was looking at, and then, at last, she said, "Sixty seconds."

My heart was pounding; if it had actually had surgical seams, it might have burst along them.

Kayla's car raced across the University of Saskatchewan campus, sending up, as she saw in the rearview mirror, clouds of dust like prairie locusts. She again told her phone, connected to the car's Bluetooth sound system, to call Vic's cell, then Jim's, but they both were still going immediately to their voice mail—and every landline number she'd tried at the Light Source had rung and rung until finally shunting to an automated attendant.

She turned left onto Innovation Boulevard and—

—*hit the brakes!* Five police cruisers were blocking the way, their roof lights flashing. Kayla skidded forward. She spun her steering wheel to keep from colliding with the closest cop car. As soon as she came to a stop, she threw her door open and hurried out. A uniformed officer approached her. "Sorry, ma'am," he said from behind aviator-style sunglasses. "Place has been evacuated."

"What? Why?"

"Ma'am, we need you to turn around and head out of here."

"Oh, Christ," she said. "It's a bomb threat, right? Somebody called in another bomb threat, didn't they?" She spread her arms. "It's a hoax."

"Ma'am, the bomb squad will make that determination when they get here."

"I'm Dr. Huron; I'm a physicist at the Light Source. I need to get in."

"Please, ma'am, you don't want me to have to—"

She scanned around and spotted a loud Hawaiian shirt about fifty meters away. "Jeff!" she shouted, but the summer wind just blew the syllable back in her face. He was with a knot of others—some in lab coats, others in jeans and T-shirts, a couple in overalls and hardhats—and no one in all black. "Jeff!"

"There's nothing he can do for you, ma'am," the cop said.

"You don't understand," Kayla replied. "I have to get in there. I have to stop them."

The cop put a hand on the Taser attached to his belt. "Please, ma'am, you need to return to your vehicle and move it out of the way."

Kayla took off, running across the grass, heading for the Light Source's entrance, a hundred meters or more away.

"Ma'am, freeze!"

She continued, legs pistoning.

And then, from behind her, a sound like fishing line being cast, and—

—something hit her in the back, the force of it impelling her forward even more quickly, until—

—her eyes bugged out and her legs stopped working and she tumbled forward, skidding face-first across the grass like a runner desperately sliding toward home. She was dazed but still fully conscious—and, she knew, for a few more minutes at least, she also had a conscience, one that was awash with guilt for not having gotten there in time.

49

THE mechanical thrum on the Light Source's experimental floor was growing louder. I had no idea what was happening in the vast ring—or in the linear accelerator off to one side that fed into it, or on the other beamlines Vic was diverting power from—but it was all accompanied by suitably impressive sound effects: a gathering storm of power. Overhead, the giant hemispherical lights flickered a couple of times, as if God himself were blinking in surprise.

When I'd changed states before—all three previous times—I'd been knocked out, and so there was a discontinuity. I'd been *here* and then I was *there*. I'd been seated, or standing, or, you know, trying to strangle someone, and then I was being carried down a corridor by a couple of professors, or lying facedown on the floor in a lab, or waking up disoriented in my bed. But this time there shouldn't be a change in perspective.

Vic kept switching from looking at Menno on the gurney and looking at the graph on the monitor, but I kept my gaze glued to the display: the single superposition spike remained rock steady as the background thrum metamorphosed into a whine, a keening of ever-increasing pitch. And then, at last, it happened: a second spike popped up on the graph, and, as it did so, the entanglement band near the top of the screen looked like a braided rope being rotated around its long axis, changing and yet remaining the same.

And then—

But then—

Just then—

Vladimir Putin paced back and forth. His generals always took seats in his presence not because he encouraged them to be at ease—far from it—but rather because the president, who only managed 170 centimeters thanks to the lifts in his shoes, disliked having to look up at subordinates.

Putin walked along the red carpeting, the same red as the bottom field of the Russian tricolor flag, and, more importantly, at least to him, the same red as used on the old hammer and sickle from the glory days of the USSR.

His communications chief swiveled in his chair. "I have the missile-silo commanders standing by to receive launch codes."

"Very good," said Putin.

And then—

But then—

Just then—

A computer display. Two spikes. A response required, but—

But what should it be? Had it always been two spikes?

Eyes were swiveled to the left, revealing someone else. Searching: a person, a woman, Asian, short, thirties, long hair, black top, black pants. A match: Vic. Victoria. Victoria Chen.

Eyes were turned back to the display. A reply, manufactured out of nothing. "Well, well, well, would you look at that?"

Menno heard the voice—"Well, well, well, would you look at that?"—and recognized it at once: Jim Marchuk. And, of course, he knew where he was: the Canadian Light Source. Pax must be nearby, as well as that physicist, Victoria.

He'd cost Marchuk half a year of his life, and that other guy, Travis Huron, two decades, but—

But, you know what? Fuck it. Dom and me, we'd been onto something huge. *Those kids were lucky to have been part of it, for God's sake.*

Menno wanted to shake his head, but nothing happened; the restraining strap remained in place. Still, what a relief it was to no longer feel guilty! After all these years! In fact—

He heard Marchuk's voice again; Vic's, too, but it was Marchuk's that was grating. Not for its tone—yeah, yeah, that was pleasant enough—but for the mere fact of its *existence*. Why was he even still alive? Fucking guy gouged my eyes out! Asshole's gotta pay for that!

When push comes to shove, you don't back down. That was the lesson young Vladimir had learned on the playground; that was the lesson he'd taught those bastards in Ukraine.

The launch sequence consisted of two parts: first a daily code word followed by a plain-Russian statement to allow the voiceprint analyzers to confirm his identity, and then a twelve-character alphanumeric code, which his Minister of Defense had already handed to him in a breakable plastic case.

Putin leaned into the microphone that arched up like the neck of a black swan. "This is the president. The dayword is *balansirovaniya*, and here is the authorization code." He cracked open the case, revealing the string embossed in red on the yellow plastic card within.

Putin spoke the first three characters—two letters and a number— and then . . .

Thoughts of his daughters Mariya and Yekaterina came to him . . .

He recited the next two characters: a number and a letter.

Mariya was expecting her first child this autumn.

Another letter. And another.

He paused, thinking. Reflecting.

"Sir?" said the Minister of Defense. "Mr. President?"

The consequences would be huge. Gigantic. No way the Americans—and the Chinese and the North Koreans—wouldn't respond.

"Mr. President? Are you all right?"

And, really, in the end, what *good* would it do?

"Sir, they're waiting on the last digit." The minister leaned in, had a look. "It's a nine, sir."

Putin scowled; he could see that perfectly well.

"Sir?"

The president opened his mouth, and said, *"Nyet."*

"Mr. President?"

"No," he said again. And then, words he didn't recall ever having said before in his entire life: "No, on second thought, I'm not going to do this . . ."

Devin Becker sat, as he had most of every day since his sentencing, on the edge of his bunk here in the Georgia D&C State Prison, hands cupping his narrow face. He was furious at the jury, the judge, and that bitch of a D.A., but, most of all, at his own lawyer and that fucking Canuck expert witness. What the hell had they been thinking, branding him a psychopath! Yeah, yeah, things had gotten a little rough that day over at the Savannah Prison, but, hell, those inmates deserved it. They're the ones who should be on death row, not him . . . well, except for that asshole he'd drowned in the sink; obviously he couldn't be here. But still.

And, besides, it was mostly the fault of the other guards. Devin had merely suggested they teach the prisoners a lesson; those brain-dead morons didn't have to actually do it!

And then—

But then—

Just then—

Devin felt something wash over him, a wave of—of . . . well, he didn't know what, but the thought he was thinking was straightforward even if it was new for him: *Maybe I shouldn't have done that.*

And, a few seconds later: *I mean, if I hadn't, I wouldn't—*

And, after that: *What was I thinking?*

And, simplest of all, and yet so novel, so strange: *Why?*

Was this . . . ? Was it . . . ? Is this what *regret* felt like? In affirming the jury's sentencing, that Jap judge had said, "Mr. Becker has shown not one iota of remorse for his heinous crimes." But now . . .

Now . . .

Devin took a deep breath. The air here was always bad: too hot, too humid, stinking of shit and piss and sweaty clothes. Still, he'd always inhaled it without difficulty, but this time it snagged in his throat, and his chest shuddered.

And again, another sucking in of rotten jailhouse air, another quaking of his chest, his shoulders cresting and falling.

And then, the most astonishing thing: his knuckles, resting against his cheeks, suddenly wet.

Face-first on . . . grass?

Pushing up, rising, the body turning.

There: a police officer, holding . . . a Taser? The cop looked at the object, his eyes wide, mouth hanging open, and then dropping the device, walking over, closing the distance. "Ma'am, I'm sorry, but you shouldn't have run."

Knees wobbling; support needed. Body rotating, revealing a view of others on the wide lawn, movements random, a flock dispersed . . .

"Let me up!" Menno said. "Let me get up!"

It wasn't *that* painful, really, but he'd changed his mind—now that he was back to *having* a mind. He wanted to get off at this stop, and not just because it might kill him if the synchrotron zapped him a second time, but because this felt so damn good—despite the splitting headache.

But Jim and Victoria were presumably both p-zeds at the moment. Of course, they'd be disoriented, but with luck they'd also be compliant. "Jim. It's me. It's Professor Warkentin. I need you to come here. Jim, are you there? Jim? Jim!"

A voice, familiar but distressed. Calling a name—calling this one's name. A response expected. And so: "Yes, Menno?"

"Thank God! Something's wrong. It hurts."

More words expected; generated: "What hurts?"

"My head. It's—Jesus, it's like a jackhammer." A grunt, then: "Turn it off! Turn it off!"

"Turn what off?"

"The beam!"

Eyes were swiveled toward Victoria; shoulders were lifted.

"Jim! For God's sake!"

Unwatched, the timer on Victoria's screen counted down the time until the beamline would fire again.

Five seconds left.

And now four.

And then three.

And two.

And just one.

And—

Wow.

Wow, wow.

I looked at my watch—a thirty-dollar Timex; Jesus, why didn't I get something nice? Something that'd impress people? I could bloody well afford it, after all!

And—yes, yes! It was like being on Mars, weighing a third of what I had before. No more guilt, no self-flagellation, no fucking burdens. The world was mine for the taking, and why shouldn't I take it? I was smarter and more cunning than everyone else, and—

And well, well, well, what have we here?

Vic.

She looked ravishing in ebony leather and charcoal silk.

Ravishing. The very word.

She'd look even better *out* of those clothes. And we were all alone here, in this big, empty place . . .

Well, all alone except for Warkentin, but that Mennonite oaf was blind, and—

And there he was, still on the gurney, head still strapped down, but—

But his mouth was hanging open, and his chest didn't seem to be moving, and his damn dog was whimpering and licking his hand.

Mildly curious, I went over and felt for a pulse.

Nada. Huh.

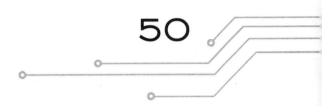

50

L YING came so easily now—and that was a good thing. When the bomb squad finally came in to search the synchrotron building, they found me and Vic and Pax, and Menno's body, which we'd moved from the gurney down onto the cement floor. We told the cops—who were discombobulated by their own quantum-state changes, I'm sure—that Menno had gone into cardiac arrest when the evacuation announcement had come over the P.A., and, of course, we'd bravely stayed behind, trying to resuscitate him. We'd gotten one of the Light Source's automated external defibrillators out of its emergency case and had deployed it next to his corpse.

Vic stayed at the synchrotron, but I was exhausted from days of negligible sleep, so she had given me her key and told me to go back to her apartment and get some shuteye. I arrived there, went to the kitchen to get a drink—and there they were, exactly where we'd left them on the pass-through, stacked one atop the other, the two green transcranial-ultrasound-stimulation pucks, and, next to them, a rugged aluminum carrying case, its lid hinged open to reveal the precisely cut black foam surrounding the quantum tuning fork.

I looked at the pucks the way Neo had stared at the red pill. I *could* go back to caring about all of humanity, eating nothing but plants, being a utilitarian, and giving twenty grand a year to starving kids.

But fuck that noise. I'm going to take Vic out for filet mignon tonight, then, when we get back, I'll show her what a real man, not some bloody p-zed, can do. I smiled, turned, headed back to the *en suite* bathroom, and ran the shower, its noise filling the air, and—

What the—?

It felt like somebody had boxed my ears. I tried to spin around, tried to see who it was, tried to—

Damn it, damn it, damn it.

I was on Vic's bathroom floor, flat on my back, looking up at a ceiling light fixture. I didn't seem to be bruised or banged up; whoever had slapped the TUS pucks on me had apparently lowered me gently to the pink tiles afterward; they'd also turned off the shower.

I'd presumably awoken on my own; otherwise, I'd have seen someone standing over me, quantum tuning fork in hand. As to how long I'd been out—well, glancing at my watch and assuming it was the same day, it was less than three hours.

God damn it. It had been so liberating being a psychopath. But there it was, bubbling up, the attribute that defined being a quick: *conscience.* The damn thing was reasserting itself, growing stronger, louder, and louder still. Christ, oh Christ, what do you do with your last few seconds of freedom?

You *savor* them—while you rage, rage against the rising of the light.

I got up, exited the bathroom into Victoria's bedroom, and there, lying on the bed, fully dressed, an ebook reader in her hand, was—

No, not Vic.

It was Kayla. She looked up as I entered.

"What the hell?" I said.

She smiled. "Hi, Jim."

"You knocked me out?"

"Uh-huh. Vic told me you were here. I figured I'd give you a chance to wake up on your own; if you hadn't revived soon, I'd have tried the tuning fork." She closed her reader's cover and got up.

"And you—you're a Q2 now, right?" I asked.

"Yes." She shrugged a little. "I recognize the feeling."

"But, then, why'd you knock me out? What's in it for you, having me boost back to being a Q3?"

"I knew you in 2001, remember. I knew you when you were a paralimbic psychopath, and I know what you did to Menno when you were briefly also a quantum one. So, for my own protection, it's better for me if you're a Q3. But watch your step, buddy-boy: I'd be even safer if I knocked you down once more, so you'd be a p-zed again."

"I'll be careful." I looked at her, trying to see if her inner change was in any way mirrored on her face—and maybe it was: the twinkle was gone from her blue eyes; even when she wasn't staring, there was now something snake-like about her gaze. "Do you know what Vic did—after, I mean?"

"What?" asked Kayla.

"Well, you're not going to like it, but . . ."

"What?" she said again.

"She erased her program—the one we used to change everyone's states. She said it was tempting fate to leave that info lying around; she didn't want someone else doing to her what we'd done to everybody. She also erased as much of the research about quantum states of consciousness as she could, including your cloud backups."

"Shit," said Kayla. But then she smiled, a cold psychopathic rictus. "Oh, well; no point in regrets, is there? What's done is done."

"What about you?" I asked. "Your brother wanted to go back to being a Q2, which I presume is what he is now. He said he preferred it. Do you? Do you want to stay a psychopath?" I gestured out the door, in the direction of the living room. "Because, you know, I can do to you what you just did to me: knock you down to the classical-physics state, and then bring you back up as a Q3. Of course, there's a risk you won't wake up at all, but . . ."

"What would you do in my place?" Kayla asked.

I was surprised by the bitterness in my voice. "You deprived me of the right to make that choice."

"Pot," said Kayla. "Seven billion kettles. Black."

I looked away.

"Anyway," said Kayla, "we'll see. It's always an option, isn't it? But until we're sure things are going well on the political front, I think I'd rather be like this. Ready for action, y'know?"

I looked at her and thought about us: two ships that had passed in the quantum night.

"Ryan's a Q3 now," I said.

"No, she'd have wrapped around like me—"

I shook my head. "Vic lied to you; Ryan was a Q1 when she tested her on the beamline."

"Oh," said Kayla. And then, after a moment: "So, what, now she's going to be all needy? Jesus."

"Well," I replied, "if you don't think you can look after her . . ."

"What? You want her?"

"Yes," I said firmly. "Yes, I do."

Kayla's head rocked left and right for a moment, then she shrugged a little: "Sure, yeah, why not? Make my life easier."

My heart was beating rapidly. "Okay; good. All right if I take her with me on a road trip to Winnipeg? I want to go see Virgil."

"Who?" asked Kayla.

Oh, right. I'd never told her his name.

"Virgil," I said again. "My son."

Travis was managing well with a walker now, and so, late one night, I drove him far out on the prairie; he didn't know anything about astronomy, and I'd offered to teach him. The moon, with its *yin* and *yang* of the Ocean of Storms and the Sea of Tranquility, had sunk beneath the horizon's razor edge, and the starry boulevard of the Milky Way cleaved the heavens.

I taught Travis how to use the Big Dipper to find Polaris, Arcturus, and Spica; pointed out the Summer Triangle of Altair, Deneb, and Vega (which, I said, was where vegans like me came from); and showed him the smudge of the Andromeda galaxy, the most distant object one can see with the naked eye, 2.5 million light-years away. That meant, I said, he was looking back in time 2.5 million years: the photons now kissing his retinas had left Andromeda at the same time the first members of the human genus, *Homo,* had appeared.

"Huh," he said. "You think there's anybody else out there?" He was leaning for support against my car's side panel—the one that had been replaced recently.

I thought again about the silence from the stars, about whether races are doomed to snuffing themselves out. "Maybe ours now has a fighting—or a *non-fighting*—chance."

I couldn't see his face, but I could hear the snort. "You think we're in some sort of utilitarian utopia now? People are people, and quantum physics be damned."

"It'll take time," I replied, as my eyes found kite-shaped Delphinus. "The new crop of quicks has to make sense of the world around them. But no one with conscience can look out at all the suffering, all the poverty, all the unfairness, without aching to do something about it. You had a conscience briefly; you remember what it's like."

Perhaps Travis shrugged. "Sort of. I can't muster the feeling again, but, yeah, it was different."

"It's better," I said firmly.

"Even with the regrets? The second thoughts?"

"Even with."

Silence for a time. I caught a meteoric streak of white in my peripheral vision, a mote of cosmic dust expiring.

"You know, you're an unusual person," Travis said. "Even among Q3s, you're an aberration. It's not like there are suddenly four billion James Marchuks out there."

My gaze dropped to the horizon, the land in front of us a great empty page. "The rioting has stopped," I said. "American troops are out of Canada, and the McCharles Act has been repealed. Other positive things will happen, too. Give it time."

"I *gave* it time once already. I fast-forwarded two decades, remember? Things got worse, not better."

"This will be different." Overhead, the constellations of summer blazed, but I flashed back to that confabulated winter sky on New Year's Eve all those years ago, the mighty hunter Orion rearing up. "Do you know when I was first knocked into a coma? December thirty-first, 2000. I missed the big party." I sang softly: *"Should auld acquaintance be forgot, and never brought to mind . . ."*

"But at least you were awake for the really big party the year before," Travis said.

I was about to launch into my "but there was no year zero" bit when it came to me. True, the numbering system had been devised using Roman numerals, which had no zero, but our system does, and this—right now—was the real year zero. All that talk about whether 2000 or 2001 had been the beginning of the new century was irrelevant: *this* was the dawn of the next millennium, the next era, with four billion people—for the first time in those 2.5 million years, the majority—uplifted from emptiness to full consciousness with conscience; truly the greatest good for the greatest number.

And, yes, there were countless challenges ahead of them; doubtless they weren't yet sure how to proceed.

But they *would* think of something.

FURTHER READING

A S the quote from David Chalmers at the front of this novel (taken from an interview with him in the Summer 1998 issue of the excellent magazine *Philosophy Now)* says, "It may be a requirement for a theory of consciousness that it contains at least one crazy idea." Throughout this book I put forward a theory that, at first blush, might seem to contain rather substantially more than just the requisite one crazy idea, so let me share this list of some of the nonfiction reading that informed my thinking. (Please note that the commentary below contains spoilers for this novel.)

First and foremost, this novel hinges on the notion that consciousness is fundamentally quantum mechanical in nature. The seed for this comes from two books by Sir Roger Penrose:

Penrose, Roger. *The Emperor's New Mind: Concerning Computers, Minds, and the Laws of Physics.* Oxford: Oxford University Press, 1989.

Penrose, Roger. *Shadows of the Mind: A Search for the Missing Science of Consciousness.* Oxford: Oxford University Press, 1994.

The first one outlines Penrose's logic (based on Gödel's incompleteness theorem) for why human consciousness has to be quantum mechanical. When Penrose first put that idea forward, he had no idea where the quantum-mechanical processes might be taking place. But anesthesiologist Stuart Hameroff had the notion that they were occurring in the hydrophobic pockets of microtubules; Penrose elaborates on that thought in the second book, and the two of them have collaborated on several papers since. A recent one that provides a good overview is:

Hameroff, Stuart, and Roger Penrose. "Consciousness in the Universe: A Review of the 'Orch OR' Theory." *Physics of Life Reviews 11* (2014) 39–78.

And for a recent update on the whole notion of quantum processes in biological systems, see:

McFadden, Johnjoe, and Jim Al-Khalili. *Life on the Edge: The Coming Age of Quantum Biology.* New York: Crown Publishing, 2015.

My novel also hinges on the notion of the philosopher's zombie, an idea most associated with Australian philosopher David Chalmers, who discusses it many places, including in these excellent books:

Chalmers, David J. *The Conscious Mind: In Search of a Fundamental Theory.* Oxford: Oxford University Press, 1996.

Chalmers, David J. *The Character of Consciousness.* Oxford: Oxford University Press, 2010.

(I've had the great privilege of getting to know both Stuart Hameroff and David Chalmers. Stuart and David long co-chaired the biennial Toward a Science of Consciousness Conference, and, when I gave a keynote address there in 2010, it was Dave who introduced me to the audience.)

Although I'm sure he wouldn't frame it this way, if you want empirical evidence that there really are multitudes of p-zeds mindlessly following authority figures, check out the work of Bob Altemeyer, a now-retired professor of psychology coincidentally at the University of Manitoba (where my character Jim Marchuk teaches). His free PDF ebook available at http://home.cc.umanitoba.ca/~altemey is compelling:

Altemeyer, Bob. *The Authoritarians*. Winnipeg: University of Manitoba, 2006.

The audio version, with a comprehensive introduction written by former Nixon White House counsel John Dean and updates and reflections added by Altemeyer, is even better; you can get it at Audible.com. For ways in which our complex behavior could be the result of things other than self-aware consciousness, see:

Duhigg, Charles. *Power of Habit: Why We Do What We Do in Life and Business*. New York: Random House, 2012.

Gigerenzer, Gerd. *Gut Feelings: The Intelligence of the Unconscious*. New York: Viking Penguin, 2007.

Hood, Bruce. *The Self Illusion: How the Social Brain Creates Identity*. Oxford: Oxford University Press, 2012.

Koch, Christof. *Consciousness: Confessions of a Romantic Reductionist*. Cambridge: The MIT Press, 2012.

Lieberman, Matthew D. *Social: Why Our Brains Are Wired to Connect*. New York: Crown, 2013.

Miller, Peter. *The Smart Swarm: How Understanding Flocks, Schools, and Colonies Can Make Us Better at Communicating, Decision Making, and Getting Things Done*. New York: Avery, 2010.

Morse, Eric Robert. *Psychonomics: How Modern Science Aims to Conquer the Mind and How the Mind Prevails*. Austin: Code Publishing, 2014.

Pagel, Mark. *Wired for Culture: Origins of the Human Social Mind.* New York: W.W. Norton & Company, 2012.

Pentland, Alex. *Social Physics: How Good Ideas Spread.* New York: Penguin, 2014.

Smart, Andrew. *Autopilot: The Art and Science of Doing Nothing.* New York: OR Books, 2013.

Surowiecki, James. *The Wisdom of Crowds.* New York: Anchor Books, 2005.

Wilson, Edward O. *The Social Conquest of Earth.* New York: Liveright, 2012.

I mention mirror neurons as one of the mechanisms supporting the notion of mindless behavior. For a good introduction to them by one of their discoverers, see:

Iacoboni, Marco. *Mirroring People: The Science of Empathy and How We Connect with Others.* New York: Farrar, Straus and Giroux, 2008.

For an opposing view see:

Hickok, Gregory. *The Myth of Mirror Neurons.* New York: W.W. Norton & Company, 2014.

Unlike Chalmers's thought-experiment zombie world, where no one has real consciousness, I posit a three-state model, with each level showing progressively more complex consciousness in successively smaller cohorts. So, cheek by jowl with my p-zeds are legions of psychopaths—and there's an enormous amount of nonfiction written about them. The seminal texts are:

Cleckley, Hervey. *The Mask of Sanity: An Attempt to Clarify Some Issues About the So-Called Psychopathic Personality.* Various publishers; five editions from 1941 to 1984.

Hare, Robert D. *Without Conscience: The Disturbing World of the Psychopaths Among Us.* New York: Atria, 1993.

One of Hare's last graduate students has a fascinating (and more recent) book, from which I drew the notion of damage to the paralimbic system being a correlate of psychopathy:

Kiehl, Kent. *The Psychopath Whisperer: The Science of Those Without Conscience*. New York: Crown, 2014.

Meanwhile, Jon Ronson looks into Hare's famed *Psychopathy Checklist—Revised* in this popular account:

Ronson, Jon. *The Psychopath Test: A Journey Through the Madness Industry*. New York: Riverhead, 2011.

As I make clear in my novel, psychopathy doesn't necessarily lead to crazed killing sprees. Hare and his collaborator have documented the existence of psychopaths in the workplace:

Babiak, Paul, and Robert D. Hare. *Snakes in Suits: When Psychopaths Go to Work*. New York: HarperBusiness, 2006.

Also on the topic of hidden psychopaths ("sociopath," as I explain in the novel, being an essentially synonymous term):

Stout, Martha. *The Sociopath Next Door*. New York: Broadway Books, 2005.

And Kevin Dutton—whom I consulted with in creating this novel—contends that psychopathic traits can even be beneficial:

Dutton, Kevin. *The Wisdom of Psychopaths: What Saints, Spies, and Serial Killers Can Teach Us About Success*. New York: Farrar, Straus and Giroux, 2012.

When I was already well into the writing of my novel, James Fallon published a book about a real-life discovery that echoed some of what my character Jim Marchuk faces:

Fallon, James. *The Psychopath Inside: A Neuroscientist's Personal Journey into the Dark Side of the Brain*. New York: Current, 2013.

And a book about the relationships between psychopathic men and nonpsychopathic women:

Brown, Sandra L. *Women Who Love Psychopaths: Inside the Relationships of Inevitable Harm with Psychopaths, Socio-paths, and Narcissists.* Minneapolis: Book Printing Revolu-tion, 2009.

The character of Menno Warkentin in this novel is an experimental psychologist. I've often said that science fiction is a laboratory for thought experiments about the human condition that it would be impractical or unethical to conduct in real life—but, in the days before informed consent, there were some doozies that put my fictional Proj-ect Lucidity to shame.

Most famous of all—and, as I argue in this novel, pretty clear evidence of philosopher's zombies in our midst—is the Milgram shock-machine obedience-to-authority study from 1961. Milgram himself recounts it here:

Milgram, Stanley. *Obedience to Authority.* New York: Harper & Row, 1974.

And his life and work are explored in:

Blass, Thomas. *The Man Who Shocked the World: The Life and Leg-acy of Stanley Milgram.* New York: Basic Books, 2004.

And for a largely opposing viewpoint on Milgram's work, see:

Perry, Gina. *Behind the Shock Machine: The Untold Story of the Notorious Milgram Psychology Experiments.* New York: The New Press, 2013.

Then there's Philip Zimbardo's Stanford Prison Guard experiment from 1971:

Zimbardo, Philip. *The Lucifer Effect: Understanding How Good People Turn Evil.* New York: Random House, 2007.

Milgram was influenced by this famous analysis of the trial of one of the Nazi war criminals, who, in the taxonomy presented in this novel, was almost certainly a Q1:

Arendt, Hannah. *Eichmann in Jerusalem: A Report on the Banality of Evil*. New York: Viking, 1963.

Two more recent books on how Q2s could influence the masses of Q1s, the latter extensively citing Bob Altemeyer:

Rees, Laurence. *Hitler's Charisma: Leading Millions into the Abyss*. New York: Pantheon, 2013.

Dean, John W. *Conservatives Without Conscience*. New York: Viking, 2006.

I'm often called an optimistic writer, and my visions of the future tend to shade toward the utopian. I like to think that's not simple naïveté, and this novel is my attempt to grapple with the notion of human evil, a topic explored in fascinating depth in:

Baumeister, Roy F. *Evil: Inside Human Violence and Cruelty*. New York: W.H. Freeman & Company, 1996.

A couple of more recent treatments, based in neuroscience:

Baron-Cohen, Simon. *The Science of Evil: On Empathy and the Origins of Cruelty*. New York: Basic Books, 2011.

Bloom, Paul. *Just Babies: The Origins of Good and Evil*. New York: Crown, 2013.

My character of Jim Marchuk is a utilitarian philosopher. Peter Singer is the best-known living utilitarian. His classic text is:

Singer, Peter. *Practical Ethics, Third Edition*. Cambridge: Cambridge University Press, 2011.

A good overview of his thought (including his famously controversial views on abortion, animal rights, infanticide, and euthanasia, some of which Jim Marchuk echoes in my novel) is:

Singer, Peter. *Writings on an Ethical Life*. New York: HarperCollins, 2000.

On the obligation Jim Marchuk discusses of utilitarians to support third-world charities, see:

Singer, Peter. *The Life You Can Save: Acting Now to End World Poverty*. New York: Random House, 2009.

And this is Singer's famous work that kick-started the worldwide animal-rights movement:

Singer, Peter. *Animal Liberation: A New Ethics for Our Treatment of Animals*. New York: HarperCollins, 1975.

Harvard professor Joshua Greene looks at the divisiveness in modern societies through a utilitarian lens in this excellent book, which also discusses the Trolley Problem at length:

Greene, Joshua. *Moral Tribes: Emotion, Reason, and the Gap Between Us and Them*. New York: Penguin Press, 2013.

Much of my novel deals with ethics and free will (for those it asserts have it). Good reading:

Cathcart, Thomas. *The Trolley Problem: Or Would You Throw the Fat Guy Off the Bridge?* New York: Workman Publishing Company, 2013.

Churchland, Patricia S. *Brain Trust: What Neuroscience Tells Us About Morality*. Princeton: Princeton University Press, 2011.

Gazzaniga, Michael. *Who's in Charge?: Free Will and the Science of the Brain*. New York: Ecco, 2011.

Harris, Sam. *Free Will*. New York: Free Press, 2012.

Part of my novel deals with confabulation—or, as one of the characters so succinctly puts it, "just making shit up." In fact, much of what we believe to be real is simply stories we've told ourselves, a faculty that defines us as a species, as explored in these works:

Gottschall, Jonathan. *The Storytelling Animal: How Stories Make Us Human*. New York: Mariner Books, 2012.

Niles, John D. *Homo Narrans: The Poetics and Anthropology of Oral Literature*. Philadelphia: University of Pennsylvania Press, 1999.

And in what must be a case of nominative determinism for the author:

Storey, Robert. *Mimesis and the Human Animal: On the Biogenetic Foundations of Literary Representation*. Evanston, IL: Northwestern University Press, 1996.

Finally, if you liked this novel, you might also particularly enjoy my other novels that deal with the nature of consciousness: *The Terminal Experiment, FlashForward, Mindscan, Triggers,* and the WWW trilogy of *Wake, Watch,* and *Wonder*.

ABOUT THE AUTHOR

Robert J. Sawyer gave a keynote address at the Toward a Science of Consciousness conference in Tucson in 2010, and he will speak again at that conference in 2016. He's also lectured about the science of consciousness at the Googleplex, the Center for Cognitive Neuroscience at the University of Pennsylvania, and TEDxManitoba, and he has published in both of the world's top scientific journals, *Science* (guest editorial) and *Nature* (short story).

Rob is one of only eight writers ever to win all three of the world's top awards for best science-fiction novel of the year: the Hugo (which he won in 2003 for *Hominids)*, the Nebula (which he won in 1996 for *The Terminal Experiment)*, and the John W. Campbell Memorial Award (which he won in 2006 for *Mindscan)*. According to *The Locus Index to Science Fiction Awards,* he has won more awards for his novels than anyone else in the history of the science-fiction and fantasy fields, and in 2013 he became the first author in thirty years, and the youngest author ever, to receive a Lifetime Achievement Aurora Award from the Canadian Science Fiction and Fantasy Association.

Rob holds honorary doctorates from the University of Winnipeg and Laurentian University, and in 2009 he served as the first-ever writer-in-residence at the Canadian Light Source, Canada's national synchrotron, a position created especially for him. His novel *Flash-Forward* was the basis for the ABC TV series of the same name, and he was a scriptwriter for that program.

A resident of Mississauga, Ontario, his website and blog are at **sfwriter.com**, and on Twitter and Facebook he's **RobertJSawyer**.